The Presidium

Michael Heath

Publisher's Note:

The Presidium is a work of fiction. The characters and all events are entirely fictional and any resemblance to actual persons, alive or dead, is entirely coincidental.

Michael Heath

The Presidium

RED WINE
THE RED WINE GROUP

CABERNET BOOKS
(A Red Wine Company)

First Published in 2014
By
CABERNET BOOKS LTD.
Bramerton Business Centre
Bramerton Road, Hockley
Essex SS5 4PJ
United Kingdom

© 2014 Michael Heath

The right of Michael Heath to be identified as the author of this work has been asserted under The Copyright Designs and Patents Act 1988

British Library Cataloguing-in-Publication Data

ISBN: 978-0-9929357-3-3

All rights reserved. No part of this book may be reproduced or utilised in any form or by any means, electronic or mechanical, including photocopying, recording or by any diffusion service, information storage and retrieval system, without prior permission in writing from the Publisher

Printed in Great Britain
by
Biddles Ltd., King's Lynn

Cover design by Andreea Barbulescu

BY THE SAME AUTHOR

Novels

The Albion Conspiracy
Legacy
Conquered Hearts
Willow Moon
Devereux ... and a question of class

Theatre Works

Silent Star
Lacrymosa
Laura
Bram
The Selfish Giant
A Christmas Carol

e eBook
The Presidium
and all the above novels are also available as e-books

About the Author

Born in Ilford, Essex, Michael has spent his entire career within the performing and creative arts. Novelist, screenwriter, director, actor, composer and lyricist, his credits include film, theatre, television, radio and the concert hall. His full c.v. can be seen on the Internet Movie Data Base. In recent years Michael has concentrated primarily on writing novels and screenplays. He is the artistic director of his own film and theatre production company.

For full details of the Cabernet Books catalogue - for both printed and e-books – visit our web site:

www.cabernetbooks.com

CABERNET BOOKS LTD.
Bramerton Business Centre
Bramerton Road, Hockley
Essex SS5 4PJ
United Kingdom

Follow us on Twitter and Facebook

Prologue

Saturday, June 1st. Shenzen, China

There were twelve seats at the large, highly-polished, teak table. The number had not been chosen at random. Twelve was the total commonly considered valid for a jury and this gathering, at least for those present, constituted a court of law. It was not, however, recognised by any judicial system, its code was not written in any statute book and the nine men and three women who occupied the plush, leather chairs were responsible to no authority other than their own.

The table itself was round. This was also not by chance or arbitrary decision. A circular table provided no 'head' seat; no natural position of command or authority. All places were of equal power and importance. Decisions made needed to be carried by a clear majority of two to one and if the critical figure of eight votes in favour was not reached, then the motion in debate was denied.

Lying in the centre of the table was an open dossier. Its contents of documents, photographs and press-clippings were spread out around it and had been the subject of detailed discussions for the previous three hours.

Each attendee had before them a folded card. The inner side contained two single-word alternatives: 'Yea' and 'Nay'. There was no place for comment or equivocation. Abstention was not allowed. It was merely necessary to place a tick by one of the two options and then the anonymous verdict was folded and placed in a small, black ballot box. When all twelve cards were deposited, two of those present would open the box and jointly count the votes. With the tally agreed, one of them would simply announce the totals for each. If the crucial minimum of eight votes in favour was secured, the motion would be declared passed.

This was the third such assembly this year. Sometimes several months would pass between meetings; occasionally, when necessity dictated, they might be only a matter of days apart. The gathering could be held in any part of the world and was often scheduled at short notice, with no more than forty-eight hours in which to travel, but there were never any vacant seats or apologies for absence. When the call came, it was answered.

On this particular bright and clear summer afternoon, the twelve were assembled in a modern, luxuriously appointed boardroom on the forty-second floor of a tall skyscraper in Shenzen, the major city in southern China's Guandong province. On three sides, original abstracts in oils hung on walls faced with expensive, imported Italian marble. The whole of the remaining flank consisted of large glass windows, running from floor to ceiling, that looked out upon the sprawling mass of the bustling, vibrant metropolis beneath, where a grey haze rose from the incessant traffic crowding the heavily congested streets. Less than 35 years earlier it had been nothing more than a suburban village but its location, directly across the causeway from the island of Hong Kong, had made it the perfect location for development by the forward-thinking Chinese. Knowing it would somehow need to accommodate the modern market capitalism that thrived in Hong Kong when the British colony reverted to China, the government in Beijing decided to pre-empt the change by building its own financial powerhouse on the island's doorstep. So Shenzen became the first 'Special Economic Zone', allowing foreign investment to flood into the region alongside the money poured in by Beijing. In a whirlwind of expansion, the village grew to be a city and the population soared in just three decades to a staggering eleven million. It was now home to numerous foreign corporations and financial institutions, where the arrival of twelve international visitors to attend a private meeting was a common place occurrence that aroused no comment or notice.

The age of those present at the table varied but fell within a fairly narrow range. The youngest was fifty-two and the oldest was sixty-nine. Between them they had amassed an extensive and wide-ranging experience across commerce and industry, finance and investment, politics and law. Though all very different individuals, of diverse nationalities, what united them was that they had each served their respective countries or national governments in some senior capacity, either in direct employment or as a consultant or adviser. Their service had, in every case, been undertaken with distinction and met with success but not a single one of them had been high profile. They had never been prominent in the media and their names were not known to the public at large. It was this comparative anonymity, combined with their proven record of judgement and acumen, that had led them to membership of this carefully selected and elite cadre.

Ten pairs of eyes looked expectantly at the two tellers.

"Unanimous" said one of them unemotionally. "Motion carried." It was the second such verdict the group had reached that day. He wrote down the judgement on a single sheet of paper in front of him. The name at the top of the page was the same as that on the front of the dossier that still lay open in front of the assembled company.

There was a clearly apparent feeling of relief in the room that there had been no dissenters and several of those present nodded gently in approval as one of the two tellers rose from his place and crossed to the door. He knocked on it three times and then returned to his seat.

A few seconds later the door opened and a man in his early forties, a white European dressed in a well-tailored dark suit, stepped silently into the room. Of above average height and slender build, his manner was confident and purposeful and his dark brown eyes stared impassively forward, avoiding contact with any of the delegates as he entered the conference room. He was familiar to all those present but they were unaware of his name and knew him only as 'The Convener'. His footsteps made no sound as he walked across the thickly piled carpet to within a few feet of the table and stopped. The teller who had announced the result handed him the sheet of paper on which he had recorded the group's decision. The newcomer looked down at the page and read the words 'Motion Carried'. His face remained expressionless and he said not a word. With a slight nod of acknowledgement, he folded the paper, secreting it in the inside pocket of his suit jacket, turned and left the room, quietly closing the door behind him.

Within a matter of days, the man whose name was at the top of the page The Convener held in his pocket, would be dead.

Chapter One

Monday, June 10th. London, England.

Dr. Luke Harvey was enjoying the early morning sunshine and walked with a definite spring in his step as he left Lambeth Bridge and crossed the roundabout to enter Horseferry Road. Making his way to the imposing Victorian portico of number 65, The Westminster Coroner's Court, he was humming contentedly as he stepped through the front doors to begin his day's labours.

The routine work of autopsy, whilst offering a divergent range of subjects, seldom posed any significant problems for a pathologist. The law required that any 'unexpected death' must be reported and subjected to autopsy but basic investigation usually showed the cause to be fairly obvious and soon established. So Dr. Harvey envisaged a reasonably stress-free day as he scrubbed-up, donned his green operating gown and then entered the mortuary's examination room to confront the first cadaver on his list.

The subject of his initial investigation was an elderly, overweight woman who had collapsed on the street. Her general condition, initial blood tests and the excess of visceral fat he quickly discovered around her vital organs supported his suspicions and they were soon confirmed by the traumatised condition of the heart muscle. He diagnosed 'acute myocardial infarction', which would be explained to her grieving relatives as a simple heart attack.

The second body for examination proved equally uncomplicated. An apparently robust and healthy building site worker had mysteriously dropped dead in the middle of his shift but it took the experienced pathologist less than an hour to establish a 'pulmonary embolism' as the cause of death. The blood clot that had travelled to block the artery to his lung had been a time bomb. It could have remained fixed where it had formed for several weeks or struck at any time but either way, undiscovered, it would inevitably take the labourer's life. As he finished sewing the corpse, Dr. Harvey nodded to his two lab assistants, Ben and Sanjev, to remove the cadaver and wheel in the final body for the morning's investigations.

The card was expensively printed on high quality material. The background was glossy black and the logo was the silhouette of a reclining woman, outlined in white and wearing lingerie. In letters of deep red the words *Elite Escorts* were embossed in the centre beneath the logo and a web address and telephone number were written across the bottom.

"This doesn't look like your common or garden hooker" said Harvey quietly.

"You'd better believe it. These girls cost well over a grand a visit."

Harvey exhaled with a slight whistle of surprise. "And you think he availed himself of Elite's 'services'?"

The detective nodded. "I know he did. I checked. He booked one of the girls for Thursday night. He evidently enjoyed himself because he immediately booked her again for the following evening but he called in on the Friday afternoon to cancel. He told the agency he wasn't very well and wanted an early night." The policeman gave a facetious laugh. "He must have really been feeling rough to call it off because the cancellation charge for less than twenty-four hours' notice was the full fee!"

"So your theory is that the previous night's sexual exertions strained his heart and it caught up with him the next evening?"

Thomas held up his hands in a gesture that said 'you're the doc, you tell me'. "It's possible, isn't it?" he asked innocently. "And I'd say that the night's activities were definitely energetic."

"Oh?"

"Fresh chaffing marks on the bedstead."

Harvey looked nonplussed and the detective gave him a condescending smile that clearly defined the pathologist as the 'innocent abroad'. "Handcuffs, Doc" he explained a little patronisingly. "They left newly-made scratches on the framework."

"Ah" said Harvey as the penny dropped. "Actually that would make sense. I found some redness on both his wrists and a very slight bruising on an ankle."

The Inspector shrugged with relief. "There you go. That's Q.E.D. if you ask me."

"Isn't booking hookers illegal?" asked Harvey casually as the afterthought struck him.

"Of course. But, officially, the agency supplies escorts not hookers. They say they charge a fee for companionship only and if the girl then wants to spend the night with the guy that's her own, personal choice. It's all bollocks of course. But you can never prove otherwise. And if I tried to shut down every escort agency on suspicion of prostitution the courts would be backed-up from now until doomsday."

Harvey stared down thoughtfully at the card. "So, in summary, what we know is that he spent the Thursday night with a hooker, indulged in some sort of handcuff fetish, felt bad the following evening, went to bed... and died."

"Yup. That's it in a nutshell."

"But you didn't include any of this sexual encounter in your report."

The detective gave him a withering look. "Well, call me old fashioned, but it's not really going to comfort his widow to know the guy got his rocks off playing away from home, now is it? So it seemed better to let sleeping dogs lie. Er... no pun intended."

Luke Harvey was fairly certain that the Inspector's reluctance to report the deceased's amorous nocturnal entertainment had less to do with upsetting the distraught widow than with avoiding the endless paperwork of unnecessary complications; but he couldn't disagree with the logic.

"So what do you think, Doc? Are we done?" asked the detective eagerly as he swallowed the last of his coffee and then stood. "Can we put this one to bed now?"

It would have been very easy for Luke Harvey simply to accede to the policeman's wishes and sign-off the death certificate there and then. He'd been a pathologist for many years, and seen a great deal, and was fully aware that it was possible for an apparently healthy heart spontaneously to give out. Sudden Death Syndrome, or SDS, was a well-observed condition; but subsequent examination would always reveal the origin of the problem. Harvey had found nothing. To encounter a heart that had simply stopped and discover no apparent cause whatsoever made no sense. Sexual activity would certainly have increased the pulse rate at the time but, in an obviously fit and healthy man, it was unlikely to have brought-on a heart attack, much less one that had occurred some twenty-four hours later. It went against his every instinct to write 'death by natural causes' on the death certificate when he knew there was nothing 'natural' about it. Reluctantly, he shook his head.

"No. I'm sorry" he apologised. "But I can't release the body yet. I'll have to go back and run further tests."

The policeman was visibly deflated. "Christ, doc. Why make a fuss? If you really think this needs more examination then just mark it as 'inconclusive' and we'll ship the body back to the Congo and let them sort it out. Then we're all off the hook."

Buck-passing was not on the pathologist's agenda. "No. Sorry" he repeated. "I need more time. I'll let you know when my tests are complete."

Ryan Thomas recognised a closing line when he heard it. With a heavy sigh, he nodded and put down his coffee cup. "Thanks for the coffee, Doc. And the wasted afternoon. No doubt I'll be hearing from you." The irritated policeman turned on his heel and stalked off.

It was two hours later when Luke Harvey finally spotted it. Re-examining the body, he was looking again at the ankle where there was evidence of slight bruising. According to Inspector Thomas this was caused by chaffing from handcuffs, and the marks were certainly consistent with the policeman's theory. As he rotated the ankle he saw it for the first time. It was a small puncture mark at the top of the big toe, just underneath the front edge of the nail. Harvey took his magnifying glass and looked carefully at the hole. Alarm bells immediately rang as he realised it was exactly the right size to have been made by a syringe. In a living body, such a small puncture would have closed-up and healed within no time so the injury had to have been made either after death or, more likely, at the time of death.

Slowly, Harvey put down his magnifying glass, gently lowered the ankle and stared at the corpse lying on his table. He didn't want to believe the sinister theory that was now forming uncomfortably in his mind but every fibre of his professional being told him it was a definite possibility.

Instructing the lab assistants to return the body to the cold store, Harvey left the examination room, removed his gown and washed his hands, and returned swiftly to his office. He made a brief telephone call and then opened his laptop. Navigating to the appropriate website, he booked himself a train ticket for the following day.

* * * * *

Tuesday, June 11th.

As he left Cambridge station and hailed a taxi from the rank, Luke Harvey took a deep breath and smiled. It felt good to be back. Sitting in the rear of the vehicle, as the taxi drove him through the familiar streets in the warm afternoon sunshine, his mind was full of memories, and all of them were good. Most medical students encounter stressful periods of one sort or another, especially on a long and arduous course, but Harvey had enjoyed every minute of his training in Cambridge and would not have changed a single day. The University's School of Medicine was an elite establishment, attached to Addenbrooke's Hospital, and it had provided the eager student with extensive practical experience under the guidance of Professor Peter Gordon. The Prof's text book, written in the early nineties, was still considered 'the bible' of forensic pathology and Luke Harvey had formed a firm friendship with his illustrious tutor that had continued long after he gained his degree. The old boy was now in his early seventies and long overdue for laudable retirement but his mind was still as sharp as a tack and he had no intention of withdrawing from his post.

The cab dropped Harvey at the main entrance to Addenbrooke's and he made his way through the grounds to the professor's office in the admin block. After the usual pleasantries and the obligatory pouring of tea, Harvey settled back in his chair to explain the reason for his visit.

"I have a problem" he began cautiously. "And, if I'm right, there's something very sinister going on. So, as is my wont, I called you because I need the benefit of your wise counsel."

The older man smiled benignly. "Well, as I've always told you, first instincts are invariably sound. So never be afraid to run with them. What's preventing you trusting your intuition?"

Harvey spent the next few minutes describing the case in detail and explaining his examination of the corpse. When he revealed he had found a puncture wound in the toe, the Professor put down his tea cup and sat up, clearly intrigued.

"Interesting" he murmured, bringing his fingertips together and settling them under his chin. "So you believe he was injected with something through the toe?"

"It seems highly probable. How else does one acquire such a puncture wound?"

"Indeed. That would also be my hypothesis."

"But if we follow that line, and assume he was poisoned by injection, then why can I find no trace of any toxin in his blood or tissues? It makes no sense!"

A gentle smile broke across the older man's wrinkled features. "It makes sense if you're looking for something that no longer exists."

Harvey was perplexed. "Meaning?"

"Sux" said the Professor quietly.

This caused Harvey to slump back heavily in his chair. "You're kidding?"

The Professor shook his head. "It wouldn't be the first time. There was a well-known case in America. And, from the conditions you're describing, it would certainly fit the bill."

Daylight began to dawn and Harvey cursed himself for not having thought of it before. Suxamethonium Chloride, commonly known in operating theatres as 'Sux', was a drug used to induce muscle relaxation, usually to facilitate tracheal intubation during an operating procedure. Administered by an anaesthetist in carefully measured doses, it would bring about short term, targeted paralysis, requiring the patient to be kept alive by ventilation support. Injected in a large, indiscriminate dose it would paralyse the entire breathing system and the patient would quickly die from asphyxia.

"It works within seconds" added the Professor casually. "Decidedly unpleasant for the victim of course because it has no sedative effect. The recipient will remain wide awake as total muscular paralysis takes place. But, more to the point, the body's enzymes break down the drug within a very short time-frame so, by the time you undertake an autopsy, there's none of it left."

"So even if we run specific tests for it, they'll prove negative."

"Exactly."

Harvey gave a disappointed sigh. "So if Dikembe Lukeba was poisoned by lethal injection of Sux, there's no way I can prove it?"

The Professor leaned forward and became a little more animated. "A few years ago that would have been the case" he said, warming considerably to his subject. "Because we didn't know what we were looking for. But not anymore. Whilst it's true that we can't establish a drug that is no longer present, we *can* detect it's metabolites."

This was a welcome surprise. "They're specific?"

"Yes. The breakdown products that are left as a result of its interaction with the body are now well documented and proven to be substance specific."

"So it has a definite signature?"

"Indeed. Unique enough to prove Sux *was* there even if it there's no longer any trace of it. If you establish the presence of these metabolites, then Sux was the culprit." The elderly man smiled. "And your theory stands up."

Harvey nodded contentedly with relief . "Thanks, Professor. I'm very grateful. Can you email me a list of exactly what I'm looking for?"

"Of course. Now what about some more tea?"

* * * * *

Wednesday, June 12th.

Luke Harvey arrived early at Horseferry Road on Wednesday morning, eager to start work and pursue his evolving theory. A quick check of his laptop showed that Professor Gordon had been as good as his word and an email showing the known and registered metabolites of Suxamethonium Chloride was sitting in his inbox. It would take a few hours for the lab to run tests on tissue samples but a confident Harvey was optimistic they would find a positive result. He rang the lab to schedule the tests and then got scrubbed up and gowned, ready to begin the day's list.

On entering the examination room, he found his two assistant's, Ben and Sanjev, patiently waiting for him.

"Before we get going, I need Dikembe Lukeba brought back" Harvey told them. "We're going to take some more of his heart and lung tissue. The lab's standing by and I'll need one of you to take the samples over. Ok?"

The two assistants exchanged a perplexed look. It was Ben, the younger of the pair, who spoke up.

"The black guy, you mean? The one from a couple of days ago?"

"Yes. We have some additional tests to run."

The confusion on the faces of his two subordinates increased markedly.

"But... we can't" said Sanjev apprehensively.

It was Harvey's turn to look puzzled. "Why not?"

"Well... because he's gone."

"What?... What do you mean 'gone'? A cadaver can't just get up and walk out."

"No, of course not. But he was taken yesterday. We thought you knew."

"Taken?"

"Yes. A couple of blokes picked him up yesterday while you were in Cambridge. Around ten-ish. To be flown back to Africa, they said."

Harvey was totally bewildered. "What are you talking about? A body can't be released without a certificate. And I hadn't signed it off. How can he have been picked-up? On whose authority?"

Ben shrugged uncomfortably and shifted nervously from foot to foot, sensing that trouble was about to come down heavily upon his shoulders. "We assumed you'd signed a release. I mean, they had paperwork and everything."

"Who did?" demanded Harvey aggressively. "Who had paperwork? Was it the police? Was it Inspector Thomas?"

The two assistants both shook their heads. "No" said Sanjev. It was a couple of suits. Ministry guys they said. They had I.D."

"What I.D.? What ministry?"

"Not sure I can remember" said Ben falteringly. "But it was all kosher" he added in a hurry. "They had an official docket with Lukeba's name on it. They said it was all arranged and they'd come to collect him. So we wheeled him out of the cold store, stuck him in a body-bag and helped them load him into a Transit they had waiting outside. It was a black job with darkened windows."

"And it had official plates" said Sanjev defensively.

Harvey was beginning to get a very uncomfortable cold feeling that was gripping his lower back and spreading slowly up his spine. "Did they sign for the body?" he demanded.

"Yes."

"Get me the paperwork!"

Pulling off his surgical gloves, Harvey stormed out of the examination room. In his office he went at once to his phone and called Inspector Ryan Thomas.

"This is Dr. Harvey" he said immediately as the call connected.

"Ah. Good. Quicker than I thought but that's a plus. Reached your verdict, have you?"

"What have you done with Lukeba?"

The voice in Harvey's ear paused for several seconds as the detective tried to make sense of this unexpected question. "Sorry, Doc" the policeman managed eventually. "I'm not with you. What do you mean *what have I done with him?*"

"The corpse was picked up yesterday. Without my knowledge or permission and presumably on your 'say-so'."

"Wait a minute" said the Inspector, irritably. "Are you telling me you've already released the body?"

"No! I'm saying the opposite. I *didn't* release the body. But it's gone. It's been taken!"

"And you think *I* took it?"

"You're top of my list."

"Oh, do me a favour, Doc" declared Thomas, clearly annoyed. "What the fuck would I want with the corpse of a dead African?"

"Beats me. But to ship it back home presumably. That's what you wanted, wasn't it?"

"Not without the proper release it wasn't. Can you imagine the fall out if there's an unauthorised cadaver sitting at the airport?"

"Then who took it?"

"I haven't a bloody clue. Didn't anyone at your end get a signature for the pick-up?"

"Yes, of course. I've sent for the paperwork."

The detective gave an exasperated sigh. "Well then, I suspect it's some daft bloody mix-up with admin. I'm sure we'll sort it out."

"I'm afraid I don't share your confidence" Harvey told him acidly.

"Why not?"

"Because since I last spoke to you I've carried out further investigations."

"And?"

Harvey took a deep breath. "In my professional opinion, Dikembe Lukeba was murdered. And I find it strangely co-incidental that his body has been stolen before I can carry out the tests that might prove it."

There was silence at the other end of the telephone as the full import of Harvey's words registered. This was not good news. Ryan Thomas had little time for the pathologist and his 'play it by the book' attitude but that didn't mean he wasn't efficient and good at his job. The last thing the detective needed was a murder enquiry but if the Doc was claiming 'foul play' then he must have good reason to do so.

After a few moments, the voice in Harvey's ear spoke again.

"You said the body was collected yesterday?"

"Yes. In a black Transit."

"At what time?"

"Around 10am."

"And I don't suppose anybody took the registration number of the vehicle?"

"I shouldn't think so."

"No matter. It'll be easy enough to find."

"How?"

"You're a spit and cough from the houses of Parliament, Doc. There's more C.C.T.V. in your back yard than anywhere else in the country."

"My assistants tell me it was two men and that they had I.D. and official paperwork. That's why I presumed you'd sent them."

"Well I didn't. And while I'm checking it out, I need you and anyone and everyone who saw what happened to stay put. Nobody goes home until I get there, ok?"

"Understood."

The line went dead as Thomas abruptly hung up.

It was four and a half hours later when a disconsolate looking Inspector Ryan Thomas eventually arrived at Horseferry Road. In Luke Harvey's office he eased himself into the chair opposite the pathologist's desk and sat back wearily as the doctor handed him a Styrofoam cup of coffee.

"Black. One sugar. Right?"

The detective nodded and gratefully took a sip of the hot liquid.

"Have you discovered anything?" asked Harvey.

The detective nodded again but it was a few seconds before he spoke.

"Cameras on Millbank recorded a black Transit turning right and heading along the north bank of the river at 10.27 yesterday morning. The registration number showed it belongs to the F.C.O."

"The Foreign Office?"

"Yes."

"So they *were* government officials. That's strange, isn't it?"

"Yes. But it gets a whole lot stranger. They took the body straight to Heathrow. It spent the night in the morgue there and left..." he glanced down at the open notebook in his hand... "on Air France flight A1381 at 6.40 this morning, bound for Kinshasa via Paris." He flipped his notebook closed. It was a gesture with an ominous finality about it.

"But they can't freight a body without a death certificate and official authorisation" complained Harvey.

"Correct. And they had both."

The doctor sat back in his chair, completely baffled. "I don't get it. How?"

"That's what I've spent the last few hours trying to discover."

"And?"

Thomas took a long draught of coffee and then stared thoughtfully across the top of the cup at the pathologist. "I'll get to that in a moment. First, tell me why you thought Lukeba had been poisoned?"

"He'd been injected. In his toe."

"But you said you found no trace of any toxins?"

"I didn't. Because there were none. But there are some substances that break down completely in the body and disappear. And one in particular that has been used before to kill."

Thomas wasn't sure he was following the logic. "But how do you find something that isn't there?"

"Precisely. That's why it had me baffled. But the body's reactions to the poison leave recognisable markers. On any normal autopsy they'd never be noticed because we wouldn't be looking for them. But a forensic expert advised me what indicators might be present and I was going to run new tissue tests."

Thomas nodded quietly to himself as the pieces fell disturbingly into place. "And the body was snatched before you could start."

"Yes. And I'm going to raise merry-bloody-hell until I find out who authorised it and why."

"No you're not" said the Inspector quietly. "Not if you value your job and your pension."

Harvey was genuinely nonplussed by the unexpected, dispassionate response. "I'm sorry. I don't understand. What are you saying?"

The detective gave a deep and regretful sigh. "I've been told to tell you that the death has been officially ascribed to heart failure and will be entered as such into the records. The body has been returned to the Democratic Republic of Congo with the condolences of Her Majesty's Government. End of story."

Luke Harvey fell silent. He felt as if a door had suddenly slammed shut in his face. A sympathetic Ryan Thomas leaned forward in his chair and spoke softly.

"I don't like this anymore than you do. And, if it's any consolation, I'd personally lay odds that your poisoning theory is right. But the paperwork that was shown to your assistants was perfectly in order because it was legitimate and issued officially. And the two guys who collected the unfortunate Mr. Lukeba were 'removal' men of a very particular kind. The kind you don't question and who will never be identified."

"And how do you know all this?" asked Harvey quietly.

"Because I've just spent an hour in a meeting that 'didn't take place' having it all carefully spelled out to me. Are you beginning to understand?"

Harvey understood all too well. But that didn't mean he liked it. He felt his fists clench. "This is *my* jurisdiction!" he whispered vehemently. "I have a duty to establish an accurate cause of death. And *nobody* can circumvent that due process. I don't care *who* they are. It's the law!"

Inspector Thomas put down his coffee cup and quietly stood. "Very noble, Doc. I applaud your ethics. But please... wise up. If you know what's good for you, you'll recognise a brick wall when you see one. This is way, way above your pay grade. And mine too." The policeman stepped away from the desk and turned as he reached the doorway. "Whatever you and I may think is irrelevant. This case is now officially *closed*."

Chapter Two

Thursday, June 13th.

Old Compton Street does not so much subtly declare itself 'pink' but rather shouts it loudly from the rooftops, thought Josh Brody with a smile as he turned into the famous road from Wardour Street and headed for Paul's, the French baker and delicatessen.

The area's unprejudiced acceptance of anyone and everyone was one of the things Brody most loved about Soho. It had always been a melting pot, offering a welcome to every race, creed and colour without criticism or condemnation. Within its narrow streets the 'haves' and 'have-nots' lived cheek by jowl; art and creativity rubbed shoulders with business and commerce, and gays and straights happily co-existed. The flesh pots and strip clubs nestled comfortably alongside the innumerable restaurants and cafés, bars and pubs, tolerantly catering for every appetite. All were accepted and all were valued. Brody liked living within such a diverse and non-judgemental atmosphere.

This particular street was the centre of the area's gay community, especially around The Admiral Duncan, and the window displays in most of the shops were aimed specifically at this clientele. Yet Brody's small flat was situated above La Gattina, a pole dancing club that, exhibiting a typically Soho breadth of palate, was situated just a short distance further along the street from the famous gay pub.

He purchased a freshly-baked stick loaf and a couple of croissants from the French deli and stepped back into the busy street. Two years before he'd written a book about Soho and so he was more familiar than most with its history. The area was originally built upon Soho fields which, according to legend, was thus named because King Charles' bastard son, the Duke of Monmouth, was prone to yelling "So-Ho!" when hunting there. Although Brody's book had briefly touched upon the origins of the place, it was concerned less with the visceral pursuits of wayward historical Royals and more with the venal activities of those considerably lower down the social strata. In its colourful past, Soho had been the major centre of London's sex trade and 'home' to the villains and gangsters that organised and ran it, along with the gambling, the drugs, the protection and most other rackets. Brody's chronicle, entitled

'Soho – The Dark Side', was a detailed and informative history of that period. It had sold well in hardback on publication and was still in print. It hadn't made him a fortune but had earned him critical laurels and helped considerably with his ever present financial problems.

By profession, Joshua Brody was an investigative reporter. Having completed a degree in political history, he joined the full time staff at The Independent and made noted progress, even winning an award on one occasion, but the salary of a staff reporter was never going to make him rich and it was now more than ten years since he made the leap of faith and turned free-lance. Being self-employed had allowed him to write three factual books, the Soho history being the most successful, and also to pen two crime novels under a pseudonym. Neither of these thrillers sold particularly well but each recovered its costs and returned a small profit for his publishers, so they were still actively supporting his career in commercial fiction. He enjoyed novel writing, and it was a necessary adjunct to his income, but it was factual and field work that was his forte and that truly fired his enthusiasm.

Brody's chief asset was his uncanny instinct. He seemed possessed of a sixth sense that was denied to most other journalists. Its stirring was never a momentous event; no beacon of light would ignite to flood his brain; there would be no Damascene revelation; it was merely that something would quietly jar and unsettle him when the facts didn't quite add up. It might at first be indiscernible, just a vague feeling that the pieces didn't exactly fit together; an indefinable discord that would nag at him and prompt him to take a second look. In the jargon of the trade, Brody possessed 'a great nose for a story', and it had served him more than well.

He was one of the first into Tunisia when the initial stirrings of the Arab Spring began to surface, filing some of the very first copy on the embryonic revolt. By the time the rest of the world was fully concentrated on what was happening, Brody was in Egypt where, at some considerable personal risk, he sought out the dissenters and began reporting back on the growing unrest. With his instinct in overdrive, he quickly moved on to Libya, working under-cover, anticipating the fall of the notorious Gaddafi regime.

The numerous trips abroad placed a frequent strain on his marriage but his copy was eagerly purchased and, all in all, his career as a freelance had provided a decent living. Then the divorce happened and life had become somewhat hand-to-mouth ever since.

Releasing the mortise and then turning the key in the double Yale lock, he opened his street door and climbed the narrow, rickety stairs to the third story landing and the door to his tiny flat. A small lounge at the front, overlooking the street, a galley kitchen, an equally undersized bedroom at the rear and a tiny bathroom where even a kitten could not be swung, now constituted his domestic world. It was a far cry from the spacious Victorian sea-front apartment he and Kassia bought when they married.

Brody was born and bred in Leigh-on-Sea, in Essex, where the wide Thames estuary flows into the cold, grey waters of The North sea, and first met Kassia during a visit home to see his parents. She was a Polish student, working as a waitress in one of the Arches cafés opposite the Westcliff beach to earn money while she completed the final term of her English course.

Brody always considered himself to be just an average looking guy, and far from the 'tall, dark and handsome' brigade, but he stood six feet in height, was indeed dark haired, had a lean frame and, when required, could turn on the charm. There was nothing false or phoney in his manner; his appeal was genuine and uncontrived and Kassia evidently proved susceptible to it as he began flirting with her over the café menu.

She was only twenty at the time, his junior by just over ten years, but her bright blue eyes, intelligent face and curiously attractive accent drew him immediately. When he then began dating her and found her to be quick-witted, clever and well-read, he was totally hooked. Within less than six months, and much to the consternation of his parents, they married.

Their daughter Serafina was born the following Spring and Brody unexpectedly found himself the archetypal doting father. Nothing in his thirty one years had prepared him for the way he felt when he first held her in his arms and, to his own amazement, he tumbled joyfully into the role of adoring parent. He knew he was fulfilling every cliché in the book and he didn't care. He had never been happier.

Domestic bliss lasted for almost three years before it gradually started unravelling at the seams. The pressure of his work, with no fixed routine and long periods of absence, certainly did nothing to help but the simple truth was they just grew apart. Even now, he couldn't put it down to any one, specific cause; it was just a combination of factors. His constantly changing and unpredictable schedule was undoubtedly a problem, but he always tried to organise his time at home to accommodate sharing the role of attentive parent and she genuinely appreciated his efforts. Her time was also pressured because she wanted to move on from her Bachelor's degree and was studying hard for an M.A., but Brody fully supported her ambition and was keen to see her complete the course. There were no real rows or arguments; and no other party was involved on either side. Yet, like the constant dripping of water on a stone, and despite their best endeavours each to accommodate the other, the relationship seemed somehow to dissolve and wear away. It appeared to be a simple case of circumstance. The irony was that he still had strong feelings for her and was fairly sure she reciprocated; but two attempts at reconciliation and a 'fresh start' failed and, after five years of marriage, he eventually reluctantly agreed to the inevitable divorce.

Saffy was now seven years old and remained the light of Brody's life. Both he and Kassia wanted her to stay in the area for her education because Westcliff boasted one of the country's best girls' grammar schools so, despite the severe financial strain, part of the divorce settlement agreed that they would each retain their half share of the apartment and would maintain the family home in situ. Brody himself moved back to his old stomping ground in London and, by a stroke of luck, secured his Spartan flat above La Gattina at a knock-down rent. Kassia heartily disapproved of her daughter's father living above 'that awful place' but, financially, Brody was in no position to consider her condemnation.

The owner of the pole-dancing club was a fourth generation Italian immigrant called Rocco Landino. His great-grandfather had owned a spaghetti house in the bad old days of Soho and many of the local crime barons were among his favoured customers. When Rocco learned that Brody was writing a history of the area he asked him, as a personal favour, not to mention the family name or refer to his *Nonno's* restaurant. The old man had not exactly been an integral part of the underworld and so Brody obliged and excluded him from the saga. Rocco was so grateful that when he learned the writer was looking to move back to London he offered him the tiny flat on the top floor of his building at only a nominal rent. Brody eagerly accepted the offer and was now a settled resident in his frugal abode.

He could hear the phone ringing as he reached the top of the stairs and hurriedly opened the front door of the flat. Carelessly throwing his shopping onto the nearby chair, he grabbed the receiver.

"Hello?"

"It's me."

"Kass. Hi. How are you? How's Saffy?"

"We're both fine. She's had a bit of a sniffley summer cold but it's nothing really."

"Oh. Well, as long as it's not serious. I'm looking forward to seeing her on the weekend."

The voice in his ear changed tone a little. "Yes. Well, that's why I'm calling. Saturday's ok but she's been asked to a school friend's birthday party on Sunday. It's an all-day thing. They're going to Adventure Island."

The vast fun fair next to the pier at Southend was one of Saffy's favourite haunts. Brody was disappointed to lose one of his precious days with his daughter but could well imagine how much she'd enjoy being there, especially with a bunch of her friends.

"Oh, right. Well, of course she must go. She'll have a great time."

"I just wanted to let you know in advance. So you would know your Sunday is free."

"Yes. Thanks. I appreciate it."

There was a pause. There was often a pause when they spoke. When discussing Saffy they were on safe, communal ground. But chatting about anything else seemed a little awkward. Neither wanted to hang up or end the conversation but neither was quite sure what could or should be discussed and a hiatus often ensued.

"Well, I guess I'd better go" she said eventually. "Lots to do."

"Yup. Sure. Well, take care."

"You too."

There was a click and the line went dead. Brody replaced the receiver with a sigh and, gathering his shopping, went to the kitchen to make a pot of coffee to accompany his fresh croissants. He'd no sooner filled the coffee maker with water than the phone rang again. Grinning, he returned to the lounge.

"What did you forget?" he asked cheerfully as he answered the call. "Does she want me to bring her some chocolate from the deli?"

"Joshua?" said a male voice.

"Oh. Sorry. Thought you were someone else. Yes, this is Josh."

"It's Luke. Luke Harvey."

This was a definite surprise.

"Christ! Luke. How are you? It's been ages."

"Yes, it has. Must be well over a year now. And I'm ok, thanks."

"How's the job?"

"Thriving. People are still 'dying to see me' and all the other jokes and clichés."

"Well *I* didn't say it!"

No. And I'm grateful. But it *is* about the job that I'm calling. Any chance we can meet for a chat?"

Brody's inquisitive instinct sprang to the fore. Luke and he were friends but had never been especially close. If the pathologist was calling then he had a reason. And if that reason required a personal meeting rather than talking over the telephone then Brody was intrigued to find out why.

"Sure. When would suit you?"

"As soon as possible. Today if you're free."

Brody's interest doubled. "What about this afternoon?"

"I can be free after two" said the pathologist.

"And I'm guessing you'd prefer somewhere quiet, without adjacent ears to overhear?"

"That would be preferable. Yes."

"Do you know the Hampshire Hotel, the Radisson in the corner of Leicester Square?"

"I think so, yes. I can certainly find it."

"Most of the customers sit outside when the weather is like this, so the downstairs bar will be quiet. Shall we say three o'clock?"

"Great. Thanks. I'll be there."

Dr. Luke Harvey first crossed Brody's path when the journalist was reporting the trial of a Brixton teenager charged with a knife murder. The case appeared to hinge on the type of blade used in the attack and the defence barrister ruthlessly attacked the pathologist's testimony, trying to get him to admit to doubts as to the identification of the fatal weapon in relation to the wounds. Harvey had calmly and courteously ridden out the fierce verbal onslaught and stuck firmly to his guns. The jury found the boy guilty, largely due to Harvey's steadfast evidence, and he was sentenced to a minimum of twenty-five years. Once in gaol, the boy subsequently admitted to fellow inmates that he'd committed the crime and one of them grassed on him. The reported confession confirmed the pathologist had been right.

Impressed with both Harvey's resolute manner and his courage, Brody interviewed him for a subsequent article on the pressures of giving forensic evidence. The two men became friendly and stayed in touch, meeting periodically and, like today, catching-up with each other's news.

Having ordered a couple of beers, they settled themselves into a quiet corner of the Hampshire hotel's foyer bar. The small talk and pleasantries were few and swiftly accomplished and Brody quickly got down to business.

"So what can I do for you, Luke?"

"I'm not sure" Harvey admitted honestly with a nervous shake of his head. "Maybe nothing. It all depends on what you feel is possible. And I certainly won't hold it against you if you tell me that there's nowhere this can go."

"Ok. Understood. So why don't you begin at the beginning and I'll tell you what I think."

Harvey took a long swig of his beer, took a deep breath, and then began to relate the strange tale of Dikembe Lukeba and the disappearance of his corpse. Brody listened attentively, occasionally jotting down a few details in his notebook, and found himself increasingly absorbed in the extraordinary story he was hearing. Fifteen minutes later, he sat back in his chair with a frown, unable to deny the obvious implications.

"So, basically, you've been warned off further questioning and told to let it go. Right?"

"Yes. Which, in itself, must mean that there is some sort of official cover-up going on."

"And you think it's concealing a murder?"

"I believe so. I can't be one hundred per cent definite because I was unable to conclude my examination. But the weight of probability is that Lukeba's death was due to foul play."

"And you want me to try and prove it?"

Luke Harvey gave a shrug. "It has to be your call. I freely admit that I dare not do so myself. I'm a state employee. And if whoever is pulling the strings on this is capable of shutting down Inspector Thomas and all enquiries then they are certainly powerful enough to bring about my dismissal." He raised his eyebrows in a sheepish look of defeat. "I have a wife and three kids to support. It hurts to admit it but I dare not step out of line and risk losing my job."

Brody nodded his understanding. "No, of course you can't. Nobody would expect you to. But you're right. There's something rotten in the state of Denmark and it's certainly worth a look to see what we might flush out."

"I was hoping you'd say that. But I don't want you to put yourself in any jeopardy or get you into any kind of trouble."

Brody grinned. "Wouldn't be the first time. But I think I can move quietly enough to avoid any major problems. Certainly with preliminary enquiries."

"But where do you start?"

"Well you can only play the hand you've been dealt. As I see it, this one holds just four cards. The first is Lukeba himself. We need to ascertain exactly who he was and what he did. If, as you suspect, he was poisoned then he definitely upset somebody somewhere along the line. If we go digging, we might throw up a motive."

Harvey nodded. "Makes sense."

"The second is Thomas, the detective. But questioning him will only announce what we're doing and that's the last thing we want. He must be made to think you've followed his advice and dropped the whole thing. Don't call him specifically but if you get the opportunity to let slip something to that effect then it might buy us a little cover."

"Ok."

"The third asset we have is you. I'll need a comprehensive report of *exactly* what you think happened. Full specifics of the suspected poison; where and how it might be obtained; any trail that procuring it might have left; and a detailed description of how it was administered."

"Understood. I'll get everything to you by tomorrow morning. What's the fourth card?"

"The only other people we know to have had contact with Lukeba before he died. Elite Escorts."

Contrary to popular perception, the great majority of girls who performed at La Gattina, and similar clubs, were not hookers. A good portion were students, supplementing their meagre grants and paying off loans; many were housewives and mothers who needed to add to the overstretched family income; others were simply resilient, strong-minded women taking advantage of the chance to store away tax-free, ready cash. What they all had in common was an awareness of their physical assets and a recognition of the simple fact that men could easily be parted from their money for the opportunity to ogle them.

The personal Rubicon that all the girls needed to cross in order to be able to do the job was detachment from nudity; to be able to view the naked body as separate from the individual within, like a costume donned in order to play a role. Once achieved, they could dance, tease and titillate yet remain one step 'removed' from the gawping and the glares and the fumbling hands that thrust five and ten pound notes into the narrow bands of their G strings. Some grew cold and hard, despising the men who pathetically spent their cash to view forbidden fruit at close quarters, but most girls were well adjusted to the work and saw it as nothing more than a lucrative way to earn a living.

Living 'above the store', Brody knew all of Rocco's regular staff and was friendly with most of the dancers. He had little interest in the performances, and was never charged admission, but would often share a late night drink and a chat sitting at the bar. The interior was not exactly 'classy'; more a poor man's imitation of a Las Vegas club; but, as the lighting was usually subdued and low level, it didn't really matter. The punters were too occupied with the girls on display to notice their surroundings and, as long as the orders for the over-priced drinks kept flowing, Rocco was none too concerned about the quality of his decor and furnishings.

The two regular bouncers on duty at the front door were known to one and all as 'Eric and Ernie'. Brody understood that one of them was indeed named Eric and so the sobriquet of the famous double-act had been applied to the pair and used for so long that no-one now referred to them as anything else. Few people, including Brody, actually knew which was which. He nodded to the two large, thick-set men as he stepped across the threshold and entered the club.

The stage area, in the centre of the main room, was relatively small but sufficient to accommodate two shiny, metal poles, with enough surrounding space for the girls to work either in pairs or individually, each going through their own well-rehearsed routine. It was Rocco's policy to schedule the performers in a varying rota, so the spectacle would keep changing, and in between their shifts the girls, usually dressed in a provocative or revealing gown, would sit in the main room or at the bar and flirt with customers, encouraging them to buy drinks and looking to pick-up extra tips.

The music was pumping loudly through the P.A. speakers and the act was changing as Brody seated himself on a stool at the bar. As the previous performer left, to cheers and whistles from the vociferous crowd gathered in the seats around the edge of the stage, a brunette dancer called Angel emerged and strutted back and forth in time to the pulsing bass of the backing track. She was dressed in calf-length boots and black stockings, with only a skimpy bikini covered in rhinestones between her stocking tops and the Stetson hat perched provocatively on her head. Like all good strippers, she knew that 'anticipation' was actually more of a turn-on than nudity itself and, for many minutes, she expertly played the floor, teasing the gawping punters. After a few energetic and impressive manoeuvres swinging around the pole, she began gyrating across the stage towards the front row of customers. With a feigned look of shocked innocence, her mime show was asking if they really expected her to remove her bra. Amid wild cheers of encouragement, eager hands reached forward holding money. Down on her knees, Angel crawled her way along the apron, collecting dozens of notes thrust into the tops of her stockings, the band of her bikini bottom and the sides of her boots.

"The dumb saps" thought Brody as he watched the girl expertly working the crowd. "So far she hasn't shown them a damn thing and she's already milking their wallets."

Angel cleverly manipulated her audience, able to raise and lower their excitement at will. The bra of her bikini eventually came off to loud applause but it was nothing compared to the reaction she engineered five minutes later when she removed the bikini bottom, leapt onto the pole and hung suspended, upside down, as she went into the splits. At the sight of her exposed, fully shaved, naked crotch, the punters broke into wild, ecstatic cheers. It was the ultimate tease. 'Here it is boys. Everything you want. But you can't have it. You can look... but you can't touch.' When she came down from the pole she repeated her crawl on all fours along the front of the apron and this time collected twice as much as her previous sortie had earned.

With a final flourish, she removed her Stetson, took a deep bow and left the stage to fervent yelling and applause.

Twenty minutes later, Brody was still seated on his stool, nursing a lager, when Angel emerged unobtrusively through the pass door and quietly entered the room. She was now wearing a long black dress with a split at the side that rose to hip level and was cut fairly low at the front to reveal an enticing view of her cleavage. Notwithstanding the celestial implications of her stage alias, Brody knew her by her down-to-earth, real name of Carla.

Carla was around thirty-two years of age and an ex-hoofer from West End musicals. She'd married a skunk and been left with a young child, an apartment she couldn't afford, and several thousand pounds of debt that her erstwhile husband had run up on her credit card. To Brody's eye, her face was attractive, if not exactly beautiful, but her body, as all the enthusiastic customers were well able to testify, was to die for. Brody reckoned she must have been one hell of a dancer in her day because, in his humble opinion, of all the girls he'd seen perform at La Gattina she was head and shoulders above the others in the skill of her routines. The punters evidently agreed with his verdict because she usually came out on top in the tally of tips. All the girls received no more than a small basic wage for each evening's work, but they were allowed to keep whatever tips the punters gave them and, in addition, Rocco paid them ten per cent of whatever drinks were ordered while they sat at a table chatting.

The main earner for the girls was the 'private dance'. There were several small rooms leading off the main salon and earnings were drastically boosted if a punter ordered a personal performance in one of these intimate chambers. These expensive, private sessions had to be booked through the house, not with the girls directly, and there were definite rules: no touching and no lewd behaviour on the premises. Eric and Ernie were on hand to ensure the punters obeyed and behaved themselves and the 'private dance' was a very popular, and highly lucrative, attraction at La Gattina. Rocco paid 30% of the exorbitant fee to the performer and the best girls were booked many times in an evening. In a really good week, working six nights, Carla could clear £3,000 in fees and tips. And almost all of it was cash in hand.

"Got a minute?" Brody asked as she approached the bar. "I won't keep you long." He was acutely aware that time was money and did not want to prevent her working the room and earning.

She smiled warmly. "Sure." She eased herself onto the stool beside him. It was actually a pleasure for her to make real conversation and switch off the 'please the punter' act.

"How was it tonight?" he enquired.

"All right, I guess" she said with a slight shrug. "The usual crop of slugs with alcohol breath and their brains in their dicks, but as long as they're spending I'll forgive them."

Brody liked Carla. He had a theory that, in common with many of the pole-dancers, she was actually performing as a means of striking back at men in general and the punters whose groping hands slid notes into her thong in particular; laughing at them with contempt for every pound they handed out to her. But such Freudian analysis was for others more qualified and didn't really interest him. All he knew was that she was a bright, attractive woman and he enjoyed her company.

"How are things with you, Josh?" she asked as Oscar, the bar tender, automatically put down her customary gin and tonic in front of her without it being ordered. "And how's little Saffy?"

"She's great. Growing up faster than I can cope with. Yesterday I was holding her in my arms, bringing her back home from the maternity ward. Today she's asking her mother when she can start wearing eye shadow. Can you believe it?"

Carla laughed. "Tell me about it. My boy is trying out for the school team and wants a new pair of football boots. I thought I'd only just got him out of nappies!"

Brody raised his glass. "To our kids. May they grow up a little more slowly!"

She chinked his glass and they both took a drink."

"May I ask you a favour?" he said gently.

"As long as you don't want to borrow money" she joked. "Sure. What do you need?"

"Information. I wouldn't feel comfortable asking the girls here about this face to face but... do you know if any of them do escort work?"

She gazed over the top of her glass at him and raised her eyebrows. "Is this a professional enquiry or for your personal delight?"

He laughed. "Entirely professional."

She shrugged. "Some do. Yes. But they're hardly likely to admit it to a reporter, now are they? Why are you asking?"

"I could tell you it's research for my next book; but I don't want to lie so I'll level with you. I need to interview a girl who undertook a gig last week through an agency called Elite Escorts. She's not in any trouble, at least as far as I'm aware, and anything she tells me will be strictly off the record. I'm just after some background on the punter she 'entertained'. So I wondered if any of the girls here know the agency and could furnish me with an intro to the girl who took the job?"

Carla shook her head and gave a little laugh. "Come on, Josh. Get real! The whole escort business works on discretion. If a girl is caught blabbing to a reporter she'd be finished. Why should she talk to you?"

Brody lowered his voice. "Because I'm keen to eliminate her from a little storm that's brewing. The police have been poking around this and an editor I know has latched onto it. If it blows open, it'll make banner headlines. The paper I'm working for wants me to get there before anybody else does. If I do, then I can control the story. So, if she'll quietly answer my questions now, I can guarantee to keep both her and the agency out of it, if and when it breaks."

He felt a little guilty lying to Carla about working for an editor, especially when he knew the police had already drawn a veil over the entire affair, but the deception seemed to pay dividends and, after a long pause, while she was clearly weighing the odds, Carla finally spoke.

"I know the guy who runs Elite" she said softly. "He keeps asking me to sign onto his books."

"I bet he does" said Brody, knowing she would be a most popular draw. "Have you considered it?"

She shook her head and turned up her nose a little. "No. That's a step too far for me. But his operation is really high class. I'll say that for him. You need very deep pockets to book any of his girls."

"Can you make an introduction for me? I promise you this is legit. There's no exposé. I won't write about the agency or its girls. I just need some discreet information on the punter. It will go no further."

Carla grinned. "You don't have to convince *me*, Josh. If I didn't trust you I wouldn't have told you I know the guy. But you'll need to make a pretty good case if you expect *him* to talk."

"So you'll help?"

"I can't promise anything. But I'll make a call."

"Thanks, Carla. You're a star!" He handed her a business card with his mobile number on it. "I can be reached here."

She nodded and took the card. Suddenly she became very serious. "Watch your step, Joshua. His agency is a class act but he's no soft touch. You definitely don't want to cross him. If you get my meaning?"

"Ok. Thanks. I'll bear it in mind."

Downing the last of her drink, she set the glass back onto the bar. "Give my love to Saffy. Time to get back to work."

She slid off the stool and made her way across the room to a corner table where two overweight Egyptians sat sprawled in a semi-circular velvet banquette.

"Gentlemen" she said warmly. "How are we this evening? How did you enjoy my dance?"

Chapter Three

Friday, June 14th. New York, U.S.A.

The meeting had been called at unusually short notice. Even though they were accustomed to last minute arrangements, the twelve members of the group found it decidedly inconvenient to re-organise their already busy schedules so unexpectedly and so soon after the previous gathering. None the less, they came.

They were assembled in a large, oak-panelled room on the ground floor of a six storey Brownstone building in midtown Manhattan. Originally built as the home of one of the city's wealthiest families, it was now the New York headquarters of a small merchant bank. The financial organisation catered for a very select and carefully protected list of clients, mostly international corporations, placing their investments and managing their funds.

The Convener was present, nodding politely in welcome to each member as they arrived, but never greeting anyone by name. Fresh coffee and tea had been prepared in four large, ornate, silver pots that were laid out on the nineteenth century oak dresser set against the side wall and, with a minimum of chat and small talk, each member helped themselves to their choice of beverage before returning with their delicate bone-china cup and saucer to take their place at the central, circular table.

When everyone was settled, The Convener handed them each a short breakdown of the single subject on the meeting's agenda before placing a bulky dossier in the centre of the table. He then took two dice from his pocket and, after shaking them briefly in his right hand, rolled them gently onto the highly polished wooden surface of the table. They came up as a three and a five.

"The reader will be seat eight" he announced. "I believe you now have everything you need" he told the group unemotionally. "As always, please leave all papers within the room and take nothing with you. Everything will be placed in the burn bag once you have departed. If you require any further information then I will be outside and at your disposal. I'll now leave you to your deliberations."

With a slight inclination of the head, he turned and left the room, closing the door quietly behind him.

The occupant of seat eight, one of the three women present, reached forward and opened the dossier. She glanced for a few moments at the first page and then cleared her throat in readiness to read aloud to the others from the text in front of her.

She would be reading at sight because it was an essential element of the procedure that no one knew in advance of the subject matter of the meeting. Likewise, the reader of the dossier was selected by the random choice of the dice throw. In this way, no preparation was possible and impartiality was guaranteed.

"Apologies are offered for the short notice given for this meeting" the woman began in clear and unemotional tones as she read. "This was caused by the unanticipated opportunity that has suddenly arisen. The accused is normally hard to reach but a previously un-announced visit to Europe will place him unexpectedly within our orbit. Should a decision be made to proceed, we will be able to take full advantage of the intended location. If the decision is to be deferred, it will be many months before this case can be reconsidered for action. It was therefore felt that this situation warranted an urgent meeting."

Most of those seated around the table nodded their silent understanding and the woman continued to read from the pages in front of her. " Inside information has been obtained at great risk and confirms that the official description of the work on which the accused is engaged is false and serves as a cover for the actual research being undertaken. This work is considered to be highly dangerous and a considerable threat to world stability."

It was a further half an hour until the reader completed her task but, once the full contents of the dossier had been read, the ensuing discussion was relatively short and quickly accomplished. Amid a general consensus that no further debate was necessary, the company moved swiftly to the secret ballot. The two tellers counted and checked the votes and the motion was declared 'passed unanimously'.

The Convener was summoned and received the verdict with his customary impassive acknowledgement. As soon as he exited the room, the meeting was declared closed and the twelve members took a brief farewell of each other and left. The entire process, from arrival to departure, had lasted just over an hour.

* * * * *

Saturday, June 15th. Westcliff, Essex, England.

Brody didn't own a car. Quite apart from saving himself the expense of petrol, insurance and maintenance, parking space in the capital was almost as valuable as real estate and to use it cost a king's ransom. Living in the heart of Soho, in the midst of one of the world's greatest concentration of transport systems, anywhere that could not be reached on foot could be accessed by tube, taxi or bus. Occasionally, at weekends, he hired a vehicle if he wanted to drive Saffy somewhere for a treat, but his normal practice for visits to his daughter was to take the Central line to Bank, then walk the half mile to Fenchurch Street and catch the C2C over-ground train to Westcliff. The whole journey took only ninety minutes and, if he left early, he could pick up Saffy in time to take her for breakfast on the seafront, which was something she loved to do.

As he sat opposite her in The Mermaid café, watching her eagerly devour her scrambled eggs on toast, he was struck again by how fast she was growing up. He treasured these moments alone with her and knew it was important to enjoy them while it was still possible. Before he could blink, she'd be a teenager and her weekends would be full of friends, boys and a thousand distractions that would all lay claim to her time. She'd always been a 'Daddy's girl', and he prayed she would ever remain so, but she was also strong-willed and independent and he had no doubt her life would quickly fill with diversions that would relegate her meetings with him to second place.

"So how has your week at school been?" he asked.

She shrugged nonchalantly. "Ok. We're doing a nature project. We're going on a trip to a farm" she said between mouthfuls. "The whole class is going. On a bus."

"That sounds exciting."

She gave an enthusiastic nod. "There'll be real animals and we can touch them and everything. I want to see the rabbits. They're my favourite."

"Really? I didn't know you liked rabbits."

"Yes. I keep asking Mum for one. But she says 'no'."

"Well, I'm sure your Mum has her reasons."

"She thinks it would be too much trouble. But it wouldn't. It's not like a dog, is it? Where you have to take it for walks and stuff. It just sits in a hutch. And I would do the feeding and the cleaning and everything!"

"Did you tell that to your Mum?"

"Yes. But she still said 'no'." There was a slight pause before a look he knew all too well arose in her eyes. "I bet she'd say 'yes' if *you* asked her."

Seven years old and already she's learned how to play one against the other, thought Brody with a sigh. It was a skill eventually developed by most children of separated parents but she'd wasted no time in acquiring it. 'Daddy's girl' or not, he was not about to pander to her aspiring manipulation.

"If Mum says 'no' to you then you can be *certain* she'll say 'no' to me."

Saffy grinned broadly. "Are you in her bad books again?"

"I hope not. But I will be if we gang up on her about a rabbit! So, as Bugs-Bunny is currently out of court, what about an ice-cream instead?"

Her face lit up. "A Rossi? With a flake?"

"You bet."

"Yes!"

They finished their meal and left the café, strolling hand in hand along the seafront to Rossi's ice cream parlour. Taking their cornets down onto the beach, they settled themselves onto the sand and watched the waves of the incoming tide breaking gently at their feet.

"You're going to Adventure Island tomorrow, is that right?" he asked her.

"Yes. It's Chloe's birthday treat. And we're getting wrist bands for the whole day. So we can go on every ride!"

"Sounds like a great time to me."

Her head tilted to one side and she raised her eyebrows. "Is it ok with you? I mean, it's Sunday and everything."

He smiled at her warmly. "Yes, it's ok. No problem."

"You won't be lonely, will you?" she asked a little wistfully.

Brody laughed. "No. I promise I won't be lonely. But thanks for asking."

Reassured that her Dad would be fine, she immediately put the subject from her mind and refocused her full attention to licking the stream of melted ice cream that was trickling down the outside of her cornet.

* * * * *

Sunday, June 16th. London, England.

Without his regular trip to the coast to see his daughter, Brody decided upon a lazy Sunday. Rising late, he went to the French delicatessen for a brunch of fresh croissants and coffee and passed a pleasant couple of hours reading through The Independent. He felt a distinct loyalty to his old newspaper and particularly enjoyed browsing the Sunday edition.

The rest of the day was taken up with a long walk along the Thames Embankment where, despite the ever present hordes of tourists, he was able to stroll peacefully in the brilliant afternoon sunshine before making his way into Covent Garden, where he passed an amusing hour watching the dynamic street performers in the piazza outside St. Paul's church.

He ate an evening meal at the Loon Tao, his favourite restaurant in China town, and then, bored with his own company, headed back to Old Compton Street and La Gattina. With a nod to Eric and Ernie, the regular forbidding sentries at the front door, he entered the club, seated himself at the bar and ordered a beer.

Weekends were busy nights and the full complement of girls was on duty to take advantage of the lucrative evening in prospect. Brody was as happy as the next man to look at an attractive woman, and most of La Gattina's performers definitely fell into that category, but knowing most of the girls on first name terms put seeing them dance into a wholly different perspective. The nudity of a total stranger could be viewed objectively, and that of a lover was a matter of intimacy, but watching the overt nakedness and provocative gyrations of friends and acquaintances left Brody feeling uncomfortably voyeuristic and faintly embarrassed. Content to remain at the bar, he paid little attention to the ever changing show and passed most of the evening chatting to the two barmen, Tim and Oscar. Unlike Brody, their disinterest in the female flesh on show was not due to any familiarity with the performers. Their blasé reaction was born of simple repetition. They had witnessed the continual parade of erotic dancing night after night until it had become mundane and a matter of complete indifference to both of them.

Angel's first show proved its customary success with the punters and she came out afterwards in a reasonably buoyant mood to join Brody at the bar.

"You went down well tonight" he told her as she slid onto the adjacent stool.

Carla grinned. "Unfortunate choice of words to someone in my profession, but thanks anyway." She gratefully picked up the gin and tonic Oscar placed in front of her but also ordered a sparkling mineral water with ice.

"Thirsty work, huh?" said Brody.

"You'd better believe it!"

She was wearing a plain, three-quarter length black dress, with simple, narrow shoulder straps. It was no more than a hundred women might wear on a myriad different occasions but, on Carla, it looked somehow enticing. As she picked up the iced water Oscar brought her and tipped back her head, taking a long swig from the glass, Brody was suddenly conscious of the curve of her neck. Strangely, he found it very alluring. A quarter of an hour earlier her entire naked body had been exposed and freely on display, and he had not been aroused. Yet as she sat so close, in an unassuming dress, the sight of her neck was beginning to stir him. 'Crazy!', he told himself and decided to dismiss the impulse immediately.

"I called Daniel Fowler for you" she told him, setting down her glass. "The guy who runs Elite Escorts. He's agreed to meet you. But you don't call the agency. You ring him on this number to set it up." She passed him a slip of paper with a mobile number scribbled on it.

"Thanks. I'm much obliged. I owe you one."

"Well, don't get too excited. I think he's only seeing you to lay down a few ground rules. I don't think you'll get much out of him."

Brody shrugged. "Perhaps not. But it's worth a try."

"Maybe. But remember what I said. He's not a guy to mess with. He came up the hard way and he's still well connected with, shall we say, the types you don't take home to meet your mother."

"I get the picture" said Brody with a laugh. "But that's ok. I never take *anyone* to meet *my* mother."

Carla made a face. "And there's me thinking you were going to invite me back home for the weekend!"

Brody grinned, but all at once the smile disappeared and, suddenly serious, he looked at her silently.

"Hey!" she chided. "I was kidding!"

"I know" he told her quietly. "But I'm curious. What would you say if I *did* invite you to spend a weekend with me?"

She stared at him, realising he wasn't making a joke. Brody held her gaze. More than one woman had passed fleetingly through his life since his divorce but none had lasted long enough to develop into anything approaching a relationship. The last 'fling' had ended more than three months since and, looking at Carla seated beside him in that strangely attractive dress, with the subdued overhead lighting reflecting shafts of different colours across her hair, he suddenly felt the need of a woman; he was all at once acutely aware of his solitary status and didn't want to spend that night alone.

The hiatus was deliberately broken by Carla as she gave a dismissive laugh and strategically turned the moment into a joke. "Hah. I'd say you were soft in the head." She turned away and stared at the back of the bar as she picked up her gin and tonic and downed it.

"You're a really nice woman, Carla" said Brody softly. "And any man would be lucky to spend the weekend with you."

She was moved by the compliment but was far too practised at maintaining her mask of self-protection to allow her reaction to show. Placing her glass resolutely back down on the bar, she turned back to him. "And you're a good guy, Josh. But this isn't Never Never Land. And I have to go to work." She slid from her stool, gave him a peck on the cheek, and sashayed provocatively towards the nearest table of punters, leaving Josh alone and reflective at the bar.

* * * * *

Monday, June 17th.

Josh spent most of Monday at his laptop. The first couple of hours passed in checking his bank account, paying bills and calculating a defence strategy against the payments that were looming on his credit card. It was a thoroughly depressing process and, at the end of it, he realised he needed some kind of lucrative assignment to cross his path very soon or he was going to fall over on his monthly maintenance payment to Kassia. He doubted the Dikembe Lukeba story would be the earner he needed but, just in case there was real substance to Luke Harvey's concerns, he went digging for any information he could find.

The web site for Elite Escorts had been well compiled. It yelled 'high class' and 'sophisticated' and made no attempt to disguise the fact that *all* its girls were expensive. The agency had evidently learned that the higher the price of an escort, the less seedy the experience of booking her felt to the punter. Each girl had her own page and each page offered numerous glamorous photographs. Several showed the selected woman wearing evening gowns but there were also shots in underwear and lingerie, and in fairly seductive poses. The possibility of "extra services" was unspoken but clearly implied and each girl had a rate card. She could be booked by the day, by the evening or by telephoning for a quotation for 'extended periods'. The photographs were all beautifully lit, had been taken by an experienced professional, and would not have disgraced the pages of the world's top fashion magazines. All in all, Elite was a very up-market operation.

Unlike his agency, trying to unearth information about the proprietor, Daniel Fowler, was something of an impossibility. An extensive Google search produced precisely nothing. There were hundreds of namesakes all over the world but clearly none of them was the owner of London's Elite Escorts. The boss of this particular agency obviously kept an ultra-low profile. After diligent exploration, Brody found a couple of minor references that could conceivably have alluded to the invisible Mr. Fowler but nothing was specific and nothing was of any value.

By contrast, the internet held numerous references to Dikembe Lukeba, a diplomat of The Democratic Republic of Congo. His native land, ravaged and torn apart by brutal war for decades, had suffered some of the worst atrocities ever seen in Africa. In 2001 the current President, Joseph Kabila, had emerged from the continual bloodshed as the leader of the nation and, according to what Josh discovered, Lukeba had been at his side ever since. Despite some hotly contested election results, and leading a country that continued to struggle in violent turmoil, Kabila was managing to cling to power and Dikembe Lukeba was clearly still part of his inner circle.

There were some strange contradictions in the articles Brody read. If the various texts were to be believed then Lukeba had undertaken several different government jobs, sometimes holding them simultaneously. Whatever the truth, his star had clearly risen. Born in the President's home province of South Kivu, Lukeba had been quickly promoted. To

Brody, it looked like a straight case of 'jobs for the boys' but, valid or not, Lukeba had successfully served his party for more than ten years and become a type of roving ambassador. His recent visit to Britain had been for trade talks at his country's embassy in Great Portland Street. Brody could find no reference anywhere to the fact he had died in London and that his body had been shipped home.

Deciding that there was not much else he could achieve until he had spoken to Elite Escorts, Brody spent the late afternoon catching up with email and running through preliminary notes for a new book he was planning. Once six o'clock passed he rang the Westcliff house and had a brief chat with Saffy, finding out how she had enjoyed her Sunday at Adventure Island. She asked again if he would speak to Kass about letting her have a rabbit but he made an excuse and declined. Investigating the sexual antics and possible murder of a foreign diplomat was one thing; attempting to influence his ex-wife to purchase a rabbit against her wishes was a far more dangerous assignment.

Chapter Four

Tuesday, June 18th.

Carla was right. Daniel Fowler was not a man you wanted to cross. His dark eyes were cold and his gaunt cheeks, on either side of an aquiline nose, gave him a somewhat 'haunted' and intimidating look. Despite his unprepossessing features, his whole appearance shouted 'money'. His slightly overlong, heavily gelled hair curled up at the collar of an expensive handmade shirt and his beautifully tailored, Savile Row pinstripe fitted his slender frame like a glove. Placing his elbows slowly and deliberately on the arms of the chair, Fowler sank back into its velvet cloth and gazed suspiciously at Joshua Brody.

If the journalist harboured any doubts as to the validity of Carla's warning, they were quickly dispelled by the presence of the minder who stood respectfully to one side of his employer but remained close enough to intercede immediately if the need arose. He was almost as broad as he was tall and, from the look of his flattened nostrils, was probably an ex heavy-weight boxer. He certainly seemed out of place within the rather elegant surroundings of the lounge of The Churchill Hotel, which was where Brody had been instructed to be at 11am that morning.

"I gather you want to talk to one of my girls" Fowler said flatly. His accent was precise and clearly enunciated but, to Brody's ear, didn't ring true. It was the acquired tone of a man who aspired to the privileged class rather than having being born into it.

"Yes" Josh replied innocently. "Just to clear up a few facts. About Thursday evening of last week."

"We've already spoken to the police. An Inspector Thomas. He told us the whole affair was 'closed'."

"Yes, I'm aware of that. This has nothing to do with the police."

Fowler looked down his narrow nose with an undisguised air of disdain. "Then, if it's closed, why are you still sniffing around it?"

Brody found both the man and his attitude unpleasant and decidedly threatening but, to a certain extent, he could understand why he was being treated to such a frosty reception. Daniel Fowler's business functioned on the margins, where the line between impropriety and illegality was conveniently blurred. His clients were high rollers who paid enormous sums to be sure of discretion and anonymity. Anything that even hinted at a breach of confidence was not to be tolerated. If he were going to make any headway, it was time for Brody to appear partisan and be somewhat economical with the truth.

"To keep my editor happy. You know as well as I do that anything with even a whiff of sex or scandal about it makes headlines, so he's asked me to check it out. But you're absolutely right. The police have closed the case. So all I need to do is to eliminate the girl from the picture. Then I can honestly report back that I've done what I was told to and confirm that the police are right. That there's no story."

"And if I say 'no'?" said Fowler coldly.

Brody gave a nonchalant shrug. "Fine by me. I'll just say I was refused an interview." He gave a knowing smile. "But we *both* know that will immediately make my editor suspicious and he'll presume the girl's got something to hide." He fixed Fowler directly in the eye. "Which is the exact opposite of what you need, right?"

Daniel Fowler made no response. For several seconds he sat motionless, like a solid, inanimate statue, as he silently weighed his decision. Finally he stood and looked down disparagingly at the journalist.

"Angel says you're ok. Otherwise we wouldn't be having this conversation. But I want you to be very clear. I run a legitimate and very exclusive business. It's taken me a long time to build its reputation and I won't allow anything to tarnish it. So if the name Elite Escorts appears in the press, in any paper at all, you will incur my considerable displeasure. And Gerry here..." he nodded in the direction of his silent minder ..." gets very upset when I am displeased. Are we clear?"

"Crystal."

Fowler nodded. "Wait here."

He turned on his heel and, with Gerry falling into step close behind him, left the lounge.

A few moments later, a tall, attractive and chic-looking woman appeared through the doorway and began making her way across the room in Brody's direction. She was expensively attired in a figure-hugging, designer summer dress in beige with a matching sleeveless coat draped across her shoulders. "Leggy" was how Brody would have described her as she moved towards him with an easy sway of the hips. He always found age difficult to assess in a stylish, well-dressed woman but he placed her somewhere between twenty-eight and thirty-five as she eased herself into the chair opposite that had been vacated by Daniel Fowler and elegantly crossed one shapely leg over the other. Her eyes were grey-green and intense and her cheekbones were well defined. It was the kind of face photographers love because it defied categorizing. She would look good in any light and in any fashion from any era. Her blonde hair settled in a gentle wave that curled under her chin as she lifted her head, gazed at the journalist and raised her eyebrows, inviting him to speak.

"Hi" said Brody in as friendly a tone as he could muster. "Thank you very much for agreeing to see me. May I order you a drink?"

She shook her head but said nothing.

"I gather Mr. Fowler has explained to you why I wanted to see you?"

She nodded but continued to remain mute. This is going to be some fun interview Brody told himself disconsolately, deciding that a more direct approach might produce better results.

"Look. I understand why you don't like talking to journalists but I promise you this is 'off the record'." He held up both palms to show his hands were empty. "I'm making no notes and I have no intention of writing about you. I just need answers to a few questions and I'll be gone. I don't even need to know your name if you'd rather not give it."

Suddenly the look of apprehension in her eyes changed and he sensed a slight lessening of tension flicker across her features.

"My name is Sophie" she told him quietly.

"Thank you, Sophie" said Brody warmly, relieved to have broken the ice. "I take it that's your professional name?"

She shrugged as if to say 'it's whatever you want it to be'.

"I believe you were booked as an escort for a Congolese diplomat called Lukeba on Thursday of last week?"

"Yes" she said quietly.

"And I presume you are aware that he was found dead in his hotel room last Saturday morning?"

She nodded.

"May I ask you if you were ever in that hotel room?"

She stared into Brody's brown eyes, clearly still unsure if she trusted him or not.

"Let me put it another way" he said hurriedly, keen to reassure her. "When he booked you as an escort did he ask you to meet him at the hotel or elsewhere?"

"In a restaurant" she said gently. "The Kiku in Mayfair. He liked Sushi. We ate a meal and then he took me to a bar a few streets away for a couple of drinks. I don't remember the name."

"Did you meet anyone or speak to anyone during the evening?"

"No. No one."

"And then you accompanied him back to his hotel?"

She sighed. "I'm sure you've checked the C.C.T.V. footage for the hotel lobby. So you know I did."

Brody had no access to the lobby T.V. footage, but she didn't know that and he wasn't going to tell her. "This is a little delicate" he said, leaning forward and lowering his voice. "Had he originally booked you for the whole night or did he arrange that with you during the course of the evening?"

"Nobody can book me 'for the night' as you put it, Mr.....?"

"Brody. Joshua Brody. But please call me Josh."

"The agency provides my services as an escort only, Mr. Brody. I am hired to join a man for dinner or to be his date at a reception or a function. I make polite conversation and interested noises and generally try to look decorative. That is what the agency's clients pay for. That is what they get. And that is *all* they get."

"I understand" said Brody, happy to play the game and allow her to recite Fowler's pre-agreed mantra. "So when he asked you to accompany him back to his hotel room, it was decided spontaneously? What I'm getting at, is that no one else could have known of this in advance. Right?"

"You are correct in your assumption."

Brody smiled. "You're an extremely attractive woman, Sophie, and *any* man would be keen to invite you back to his room. And I gather he enjoyed your company so much that he then also booked you for the following evening. For the Friday."

"He did. But that was much earlier, during dinner. He called the agency from the restaurant and told them he was so delighted with me that he wanted to ensure I was available for the next night. It was just bravado, of course. He was showing off; trying to look big. And, as I'm sure you already know, he called the next day and cancelled on me."

"But the agency still charged him the full fee."

"Of course. Once he'd booked me the agency closed my diary and took no further engagements for that evening. Anything less than twenty-four hours' notice incurs a full charge."

"Were you given any replacement engagement for the Friday evening?"

She smiled and, for the first time, he saw the mask slip and felt the real Sophie was answering him. "No. I spent the evening alone, watching T.V. in bed. It was delightful."

Brody grinned and sat back in his chair. "I'm sure it was." He looked across at her beautiful face, feeling decidedly awkward and impolite for putting her through this inquisition. He badly wanted to try and put her at her ease. "Sophie, please believe me when I tell you that I take no pejorative view of your profession. In my book, any man who gets to take you on a date is a lucky son of a bitch and there's nothing wrong with him paying you for the privilege. And if during the course of that date he wants to be extra generous and you feel like being extra grateful for that generosity then it's nobody's business but yours. And I *mean* that."

She smiled again. "Thank you, Mr. Brody. And please believe me when I say I neither care about your opinion nor seek your approval... but I appreciate your effort in expressing it."

Josh laughed and felt they finally understood each other. He hoped he had secured enough of her trust for her to reveal the final facts that he needed to confirm.

"I have one last question, Sophie. Then I'm done."

She seemed relieved. "And then this is all over? I mean, there will be no mention of me or the agency in the press, right? That's what Daniel told me."

"That's right. I give you my word."

She nodded her approval. " Good. What do you want to know?"

"The police report states that Dikembe Lukeba died from a heart attack. Their conclusion is that it was brought on following sexual exertion as a result of spending the previous night with you. I won't presume to ask you to describe any details but do you think that's a reasonable assumption?"

Her jaw dropped open and she was genuinely taken aback. "Are you kidding me?"

"No. I'm perfectly serious."

She shook her head and laughed. "Mr. Brody, most of the men who book the services of an escort do so for the sake of appearances; to fool the people around them into believing the girl is their social partner. The trouble is, a great many of them are also fooling themselves."

Brody inclined his head and frowned. "Meaning?"

"Meaning, whilst their money can buy them an attractive woman on their arm, it can't buy them a performance in the bedroom. A great many of the men who are 'generous' to me are nervous, inhibited and often simply incapable. I spend as much time nursing broken egos as I do indulging passions. Mr. Lukeba's heart attack might well have been brought on by sexual *frustration*... but it certainly wasn't due to sexual *exertion*. Not with me anyway. It was all he could do to function at all."

Brody sat bolt upright, totally unprepared for this revelation. "But the handcuffs" he said, perplexed. "I assumed he was into bondage games and..."

"Handcuffs?" she interrupted, cutting across him directly with a genuinely incredulous look on her face. "Do I look stupid to you?"

"No. Of course not."

"Then stop and think. It was the first time I'd met him. Do you think I'd allow the use of handcuffs with a stranger?"

"Not on *you*. On *him*."

"Not on anybody!" she said vehemently, shaking her head in disbelief. "You don't get it, do you? A girl is very vulnerable in a man's room. Especially if he's a big powerful guy. So you *never* lose control. I've got nothing against anybody playing bondage games if that's what they enjoy. But not with a stranger and *never* on a first booking. Believe me. If he'd produced handcuffs I'd have been straight out the door!"

It suddenly all made uncomfortable sense. And Brody was certain she was on the level.

"So, what you're telling me is that nothing took place on that Thursday night that might have over exerted Lukeba?"

Sophie gave a derisory sniff and lowered her voice to a whisper. "What took him three-quarters of an hour to get started was over in less than a minute. He then fell asleep and I left him to his slumbers. I wouldn't call that over exertion, would you?"

Brody slowly shook his head. "And do you think that's why he cancelled on you for the following day? To avoid the embarrassment of another failure?"

She shrugged. "I presume so. But frankly I don't care. I still got paid and I was spared the ordeal of a repeat performance. Or rather non-performance. I wish more clients would cancel at short notice."

"I'm sure that's a very rare event" said Brody with a smile. "But thank you for your time, Sophie. I'm much obliged."

She stood. "Are we done? Am I free to leave?"

He raised himself to his feet and nodded. "Yes. Unless I can buy you a drink?"

It was Sophie's turn to grin. "I wouldn't recommend it. Not with Daniel waiting for me outside in the car. He'd charge you by the hour."

Brody laughed. "Good point. Some other time, maybe."

"Maybe" she said with a smile. With no further word, and no attempt at a farewell, she turned and left.

Admiring the feline way she moved, Brody watched her walk away across the hotel lounge, wondering why a woman like that had opted for the profession she was in, and wishing he didn't find her so stunningly attractive. His eyes followed her every step of the way until she disappeared through the far doors.

Sitting back down in his chair, he considered the unexpected revelation supplied by the charming Miss Sophie and tried to slot it into the known facts. It made no sense. He needed a strong coffee while he tried to gather and organise his thoughts. Reaching out to the low table beside his chair, he picked up the lounge menu card. On discovering a pot of coffee for one was £6, plus a 15% service charge, he rapidly put the card back down again and left, deciding to head for the nearest Starbucks.

As he walked out of the room, heading for the front doors, he cast his eye around the lobby to see if Sophie and Fowler, and the ever-hovering Gerry, were still in the hotel. An Asian woman was at the reception desk, checking-in while a liveried porter piled her considerable luggage onto a trolley, a solitary man was seated by the window reading a copy of the Times, and a harassed couple, whose accents immediately betrayed their American nationality, were remonstrating with their two unruly children, trying to get them to stop running around the Churchill's lobby. But there was no sign of the three from Elite Escorts.

Brody left the Portman Square hotel and turned right, making his way down to Oxford Street, where he crossed the road through the crowds of shopping tourists and headed south in search of caffeine. The Starbucks on the corner of North Audley Street and Green Street provided a welcome refuge and, with a double shot Americano, he settled himself at a table by the window to try and clear his head and re-run what he now knew following his interview with Sophie. He took out his notebook and, as was his custom, began carefully listing what he had so far established. For the next quarter of an hour, he wrote down his thoughts point by point to clarify the current state of his investigation.

Fact. Dikembe Lukeba books Sophie, a high class call girl, from Elite Escorts for Thursday evening.
Fact. After splashing his money around and booking Sophie for a second night, even before he has sampled her talents, Lukeba is semi-impotent and the proposed night of passion is an embarrassing failure.
Fact. Lukeba calls the agency the next day, Friday, complaining of feeling unwell, and cancels Sophie's services for that night, even though he knows it will cost him the full fee.
Fact. Lukeba is found the following morning, dead in bed.
Fact. The police find fresh scuff marks on the bed frame suggesting the use of handcuffs or restraints. Luke Harvey finds bruising on Lukeba's wrists and ankle that would point to confirming this.
Fact. If handcuffs or restraints were used in Lukeba's bed, then it wasn't during Thursday night's fiasco with Sophie.
Assumption. Lukeba was too embarrassed by his sexual inadequacy to risk another night of failure with Sophie. So, having cancelled her, he books another girl, as yet unknown, and decides to employ handcuffs or restraints to get himself turned-on and encourage his performance.
Assumption. The police presume his sexual efforts have brought on heart failure.
Fact. Luke Harvey can find no sign of a heart attack.
Fact. Luke Harvey discovers a puncture mark in Lukeba's toe, suggesting he was injected with a syringe.
Assumption. Harvey presumes this was to administer a poison that induces heart failure but disappears from the body.
Fact. Lukeba's body is removed and shipped back home without Harvey's knowledge or permission.
Fact. The police tell Harvey the removal of the body was official and the case is closed.
Assumption. The police did not want Harvey to be able to prove foul play.

Brody sat back and looked at his list as he took a deep draught of the strong coffee. Having read it through twice he drew a line under the text and began writing again.

Question: Is it possible that Luke Harvey is mistaken and the puncture mark he found in the toe is not significant and due to some other cause? Check this again with Harvey.
Question: If Harvey is mistaken about poisoning and the death was indeed due to a heart attack, why would the authorities hurriedly remove the body and ship it home?

Question: Are we simply reading too much into this and was it just an admin mix-up?

As he looked down at his questions, Brody reckoned that the obvious scenario was emerging as the most likely answer. A foreign diplomat, indulging in a sexual fetish with a call girl, dies of a heart attack. It would make headline news, fill the front pages of the tabloids and cause embarrassment all round for the U.K. and the Democratic Republic of Congo. Much easier to send the body home and quietly forget the whole business. After all, Harvey had found no trace of any toxin in the body. His whole conspiracy theory hinged on finding one small puncture mark in Lukeba's toe. It was crass. Maybe the diplomat had stabbed himself with the point of a pair of scissors while trimming his toe nails? Either way, there was nowhere to go with any of this. You can't investigate conjecture. The whole affair was a dead end.

Brody's list had filled two sides in his notebook. With a reluctant sigh, he firmly drew a line through both pages and closed the pad. He took another swig of coffee and stared disconsolately out of the window. He needed employment; he needed a story; but this wasn't it. He decided he would call Luke Harvey and tell him, regretfully, that the whole business was closed.

It was then that he saw him. There were tables and chairs on the pavement outside the café occupied with several people relaxing and enjoying the summer sunshine as they idly chatted, drinking their teas and coffees. At the table nearest the front door was a solitary man reading a copy of the Times. Brody recognised him at once. He had been seated in the lobby of The Churchill Hotel not half an hour earlier, reading the same newspaper. For a few seconds, the true significance of this apparent coincidence evaded him but he quickly realised that the odds on this being pure happenstance were ridiculously long. There was no mistake. The guy had copper brown hair and was wearing a grey jacket with a very small check in the material. It was definitely the man he had seen in the Churchill lobby. An uncomfortable ripple ran the length of Brody's spine as he realised, with an icy-cold lucidity, that he was being followed. The man was sideways-on to Brody, with his seat positioned facing the Starbucks front door, presumably waiting until the journalist emerged. Brody felt his insides tense and his heart rate begin to rise.

Reaching into his hip pocket, he took out his mobile phone and navigated through the screen to the camera function. He carefully deactivated the flash, to avoid announcing his shot, and then held the camera to the window. The auto-focus was having trouble dealing with the glass so he switched it off and played with the position manually until the image became clear. It wasn't pin sharp, the window wouldn't allow such clarity, but it was sufficiently in focus for the man's features to be plain and obvious and, more importantly, recognisable. Brody pressed the control button three times and then checked the results. Each shot was good enough and he replaced the phone in his hip pocket.

He looked down at his closed notebook. He had been on the point of disregarding its contents and telephoning Luke Harvey to tell him he was facing a dead end. But if someone was now following him then they had a reason for doing so. The indiscreet behaviour of a diplomat was insufficient cause. The presence of the guy outside the café, silently reading a newspaper, was shouting at him loud and clear. It seemed somebody, somewhere, didn't like a journalist asking awkward questions. Somebody, somewhere, must therefore have something to hide. And their need to conceal their secret was sufficient to have him followed.

It was simple to confirm the hypothesis.

Brody got up from his seat and walked calmly to the door. Keeping his eyes front and forward, and attempting to look as relaxed and unconcerned as he could, he turned left and headed back up towards Oxford Street. Keeping his pace measured and unhurried, he crossed the main thoroughfare at the junction. He needed a reason to turn around so he walked up to the front doors of the large branch of Marks and Spencer on the opposite corner. When a large, overweight woman began exiting the store with both hands carrying shopping bags, Brody stood to one side and politely held open the door for her. As she thanked him, he was able to turn his head and nod to her. There was no mistake. The guy in the grey check jacket was crossing the road behind him, preparing to pursue him into the store.

Now certain that he was being followed, the natural impulse was to go to ground and hide; but Brody knew it was important to act entirely as normal if he were to avoid letting his tail know that he had been spotted. Despite the tension rising in his gut, he forced himself to appear relaxed. He bought a pair of socks in the men's department of Marks and Spencer, to create a valid reason for having entered the store, and then calmly retraced his steps and left through the main doors.

In contrast to his seemingly untroubled demeanour, Brody's mind was in overdrive. He was furiously trying to consider his situation from all aspects. Luke Harvey had told him that the clampdown on the Lukeba case had been 'official'; that the closure had been dictated by the authorities. With uncomfortable clarity, he realised that his current shadow might also be acting at the behest of the authorities. If so, then it was not beyond possibility that his calls were also being monitored. There were numerous phone shops along Oxford Street and he entered the first one he came across.

"I want the cheapest pay-as-you-go mobile you've got" he told the smiling assistant.

The young salesman was not so easily deterred. "Well, if you don't mind me saying so, sir, that's never a good option. You see, the cheaper handsets don't provide..."

In no mood to hear this spiel, Brody cut him short. "Look son, let me be clear. No music, no camera, no internet or email. No bells and whistles and no contract. I want a bog standard, pay-as-you-go phone that just makes calls and sends texts. Ok?"

Visibly disgruntled, the assistant reached behind him and withdrew a box from the shelf. "This is the very bottom of the market" he said pointedly as he placed it onto the counter in front of Brody. It's on special offer at £19.20.

"Great. I'll take it. And let's put £20 onto the card."

As the salesman processed the SIM card, Brody removed the phone from its packaging and switched it on. There was not much charge in the battery but it would be sufficient for a couple of calls. Five minutes later he left the shop with the new mobile in his pocket.

Walking back through London's West End towards Soho, he took out his original handset and navigated through the contacts file to find Luke Harvey's number. Then, using his new phone, he sent him a text message: *Urgent we meet. Same venue. 6pm today. Text only 'Yes' to confirm' and use only this number to reply. Josh.* The affirmative response arrived some ten minutes later, just as Brody was entering Old Compton Street.

Chapter Five

From the front window of the main room of his flat, Brody could see the opposite side of the street below but there was no sign of his shadow. He presumed that Mr. Copper Hair was ensconced in one of the numerous cafés, watching his front door.

Brody was aware that, if his tail was to be effective, then whoever was organising it would periodically change those undertaking his surveillance and his Times-reading friend in the grey check jacket may well have already been substituted. He also realised that, as long as his pursuers were ignorant of the fact he knew they were watching him, he held an advantage.

Using his new telephone, he put in a call to The Independent and asked for the World Affairs desk. He immediately recognised the gruff, impatient sounding voice that spoke in his ear.

"World News."

"Hello Alan. This is Josh Brody. How's tricks?"

"Josh! What a surprise! How the hell are you?"

"Oh, ducking and diving. Managing to scrape a living. But nothing that'll put me in line for a Pulitzer."

"Tell me about it! How's that family of yours? Do you get to see much of them?"

"Weekends. And they're fine thanks. Saffy is seven now."

"Never! It seems like only yesterday we were toasting her arrival. Tempus fugit, eh?"

"And how!"

Brody liked Alan Denton. On the surface he was a tough, no-nonsense editor whose department ran with clockwork efficiency, but once you got to know the real man beneath the surface professional you discovered one of the most compassionate human beings Brody had ever met.

"So what can I do for you, Josh" asked the newspaperman.

"I was hoping for an update on Sean Finnegan. I know he was away covering the Sudan crisis but I'd heard a rumour he might be back."

"Yes, he is. He flew in a week or so ago. And with some truly amazing pics. Shall I put the word out that you're looking for him?"

"No. Don't worry. If he's back in London then I know where I can find him."

"Yes. But will you find him sober? I doubt it. You know Sean."
Brody laughed. "Indeed I do!"
They chatted for a few more minutes, making a promise to meet soon for a drink that both of them knew they were highly unlikely to keep, and then brought the conversation to a close. Brody was pleased with the outcome of his call.

All the dwellings in the original construction of Old Compton Street were erected many years before the notion of an alternative means of escape in the case of fire was part of standard design. So the building housing Brody's small, third floor flat had only a small street door and entrance passage to the staircase, and no alternative exit from the upper storeys. The later introduction of fire regulations caused an iron frame staircase to be added to the rear of the structure which, from Brody's residence, was reached by climbing through the bedroom window. He had, thankfully, never had reason to utilise this awkward method of egress but the morning's unsettling revelations made him now unexpectedly grateful for its existence.

At 5.30 pm, Brody released the lock on the bedroom window and tried raising the lower section. It was stuck fast. Every night, he lowered the top half a few centimetres to allow fresh air into his cramped sleeping quarters but the bottom half of the window had remained closed ever since he'd moved in. It took several hard thumps with the flat of his hand to finally get the obstinate woodwork to shift and, as the sash cord in the side-frame grumbled and squeaked, he lifted the lower section and climbed out onto the fire escape stairs. Anticipating he may need to return via the same route, Brody left a small cardboard wedge in the bottom of the frame as he quietly allowed the window to fall and brought it carefully to rest.

The iron staircase led to the narrow service alley at the back of the club and he followed it through into Dean Street, where his unobtrusive exit was beyond any watching eyes. From there it was only a matter of a few minutes' walk to Leicester Square.

Luke Harvey was punctual and appeared in the bar of The Radisson Hampshire at a couple of minutes after six. Brody had ordered a beer for him and it was waiting on the table as the pathologist lowered himself into his seat.

"Your text message was a little staccato and furtive" he said with a smile as he gratefully picked up his half pint and took a long draught. "What's all the mystery?"

"I'm being followed" Brody told him evenly, trying to make it sound as un-dramatic as he could. "So it's not beyond the realms of possibility that my phone is also being monitored and perhaps my messages are being read."

Harvey put down his beer in astonishment. "Are you serious?"

The journalist took out his phone and brought up one of the three photographs he had taken from within the Starbucks café. He passed the handset to Harvey.

"Taken this morning. There's no mistake. He was waiting in the lobby when I left The Churchill Hotel, he sat outside Starbucks while I had a coffee and then tailed me in and out of a store on Oxford Street. Do you recognise him at all? Have you seen him before?"

Harvey gazed down at the picture and slowly shook his head. "No. I've never laid eyes on him." He looked up again with a deeply worried expression. "Josh, I'm not sure what's happening here but it was never my intention to bring trouble down on your head. If you're being followed then, clearly, we're getting out of our depth. I think we'd better do as Inspector Thomas suggested and just forget the whole thing."

A wide grin creased Brody's face. "Are you kidding? I'm just getting started!"

The journalist spent the next half an hour bringing Harvey fully up to date on his meeting with Daniel Fowler and Sophie and then pointedly retracing and confirming every step of the story that had gradually unfolded since the corpse of Dikembe Lukeba had first been wheeled into the pathologist's examination room. When he felt he had covered everything they currently knew, he ordered two more beers and settled back into his chair.

"So somebody doesn't want us poking around. That means they have something to hide. And I intend to discover what it is."

"I'll be honest with you, Josh. I don't like it" said Harvey sincerely as a waiter appeared beside him and delivered their drinks. The pathologist waited until they were alone again before continuing. "And, frankly, I don't want to be involved in anything this sinister."

"You won't be. In fact, it's essential that you and I have as little contact as possible from now on. Keep your eyes peeled, of course. Try and register anything suspicious, like the same car appearing behind you when you're driving, or maybe seeing the same man or woman at different locations in the street, but otherwise just live your life as normal. If I should need to reach you, I'll use the landline at your workplace and leave a message asking you to call at a designated time. I'll leave a different name and number whenever I need to speak to you. When you return my call, you must always use a public call box. Never phone from home, or work or using your mobile. Understood?"

Harvey nodded reluctantly. "Yes. But I still don't like it. And I don't see how you hope to investigate this any further. If the Lukeba thing is being stonewalled from on high, then they'll have closed every door. How do you propose to move forward?"

"I take a closer look at Lukeba himself. He's currently all I've got to go on."

"But he's dead. And we know next to nothing about him."

"True" said Brody with a smile. "But I'm hoping to rectify that problem a little later tonight."

Sean Finnegan was an Irish photo-journalist of rare talent. His work first came to prominence during the Gulf War of '91 but he then found himself on assignment in Africa and seemed to discover his natural environment. He felt an immediate and strong affinity with the dark continent and, with almost evangelical fervour, skilfully used his lens to alert the rest of the world to its pain and suffering. Over the next two decades he recorded the horrendous Rwandan Genocide, the rise of the R.U.F. in Sierra Leone, the endless years of fighting in the Congo, and the turmoil and disintegration of Somalia. His powerful pictures were graphic but always managed to reach out and touch the viewer, adroitly capturing the individual human pain and torment beneath the military headlines. His most famous shot was of a mother cradling her injured baby in her arms and begging for medical help, unaware that the child was already dead from the bullet that had pierced its tiny, undernourished body. That photograph reached almost every national newspaper in the world and garnered several awards.

Sean's trips back to the U.K. were infrequent but always eventful. Possibly as a reaction against the appalling horrors he continually witnessed at close hand, his London visits often consisted of one continuous bender. Among his friends, his capacity for alcohol was legendary and nobody could keep pace with Sean when he was on a roll. It took twice the amount of Guinness any normal mortal could consume before Finnegan entered even the preliminary stages of inebriation but, none the less, if you wanted anything approaching a sensible conversation with him, it was advisable to catch him early in the evening. So it was just before 8pm when Brody pushed open the wide doors of O'Neill's Irish pub in the central section of Wardour Street and stepped into the crowded, bustling interior.

Sean's favourite watering hole did a roaring trade, especially on 'live music' nights, and Brody had to elbow his way through the buzzing throng to reach the bar. The five-piece band, squeezed onto the little stage in the corner of the room, boasted a violin, a guitar, a mandolin, a bodhran, and a tin whistle. The instrumentalists were all skilful musicians and performing with impressive drive and energy, but it wasn't the lively playing that caught Brody's attention. It was the familiar, raucous tone of the voice that was pouring through the p.a. system and leading the band in song:

As I was a going over Cork and Kerry mountains
I spied Captain Farrell and his money he was counting
First I drew my pistol and then I drew my rapier
Saying 'Stand and deliver' for he were a bold deceiver

With no need of urging, everyone in the pub, including the bar staff, then joined the chorus with gusto and filled the room with enthusiastic singing:

Musha ring dumma do dumma da
Whack for the Daddy O
Whack for the Daddy O
There's whiskey in the jar!

Brody was fairly sure that, like him, most people present hadn't the faintest clue what 'Whack for the Daddy O' might imply, much less any idea as to the meaning of 'Musha ring dumma do dumma da', but it was patently unimportant. At the microphone, Sean Finnegan, pint of Guinness in his right hand while his other was held cupping his left ear, was in full flight and, to the delight of the audience, gave his inimitable rendering of all six verses of the famous Irish ballad. At the end, everyone sang the chorus twice for good measure before the band finished with a flourish and the entire crowd broke into cheers and applause. As Finnegan stepped down from the small raised stage, Brody worked his way through the crush and waited until the backslapping and congratulations were over before he tapped the Irishman on the shoulder. Finnegan's face lit up with genuine delight as he turned and saw his old friend.

"Brody, me bucko!" He engulfed Josh in a crushing and affectionate embrace. Years in Africa hadn't changed Sean's accent one iota and his melodic Irish brogue was as welcoming and to the point as always. "How the fuck are you? Let me buy you a drink!"

The photographer's regular moustache and chin beard were accompanied by several days' growth of stubble on his cheeks and his long, curly auburn hair hadn't seen a comb in a considerable while and was as unruly as ever. He looked as if he had rolled out of bed and trundled straight into the pub, which may well have been the case. Notwithstanding his somewhat dishevelled appearance, his eyes were bright, full of energy and shone like diamonds as he slapped Brody on the back and led him to the bar yelling: "Landlord! A pint of the dark nectar for my friend!"

There was nowhere in the heaving bar to chat quietly but, ensconced in a far corner with their pints of Guinness, they spent an animated half-hour catching up on each other's news. The journalistic fraternity is more 'tight-knit' than most professions, especially among the free-lancers, and word of who is doing what, and where, frequently passes between the community as people bump into each other at functions and gatherings, or at airports en route to assignments. So each of the two men had a vague notion as to what the other had been doing, but it was good to fill in the gaps and bring themselves up to date.

It was not easy for Brody to prise Sean away from O'Neill's but, with a promise to bring him straight back and pass the rest of the evening in a river of Guinness, the Irishman reluctantly agreed to step outside and find a place to talk in private. They walked five doors down to the Costa Coffee on the corner of Shaftesbury Avenue and, armed with a couple of Americanos, Brody steered the photographer to an empty corner table and they seated themselves.

"So what is it that's so all-fired important?" Sean asked, his face distorting in a grimace as he sampled the non-alcoholic drink.

"You're an old Africa hand, Sean. And I need to pick your brains."

"Be my guest!"

"I'm trying to nail down some info on a Congolese diplomat."

"Most of 'em *should* be nailed down. Permanently. Which particular specimen did you have in mind?"

"A guy called Dikembe Lukeba."

"Hah! Tweedle-fucking-dum" he declared with undisguised disdain. "Now you *are* scraping the barrel. Him and his brother, both. The terrible twins."

Brody sat up sharply. "Twins?"

"Yes, of course. Known to the press corps as Tweedledum and Tweedledee. Between 'em they've screwed more money out of Congo than you could stack in Fort Knox."

"*Identical* twins?"

"Yes. Didn't you know? Dikembe and Fabrice Lukeba. Africa's very own two-headed Janus. Each watching the other's back while they both line their pockets. God's little joke on the Congo."

Suddenly Brody realised why he'd found apparently conflicting articles on 'Lukeba' on the internet, describing different roles and locations. There were *two* of them. But they looked like the same guy in all the photographs because they were identical twins. "And they're really bad news, huh?" he asked.

Sean nodded dolefully. "A real dose of double-trouble. Or at least, they *were*. But I assume that's why you're asking?"

Brody was momentarily thrown. "How did you know? There's been no release of it anywhere."

It was Sean's turn to look puzzled. "Well, it's no secret. Gerhard Weber told me. He called me a few days back from Vienna."

"Vienna?"

"Yes. He's thinking of doing a piece on it."

Brody was thoroughly confused and beginning to wonder if Finnegan had consumed more Guinness than he'd realised. "Sean. I think maybe we're at cross purposes" he said carefully. "Dikembe Lukeba was found dead in his London hotel room just over a week ago. The pathologist who examined him suspected foul play but the authorities declared he'd suffered a heart attack and shipped his carcase back to the D.C.R. before anyone could prove otherwise. And they've hushed the whole thing up. So how the hell can Gerhard be doing a piece on it?

Sean sat back in his seat, genuinely shocked. He was clearly stone-cold sober. "Dikembe?" he asked quietly.

"Yes. That's why I came to pick your brains. I'm trying to build a profile of him."

Sean wasn't really listening. He was thinking hard. "Fuck" he said softly. "Then they've got 'em both."

"Both?" enquired Josh apprehensively.

The Irishman nodded slowly. "Fabrice Lukeba shot himself last Wednesday night. In a Vienna hotel."

Brody felt an unwitting shiver tingling his neck. "Last Wednesday? And Gerhard told you it was suicide?"

Sean nodded again. "That's the story... But only if you believe in Father Christmas and the Tooth Fairy."

Several moments passed in silence as they both tried to take stock of what they had each just learned. Eventually, Josh spoke. "I'll get two more strong coffees. Then, if you're up for it. I'd like to hear everything you can tell me about Tweedledum and Tweedledee."

For the next half-hour, Sean Finnegan dutifully gave a full account of the notorious Lukeba twins and their nefarious career in the D.C.R. Brody took notes, interrupting only occasionally to check a detail or spell a name. It was a depressing saga of large scale corruption and violent intimidation.

"How do they get away with it?" he asked as Sean finished his sorry tale.

"To understand that, you have to understand Africa. You can't judge it by western criteria. Its whole ethos is still fundamentally tribal. They can't help it. It's in their D.N.A. There's still a greater instinctive loyalty to kith and kin than to the ballot box."

"But they can't *all* be like that" protested Brody. "This is the 21st century."

"Yes" Sean agreed bitterly. "And if we'd educated and supported the continent in the last two hundred years instead of pillaging it to death, it might be more a part of the modern world. But instead, we've just swapped colonial rape for industrial and commercial rape. Those

Africans who have risen to power have learned the lessons of their exploiters all too well."

"So corruption is endemic. Is that what you're saying?"

"Pretty much. I mean, a lot of it is fairly small scale. What you and I would see as corruption, most of their politicians genuinely see as just perks of the job and nobody bats an eyelid. It's the tribal mentality again. Like a village chieftain, or a council of elders, receiving these perks is what confirms their status. It's considered perfectly normal. It's even expected. But then there's the big boys. The clever ones who have learned how to take advantage of their position on a massive scale. They screw the Bejeezus out of it. And they don't allow anyone or anything to get in the way of their personal gravy train."

"Like the Lukeba brothers?"

Sean nodded. "They remained diplomats and never took ministerial office. They were far too clever for that. They kept their heads permanently below the parapet. But, between them, they controlled virtually all the licences for excavation and mining. If you were a foreign multi-national looking for mineral rights in the Congo then it was almost impossible without gaining their approval."

"Which, naturally, came at a price?" asked Brody.

"Is the Pope a Catholic?" asked Sean, with a sardonic look. "Over the last ten years they've amassed a considerable personal fortune. Most of which is doubtless sitting in numbered bank accounts in Geneva. But stashing away backhanders is standard stuff. What singles out the Lukeba brothers is what they did last year."

"Which was?"

Sean took a deep swig of his coffee and shook his head, almost as if he himself could still not believe what he was about to relate. "A Chinese company surveyed an area near the Sankuru river. They found Thorium."

"What's that?"

"It's a mineral with a lot of industrial applications. It's been known and used for donkey's years but it's recently been put forward as an alternative to Uranium in nuclear fuel production."

"So it's likely to be in demand?"

"Exactly. And, according to the grapevine, the Chinese paid a pretty penny for the mining rights. The trouble was there were two villages within the proposed excavation area. The people didn't want to move and they didn't want their land excavated. They claimed ancient rights and insisted on staying put."

"Did it go to court?"

Sean raised his eyebrows and looked up at his friend. "Brody, you're a darlin' boy and bless you for your naivety. But 'no', it didn't go to court. Both villages were razed to the ground. All the men, women and children were massacred. Even the animals were killed. Everything. The whole kit and caboodle. Just eradicated. Wiped from the map."

Josh experienced a sickly feeling in the centre of his stomach. "How can that be?"

"Very simple, really. It was blamed on guerrillas. When you live in a country that is permanently being torn apart by violence, where war and revolution are as natural as mother's milk, nobody pays much attention to just one more atrocity."

"And that was the official story?"

"The authorised version of events. Oh, Tweedledum and Tweedledee underwent a very public breast-thumping and displayed various manifestations of grief. Troops were despatched to 'root out the perpetrators of this heinous crime', and various outraged party members vowed to bring them to justice. In the meantime, the Chinese mining company quietly moved in and started excavations."

Josh sat back in his chair. "So the Lukebas got away with it?"

A knowing look broke across Sean Finnegan's unshaven features. "Not any more. Looks as if justice finally caught up with them, doesn't it? And I, for one, will raise a glass to that!"

"Who do you think did it, then?"

The photographer shrugged. "Don't know. Don't care. There are more armed bands of fighters in the D.C.R. than flies on a Kerry cow pat. Any one of them could have done it."Brody shook his head in obvious doubt. "That's just the point Sean. If it was one of the rebel groups then they wouldn't think twice. They'd shoot the Lukebas there and then on their home turf. God knows there'd be ample opportunity. It would just be another African political killing. Why would they follow them abroad and set up a couple of phoney deaths in hotel rooms? And, more to the point, where does a rebel guerrilla group get the resources to plan and fund trips to London and Vienna? It makes no sense."

"When did anything in Africa make sense?" asked Sean with a disparaging look. "All I know is, they've paid for what they did. And I'm glad." He laughed. "Christ! I'd have pulled the trigger myself given half a chance!"

"But it doesn't add up. I don't buy it. There's something else going on here."

Finnegan raised his hands in a gesture of surrender. "Well, you may be right, me bucko, but I don't have time to argue about it with you now. I promised the band I'd be back to give 'em 'Danny Boy' and, as I can't stomach anymore of this coffee and need a sharp intake of the dark nectar, I think it's time we vacated this excuse for a watering hole and went back to the pub. What d'ya think?"

With a reluctant smile of acceptance, but still deeply concerned and unhappy about all he'd heard, Josh agreed to accompany his friend back to O'Neill's, bracing himself for the inevitable onslaught of Guinness.

Chapter Six

Wednesday, June 19th

Brody slept unusually late and it was 10.15 am before he managed to drag himself reluctantly from under the warm comfort of the duvet. His head was decidedly fuzzy and the tension in his neck instantly informed him that he had, thankfully, ceased his consumption of alcohol the previous evening in the nick of time. Had he taken even half a glass more, the nascent hangover that was ominously threatening would be surging to engulf his clouded brain. As it was, a trip to Paul's deli and a strong black coffee restored some degree of clarity and allowed him to reconsider his notes and write up all he had learned from the exuberant Sean Finnegan.

On their return to O'Neill's the previous evening, the Irishman had said very little more relating to the Lukeba twins. This was partly because Sean, personally, cared little about their recent fate but, mostly, because his time was largely taken up with his musical duties. As promised, he joined the band to give his rendition of The Londonderry Air, better known as 'Danny Boy', and drew wild cheers of approval from the packed and boisterous pub audience, eliciting several cries of 'more' and 'encore'. To Brody's surprise, Finnegan's subsequent performance of 'The Mountains Of Mourne' had precisely the opposite effect of his previous rendition and appeared to move the revellers profoundly. It wasn't that Sean was blessed with anything remotely approaching a beautiful voice. On the contrary; his rough and ready tones were hardly the mark of the singer's art; but there was something in his raucous and untrained delivery of the simple lyrics that reached out to all present and that even Brody found decidedly touching. Several of the large, macho types among the crowd surreptitiously wiped away a tear before anyone could detect it and the applause at the end of the song was long lasting and deeply appreciative. Sean Finnegan, photo journalist and jaded old Africa hand, was definitely the star turn at O'Neill's that night.

As his fragile head slowly cleared and returned his consciousness to the land of the living, Brody ordered croissants and more coffee and went carefully back through the pages of his notebook from the very beginning. Attempting to reassess everything from a fresh, unbiased perspective, with no preconceptions, he re-read everything he'd been told by Luke Harvey, the escort Sophie, and then the newly added information provided by Sean Finnegan. The conclusions were undeniable and screaming 'conspiracy' at him like a neon sign flashing in a dark night.

The death of the Lukeba brothers within a few days of each other, both apparently without the interaction of a third party, was too much of a co-incidence to be credible. The inconclusive condition of Dikembe's corpse, coupled with its unscheduled removal, reinforced Luke Harvey's theory of 'foul play'. That, in turn, suggested that the apparent suicide of the twin Fabrice was also highly dubious. Inspector Thomas' frank and candid conversation with Luke Harvey confirmed that the U.K. authorities wanted to keep a lid on the whole affair. The first question was: why? The second question was: are the Austrian authorities acting in similar vein?

Like Sean Finnegan, Brody didn't buy the story of suicide in Vienna. Given the recent events near the Sankuru river in the D.C.R., it was highly plausible that the brothers had both been murdered as a reprisal. But, unlike Finnegan, Brody couldn't accept that the killings had been carried out by a dissident guerrilla group. Most of Africa's rebel bands operated as a pretty blunt instrument and the notion of mounting a sophisticated assassination operation in not one, but two, foreign capitals, didn't fit the profile. The resources and expertise necessary to carry out such attacks were patently beyond the reach of a rebel group in the D.C.R. In Brody's analysis, the balance of conjecture was leaning towards a double hit by organised crime; probably the Russian or Balkan Mafia. But, if true, why would such criminal factions carry out reprisals on behalf of some obscure, rural African community?

Or perhaps the Sankuru river affair was merely a coincidence? Maybe the motive for murder stemmed from a completely different event? The myriad opportunities to exploit the wealth of Africa were a big attraction to criminal elements and, with the crooked twins' nefarious background, it was not unlikely they had crossed swords at some time with Mafia interests. But the nagging doubt in Brody's mind, the jarring little piece of the puzzle that didn't quite fit, was the inescapable conclusion that the British authorities, and probably also the Austrians, knew the truth about the deaths and were attempting to draw a veil over it. Why? Why would two governments be covering up murder to protect organised crime? It simply made no sense.

The time for equivocation had passed. If Brody was going to investigate the mystery further then it was time to put his work on an official footing. That would not only give him a degree of back-up but, more importantly, would furnish him with the funds he needed to do what he was now certain had to be done. Ordering another coffee in a take-away cup, he settled his bill at Paul's and walked back to his flat. A Google search of "What's On" in Vienna turned up what he was looking for within seconds. He then made two quick telephone calls to set up appointments for that very afternoon before checking available flights from Heathrow.

One of the advantages of living in Soho was that most of Brody's contacts were within a stone's throw of his flat. It took the journalist only five minutes to walk to Poland Street to the office of Adele Sanders, his literary agent. Now in her mid-fifties, she was an elegant woman who always dressed well, even if she was due to spend the day alone in her office with Ella, her secretary cum general assistant, but her ever neat and well-ordered appearance belied the strong-willed woman beneath. She was what American writers would have described as 'a tough old broad' and Brody held an immense admiration for her. He was of the opinion that a good agent required certain well defined attributes: impeccable manners, the ability to converse at all levels and within all situations, an inherently cunning and devious nature, and the facility to lie like a trooper in the interests of a client. Adele held all these qualities in spades. She was a black widow spider in a Karl Lagerfeld attired web, and Brody loved her for it.

"Daahling" she greeted him enthusiastically, with an air kiss on each cheek, "it's been too long since I saw you. Take a pew and tell me everything that's happening in your life."

Brody settled himself in the chair opposite her desk but before he could speak she pre-empted him to enquire as to what she really wanted to hear.

"How's the new novel coming? Orion is keen to have the manuscript."

Orion Publishing dealt in both fiction and non-fiction. The firm had published Brody's Soho history and also his two crime novels, written under the pseudonym of Ian Magen. The publishers requested the nom de plume because they wanted to keep the commercial fiction separate from the academic work, telling Josh that if he became well established as a novelist then the truth could be revealed later and used as a publicity angle. If, on the other hand, fiction sales were slow then the apparent lack of success would not be detrimental to his non-fiction career. Brody, always a crossword fan, has chosen the name Ian Magen because it was an anagram of 'an enigma'.

"I can't believe Orion is exactly champing at the bit" said Brody with a grin. "The last two didn't sell that well."

"They got back their advance and then a little extra. So they're not complaining. Anyway, that's not what it's about. They expect to nurse a novelist through the first couple of books. It's the long haul they're interested in. But I can't send them what I don't have. I was hoping for a first draft by now." She peered at him over the top of her glasses, which she wore on an ornate gold chain around her neck, addressing him like an admonishing headmistress confronting a miscreant pupil. "Are we having problems?"

He shook his head. "It's progressing. But I think I need to put it on hold."

She raised a censorious eyebrow. "Oh?"

Adele understood that her client's journalistic work enabled him to put food on the table and pay the rent but she would have preferred Josh to set journalism aside completely and concentrate on fiction. She sincerely felt he had the ability to carve a successful career as a novelist and was always concerned that Brody himself did not have sufficient self-belief. It wasn't that she wanted him to starve in a garret, suffering for his art, although that was uncomfortably closer to the truth than she realised, but she knew that, like many writers, he needed constant motivation and no distractions. When he got going and was on a roll his work was good; but he would always find a hundred excuses to defer the task of simply sitting down and beginning to write, and Adele was not in the mood to hear yet another pretext for postponement.

"New novels don't write themselves, darling" she chided . "It's perspiration, not inspiration, that gets the job done. What's the hold up? Please tell me you're not shipping out to Syria to cover that dreadful war!"

Josh gave a dismissive shake of the head. "No. I've had my fill of Arab conflicts. This is different. I'm onto something. And if it breaks the way I think it might, we'll have a very hot story. There'll be a newspaper exclusive, a book and probably a T.V. documentary."

This was music to the agent's ears. "Tell me more" she told him enthusiastically.

"I can't say too much now. But I will make you a promise. If this story leads up a blind alley then I'll abandon it and knuckle down and get the new novel finished in double quick time. I'll start work on it as soon as I get back."

"Back? Where are you going?"

"Vienna. And I need your help to set up the visit. The University of Wien is staging an English language book fair this month. I've checked the web site and Orion has a stand there. I want you to find out who's running it and then tell them I'll be in Vienna next week and that I'm happy to put in a personal appearance. A 'Meet the Author' sort of thing. You know the drill. It runs until the 28th so we should get in just under the wire."

"Not to put too fine a point on it" said Adele tactfully as she folded her arms across her ample bosom, "but they may not have your book with them on the stand."

Josh laughed. "I'm sure they haven't! But these fairs are as dull as ditch water. I'd wager they'll jump at the chance to break the monotony and have an author present. Especially if you are applying your particular talents to persuading them that it's a great idea. All they need do is DHL a few copies out to Vienna and I'll turn up and sign them. What have they got to lose?"

Adele took an audible intake of breath. "I don't like offering freebies, darling. It sets a bad precedent. And I doubt I can screw a fee out of this when it's me making the approach to them."

"A fee is not important. I need a valid reason for being in Vienna and this is the perfect cover."

The word 'cover' brought a smile to the agent's face. "Sounds very cloak and dagger! Still, if it will kick start your writing then I'm all in favour. Ok. I'll try to set it up and I'll call you later today."

Brody stood. "You're a star. While I'm away I'll be checking email but feel free to call at any time on the mobile."

If his calls *were* being monitored then it would serve his purpose for those listening to hear him discussing a legitimate reason for his presence in Vienna.

"Ok" said the agent reluctantly. "I'm not totally sure what is going on here but if this is what you want then I wish you luck with it."

"Thanks, Adele" said Brody with a wink. "I'll bring you back some Viennese chocolate."

"Never mind the sweeties, darling. Just bring me back a manuscript."

He blew her a kiss and left the office. She was already on the phone to Orion before he was through the door.

An hour later, Brody stepped out of the station onto the Isle Of Dogs. A few minutes' walk took him to the grand, impressive, glass-fronted offices of The Independent that rise majestically in Marsh Wall alongside the now defunct West India Dock. It gave him a strange feeling to be re-entering his old place of work but, as he made his way through the front doors and into the entrance lobby, he could sense the same 'buzz' he'd always experienced during his years as a rising young reporter. There was a definite, recognisable smell in the air. Maybe it was the polish the cleaners used on the marble floor, or maybe it was just something emanating from the very fabric of the building itself, but there was a familiar scent that filled his nostrils; it was redolent of youth and promise; of optimism and possibilities; and he liked it.

Alan Denton's office was situated in a corner at one end of the main news room. It was small but it was tidy and well organised, which was typical of the man himself and the operation that he ran with particular efficiency. Brody eased himself into the chair he was offered as Denton closed the office door to extinguish the noise of the outside news room and afford them some privacy.

"I'm tight for time today" he explained as he retook the seat behind his broad desk. "But you said it was urgent so I've cleared twenty minutes. Will that be enough?"

"More than enough" Brody told him gratefully. "But I'll come straight to the point."

It didn't take long to give Denton a résumé of the situation and a concise picture of events as Brody knew them. The editor was clearly intrigued and occasionally jotted down details on his notepad.

"And this pathologist has the paperwork to prove that the body was *officially* removed from the Westminster morgue?"

"Yes."

"Before he could carry out further tests?"

"Yes."

"And then you start asking questions and suddenly find you're being tailed?"

"Yes."

"And you're *certain* about being followed?" Denton asked pointedly. "I mean there's no possible chance you could have been mistaken?"

Brody shook his head. "None."

"Hmmm." The editor sat back in his chair with a concentrated frown on his face, slowly twirling a pencil between the fingers of his right hand. "Somebody 'upstairs' doesn't want you disturbing the status quo."

"Exactly. And that's precisely why I want to go digging."

The editor nodded. "And now we have the apparent suicide of the twin brother in Vienna."

"Which I'd lay a hundred to one is another cover-up."

Denton nodded again. "I agree." He looked across the desk at his friend. "What do you need?"

"A stake. To get me to Vienna and to follow up whatever I find. To be perfectly frank, I simply don't have the resources to do this on my own. My alimony won't allow it."

Alan Denton grinned from ear to ear. "*That* I can appreciate. So let's cut to the chase. You know I'll help you if I can. But in these days of budget cuts and falling sales I have to justify every single penny that passes across this desk. What exactly are you offering me?"

"Exclusive print rights to the initial story and a ten per cent cut, with prior editorial approval, of any media spin-offs if whatever I discover leads to a T.V. documentary or magazine articles. If it proves to be big enough for a subsequent book deal then the rights are entirely mine but the Indie will get full credits and honourable mention."

"And in return?" asked Denton.

"I need a commissioning fee. Fifty per cent guaranteed and the remainder payable if we get the story we want. You take care of *all* incidental expenses. You know me well enough to know the ex's will be legit and I'll keep to within a sensible margin but, as my pockets are currently empty, I need everything covered."

"All right. Sounds good to me. Anything else?"

"Yes. We have to keep this whole thing between just the two of us. I want the authorities to think I've walked away from it."

"Won't that be a little difficult when you suddenly arrive in Austria's sunny capital?"

"I've covered that. I'm doing a p.a. at an English book fare. A 'meet the author' sort of thing."

"You think they'll swallow that?"

Brody shrugged. "Probably not. But it gives me a valid reason to be there if I have to make excuses at some future date. I can lie about the purpose of the trip but I can't lie about actually being in Vienna. This covers my back."

Denton nodded slowly. "Ok. Makes sense. But I still think you need to be careful. We don't yet know how high up this might go. And we don't want you ending up in a hotel room with a puncture in your toe!"

"Too right!" agreed Brody with a laugh. "But I doubt that's likely. As long as whoever is watching me thinks I've turned up a big fat nothing, then I'll be fine."

"None the less. You be careful out there." There was a genuine note of concern in the editor's voice and Brody was grateful for it. "Is there anything else you need?" asked Denton.

"Yes. I don't want any official record of the fact that I'm working for you. So I'd like you to open a new bank account, but not in my name, and to pay all monies for expenses into it, so there's no trace of me receiving any direct payments from the Indie. I'll need a cash card and a credit card for the account and PIN notification."

"That's not difficult. We can open a 'project account'. How soon do you need it?"

"As soon as you can possibly set it up. The cards will probably take a few days to come through, so I'll need you to courier them to me. I'll text you the address when I've found a hotel. I'm using a different mobile number until all this is over. So keep a note of it and don't use the one you have on file."

"Got it. Anything else?"

Brody looked a little sheepish as he reluctantly said: "A small float would help. I can put the flight to Vienna on my own credit card but I'll need cash for when I'm there until you can mail me the cards for the new account."

"No problem" Denton told him and unlocked and opened the top drawer of his desk. He reached in a withdrew a wad of twenty-pound notes, tied up with a rubber band. He placed it lightly on the desk in front of Brody. "That's five hundred. It's the most I'm allowed to authorise in cash without a nod from upstairs."

Brody gratefully picked up the money and placed it carefully into the inside pocket of his jacket.

"Good hunting, Josh" Denton wished the journalist and offered his hand.

Brody stood and shook his friend warmly by the hand. "Thanks, Alan."

Adele called him at just after 6 pm. "It's all fixed, darling. They'd love to see you and they want to set up a little signing session. They've arranged for the courier to ship out twenty-five copies of the Soho book overnight. Do you think that'll be enough?"

Josh laughed. "More than enough. I'll be surprised if we sell a single book. Why would the Viennese want to read about the history of Soho?"

"Who knows anything about anything, darling? If we knew what makes people buy a particular book we could write them to order and all retire! Just smile nicely at everyone, kiss the babies and sign the books. The sooner you get done, the sooner you are back and can get down to writing."

"Thanks. I will, I promise."

"Your contact is a Miss Bryony Gregg, by the way. She's expecting you."

"Bryony Gregg" repeated Josh as he scribbled down the name. "You're the best, Adele. Many thanks."

"All part of the service, darling. Keep safe. Bon voyage."

She hung up and the line went dead.

Brody had no idea how long he might be in Vienna so he threw enough clothes into his case to see him through ten days. He rarely dressed formally but it was always wise to have one smart suit to hand in case of need and he opened the small wardrobe to survey the hanging rail. As he only possessed two suits, the choice was not difficult. Selecting the plain black in preference to the slate grey, he folded it carefully and laid it on the bed, ready to be placed last of all into the suitcase. He wrapped a pair of black brogues into a plastic Tesco bag and stowed them alongside his leather toiletries holder, before placing the suit on top of everything and then firmly closing the lid and clicking the locks into place. Taking a long red webbing strap, he threaded it through the handle and around the entire case before buckling it. Modern day suitcases were all mass produced and it was possible to find dozens of identical bags tumbling down the carousel at an airport. The red strap would allow him to readily identify his own and avoid anybody inadvertently making off with his luggage.

By 7.30 pm, his packing long completed, he was ready to eat but, before walking out to Chinatown, he seated himself in the lounge and put through a call to the family home.

"Hi. It's me" he told Kassia as the call connected.

"Hello. We don't normally hear from you on a Wednesday. Is anything wrong?"

"No. Everything's fine. I just wanted to let you know that something's come up and I'll be a way for a few days."

"Oh, really?... There was a momentary pause. "Is it work?"

It was a simple question. But the subtle change in her voice as she delivered that single word 'really?' was loaded with overtones. She wasn't actually asking if his absence would be due to work. She was in fact saying 'are you going away alone or with another woman?'

It always struck Brody as strange that Kass had divorced him precisely because she wanted to dissolve the bond that held them legally together, severing the tie of marriage and recasting them both as single individuals, yet, whenever there was the slightest intimation that another woman had crossed his path or might be taking an interest in him, her manner instantly changed and became icy. He liked to think that if she met someone new then, although he wouldn't exactly enjoy the situation, he would have the grace to accept it and wish her well. Not that there was much chance that his tolerance would be put to the test in the foreseeable future. Kass was still determinedly locked into her 'I don't need a man' phase. He just wished that, having opted not to be with him herself, she would be a little less frosty about him being with someone else. But it was never wise to address the subject.

"Yes, it's work" he answered quietly. "It's a book fair in Vienna. Adele wants me to put in an appearance. Seems to think it would be good for raising my profile or something."

"Ah. Well, I'm sure you won't object. You always loved the place."

Brody had taken Kass to Vienna for a romantic weekend, back in the amorous days when they first began dating. It had been one of the 'good' times and he still had fond memories of their time in the Austrian capital. He hoped she did too.

"Yes. I'm not complaining."

"Will you be gone long?"
"Don't know. Maybe a week."
"Oh. Ok. Good."
"I just wanted to let you know I'll be away and to have a brief word with Saffy."
"Yes, of course. Well... I'll say goodbye. Have a good trip."
"Thanks. I will."

Kassia called Serafina to the telephone and the little girl chatted eagerly with her Dad. She told him all about school and regaled him with a detailed account of the latest class nature project. The bus trip to the farm had evidently been a huge success and they were now following it up with geography, history and art work, all related to the animals they had seen. Brody was pleased she enjoyed school so much and delighted that she seemed to be such a bright and keen student.

"And Mum says that I can have a rabbit after all!" she told her father excitedly.

This was a genuine surprise. "She does?" asked Brody in amazement. "Why did she change her mind?"

"Well Chloe got a puppy for her birthday. Her uncle's dog had six puppies and he was giving them away. I asked mum if we could take one but she said we couldn't afford a dog and they need too much looking after. So she said we could have a rabbit instead! Isn't it great?"

Brody laughed inwardly at his ex-wife's predicament. Faced with the prospect of vets' costs and food bills for a puppy, never mind the daily walking and exercise routine, she had realised that keeping a rabbit was considerably the cheaper and lesser of two evils. He harboured a vague suspicion that Saffy, even at seven, was canny enough to have realised the dilemma and to have pushed hard for a puppy precisely to secure the longed-for rabbit. Either way, he was glad that such decisions were outside his ambit.

He explained to his daughter that he would be away for a few days and, with typical resilience, she accepted the fact without a second thought.

"Where is Vienna?" she asked calmly. "Is it far?"

"About a couple of hours by plane. But I'll only be gone a few days. And I'll bring you back some Mozart Kugeln. Little round balls of chocolate with sweet centres."

"Oh, good. And some for Chloe?"

"Yes. Ok. Some for Chloe too. So be a good girl for your mum and I'll call you as soon as I get back. All right?"
"Ok Dad."
"I love you lots."
"Love you too, Dad. Bye!"

She hung up and Brody slowly replaced the receiver into its cradle. He hated saying goodbye to Saffy. There was something about putting down the phone and instantly severing the connection that made him acutely aware of the lack of her physical presence. Suddenly, in an instant, she was gone and he was alone; an absent father. He loathed the very words. Yet it was his uncomfortable reality. She wasn't there beside him. He couldn't pick her up and cuddle her; couldn't kiss her goodnight as he tucked her up in bed. He wasn't there when she rose to wish her 'good morning' and hold her hand while he walked her to school. He knew all the reasons why. He'd been through the conversation and the reasoning a thousand times. It made no difference. What he felt was akin to a form of mourning for what he'd lost. No amount of logic or common sense could comfort him or replace all that he was missing as she grew through childhood. The status quo was simply his cold, hard reality and, one way or another, he had to deal with it. Work afforded some consolation. At least when his mind was occupied he wasn't thinking about being an absent father. Brody cast his eye across the room and looked at his packed suitcase with a certain degree of relief. Tomorrow's trip would give him plenty to occupy his mind.

Chapter Seven

Thursday, June 20th. Vienna, Austria.

Austrian Airlines flight OS452 touched down smoothly onto the runway at Vienna Schwechat at 12.36 pm, precisely four minutes ahead of schedule. To his surprise, Josh's bag was one of the first to emerge onto the carousel and he found he was swiftly through customs and arrivals less than twenty minutes after leaving the aircraft.

He went directly to the Wechsel Bureau and changed the five hundred pounds cash Alan Denton had given him into Euros before heading for the train. Vienna's airport lies some 18 kilometres south of the city but, like Heathrow, has a railway station within the concourse, providing quick and easy transfer to the centre. The express CAT train was not due to leave for another quarter of an hour so Brody caught the slightly slower S7 Schnellbahn and enjoyed an uneventful ride into Wien Mitte.

He'd left his London flat early that morning, again using the fire escape exit. He was almost certain that his departure had not been seen by any possible watchers but, just to be sure, he took a taxi to Paddington station, making it look as if he was undertaking an inland train journey. Once inside, he slipped quickly through the crowd to the Underground and took the District line to Hammersmith, where he changed onto the Piccadilly line and caught the tube to Heathrow. It was a long and convoluted route that more than doubled the time of his journey but, if he was being followed, he was sure he'd given his tail the slip. They would soon enough discover that he was in Vienna but the longer it took to confirm his whereabouts the more time he had to move freely, and the easier he felt.

Walking out from Wien Mitte station into the bright Vienna afternoon, he crossed the Landstrasse Hauptstrasse in front of the striking, modern facade of the Vienna Hilton. The impressive looking, five-star hotel was well beyond his meagre resources and, with a distinct pang of regret, Brody walked around it and crossed the bridge along the northern edge of the Stadt Park. He knew exactly where he was heading and was pleased to find he could recall the back streets of the old part of the city with a fair degree of familiarity. A few minutes later he branched into the Fleishmarkt and strolled to the three-star Hotel Post. He had stayed there with Kass on their long weekend in Vienna and they had found the hotel reasonably priced, clean and comfortable. He was delighted to discover it had undergone something of a face lift since his previous visit and was looking considerably smarter than its modest rating would imply.

Brody's German was not exactly fluent but he knew enough to get by and was quite happy to use it to attempt the checking-in process. As usual, after beginning the conversation with no more than the simple traditional Austrian greeting of 'Grüß Gott', the girl at the reception desk recognised his native accent and immediately addressed him in perfect English. Thereafter, the entire procedure was completed in his own language, which the receptionist spoke as well as he did. He told her he needed a room for a few days, possibly a week, and asked if he could leave his reservation open ended. She was polite but told him that, as it was high season and the tourist trade was in full swing, she had only one or two vacancies and could not hold a room for him without a pre-paid reservation. He decided to book-in for six nights. If he needed to extend his stay in the city then he'd have to risk the continued availability of his accommodation.

His second floor room was simple, but comfortable, and looked out from the front of the hotel over the Fleishmarkt. He hung his suit in the wardrobe but didn't bother to unpack anything other than his toiletry bag. Having quickly washed his face and hands to freshen up, he made his way downstairs to the hotel's café, where he ordered a large black coffee and a slice of Strudel with Schlagobers, which meant a heaped topping of thick, whipped cream.

The pastry was delicious and the coffee was strong, the way he liked it. It was served, as always in Vienna, with a glass of fresh water by the side of the cup. It was a custom Brody liked and wished the English would adopt. His culinary indulgence over, he left the café and set out to stroll through the city streets.

Vienna is divided into various Bezirke, or 'districts', and each is designated by a number. The main city centre comprises the first district and, like the West End of London, is the 'up market' area of the capital. None the less, unlike Mayfair, where everything costs an arm and a leg, Vienna's first district was not exclusively the province of the rich and wealthy and it did not take Brody long to find a small telephone shop where he purchased a local network SIM card for his second phone. He had both mobile phones with him. His normal handset for ordinary calls that might be monitored and his new unit for anything that needed to be anonymous and should not be overheard.

With the new SIM card fitted into his phone, Brody made his way to Stephansplatz and seated himself at a table in a pavement café opposite the huge wooden doors at the front of the great cathedral. With a second cup of Viennese coffee in front of him he first sent a text message to Alan Denton, to give him the address and co-ordinates of the hotel, and then put through a call to Gerhard Weber. Whilst they had never shared the kind of relationship Brody enjoyed with Sean Finnegan, the Austrian journalist was as friendly as ever and delighted to hear that Josh was in Vienna. The two arranged to meet later that evening in the café bar of the Hotel Post.

Wanting to establish as soon as possible his bona fide reason for being in the Austrian capital, Josh took a taxi to the University campus on the Ring. There were numerous posters and small banners advertising the book fair and he simply followed his nose and quickly came to the hall where the event was being held. The fair had been organised by the University's English language department and was being staged in partnership with The British Publishers Association, whose members were represented at the thirty or so stands that Brody estimated were spread around the hall. It was a smart move on the part of the University. Its courses were being promoted and publicised by the fair but the whole event was being paid for by the contributing publishers, who all paid a substantial rent to secure their presence.

Brody soon found the Orion stand, manned by a couple of the company's representatives. One was a guy in his early twenties, the other, whom Brody took to be Bryony Gregg, was an efficient looking woman in her mid-fifties with short, greying hair and dressed in a smart two-piece suit. Her appearance was neat and precise and definitely academic. The two were standing, idly chatting, as Brody approached and introduced himself.

"Miss Gregg?"

She looked up and smiled. "Yes. How can I help you?"

"I'm Josh Brody. I believe you're expecting me."

"Mr. Brody. Of course." Smiling warmly, she extended her hand and Josh shook it. "Welcome. How nice to see you. Won't you sit down?"

The Orion stand was on a tiny raised rostrum, about ten centimetres above floor level. It was hardly large but sufficient to accommodate a small table and two chairs at its centre, and was surrounded by shelves of the company's books. As Brody seated himself opposite Miss Gregg, he spied a pile of 'Soho – The Dark Side' lying in the far corner, surrounded by bubble-wrap where the copies had recently been unpacked.

"We'll be putting your books at the front of the stand this afternoon" she told him enthusiastically. "And we thought we'd look at a signing on Monday, if that's all right with you? It gives us a few days to get a modest promotion underway and try and make a little event of it. We thought from 12 noon to 2pm ought to be about right. Quite a few people look in during their lunch break."

"That's fine" Brody told her amiably. "I'm happy to fit in around you."

They chatted for a quarter of an hour or so. The experienced and very pleasant Miss Gregg was clearly accustomed to dealing with authors and signings and the general rigmarole that accompanies a book fair. She was more than adept at small talk and polite conversation and, although he was certain she had never read it, dutifully waxed lyrical about Brody's Soho book and what an asset it was to Orion's list.

Brody gave her the number of his mobile telephone in case she needed to reach him and, with a promise to return promptly in time for the Monday signing, took his leave. With the warm sun shining brightly in the cloudless Viennese sky, he opted to enjoy the role of tourist and walk back to his hotel. Crossing the Ring, he strolled through the Volksgarten and on through the grandeur of the Hoffburg Palace grounds, making his way leisurely back to the first district.

At the Hotel Post he checked his email, took a shower and then settled down to await his evening appointment and get to the real purpose of his visit to Vienna.

Gerhard Weber was a large individual. Something of an athlete in his college days, he had remained a reasonably fit and agile man when Brody had first met him ten years before. The past decade had not been kind however and middle age had seen his once muscular frame become decidedly flabby and out of condition. The manner in which Gerhard's shirt buttons were now stretched over his considerable paunch told Brody that his penchant for Weissbier, the wheat based ale that is a favourite of the Viennese, was a habit that he clearly still indulged. A fact that was reinforced by the two large glasses of the pale gold liquid that he ordered the instant he seated himself at Brody's corner table.

Weber's obvious increase in weight had done nothing to dent his jovial manner and Brody found him as convivial as ever as they chatted and sipped their ale.

"So, Josh" Weber asked after some half an hour of small talk. "What brings you to Wien?"

"An English book fair. My agent seems to think it might encourage the noble Viennese to buy a few copies of my Soho book if I put in an appearance. Personally, I think she's pissing in the wind but hey, I wasn't going to quibble if it meant a trip to Wien! The chance to travel is one of the reasons we do the job, right? God knows it can't be for the money!"

"Too true! Last year I made less than a driver on the U-Bahn. Can you believe that?"

"Yeah. I can." Brody grinned at his friend. "But you wouldn't want to drive a train, Gerhard, now would you?"

"I couldn't! I wouldn't fit inside the verdammter cab!"

The both laughed and Brody noticed that the whole of Weber's upper body shook, perceptibly straining against the confines of his jacket.

The Austrian raised his glass in a toast. "To dedication! Or whatever it is that keeps us both doing this crazy job!"

As Gerhard set his glass back down on the table he gazed across at Brody and raised a quizzical eyebrow. "You know, Josh, if you knew you were coming to Wien, you should have picked up a commission from one of the London broadsheets. I don't know... 'a Londoner's view of Austrian politics' or something like that. The rise of the right is causing big problems over here. A writer with your ability could have turned it into something interesting and sold it."

Brody sensed the opportunity he had been waiting for and seized it with alacrity. He looked up from his beer glass and spoke with as casual a tone as he could muster.

"In a way, I *am* looking at a possible story while I'm here. It's not a commission or anything. Just something I thought I might check out. But I think you may have beaten me to it."

"Oh?"

"Fabrice Lukeba" said Brody slowly, carefully enunciating the name. "Sean Finnegan tells me you are thinking of doing a piece on his death."

The Austrian nodded. "I was. Yes. I was intrigued. He'd only been here a matter of days and then he apparently shot himself. It's not the sort of thing you do on impulse, is it? I mean, if you are depressed enough to take your own life then you've probably been down for some considerable time. So it struck me as odd that he would come all the way to Wien just to commit suicide. I thought it might be worth looking into."

Brody nodded. "I agree. So, what did you find?"

Gerhard took a large swig of his beer and then wiped the back of his hand across his mouth. "He was a bad guy. Corrupt politician. Milking the state coffers. You know the kind of thing. So he was not your usual suicide type and I thought I might be onto something. But then I discovered he was a twin and news reached him that his brother had suddenly died in London. That was the motive. He couldn't live with the loss."

"Why do you say that?" asked Brody, leaning forward in his seat.

"He left a note. 'Can't go on without my brother. Too much to bear. No future.' "I'm not quoting verbatim, you understand, but that was the gist of it."

"Did you get to see the note for yourself?"

"Yes. It was only a few sentences but it made the point clearly enough."

"So you believe it was genuine."

Weber gave a shrug of his large shoulders. "Ach. I see no reason to doubt it. Twins are strange that way. They have this telepathic thing don't they? They sense each other's emotions. When one is hurting the other one feels the pain. All of that stuff. And these two were particularly close, so I'm told." Gerhard's chubby features creased into an inquisitive frown. "But why are you asking? What's your interest in this?"

Brody had no wish to reveal his hand. If he was to be effective in his enquiries, he needed to conceal as much information as he could; but Gerhard was no fool and the mere fact that Brody was asking questions would indicate his suspicions to the Austrian. A little dissembling was required. He leaned in across the table and spoke in almost a whisper.

"This can't go any further. Ok?"

Gerhard nodded. "Of course."

"The death of the brother in London was a little sordid. There was a call girl. There were rumours. You know the sort of thing. It wasn't straight forward. Sean Finnegan thinks the guy in London could have been hit by one of the rebel groups from the Congo."

"With a hooker as cover?" asked Gerhard scornfully.

"Uhuh."

"That's crazy. A rebel group would just have shot him dead in his own back yard."

"That's what I told Sean" Brody reassured him. "But when Lukeba's brother died here in Vienna within a few days it all seemed a little too much of a coincidence and Sean was insistent. To be fair, nobody knows more about Africa than Sean. So, when I knew I was coming to Vienna, I promised I'd check it out."

"You mean... see if there are any similarities?"

"Exactly."

Gerhard gave a sniff and a slight grin. "Well, there was no mention of a prostitute here. At least, as far as I'm aware. Otherwise I would have dug a little deeper. He was over here for a U.N. trade conference, out at the International Centre on the Donau. He'd attended all of the sessions. No unusual behaviour. Then he gets the news about his brother and"... he formed his thumb and two fingers into the shape of a gun and held them to his head... "bang!"

It was time for Brody casually to slip into the conversation the real question he needed to ask. "And when you dropped the story, it was entirely because you thought it wasn't worth it? You were not pressured at all by the police or anyone to leave it alone?"

The Austrian looked surprised by the suggestion. "No. Not at all. In fact the police were unusually co-operative. They made the note and all the evidence available to me without my even asking."

Brody experienced a ripple of doubt. Weber's last sentence jarred in his head as soon as he heard it. The police had made the suicide note available without even being asked to do so. Gerhard was right. That was indeed 'unusually co-operative'. Josh's instinct was telling him that something was wrong.

"Do you have the contact details for the case officer?" he asked casually.

"Sure. It was guy called Kleist. He's an Oberkommisar with the Kriminalpolizei. I can give you his number if you want it."

"That would be great. Thanks."

Gerhard grinned and shook his head. "Let it go, Josh. You and Sean are chasing shadows. God knows it's not hard to pick up a hooker here in Wien. A short drive to the Gürtle will find you any sort you want. There are dozens of them on display on the sidewalk. But do you really think a rebel group in the D.R.C. knows that? And even if they do, can you see them organising a call girl to cover a hit? They couldn't set that up at home never mind here or in London. It doesn't add up!"

Brody laughed. "You're right, Gerhard. But you try telling that to Sean. Especially when he's had a few glasses of Guinness! I'll check it out with the police, just so I can tell him I've done it. Then I'll get down to the serious business of the book fair." He raised his beer. "Until then... let's stop worrying about our Irish friend and sink another glass of this excellent Weissbier!"

* * * * *

Friday, June 21st.

After a breakfast of coffee and rolls, Josh put through a call to Oberkommisar Kleist at the number Gerhard had given him. He used his secondary mobile with the Austrian SIM card to make the call.

"Kleist." The voice was deep and sonorous and even from just the one word, Brody formed an instant picture in his mind of a large, thick set individual.

"Guten Morgen, Herr Kleist" began Josh, employing his best German accent. "Ich heisse Brody. Josh Brody. Ich bin ein Kollege Gerhard Weber's. Sprechen Sie English?"

There was a momentary pause before the reply came. "Yes. I have a little English."

Josh was relieved. His German was reasonable but would not stretch to any detailed questions regarding the Lukeba death. "I'm a journalist from London. I wonder if you can spare me a little time to answer a few questions about Fabrice Lukeba? I understand you are the officer who handled the case."

There was another pause. When Kleist spoke again there was a clearly discernible note of caution in his tone. "Why do you have questions about this?"

"Oh, it's only to check a few details" Josh replied as nonchalantly as he could. "I'm writing a piece on identical twins. How they often do the same things even though they're miles apart; wear the same clothes; read the same books and so forth; the apparent telepathic link between them. I expect you know that Lukeba's twin brother died in London a couple of weeks ago? It's such a co-incidence that they both died within a few days of each other, so I thought I'd include a couple of paragraphs about it in my article."

The voice at the end of the line gave a distinct sniff of derision. "You think they had some sort of mental connection that made them both die?"

Brody laughed. "No. Between ourselves, I think it's a crazy idea. But it makes good copy and helps me to sell the article. So, do you think we might meet?"

Kleist made no attempt to hide the sigh he gave before answering. "I can give you a few minutes maybe. Tomorrow morning. My office is in the 9th district. Wasagaße 22. Close to the Freud museum. Do you know it?"

"I'll take a taxi" said Josh, scribbling down the address. What time would suit you?

"Ten o'clock."

"Thank you. I'll be there."

Kleist hung up without a word of goodbye.

With the rest of his Friday apparently free, Brody was deciding on how best to spend the day when his English phone rang. The display showed it was an Austrian number. He didn't recognise it as belonging to Gerhard Weber, so presumed it had to be a call from Bryony Gregg at the book fair. He pressed the connect button.

"Hello?"

"Mr. Brody?"

The voice speaking in his ear sounded English and was indeed female, but did not belong to the efficient Miss Gregg.

"Yes" said Josh tentatively.

"I hope you don't mind my disturbing you but I got your number from Adele Sanders, your agent. She said it would be ok to call."

Trust Adele to milk every opportunity she can, thought Brody and wondered just what scheme she was concocting to utilise his time in Vienna. Whatever it was, he was sure there would be potential book sales at the end of it.

"Yes, it's fine" he told the caller. How can I help you?"

"My name is Shelley Anderson. I'm with the British Council. We're supporting the English book fair at the University and I understand you're putting in an appearance there?"

"That's right. I'm doing a signing on Monday."

"Well, I don't know how long you'll be in Wien, and I hope you don't think I'm imposing, but we were wondering if we might inveigle you to do something similar for *us*?"

"A signing you mean?"

"More of a talk really. Although I'm sure signing will be involved. As you probably know, our remit is to promote British art and culture and we often hold little events. Nothing major. Just enough to generate a bit of publicity and support the cause. Having an author in town is too good a chance to miss, so we were hoping you might agree to give a brief discourse on your work. It wouldn't be too grand or daunting. Just twenty minutes or so on your methods of working, the topics that interest you etc., and then a brief Q and A afterwards. I'm sure you've done this sort of thing before."

"One or two" said Josh knowingly.

"There's no fee I'm afraid. Budgets simply won't stretch to it. But these talks are always well attended and you're bound to sell some books. And we find most authors really enjoy the chance to meet with their readers and discuss their work. Your agent seemed to think it was a great idea."

"I'm sure she did" said Josh with a smile. "And she's right. Of course I'd be happy to help."

"Thank you! I'm so pleased. I'll get down to organising it right away. Can you let me have your email address and I'll copy you in on the details as we set them up here." They exchanged email addresses and Josh jotted hers down in his notebook.

"Could we meet for a coffee sometime and chat through the basics?" she asked. "I can prep you on the format and explain the general drill."

"That would be useful" Josh told her, glad that his free Friday now had an agenda. "I'm around this afternoon if you can manage it."

"Perfect. Where can I find you?"

Like most journalists pursuing a story, Brody preferred not to disclose his exact location until he was sure of the person he was telling. "Well I'm doing a little sight-seeing today anyway so I can come to your office if you like."

"Are you sure?"

"Absolutely."

"That's so kind. Thank you. We're in the seventh district. Siebensterngasse 21. There's a tram stop just a few metres away at the end of the street."

"I'll find it. What time would suit you?"

"Around 2pm?"

"That's fine. I'll see you then."

"I'll look forward to it. Goodbye."

Josh clicked off the handset with a satisfied grin. Chance, and the acquisitive instincts of his indefatigable agent, had unexpectedly provided another valid reason for his presence in Vienna. It would afford extra cover for his true purpose and was far too good an opportunity to miss.

"Mr. Brody?" she asked with a broad smile as she eagerly extended her hand. "I'm Shelley Anderson. I can't tell you how delighted we are that you're able to help us."

Her appearance was far from the image Brody had anticipated and he realised, with a marked degree of self-admonishment, that he was guilty of stereotyping. Something in his subconscious had automatically assumed that a representative of The British Council, organising a literary event, would probably resemble the efficient Miss Gregg of Orion Publishing and appear somewhat 'bookish' and something of a 'blue stocking', neither of which epithets remotely applied to the young woman shaking his hand.

She was slim and stylishly dressed in denim jeans, with a powder blue cotton jacket over a crisp white T-shirt. Her sparkling eyes were bright and intelligent and her shoulder length hair was naturally fair, not exactly blonde but too light to be called brown. She was an attractive woman and Brody found something in her manner instantly appealing. He estimated her to be somewhere around thirty years of age and, as he shook her right hand, found himself inexplicably noting that she wore no wedding ring on her left.

"It's a pleasure" he told her warmly. "Only too glad to help."

"You found us all right? No problems?"

"None. Although I must confess, I just got into a taxi and gave him the address."

She smiled at him and her whole face seemed to light up. "Very sensible. That's pretty much what I do." She gestured towards the front doors. "Shall we head outside? It's a beautiful day and there's a great little café in the park just around the corner."

"Perfect" said Josh.

They left the reception area and he politely held open the door for her as they stepped into the street and entered the warm afternoon sunshine.

"Are you permanently based in Vienna?" he asked.

"No. I'm just in town to help with the book event. I'm fairly peripatetic. They tend to send me here, there and everywhere. What about you? Will you be in Vienna long?"

Brody shook his head. "Just a week or so."

"Are you staying in the city centre?"

"Yes. In the first district. The Hotel Post in the Fleishmarkt." Brody now had no reservations about revealing his location to this particular enquirer.

"Really? That's very close to me."

"Oh?" enquired Josh, trying to conceal the fact that he was pleased to discover she was staying near his hotel.

"The Council has an apartment in Bäckerstrasse. It's just a block away from you."

"Well then, as we're neighbours, we'll have to meet for dinner or something."

"That would be nice" she answered politely. Her manner gave nothing away and Brody couldn't tell whether she was actually keen to have dinner with him or was merely saying so as a matter of form and part of the necessary etiquette of her job.

"Are you in town just for the business of the book fair or is this also something of a holiday?" she continued as they strolled.

"A little of both" he casually lied. "I'm doing some research. Nothing major; just some background stuff; but I love this city so I'll also spend a few days doing the tourist bit."

"I don't blame you. It's one of my favourite places too."

They turned into Sigmundsgasse and entered Siebenstern Park, where several large, bright-orange table umbrellas a couple of hundred metres away ostentatiously revealed the location of the park's busy café. Vienna was one of the first European cities to develop the notion of a coffee house, a residue of one of its invasions by the Turks in the late seventeenth century. These early establishments were the corner stone of what would eventually become 'the café society' and the tradition had thrived and continued in the city ever since. Rather than a mere convenience, providing a place to drink a beverage, cafés in Vienna serve as a social centre where people meet to chat, read the day's newspapers, eat a snack or a full meal, and generally pass away the time. The quality of food and pastries, even in a simple park café, is as good as any restaurant and the service is usually first class, with waiters and waitresses dressed in formal black and white and keen to earn the tips, or 'Trinkgeld', that is customarily given.

By the time they seated themselves at a small table on the edge of the decking, Josh and Shelley were on first name terms and chatting freely. A smiling waitress took their coffee order and they got down to discussing the purpose of their meeting.

"I thought we might look at next Tuesday" she began. "We've had several different talks by authors during the month of the book fair and they've all been quite successful. Yours will be a great finish to the series. Somewhere between twenty minutes and half an hour is usually about right. Then a quarter of an hour for a Q. and A. Would that be ok?"

"That's fine. But it's not as if I'm well known. So, I must confess, I'm not exactly expecting a crowd. Do you think anyone will turn up?"

She laughed and he wondered why he noticed the way her hair fell across her shoulders as she gave a slight shake of her head.

"You'd be surprised" she told him with a grin. English literature is very popular here. The last speaker drew over a hundred in the audience."

This was indeed a revelation to Brody, who had genuinely anticipated he would be addressing just a few old ladies, and maybe a dog, if he was lucky. "Really? I'm amazed!"

"We tend to think other countries are like our own, where learning a foreign language is generally treated as an inconvenience. But most of Europe sees English as a necessity in the modern world and original language books sell well; especially here in Vienna. The city even has a full time English-speaking Theatre. And most American and English films can be seen in cinemas with their original soundtrack."

"I think I'd better brush up on my notes" he said sincerely as the waitress brought their coffees and set them down on the table.

"About fifty per cent of your audience will be students who are reading English at the University, the rest will be interested members of the public. I'd bring several copies of your book, if I were you. I'm fairly sure they'll all be sold; especially if you sign them. But we'll have order forms to hand anyway, so anyone wishing to do so can buy a copy through The British Council and we'll arrange to send it to them."

"You've done this before" said Brody with a smile.
She nodded knowingly. "Just a bit."
"So what exactly is it that you do?"
"Well my official title is 'British Council Liaison Officer for the Department of Culture, Media and Sports'. So you can see why I never use it!"
Josh laughed. "Can you actually get all that on a business card?"
"No" she declared, smiling. "So mine just says 'British Council'. And, despite my impressive designation, I have nothing to do with sports or media. My activities are confined solely to the arts. So I cover theatre and film, music, literature and visual arts like painting and sculpting."
"And are you based in London?"
"Head office is in London, yes. But the purpose of The British Council is to promote U.K. culture around the world so I can pretty much be sent anywhere. Of course we're nowhere near as widespread as we used to be. In these days of cutbacks our budgets have been slashed like everyone else's. But, thank God, we're still seen as an important source of promoting trade and tourism. So I'm not out of a job yet!"
The conversation went on, flowing easily, and Brody felt genuinely relaxed in Shelley Anderson's company. They ordered a second coffee and continued to sit and chat for over an hour before she reluctantly checked her watch and told him she needed to get back. Brody paid the bill and they walked out through the park.
"Have you discovered the Kammeroper yet?" she asked as they strolled.
Josh shook his head.
"Oh, you must pay it a visit. It's in your building."
Brody raised a surprised eyebrow. "In the hotel?"
"Yes. The original structure was damaged in the war but the ballroom was untouched. It was separated off when the hotel was reconstructed and was turned into a charming little opera house. It's only small of course. It holds around two hundred and fifty or so, I believe. But they do some good things. They tend to find young singers at the start of their careers and give them their first break. I've seen some excellent productions there." She looked across at Josh's concerned expression. "Or maybe opera is not your thing?"
"Not at all" he said hurriedly. "The little I've heard, I've generally liked very much. But I'm just thinking about it and, if I'm honest, I must

shamefully admit that I don't believe I've ever been to a live performance of a full opera."

"Then you have the perfect opportunity! It's literally on your doorstep."

He nodded. "But I think I might need a little guidance, don't you? Don't they say that you should always see your first opera with someone who knows all about it?"

She looked up at him and grinned. "Do they?"

It was a moment they both understood, and each knew the other had registered the fact, but neither spoke. He wanted to know if she would go with him to the opera and she knew that was what he was wondering. The silence prevailed while he tried to second guess her reply. They had clearly enjoyed each other's company for the last hour but he was acutely aware that socialising was an important part of her job, and he was honestly unsure as to whether her relaxed and comfortable manner was an indication that she genuinely liked him or merely an aspect of her professionalism. He opted to hedge his bets.

"Do you think they might have a couple of tickets available?"

Her eyes widened a little. She was enjoying the verbal fencing. "They *might*" she said lightly. "But the theatres here run what they call Abonnements. It's a subscription to tickets that means seats are always available to the holders so, quite often, everything is pre-sold; especially in a tiny house like the Kammeroper."

"Ah" said Brody resignedly, deciding she was politely stepping back from the possibility of joining him.

"On the other hand" she added with a distinct gleam in her eye, "The British Council has a good relationship with all the city's theatres so, if you'd really like to see something there, I could call the Kammeroper and probably get a couple of house seats."

Brody could not conceal the grin that broke across his face. "That would be terrific" he told her happily. "Maybe I could buy you that dinner we mentioned and then we could see the performance?"

"That sounds good" she said, allowing herself a smile. "I'll make a call."

Chapter Eight

Saturday, June 22nd.

Unlike Brody's misplaced preconception of Shelley Anderson, Oberkommisar Dieter Kleist proved to be everything the journalist expected to find as he was ushered into the policeman's office and seated himself opposite the Detective Inspector's desk.

He was a big man, over six feet tall Josh estimated, with broad shoulders and large hands. Brody was fully aware of Kleist's vice like grip as they shook hands in greeting. Unlike the over-weight, unfit, Gerhard Weber, who was also not a small individual, this Austrian policeman looked to be in good physical condition and no villain would relish confronting him. He had a head of thick, wavy hair that was combed back without a parting and displayed the first, encroaching shades of grey at his temples. Josh presumed he was around forty years of age and, from his somewhat reticent manner, none too keen to be interviewed by a British reporter.

"How exactly can I help you, Mr. Brody?" the detective enquired a little coldly.

"Well, as I mentioned to you on the telephone" Josh began, adopting as friendly a tone as possible, "I am writing a piece on twins and the coincidences that seem to occur in their lives. I'd like to include something about the death of the Lukeba brothers. As Fabrice passed within a few days of his twin, it seems like another of these extraordinary, simultaneous, fluke occurrences."

Kleist gave a shrug of his large shoulders. "He couldn't live without his brother so he shot himself. Tragic, I agree... but hardly a coincidence. More just a case of cause and effect, wouldn't you say?"

"You're probably right" said Josh with a nod as he opened his notebook. "Is that all that the suicide note said or was there anything else written?"

With a look that did not conceal the fact he felt his time was being wasted, Kleist reached onto his desk and opened a file that was set out in preparation for this interview. Withdrawing a sheet of paper, he passed it across to Brody.

"Read it for yourself."

Josh was surprised to receive such evidence unbidden and gratefully took hold of the sheet. It was not a photocopy. It was the original letter, on in-house, headed notepaper with the words 'Intercontinental Hotel Wien' emblazoned across the top in dark blue. Written in English, the handwriting was far from neat, as though scribbled in something of a hurry, and the rather cursive penmanship was light in character and a little florid in the sweep of the strokes. It said simply:

The death of my brother is too much to bear. We have shared every moment of our lives together and I cannot see a future without him. My apologies to all. But I wish to join him in a better place. F.L.

"Very sad" said Josh quietly as he quickly scribbled down the text and then passed back the note. "And he shot himself in his hotel room, is that right?"

"Yes. The chamber maid found him" replied Kleist matter-of-factly. "Our pathologist estimates the death to have been somewhere between ten o'clock and midnight. The maid found him at approximately nine-thirty the following morning."

"His brother was also found in a hotel room" said Brody. "In bed. Did Fabrice shoot himself in bed?"

"Looking for more coincidences?" asked Kleist in a clearly evident tone of disdain.

"Just trying to establish the facts" Brody replied with a polite smile.

"The 'facts', Mr. Brody, are these." The policeman again reached into the file and withdrew several photographs, which he slowly and deliberately set out on the desk in front of him, all facing the journalist. The colour pictures, taken from various angles by the police photographer at the scene, showed the body of Fabrice Lukeba lying slumped back in a chair facing the dressing table in his hotel room. The photographs were particularly gruesome and, Brody presumed, Kleist fully intended to shock his guest with the graphic images.

There was a great deal of staining across the front of the corpse from the large blood flow that had issued from the side of the head, much of which had been blown away by the force of the bullet. Lukeba was positioned at an angle, with his head back against his left shoulder. The gun was lying in his lap where, presumably, it had fallen once he had shot himself.

"As you can see," said Kleist unemotionally, "he stuck the barrel of a Sig Sauer automatic in his mouth and blew his brains out."

"Any idea where he obtained the gun?" asked Brody.

"We presume he brought it with him. Probably in his diplomatic bag. We traced the serial number to a shipment of arms that originally went to the Kenyan army. But, as you might imagine, the paper trail came to an end once the pistol entered Africa."

"And you dusted it for prints, of course?"

Kleist looked down his nose a little contemptuously at the journalist. "Of course" he replied quietly. "Only one set. Lukeba's."

"And what was the official reaction to the death?"

"Excuse me, please?"

"Well, he was a visiting diplomat. An official guest in your country attending a U.N. conference. It's a little messy for both governments when he unexpectedly goes and shoots himself. I wondered if the authorities here or his colleagues back in the D.R.C. issued any statements?"

"The normal condolences were passed by my government to the Africans."

"But did they pressure you to get it all sorted quickly? Did they want a swift conclusion and a minimum of fuss? You know the sort of thing."

There was a pause of a few seconds before the detective replied. His eyes narrowed and he was unable to prevent the clear look of suspicion that materialised in them. "What does the official attitude to this suicide have to do with the idea of twins and their... I don't know the English word. We say 'Synchronismus'."

"Synchronicity" said Josh helpfully, trying to deflect the question. "Nothing really. Only the English authorities were clearly uncomfortable with the notion of a dead diplomat on their doorstep. I just wondered if the Austrians felt the same. I'm looking for possible coincidences again, do you see?"

Kleist shook his head. "My government felt no such embarrassment. Merely sadness."

"Of course. Yes. I understand. And is the body still here in Vienna?"

"No. It was sent home for a family burial."

"When was that?"

Kleist gave a puzzled look but reached to the file in front of him and checked the documentation. "It was flown back to Africa on... Sunday the 16th" he said, reading from the report.

"Really? That's only three days after it was found" said Brody. "Isn't that a little fast?"

Kleist gave a shrug. "That is not my department. But it would have been sent back at the request of the D.R.C. government. I'm sure my colleagues did it quickly to ease the distress of the family."

"I see. Yes. That must be it. Austrian efficiency, as always." Brody felt it was time to leave. He stood. "Well, thank you so much for your time Oberkommisar. I'm extremely grateful." He extended his hand in gratitude and the Austrian rose from his seat and shook it.

"How long will you be in Wien?" asked Kleist.

"Only a few days. I have all the information I need. But I thought I might grab some time to do a little sightseeing before I fly back to London."

The Austrian nodded. "Then I wish you an enjoyable stay and a safe journey home."

It was as Brody withdrew his hand from the big man's grasp, and took a final look down at the photographs on the desk, that it suddenly struck him. Something had bothered him when he first saw the disturbing images but he had been unsure as to what. It wasn't the sight of the dead man, unpleasant as it was, it was something else. Something indefinable that nagged at him. Now, all at once, he knew. It took every ounce of self-control not to react visibly, but the revelation hit him hard, striking his nerves like a cold shower.

"Thank you again Herr Kleist" he managed to utter, and quickly turned and left the room.

As he walked back down the corridor he could feel the tension mounting across the back of his neck. He had the distinct feeling that Kleist would be standing in the doorway, watching him depart, but he kept his gaze forward and didn't turn to check. Handing-in his visitor's badge to the clerk at reception, he signed himself out in the daily log book and then stepped gratefully through the large front doors and onto the street.

The air felt clean and fresh and the warm June sunshine eased some of the tension that was coursing through him. Turning the corner into Berggasse, he hailed a taxi and told the driver to take him to The Hotel Post. He would check the details once he was back in his room, but he already knew what he would find.

Twenty minutes later, seated on the side of his bed, he opened his laptop and logged onto the internet. Checking his notebook for the references he had previously found, he navigated to the appropriate web pages. There was no mistake. In every photograph showing one or the other of the twin brothers signing different trade agreements, on separate dates, the pen was always in the left hand. Tweedledum and Tweedledee were both left handed. But it was the left side of Fabrice's head that had been shot away. The gun had been placed in his mouth from the right hand side and the bullet had exploded up into his brain and exited via his left temple. No left handed person could have committed suicide that way. Fabrice Lukeba had been murdered.

For a full half an hour, Brody sat silently in his room trying to gather his thoughts. He methodically pieced together the various events that were now slowly forming like a jigsaw puzzle to reveal an obvious conspiracy. Two deeply unpleasant individuals had been murdered. From what he knew of their nefarious activities, they had caused the death of hundreds of people and the suffering of countless others, so there would be no shortage of candidates with sufficient motive to strike down the twins. The potential suspects list was probably endless but the prevailing issue was not so much *who* might have wanted to see the Lukebas dead; the question that needed to be answered was why the killings were being covered up and swept under the official carpet.

Unlike Inspector Ryan Thomas in London, who had admitted to Luke Harvey that he had been 'leaned on' by his superiors, Kleist had given nothing away. But the swift removal of the body by the Austrian authorities was a clear indication of a whitewash. It was a carbon copy of the repatriation of the London corpse. Neither country wanted incriminating evidence remaining on their soil. Why?

Brody looked again at his notebook and re-read the text of the apparent suicide note. It was signed 'F.L.'. Why had Lukeba supposedly signed his initials instead of his signature? Because a signature was identifiable. In the modern era of email and electronic communication it was perfectly possible that there were no readily available examples of Lukeba's handwriting for comparison with a suicide note. But a signature? There would be numerous samples to hand. His passport, his registration at the hotel, documents he had signed during the days of the conference; all of them could provide comparisons. But two simple initials would allow no such evaluation. It was another plain indication that the suicide note was fake and almost certainly written by the killer.

Brody had to think; to clear his head. He decided he needed fresh air and to escape the confines of his hotel room.

The wide expanse of the Stadtpark was a peaceful oasis in the midst of the capital's busy streets. Like any major European city, Vienna was teeming with traffic yet, despite the crowded roads that encircled it, the park was quiet and the noise of vehicles was reduced to nothing more than a faint, distant hum. Brody could hear birds singing in the trees and the sound of children laughing as they played games of chase on the wide, open stretches of grass. It gave him space to breathe and to try and relax as he attempted to formulate his next move.

He seated himself on a wooden bench alongside the central lake where, just a few metres in front of him, ducks and geese were noisily flitting in and out of the water, struggling against each other to win the scraps of bread that various passers-by threw to them. To his right, at the southern end of the park, the distant Intercontinental Hotel on Johannesgasse stood facing him. He didn't know which room Fabrice Lukeba had occupied. Maybe it was at the front of the hotel, overlooking the park. Perhaps Lukeba had stood, gazing from the window of his room, looking at the very bench where Brody now sat. Maybe a glimpse of the park had been the last thing Lukeba had seen of the outside world on the night he was murdered; the night when an assassin entered his room, placed a Sig Sauer pistol in his mouth and blew his brains out.

How did the assassin gain entrance to the room?, Brody wondered. Had he forced his way in? Or had Fabrice allowed him entry? And if so, why? Kleist would offer no further details. He had fulfilled his official obligations and, from now on, would be a closed book. As Brody sat gazing across the wide expanse of the park at the distant hotel, an idea struck him. It was certainly worth a try. He got up from the park bench and began heading south with a purposeful stride.

"I wonder if you can help me please?" he asked in English as he approached the reception desk and held out his British press card. "I'm writing an article for a London newspaper and I need a little information."

The Empfangschef, the chief concierge and head of the reception staff, was dressed in the hotel's full livery of coat, trousers, waistcoat and company tie, which was neatly knotted beneath an immaculate white collar. He was around forty to forty-five years of age and his black hair was well groomed and slicked back close against his head. Probably ex-army, thought Brody as the man took an immediately suspicious look at the proffered press card and his features adjusted into a polite but perfunctory smile.

"How can I be of assistance?" he enquired in excellent English.

"May we speak in private?" asked Brody quietly.

The man nodded and indicated that Brody should follow him. He led him to one of the many tables in the area of the foyer bar. When they were both seated, the concierge raised an expectant eyebrow, waiting for Brody to speak.

"There was an unfortunate incident here ten days ago. A suicide in one of your rooms." The man visibly bristled and his eyes narrowed as Josh continued. "I am reporting it for my newspaper and would like to ask you a few questions."

"I'm afraid I cannot help you" came the immediate and somewhat frosty reply. "Only the hotel's press officer is allowed to make a statement on such things. And, unfortunately, she is not in Vienna at present. She is on holiday until next month."

"I understand" said Brody. "But I was hoping to keep the hotel's name out of this entirely. If I wait for a statement from your press officer then of course I will have to say who she is and where she works. If I simply say 'a hotel in Vienna' then I don't need to mention the Intercontinental by name... or its staff" Brody added pointedly.

"That would be best" said the Empfangschef curtly.

Josh reached into his inside pocket, withdrew his wallet and casually took out a one hundred Euro note. The immediate change of expression in the eyes of the man opposite instantly told Brody that he had guessed correctly. All concierge staff in top class hotels expect tips, for services rendered, as a fundamental and important part of their wages. These cash-in-hand payments are an essential source of income and the head of the reception staff sitting across the table was no exception to the general rule.

"Of course, it would greatly assist me if I could obtain one or two answers to just a few simple questions" explained Josh. He unobtrusively placed the hundred Euro note inside the menu card that sat on the table, as if settling a drinks bill, and then closed it and laid it flat, concealing the money.

"No names?" asked the concierge.

"No names" replied Brody quietly and used one extended fingertip gently to slide the menu card forwards across the table.

The chief concierge reached forward and calmly picked up the card. He covertly slid the hundred Euro note from inside into the palm of his hand, which then disappeared into his pocket, before replacing the menu onto the table. "How may I help?"

"Do you have C.C.T.V. coverage all around the hotel?"

"Yes. The main cameras are on the landings by the lifts. But there is a single camera at the start of every corridor."

"And coverage in the reception area?"

"Yes, of course. In all the public areas."

"Did anyone from the police or the authorities ask to see any of the recorded footage for the night of June 12th?"

The Austrian shook his head. "No."

"Does the hotel still have it?"

"Yes. The recordings are kept until the end of every month. Then the hard disk is wiped and recording begins again on the 1st."

"If I need to see the footage for the night of the 12th, can that be arranged?"

The man gave a slight smile. "I'm sure our security staff will be able to assist you if I ask them to help."

I'm sure they will, thought Brody. The only question would be how many palms had to be greased before he could see what he wanted. Brody withdrew another one hundred Euro note from his wallet.

"I'd like to arrange that as soon as possible. And I'm sure I can rely on you to make sure the security staff are not too demanding." He took out a pen and hurriedly scribbled the number of his Austrian mobile on the Euro note. This time he held it in his hand. "I can be reached at this number."

The concierge nodded. "I'll see what I can do."

Before he set down the money, Brody withdrew a third one hundred Euro note and added it to the one in his hand. "I'd also like to speak with the chamber maid who found the body. Is she available?"

The Austrian checked his watch. "She's on until three. So I believe I might be able to find her."

Brody reached forward and, as before, slipped the two notes into the menu card on the table and slid it across. "I'd like to see her now, please. And, unless she speaks good English, I'll need you to translate."

The man looked towards to the bar and clicked his fingers at one of the waiters, who immediately hurried across to the table.

"Please order a drink while you are waiting" the concierge told Brody as he stood and smoothed down his coat. "Compliments of the house, of course. I will return in ten minutes."

As his boss disappeared, the waiter took Brody's order of a small beer. At three hundred Euros, it would be the most expensive drink he'd ever tasted; but worth the price if it produced the results he was seeking.

A quarter of an hour later, the concierge returned with a sheepish looking young girl in tow. She looked to be around twenty years of age and was dressed in a neat grey housecoat with white collar and white cuffs on the half-sleeves, which Brody took to be the hotel's uniform for chamber staff. She seated herself nervously at the table as the concierge eased himself into the chair beside her.

"This is Gabrielle" he said by way of introduction. She is from the Czech Republic. She has no English but her German is good. I have explained that she is not in any trouble and has only to answer a few questions."

As he took out his notebook, Brody smiled warmly at the anxious young woman, trying to put her at her ease. "Thank you for agreeing to see me" he began gently. "I have just a few questions. Is that ok?"

The manager translated and the girl nodded meekly.

"I'd like to ask you about the morning you found the body of the man who shot himself."

The girl's answers, through the manager, were hesitant, often little more than a variation of 'yes' or 'no', but as Brody persevered and carefully probed he gradually established exactly what she had found on entering Lukeba's room. It seemed she had twice knocked on the door, according to the hotel's instructed routine, and awaited a reply. Receiving no response, she presumed the room was empty and let herself in with the pass key. As was her custom, she set down her carrier of cleaning equipment by the bathroom door and then stepped into the room proper to begin making the bed.

It was several moments before she suddenly realised there was a body lying in the chair by the dressing table. On being confronted with the appalling sight of Lukeba's blood covered corpse, with half the side of the head missing, she let out a scream and ran for help. The senior chamber maid for that floor of the hotel calmed the girl and then took charge and called the head manager. When the police subsequently arrived, they cordoned-off the whole corridor, not allowing anyone near the scene, so, apart from the initial shock moments when she first discovered the corpse, Gabrielle could provide Brody with no real further information. She had been so distressed by the find that she had been off work for more than a week and had only returned two days previously.

"I want you to think very carefully please, Gabrielle, before you answer my last question" Josh told her as encouragingly as he could. "Please try to remember. What was the room like when you first let yourself in? I know the man was sitting slumped in the chair. But did you notice anything about the rest of the room? Did it seem as if there had been a fight or a struggle? Or was everything neat and tidy?"

Gabrielle began shaking her head as the concierge translated. She then replied, and her answer was interpreted for Josh: "No. There was no sign of a struggle. The room was normal and everything was laid out as it should be."

Suddenly the girl looked furtively at her boss and then back at Josh. It was clear she wanted to say something but was unsure if it was permitted.

"What is it, Gabrielle?" asked Brody.

She again looked from one to the other but made no reply.

"Tell her it's all right" Brody instructed the manager. "She can say whatever she wants to."

The Austrian nodded his consent at the girl.

Nervously, she began to speak and her reply was translated: "The bed was wrong. We have a special way of making the bed and folding the covers. I do it every morning. This bed seemed as if it had not been slept in. But the covers were not right. Someone had put them on the bed to make it look as if it was still freshly made. But the folds were all wrong."

Brody thanked the girl for her time and, greatly relieved her ordeal was over, she sought the manager's permission to leave and hurried away. Brody stood.

"Thank you for your time, Mein Herr. I will wait for your call regarding the C.C.T.V. footage."

The concierge bowed his head politely and Josh left the hotel.

There must have been some kind of struggle, he told himself as he walked back through the green spaces of the Stadtpark. The bed must have been disturbed, as was probably the rest of the room. Then, when the killer had shot Lukeba, he must have calmly remade the bed and set the room to rights. He would then have written the suicide note and departed. If the police swallowed the set-up, and believed the death was suicide, they would have had no reason to ask to see the corridor C.C.T.V. footage, which is why it had not been checked. It was now more important than ever that Josh had sight of the video recording for that night. Whatever it cost in bribes, it was a price he would have to pay.

It was past 1pm when Brody, still deep in thought, walked back into the foyer of the Hotel Post. He entered through the glass front doors and went straight to the reception desk to ask for his key. The bright faced young woman behind the counter was new to him.

"Herr Brody?" the girl enquired as he gave her his room number and she retrieved the key from the rack behind her.

"Yes."

"Sie haben ein Paket bekommen."

"A packet for me?"

"Yes. It is this morning arrived" the girl managed in a brave attempt at English.

From the size and shape of the padded envelope she handed him, Brody guessed it was the card for the new bank account and had been couriered, as promised, by Alan Denton.

"Any other messages?" Brody enquired.

"Nein. Aber ein Mann hat sich nach Sie erkundigt."

Brody frowned. He was uncomfortably sure he had understood but wanted to be certain. "In English, please."

The girl braced herself to begin. "Er... a man... he is asking after you."

"A policeman? Er... Polizei?"

The girl shook her head. That ruled out Kleist.

"A big man? Fat? Brody spread his arms, gesturing to try and denote the size of his overweight friend Gerhard Weber.

"Nein." The girl held her hands a short distance apart, indicating a slim individual.

Concerned, Brody moved a little closer to the desk and leaned in towards the girl. "What did he look like?" he asked quietly. "Er... Wie sieht er aus?"

The girl shrugged. "Ziemlich normal." There was a short pause before she suddenly corrected herself. "Oh... aber er war Glatzkopf!"

Brody's face screwed up in incomprehension. "Sorry?"

"Raziert!" said the girl. She ran the flat of her hand across her head and made a 'zzzzzz' noise, imitating a motor. "Raziert."

"Oh. A shaved head!" said Brody. "OK. I understand." This was puzzling. Brody knew nobody in Vienna of that description. "But he didn't leave a message?"

"No. He ask if you stay here. I say 'yes' but you not in room. He say he come back."

"Nothing else? He didn't leave a name?"

"No. No name."

"All right. Thank you. But if the gentleman returns, please make sure you ask his name. Dankeschön. "

Gathering his envelope, Brody took the stairs and walked up, pensive, to the second floor. The only people who knew he had checked into the Hotel Post were Alan Denton, Gerhard Weber and Shelley Anderson. Denton was at home in the U.K. and Shelley Anderson had his mobile number if she needed to reach him. There was an outside chance that Weber might have sent someone to see him, or passed on his location, but he was sure the journalist would have called him first to check it was ok. A quick call to Gerard could clarify the point. The only other possibility was that Oberkommisar Kleist had tracked him down and sent a man to see him, but the girl at the desk had said the visitor had not claimed to be a policeman so he had evidently not shown a warrant card; usually the first thing a copper does when making an enquiry.

As soon as he was in his room he put through a call to Gerhard Weber. The journalist was in the middle of a game of golf and none too delighted to be interrupted. Brody apologised and, keeping the call short, simply asked if Weber had sent someone to see him or maybe mentioned his whereabouts. As expected, the answer was a pointed 'no'.

Brody was a little uneasy. He had the same uncomfortable feeling he experienced in London when he first realised he was being tailed. Stepping to the window, he eased the net curtain to one side and looked down into the street. The Fleischmarkt was as normal as ever, with pedestrians moving to and fro. More to the point, nobody was hanging around on any corner and watching the hotel. Just as he was deriding himself for an overactive imagination, and deciding there was nothing especially sinister about someone asking for him at the reception desk, his mobile rang. He recognised the number.

"Hello?"

"Hi. It's Shelley. I called the Kammeroper and we're in luck. They've reserved two house seats for us for Monday night. Is that ok with you?"

"It's terrific. Thank you. What time?"

"It's curtain up at seven-thirty. So if we meet at, say, seven, we can pick up the tickets and have a quick drink. How does that sound?"

"Perfect. But why don't we make it six and I can buy you dinner before we go in?"

"Even better. It's a double bill, by the way. 'Gianni Schicchi' and 'Il Tabarro'. Both by Puccini, so you're in for an easy baptism. Bags of great tunes and each one only an hour long. And one is a comedy, so there'll be a few laughs thrown in for good measure."

"I'm looking forward to it already" said Josh. And he meant it.

"So what's your programme for tomorrow?" she asked casually. "Anything planned?"

"Nope. I'll probably just go for a wander around the city. What do they call it over here? There's a funny word for it, isn't there?"

She laughed. "You mean a Stadtbummel?"

"That's it! Yes. It's a great word, isn't it? To English ears, merely the sound of it seems to imply something lazy and relaxed, which is just what you want for an idle wander."

"I've never really thought about it. But now that I do, I guess you're right."

There was a pregnant pause for a moment and then she spoke again. "Look... it's Sunday tomorrow, so the office is closed. If you have nothing special on your agenda and don't mind some company, maybe we could both undertake that wandering."

Josh felt a distinct lifting of his spirits. "You mean, take a Stadtbummel together? That sounds like fun to me."

"Do you know the Cafe Landtmann? It's on the Ring opposite the university."

"I think I remember seeing it. Yes. But I've never been there."

"Well, if we're going to do the tourist thing, why don't we start there? They do a great lunch. And the pastries are to die for. Do you think you can find it?"

"I think I might manage that little piece of navigation."

"How does one-thirty sound?"

"Sounds good."

"Ok. I'll see you then. Take care, Josh. Tschüs."

She hung up.

Brody sat down on his bed and looked with a smile at the phone in his hand. Despite its more ominous true purpose, he was beginning to feel very pleased he'd made the journey to Vienna.

Opening the padded envelope sent by Alan Denton he found something else to brighten his day. Not only had the editor sent him the cash card for the new account but he had included a brief note saying that he had opened it with £5,000 as a down payment against fees and expenses. The PIN number for the card arrived by text message an hour later. Brody took a short walk to the nearest ATM machine and made a large withdrawal. He was 'in funds' and able to operate as he needed to. This investigation was looking up.

Chapter Nine

Sunday, June 23rd

Brody's new mobile with the local number rang loud and clear at 8.30 am, its annoyingly insistent beep rousing him unceremoniously from slumber. Bright sunlight was forcing its way around the edges of the drawn curtains to illuminate the darkened room as he forced open his eyes and reached out sleepily to grab the handset.
"Hello?" he murmured throatily into the receiver.
"Herr Brody? I hope it is not too early to call."
"Who is this?"
"This is your friend from the Intercontinental. I have organised the information you requested."
Brody was jerked into clear consciousness and sat himself upright in the bed. "That's good" he said hurriedly. "Thank you."
"It would be helpful if you could be here at 9 am. That is when the shift changes."
Snatching a quick look at his watch, which was lying on the bedside table, Josh decided it was just about possible. "Yes" he answered quickly, throwing back the duvet and hauling his protesting body out of bed. "I'll be there."
"I will make the arrangements." The line clicked off.
Brody grabbed the house phone and hit 9 for reception.
"I need a taxi please" he said urgently as the call was answered. "Can you have it outside in twenty minutes?"
"Certainly" the receptionist told him and, with a hastily murmured 'thanks', Josh quickly dumped the receiver back into its cradle and darted for the bathroom. With a swift brushing of his teeth and a lightning quick soaping under the shower, he managed to be dressed and leaving the foyer just as the taxi pulled into the kerbside in front of the hotel."
Being Sunday morning, the roads were uncrowded and free from the usual heavy throng of traffic. The driver made the journey in less than ten minutes and Josh was climbing the front steps of the Intercontinental at the moment a disparate choir of local bells could be heard announcing the various nine o'clock services at the many nearby churches.

The head concierge was behind the front desk dealing with a guest when he saw Josh arrive. With a discreet nod of his head to the right, he indicated that Josh should take a seat in the foyer. It took no more than a few minutes to conclude the matter in hand and the concierge then left the counter and made his way across the reception area. As he reached Josh's chair his pace didn't falter and he walked on past, simply uttering a quiet "Please." Brody allowed him a couple of additional paces before rising and setting off behind him. The man went through a far door into one of the downstairs corridors and Josh followed suit. Once they were clear of the foyer and possible prying eyes, the concierge turned and spoke.

"The man on duty is called Bernd. I have told him what is needed and he will co-operate. But you must understand that this is not hotel policy and he is taking a great risk. If the management learns what he has done he could lose his job."

"I understand" replied Josh. "I will make it worth his while."

They came to a door at the end of the corridor where the concierge stopped and knocked."

"Herein" came a voice from within and the concierge opened the door and led Josh into the room.

The interior was dark, with no outside windows and lit only by two low wattage lamps in each of the far corners, but the area in front of the main mixing console was illuminated by the light of the twenty or so T.V. monitors that were ranged in three banks above it. Seated beneath the screens, in the reflected glow of the black and white images that shone from overhead, was a solitary individual who looked up expectantly as Josh entered the room with his companion.

"Dieser Mann ist Herr Brody" said the concierge. The security guard nodded.

Josh pulled a one hundred Euro note from his pocket and handed it to Bernd. "This will not take long." The security guard took the note as he looked to his boss for translation.

"Wir brauchen nur kurze Zeit" the concierge told him. The guard nodded again and swivelled his chair around. Pushing his feet into the ground, he propelled himself across the wooden floor to arrive at the rear desk some four metres away where there were three larger monitor screens and two computers.

"Was möchten Sie anschauen?" he asked Josh.

The files were all stored on the hard drives in date order and, with Josh prompting and the concierge translating his instructions, Bernd navigated through them until they reached and opened the folder for June 12th. The hotel had a total of forty-eight cameras, subdivided into floor levels, and each one had its own contents file against that particular day. Lukeba had been in room 311, which meant the third floor, corridor one. The police Kommisar, Dieter Kleist, had told Josh that the estimated time of death was between 10pm and midnight so, allowing plenty of leeway, Josh asked the guard to roll back the recording to 6pm and then scroll through the footage. It was a simple process to run the pictures at high speed until someone appeared in the corridor, then to slow to normal tempo to check the images. Nothing of any significance showed until the time code running across the bottom of the screen, delineating hours, minutes and seconds, showed 20.47. 09.

Fabrice Lukeba appeared at the beginning of the corridor and walked its length to his room, which was the last door on the left. Josh wrote down the time in his notebook. The man's gait was relaxed and casual and his shoulders rolled slightly in something approaching a swagger. It was not the movement of a man so depressed that he was about to commit suicide. The pictures that followed showed a couple leaving a room half way along the corridor and walking in the direction of the landing to take the lifts and, shortly afterwards, a room service waiter delivering a tray of food to room 305. Otherwise the image remained clear until just after 9.30 pm.

Entering the screen from the bottom of the picture, and walking slowly along the corridor, occasionally turning her head very slightly to check on the door numbers, a female appeared. As the guard slowed the shuttle control to normal speed, the three men watched while she made her way to the last door on the left and knocked.

"Hold it!" yelled Josh, and the guard put the picture into freeze-frame. Brody stared at the screen in amazement and cursed himself for his own stupidity. Without thinking, and with not one shred of evidence to support the notion, he had automatically assumed that Fabrice Lukeba had been shot by a man. It was an assumption based on pure pre-conditioning and totally without substance. He had immediately presumed that an assassin, a murderer who could place a Sig Sauer automatic in the mouth of his victim and calmly blow out the man's brains, would be male. A glance at the shock registering on the face of the concierge told Josh he was not the only one guilty of unfounded supposition. Not only was the Austrian surprised to discover an unknown visitor calling at the room of the apparent suicide, but he was clearly also astonished to find the figure was a woman.

"Eine Frau?" he said in a disbelieving tone.

"Let it roll" instructed Josh, and Bernd hit the play button.

The recording slipped back into movement and they continued to stare at the screen in concentrated silence as they saw the door of room 311 opened from within. After a pause of just ten or twelve seconds, during which a few brief words were obviously exchanged, the women stepped across the threshold into the room and the door was closed behind her.

"Ask him to fast-forward until we see her leave" requested Josh.

The security guard did as he was bidden and all three men eagerly scanned the footage. The couple from the earlier pictures were seen returning to their room but otherwise the corridor was empty and free of activity. Finally, the door to room 311 opened and the same woman left, calmly closing the door behind her and walking at an unhurried pace back towards the lifts.

"Freeze it!" snapped Brody. He read the time code at the bottom of the monitor screen and wrote it into his notes. The print-out stated 22.49.26. "Can you enlarge her image?"

With prompting from his boss, the guard understood what was required and magnified the picture. It was a little grainy, due to the low light in the corridor, but it was clear enough to see the basic figure.

"Now put it into slo-mo" Josh ordered. As the picture clicked slowly through the screen, frame by frame, Brody realised the woman was fully aware of the security cameras in operation and was deliberately keeping her head down. The recording of her arrival, approaching the room, had only shown her from the rear and had not revealed her face, but her departure meant walking *towards* the camera, so she was holding her head bent low, hiding her features. She was of a diminutive height; Brody estimated her to be about five foot two or possibly five foot three. Under a light summer coat she was wearing an elegant evening dress that must have incorporated a split at the side because the act of walking revealed her leg up to the thigh. But her face was simply not visible. All that could be seen was a downturned head of thick, dark hair."

"Pause it there please" requested Josh. "Can you save that image?"

The concierge gave the instruction and the guard nodded and tapped away at his keyboard, logging the still shot as a jpeg.

Brody took a deep breath. Whoever the young woman in the image may be, she was about to be exonerated or condemned for murder.

"Now" said Josh quietly. "We need to roll through the footage to see if anyone else goes in or out of this room."

The recording was shuttled at high speed while all three watchers stared intently at the screen. Anyone appearing in the corridor was ignored unless they entered room 311. Nobody did. The digits of the time code continued flashing endlessly through at breakneck speed until an image of Gabrielle, the chamber maid, could be seen wheeling her trolley along the corridor. At 09.24.59 she entered Lukeba's room.

The three men exchanged a knowing look. Each was fully aware of the significance of what they had discovered.

"I need him to switch to the foyer cameras that cover the reception area" Josh told the concierge urgently. "Run everything you have for the two hours between 9 pm and 11 pm. We're looking for a good, clear image of her entering or leaving. If we can't find her in the foyer, it means she came in through another entrance. So we then move to whatever coverage you have for outside."

It took a further ten minutes or so of careful shuttling before the foyer recordings identified their quarry. She was exiting the lifts and crossing the reception area and, as before, her chin was held firmly to her chest, keeping her face hidden from view. Whether maintaining her gaze firmly towards the floor was a mistake, or whether it was a simple case of Brody getting lucky, he didn't know, but Fate handed him a bonus. The woman was half way across the foyer when she inadvertently bumped into the shoulder of a large, overweight man in a dinner jacket who was escorting his equally rotund wife in the direction of the bar. The collision was nothing more than minor contact but it was enough to startle the departing woman and she momentarily lifted her head in surprise.

"There!" yelled Josh triumphantly. The security guard froze the picture and in front of them, for the first time, they were able to see the woman's face in full view. Her appearance was clearly oriental, almost certainly Chinese and, despite her expression of wide-eyed surprise, her features were soft and delicate. She was pretty. Brody estimated her to be somewhere in her late twenties, perhaps thirty at the most.

The guard enlarged the picture and all three men stared uncomprehendingly at the image. It was a total paradox. The attractive young woman before them, whose slim face and high cheek bones might have belonged to a fashion model and reflected no inherent malice or threat, had almost certainly just coldly and callously killed a man, blowing out his brains with a gun forced into his mouth. None of them could make sense of the incongruous scenario; but it was staring out at them clearly in black and white from the monitor screen. It was, quite literally, merely necessary for them to believe their own eyes.

Brody turned to the concierge. "We need to keep this footage separate. And it must be stored somewhere safe and not wiped for the monthly turn around." He reached into his pocket and withdrew a USB memory drive, which he then handed to the security guard. "I need a video copy of her in the corridor and in the foyer, and jpegs of all the stills freeze-frames."

Jpegs and Video were words the guard understood and he nodded to Brody.

"Will you show all this to the police?" asked the concierge warily.

"Not yet" said Brody, taking out his wallet. He produced two more one hundred Euro notes, handing one each to the other two men. "This remains *our* little secret until I can get all the evidence together. You two have to remain totally silent about what we've found here today. Is that understood?"

"Understood" replied the concierge.

Twenty minutes later Brody was walking back through the Stadtpark with the memory stick in his jacket pocket.

Safely ensconced in his room at the Hotel Post, Brody sent an email to Alan Denton, knowing it would be awaiting his return after the weekend.

Post gratefully received. Research going well. There is indeed gold at the end of the rainbow. Will call asap. J.B.

Brody then opened the room safe that sat on a shelf within the wardrobe unit and reset the combination. He normally used Saffy's birthday for any passwords he needed but, being ultra-cautious, on this occasion decided to do nothing remotely predictable or decipherable and to choose a number totally at random. He glanced across the room to the bedside table where the red illuminated figures on the digital clock showed the time as 11.45. He typed 1145 onto the keypad and the mechanism whirred and accepted the new code. He placed the USB memory stick inside the safe and then locked the door.

His hurried departure earlier that morning had meant he had not yet eaten and his stomach was looking forward to his lunch with Shelley almost as much as Josh himself. His swift exit from the hotel also meant he had not shaved and, rubbing his hand across the prickly stubble on his chin, he decided he was in urgent need of his razor. There was something about the efficient and attractive Ms. Anderson that, surprisingly, prompted him to try and make a good impression. His normal attitude with women was very much 'take me as you find me', and most females seemed to respond favourably, but, as he soaped his face and then ran the blade carefully over his upper lip, he felt a little like a nervous high school student preparing for a date; and he didn't know why.

Shelley was right. The Café Landtmann was everything a tourist would want to find in a traditional Viennese coffee house and restaurant. Its elegant, nineteenth century exterior was surrounded by pavement tables and chairs, where customers sat basking in the early afternoon sunshine, idling away their Sunday, just as they had done a hundred and forty years earlier when the café first opened.

Between the pavement tables and the entrance, the recent addition of a glass canopy provided shelter to accommodate outside patrons in the colder winter months but, once through the large, ornate front doors, all modernity was left behind and the customer stepped back in time to a bygone era. High, chandeliered ceilings looked down upon wood panelled walls of beautiful inlaid marquetry that ran the length of the café's long interior. Crisply laundered, white cotton cloths adorned the tables and all the seats were plush, padded banquets. The six tall, arched windows of the main room were hung with thick, green velvet drapes and their incoming light was reflected and magnified by large mirrors that were set into the opposite walls. Brody would not have been surprised to see nineteenth century ladies in tightly-wasted long dresses, with broad-brimmed hats and furled parasols, flitting between the tables to make polite conversation. It was picture-postcard perfect; a dream for every graphic artist that had ever needed to compile a travel brochure and evoke the glories of Hapsburg café society.

"Well, you were right," Josh told Shelley as the waiter led them to the table she had booked and they gently lowered themselves into the deep upholstery of their seats. "If we're going to do the tourist bit, then this is the ideal place to start!"

"I thought you'd appreciate it" she told him with a satisfied grin. "Even a down-to-earth pragmatist like you couldn't object to a little self-indulgence once in a while."

"Too true!" he agreed with a laugh. "I'm sure places like this were built for the rich, hedonistic, decadent upper classes. But if the strudel is as impressive as the decor then I'll happily put aside my egalitarian principles and demand a large helping!"

"Then let's first order a glass of wine and raise a toast to 'extravagance'. At least for today!"

The meal was every bit as good as anticipated and the time flew by un-noticed. Josh was truly relaxed in Shelley's company and was unaccustomed to feeling so at ease with someone he had known for such a brief period of time. The conversation flowed freely from the deep and profound to the trivial and superficial and back again, and all of it was effortless and comfortable. Their career paths could not have been more different yet, as they talked, they discovered shared attitudes and opinions, common likes and dislikes, and seemed to find a natural, unforced accord in almost everything they discussed.

After they left the café, they strolled around the Ring for a couple of miles, leisurely enjoying the afternoon sunshine. They bought two ice cream cones from the Eissalon at Schwedenplatz, almost oblivious to the teeming crowds of tourists and sight-seers that swarmed about them, and then crossed the Aspernbrücke bridge over the grey, gently rippling water of the Donaukanal, heading north towards the Prater Park.

Shelley was keen to learn all she could about Josh's experiences in Egypt and Libya, and the life in general of a writer and journalist, while he, in his turn, wanted to know all about her work in the arts and her travels around the world for the British Council. Their interest in each other was genuine and sincere and Josh increasingly felt as if he'd known her for a few years rather than a few days. Twenty minutes after crossing the Kanal, they caught their first sight of the Riesenrad, Vienna's famous Ferris Wheel, looming above the roof tops at the end of the street.

"As soon as I see it, my head fills with zither music and 'The Third Man' theme!" declared Shelley with a laugh. "It happens every time!"

"It's one of my all-time favourite films!" Josh told her, delighted to discover yet something else they had in common. "I can even quote you most of the significant lines. Now how nerdy is that?!"

As soon as they entered the park, they made their way through all the various stalls and side shows and headed directly for the big wheel. As Brody bought two tickets at the kiosk, they found there was an English speaking guide on hand to point out which of the gondolas had been used in 'The Third Man' and which had been used in the Bond movie 'The

Living Daylights', and offering to accompany passengers and provide a commentary on the surrounding city for a small additional charge. His spiel must have been effective because the twenty or so people queuing all opted to wait and travel in one of the two gondolas that had been used in the famous films, so Josh and Shelley unexpectedly found they had a car all to themselves.

The gondolas were unchanged from their original design and it was akin to stepping back in time to sit on their wooden benches and watch the wider city beneath gradually appear all around as they rose ever higher. The car creaked and groaned as it swung gently back and forth within the iron frame of the wheel, making its very slow and sedate circular progress, just as it had done for over a hundred years. They moved from side to side of the car, looking from all the windows at the amazing view surrounding them.

When the gondola reached the highest point of the wheel, Josh took Shelley's hand and pulled her gently towards the door.

"This is where Orson Welles suddenly slid open the door and Joseph Cotten immediately grabbed the window frame, in case Harry Lime was thinking of throwing him out of the car."

Shelley glanced down at the fairground far below them and gave a little shiver. "That's a hell of a long way to fall!" She looked up at Josh and grinned at him. "So don't get any ideas. There are much easier ways to get rid of me than throwing me from a Ferris Wheel!"

Brody smiled but his voice was low and gentle as he said: "There are several people I might like to remove from my life... but you certainly wouldn't be among them."

She saw the change of mood in his eyes and it was a few moments before she spoke. "I'm glad" she replied softly.

"In fact, for the last couple of hours, I've been trying to think of ways in which I might conspire to bring you further into it."

"Really?"

He nodded slowly. "Really... and I've also been wondering how I might possibly do this."

Brody was still holding her hand and he gently pulled her towards him as he lowered his head and kissed her. It was a little tentative at first but she responded immediately and began returning the kiss. His arms went around her and he held her close.

"I think I've wanted to do that since the first day I met you" he whispered as their lips parted.

She smiled warmly. "Then I'm glad you finally decided to do it."

As they strolled back through the fairground, Josh took her by the hand, intertwining their fingers. Walking hand in hand like a pair of teenagers was not something he had often done, even with Kassia when they were first together, but with Shelley it seemed somehow natural and right. She appeared to feel the same way and was content to leave her hand linked to his. When they reached the Praterstraße Josh hailed a cab. It appeared to be tacitly agreed that their Stadtbummel had come to an end and it was time for a taxi.

"Wohin?" asked the driver as the two of them sidled into the back seat.

"Bäckerstraße" Shelley told him at once and then turned suddenly to Josh. "If that's all right with you?... I thought you might like to see my apartment."

Josh smiled and gently nodded. "Sounds good to me."

Twenty minutes later the cab pulled into the kerb outside number seven Bäckerstraße. On the outside wall, four small, red and white Austrian flags were suspended above a white plaque that stated 'Barockes Bürgerhaus - Nach 1712 Erbaut.' Josh could tell from the sign that it was a listed building but nothing prepared him for what he was about to see. Shelley led him through the large wooden doors of the arched entrance and, to his amazement, he emerged from the shadows of the low ceilinged passageway to find himself standing in a beautiful, early eighteenth-century Renaissance courtyard. It had been recently renovated but the refurbishment had been painstakingly carried out to accurately restore every aspect of the original design. Josh stood open mouthed as he gazed up at the iron framed balconies of the three floors.

"It's stunning" he told Shelley sincerely. "I'm half expecting to see Juliet appear from one of the windows and call out to Romeo."

"Well it doesn't quite go back that far but I know exactly what you mean. It grabbed me the same way when I first saw it."

She led him inside and they climbed the stairs to the third floor where the British Council rented an apartment. The interior was tastefully furnished, with every modern convenience, but all the original features of the structure, the curves and arches of the ceilings, doors and windows, had been preserved.

"It's kept for V.I.P.s and the like when we need to accommodate them" Shelley explained. "But, if it's free, visiting staff are allowed to use it when we're in town."

"One of the perks of the job, huh?"

"Yes. There aren't that many. But this is definitely one of them!" She turned to him and smiled. "Would you like the guided tour?"

Josh shook his head slowly. "No. You can show me the apartment later. Right now, I'm more concerned with its current resident."

"Really?" she said with mock surprise and in a deliberately coy voice. She stepped closer to him. "Well, that particular tour begins in the bedroom. Would sir like to follow me?"

"Sir would like that very much."

With a grin spreading across her face, she took him gently by the hand and led him along the hallway to the tall panelled doors of the bedroom.

Josh had known several different women since the break-up of his marriage but never had he felt so relaxed and at ease with a partner. He took her in his arms and kissed her and gradually their hands began to explore each other's bodies. As he slowly undressed her and removed her clothes he was struck by the beauty of her nakedness and the way it moved him emotionally as well as arousing him sexually. The smooth, flawless skin of her breasts and the delicate curve of her narrow waist felt perfect to his touch as he tenderly ran his mouth and his hands over her flesh and experienced the exquisite joy of discovery; the wonderful sensation of newly found intimacy.

Their love-making was fervent and exciting but was far more than simply satisfying sex. There was a closeness between them that seemed, even at the height of eager passion, to draw them into an unspoken bond. As they lay together afterwards, her head resting on his shoulder and his arm around her waist, they each knew that this was the beginning of something. Neither wanted to articulate what they were feeling; it was enough to lie calmly together, intertwined, knowing that, whatever the future might hold, they were content to allow it to arrive.

"Did you never want to write fiction?" she asked casually as they lay staring up at the ceiling.

"Ah... True confessions time" he murmured, keeping his eyes fixed upwards. "I did. And I do."

"Really?" she eased herself up onto one elbow and stared at him in a mixture of shock and excited surprise. "When?... And what? I mean... how do I not know this?"

"Detective fiction" he admitted a little sheepishly. "Two published so far. But I write under a pseudonym."

"Why? Don't tell me your embarrassed by it? Some of the world's best authors write detective stories."

"It's not that. Actually, I'm quite proud of them. But my publishers didn't want it to detract from sales of my factual work. And I think they were right because, up until now, neither novel has sold particularly well."

"So what's your pen name?" she asked eagerly.

He grinned. "Ian Magen."

Her face creased into a frown as she puzzled over this new identity. "Ok. So where did that come from?"

"I'm a crossword nut. It's a tease."

"It's an anagram!" she exclaimed. "Wait... don't tell me!" Her eyes suddenly shone extra brightly, full of energy and life. "Er... 'imagine'? No! Only one letter 'i'. Wait a minute... 'Enigma'! No, hang on... Oh! '*An* Enigma'!" Brody nodded and she laughed aloud. "I like it! That's great! Now I want to read them both." She beamed at him. "So, Mr. Ian Magen. Are they still in print? Can I buy them at a book shop?"

"Well I doubt you'd find them here in Vienna. But they still have a few copies on the book stands at airports and the like."

"Then I shall get them as soon as I land at Heathrow!"

"When are you flying back?" he asked, suddenly a little depressed to think that his idyll with her in Vienna would be limited.

"Well the book fair closes on Friday afternoon. So I'll spend Saturday tying up the loose ends and closing down the paperwork and fly back next Sunday morning."

He adjusted his position and turned to her. "You mean, you'll be gone in a week?"

She nodded. "That's when my flight's booked."

"Hmmm... well, I don't know about you Miss Anderson, but I was hoping this might be the start of something longer than just a few days. So, I'm not so sure I can let you slip out of my grasp that soon."

She smiled warmly and her whole face seemed to light up. "Then you'd better make a point of tracking me down when you get back to London. It shouldn't be so hard for an investigative journalist, should it? I thought you were good at research?"

He rolled over and eased himself lightly on top of her. "This is true. And right now, I'd like to conduct some further enquiries into this particular body of evidence."

He lowered his head and kissed her breasts and then began moving slowly down the delicate contours of her body.

They lay close together in bed throughout the night, not falling asleep until well into the early hours. They made love twice more but most of their time was spent in idle, desultory chatter. She told him all about her life from childhood, through university and on into her career. He learned that her current home was a rented apartment in Putney, just south of the river, but that she spent more time away from it than in residence. He in his turn related a brief version of his history, recounting his marriage and his daughter Saffy, and his precarious existence as a freelance journalist and writer.

Each felt comfortable and at ease with the other. It was a very long time since Josh Brody had known such a sense of contentment and, as his heavy eyelids finally closed, he drifted into a deep and restful sleep.

Chapter Ten

Monday, June 24th.

The next morning, in the secluded Bäckerstraße apartment, Josh and Shelley rose early. She had to be at The British Council offices by 8.30 am and Josh needed to make telephone calls before readying himself for his signing appearance at the book fair at noon. They shared a quick cup of coffee together and then she rushed to shower and dress while he departed to walk the short distance back to his hotel.

En route, in lieu of breakfast, he bought a coffee and a Käsebrot at an Imbiss, one of Vienna's numerous small snack cafés where there are no seats, just some tall stands where patrons eat and drink on their feet, and arrived back at the Hotel Post by 8.15 am.

He took a leisurely hour to shower and shave and then, having dressed in a clean white shirt and his black two-piece suit, he settled himself on the side of the bed and took out his mobile phone with the Austrian SIM card. The local time was just after 9.30 am and Vienna was an hour ahead of London so he knew Alan Denton, who was always at his desk promptly by eight, would long ago have arrived at work.

"Morning boss" he said as the editor answered his call.

"Ah. The Prodigal calls home!" replied Denton with a smile in his voice. "Your email sounded promising. But I trust you are not being too profligate with my money!"

"As miserly as Scrooge himself, I promise you. But what I *have* spent has provided us with a serious shopping basket."

"Good. How soon will you be bringing home the bacon?"

"All being well, in a few days. But first I need a favour."

"Shoot."

"The pathologist who first set the ball rolling on all this is called Luke Harvey. I promised to keep him out of the picture so, now that this is getting murky, I'm going to close him down and break all contact. I shouldn't need to reach him again but, if I do, I'll need you to act as intermediary. He operates out of the Westminster Coroner's office."

"Got it" said Denton, scribbling down the name and the details as he spoke. "Anything else?"

"No. That's all for now."

"Then, work aside, how's the trip? Enjoying Vienna?"

"Very much" answered Brody, with a just detectable trace of contentment in his voice.

"Aha" exclaimed Denton wryly, not mistaking his ears. "I recognise that tone. So please remember that your expense account is for business and not for entertaining the fair Fräuleins of Wien!"

Brody laughed. "Duly noted!"

"Then take care, Josh. And bring me back some goodies as soon as you can."

"Will do. And thanks." Brody clicked off the phone and then immediately put through a call to the Westminster Coroner's Court. He left a message with the receptionist for Dr. Luke Harvey to call 'his cousin' and gave the number of his Austrian mobile. He told the girl he could be reached before 11 am or after 1pm London time. The receptionist promised to relay the message and Josh hung up. In less than twenty minutes, Brody's mobile rang and the display showed a London number. He hit the receive button.

"Hello?"

"Josh?"

"Yes. Hello Luke. How are you?"

"Ok. I got your message."

"And you're ringing me from a call box as agreed, yes?"

"Yes. I made an excuse about nipping out to post an important letter before the mid-day collection. But I don't have long. Is there any news?"

"Plenty. I don't want to involve you in the detail. There's no need. But I wanted you to know what I've found. Lukeba had a twin brother called Fabrice. He was murdered on June 12th at a hotel in Vienna."

There was an immediate ensuing silence of several seconds and Brody knew that the pathologist had been severely shaken by what he had just heard. He could feel Harvey's unspoken fear even though he was half a continent away. "Luke?" he asked calmly. "Are you ok?"

"Yes" Harvey replied quietly, attempting to gather himself together. "Is that where you're speaking from? Vienna?"

"Yes."

"And you're quite sure of the facts? I mean... there's no mistake?"

"No mistake. He was murdered. And I can prove it."

There was a heavy sigh at the end of the line. "So Dikembe is likely to have been murdered too."

"Almost certainly. I just wanted you to know that you were right, that's all."

"Then where do we go from here?" asked Harvey nervously. "This is going to stir up a real hornets' nest, isn't it?"

"Probably. Yes. But you needn't worry. You won't get stung."

"How can you be so sure?"

"Because I'm keeping you out of it. I can come at this from the Vienna end. Nobody will know the tip off came from you. That's a promise."

"Thanks" said Harvey meekly, the relief very evident in his tone. "It's not that I'm ducking out on you. It's just that I can't risk my job. The family..."

Brody cut him short. "It's ok. Don't apologise. I understand. And you're right. So relax. I won't call you again. If I absolutely need to get in touch then I'll do it through a third party; a journalist colleague called Alan Denton. If he calls you, you'll know it's safe to speak to him. Otherwise, you're completely out of the loop. Ok?"

"Ok... and thanks for the confirmation."

"No problem. Take care."

Brody clicked off the call button and stared knowingly at the handset. Harvey was a clearly worried man. Josh didn't blame him. In the modern era of financial uncertainty, no job was truly secure and Luke had already felt the warning cold wind of pressure from above. As a freelance, Brody was immune to such threats. His own career wove in and out of recession on a semi-permanent basis and the world's present financial crisis held no particular fears of redundancy. The sole advantage of his precarious income stream was that it couldn't get any more unreliable than it already was, so what did he have to fear?

Brody's taxi pulled to a gentle halt outside the University at exactly 11.45 am. He made his way to the hall housing the book fair and found the ever friendly Ms Gregg as fully prepared as expected and patiently awaiting his arrival at the 'Orion Books' stand.

"Mr. Brody. How nice of you to be prompt." She extended her hand in welcome and Josh shook it politely. "I've placed the desk here for you, at the front of the stand, and we have copies of your book arranged on display. May I find you a coffee?"

Josh declined the offer of coffee and seated himself at the desk. To his genuine surprise, a small line of around six or seven people soon began forming in front of him and, as the large clock on the far wall of the hall resoundingly began striking noon, the first in the queue stepped forward, holding out a copy of 'Soho – The Dark Side'.

Fully aware of what was required of him, Brody greeted the young male student with a warm smile.

"To whom should I sign it?" he asked.

"Please write 'To Friedrich'" came the heavily accented reply.

Josh began writing *'To Friedrich – with all good wishes. Josh Brody'*.

"I am studying English here at the University" explained the student. "And I will spend next semester in London. So I am happy to read your book and learn about this part of your capital."

"I'm delighted to be able to help" said Josh, handing back the now autographed book. "I hope you enjoy your trip."

The next in line, a woman in her thirties, stepped forward and Brody put on an equally welcoming smile as he took hold of the proffered copy and once again asked for the name of the recipient. The process continued and half an hour later, contrary to his expectations, Brody found he had signed no less than fourteen copies of his book. As the last autograph seeker walked away, Bryony Gregg approached him.

"How about that coffee now? It's only from the machine in the vestibule but it *is* real coffee."

He nodded gratefully. "That would be perfect. Thank you."

"I'll be back in a couple of minutes." She stepped from the stand and made her way through the exhibition to the exit doors on the far side. As she disappeared from view, a man walked up to the Orion stand holding a copy of Brody's Soho book. Stepping quietly onto the low rostrum, he placed the book carefully on the desk in front of Josh.

As Brody opened the cover and turned to the title page, ready to sign, he looked up and flashed the newcomer his customary smile. There was no reaction. Instead of returning Brody's greeting, as all the previous book buyers had done, the stranger remained impassive. He was dressed in a black suit, not dissimilar to Josh's own, the jacket of which was unbuttoned to reveal a plain, black T-shirt beneath. His dark-brown eyes seemed cold and remote and looked out from beneath a shaven head.

"Mr. Brody?" The voice was impassive and devoid of emotion. The accent was English and bore not the slightest trace of Viennese colouring.

"Yes. To whom shall I sign?" replied Josh a little tentatively

"Please write: 'To Jalil'"

Brody was unsure if he had heard correctly. "Jalil?" he repeated.

"J-a-l-i-l" spelled out the stranger deliberately.

Josh did as he was bidden and began the customary inscription. "An unusual name" he said, making conversation as he wrote without looking up. There was no comment or reply. Josh completed his signature with his regular flourish and then closed the book. He picked it up and held it out towards the taciturn man. "Thank you for buying the book. I hope you enjoy it."

With no word or acknowledgement, the stranger calmly took the copy with his left hand and, with his right, reached simultaneously into the inside pocket of his suit jacket. He withdrew a small sheet of note paper and placed it slowly and deliberately onto the desk.

"Please write" commanded the man evenly. "Apartment 3. Tiefer Graben 8."

"I'm sorry?" said Josh, perplexed.

"If you want further information concerning your enquiries, be there, *alone*, at 11 am tomorrow."

"Wait a minute" Brody told him urgently and stood, realising at once that this must be the same shaven headed guy who had been asking after him at the hotel. "Just who are you and what is this all about?"

The visitor exhibited no reaction and merely coolly repeated his previous words: "Apartment 3. Tiefer Graben 8. 11am." Saying nothing more, the man turned and began to walk silently away.

Pushing back his chair, Josh stepped out from his seat. "Just a minute..." he called. The disappearing stranger made no attempt to turn or respond and continued into the crowded floor of the hall. Brody was about to set off in pursuit when a young girl stepped up onto the rostrum gripping a copy of the Soho book, closely followed by Bryony Gregg who was holding a large Styrofoam cup of coffee.

"Black, no sugar. That's right, isn't it?" she said, proffering the cup.

"Er... yes. Thank you" said Brody reluctantly accepting the coffee.

"And I see we have another fan wanting a signature. It's going really well, don't you think?"

"Yes" agreed Josh as he unwillingly settled himself back into his chair and watched the stranger disappear through the exit doors on the far side of the hall. He picked up the slip of paper in front of him and hurriedly scribbled down the address before he forgot it. Placing the note carefully inside his jacket pocket, he greeted the young woman waiting patiently for him with a manufactured smile and made ready to sign her copy.

The remainder of the two hours passed without incident and, as planned, the efficient Ms Gregg called a halt to proceedings at exactly 2pm.

"Thank you so much" she told Josh as he shook her hand in farewell. "It's been a very effective promotion."

"I'm happy to help."

"Well, you'll be pleased to know that I have some good news. The University has ordered a dozen copies for their English library. Isn't that marvellous? We couldn't wish for a better shop window!"

"Marvellous" agreed Josh, anxious to take his leave as soon as he could politely do so. "Adele will be delighted."

With the usual promises to stay in touch and expressions of looking forward to their next meeting, Brody finally departed and left the University hall. He was seated in the back of a taxi, heading back around the Ring towards the first district, when he had the first opportunity to take the note from his pocket and open it. He stared down at his hurriedly scribbled scrawl. *Apartment 3. Tiefer Graben 8. 11am.* He had no idea who the baleful-looking man was who had delivered the instruction but clearly Josh's investigation had rattled someone's cage. Perhaps the following morning's rendezvous would provide him with some answers.

That evening, as arranged, Shelly Anderson arrived at the Hotel Post at 6 pm and she and Josh seated themselves at the table he'd booked in the hotel's own restaurant. They had a full ninety minutes before the curtain rose on Puccini's opera double-bill, so their meal was unhurried and they chatted freely. Brody tried hard to keep his manner light and unconcerned but his dinner partner was far too astute not to notice that he was more than a little preoccupied. There was a marked change in him since the previous evening.

"What's wrong, Josh?" she enquired eventually. "Something's bothering you, isn't it?"

"No. Nothing" he lied. "I'm fine."

She looked down at her glass of wine. "I'm a big girl now, Josh" she said gently. "Not some naive prom date. If you're having regrets about last night, then I'd rather you just say..."

"What?... " he interrupted with alarm. "Oh, God no." He reached out and took her hand, squeezing it tightly. "Shelley, you're the best thing that's happened to me in a very long while."

She lifted her head, clearly relieved. "Then what's the matter?"

He stared at her. He cared too much to allow her to jump to wrong, if understandable, conclusions but he also didn't want to involve her in what was fast becoming an ominous and sinister trail of events. Realising he owed her at least some form of explanation, he opted to tell her just enough to try and set her mind at rest.

"I told you I am doing some research while I'm here in Vienna."

"Yes."

"Well something happened today, connected to that research."

"At the book fair?"

"Yes. It's probably nothing. But I'm dealing with something unpleasant and it almost certainly involves some very unsavoury people. So it's been playing on my mind a little. But that's no excuse for my bringing it into our evening together. I apologise."

"Can you tell me what it's all about?"

"I'd rather not. And that's not because I don't trust you" he added hurriedly. "It's because what you don't know can't hurt you. And until I'm certain of just what I'm dealing with, I want to play it safe. But, whatever else you may imagine, please don't think it has anything to do with yesterday. Last night was very special. Nothing could ever make me regret it."

She lifted her hand, that he was still gripping, and gently kissed the back of his fingers. "I feel the same way, Josh. So it worries me to hear you are getting involved in something serious. You're not in any danger, are you?

He grinned. "Not so far."

"That's not good enough. Please don't joke about this. I don't want you taking risks."

Brody laughed. "Then let me reassure you. I'm a reporter, not a hero. I detest violence, and especially if its directed at me! So the minute trouble starts to arrive, I'm the first one out of the back door. How do you think I managed to survive in Egypt and Libya? Putting myself in harm's way is definitely *not* on my agenda."

She seemed genuinely reassured. "Good. I'm glad to hear it. But even so, I want you to promise me that if this present enquiry, whatever it is, turns sour, then you'll drop it before you get hurt."

He reached out and closed both his palms around her hand. "I promise."

They looked into each other's eyes and she nodded gently. "Ok."

He raised an eyebrow. "May I ask you something serious?"

"Yes."

"Do you think we have time for Strudel and Schlagobers before the show?"

The pristine auditorium of the Kammeroper, with its beautiful arched plaster work trimmed with gold leaf, and the elaborate wrought-iron balustrade of its narrow horseshoe balcony, was both elegant and evocative of a bygone era. Like much of the arts scene in Vienna, the little chamber opera house was well supported and almost all of the velvet-faced seats were occupied. Shelley had secured a pair of the management's house seats, kept available to accommodate unexpected guests and V.I.P.s, and she and Brody settled themselves into the two vacant places at the end of the centre row. A few minutes later, the auditorium lights faded and a hush fell over the audience. The conductor emerged to take a brief bow and receive his welcoming applause before he raised his baton and brought the orchestra instantly to life. Gianni Schicchi has no overture and, after just thirty seconds of establishing music from the pit, the curtain rose to reveal a group of grieving mourners gathered at the bedside of their relative, who had just died. It struck Brody as a strange beginning for a comic opera but, as the initial expressions of grief quickly gave way to squabbling over the dead man's will, the action sprung swiftly into the true nature of the farcical plot.

To his delight, and genuine surprise, Brody's first experience of live opera was a revelation and an immense pleasure. The voices were strong and powerful and the quality of the singing was stunning. He was listening to a German translation of an original Italian libretto but the power of the music and the performances made the action and the story obvious and, despite the language issues, he found himself deeply involved. He was thrilled to recognise the famous aria 'O Mio Babbino Caro' and hadn't realised that the tune he knew so well was from this particular opera. The music captivated him and, for an hour, he escaped all thoughts of the strange meeting of earlier in the day.

The second half of the double bill was 'Il Tabarro', which he also truly enjoyed, and after the performance, as he walked Shelley back to her Bäckerstraße residence, Josh was still humming one of the themes that continued to course through his head and was in a relaxed and greatly improved frame of mind.

At just after 10.30 pm, as Josh and Shelley were opening her apartment door and stepping into the hallway, another front door was being opened at a city centre apartment less than a kilometre from the Renaissance building in Bäckerstraße.

"Happy Birthday" said the girl breathily in accented English as she stood in the doorway. "I am supposed to come gift wrapped... but there wasn't a big enough ribbon."

The man who had opened the door was more than a little taken aback to discover the woman in front of him, although the surprise was far from unpleasant. She wore a coat draped around her shoulders but it was open wide at the front, exposing an evening dress beneath that was cut low, amply revealing the top of her fulsome breasts, and had a side-split from the hem to the top of the thigh, showing that her slim and shapely legs were wearing black lace stockings. She was carrying just a small leather handbag that matched the black of her coat.

It was several seconds before a narrow smile broke across his face. "But it is not my birthday" he uttered quietly.

She gave an exaggerated shrug and seductively raised her eyebrows. "Well your friends seem to think it is. You are Doctor Nazari aren't you?"

He nodded silently.

"Then I'm in the right place. They told me it was your birthday and booked me to come and give you a little party." Her mouth creased into a slight pout of feigned disappointment. "Aren't you going to invite me in?"

The smile on his face grew broader and he stepped to one side and extended an arm in the direction of the interior. "Please."

Her high-heels clicked provocatively on the wooden parquet flooring as, with a subtle swaying of her hips, she sashayed through the apartment's entrance and, without asking, continued directly on through the interior glass panelled doors into the lounge. She slid the coat from her shoulders, flinging it carelessly across the back of an easy chair where she likewise placed her handbag, and then seated herself theatrically on the sofa, extending both arms along the back rest and crossing one slender leg over the other, causing the split in the side of her dress to gape and reveal the black lace top of her stocking. "Do you have something to drink?" she asked.

"Yes" Nazari told her, crossing to the drinks cabinet in the corner of the room. "I have whisky, gin and vodka, or there is also wine if you prefer."

"Gin and tonic. Plenty of ice."

He nodded obediently and picked up the large green bottle of Gordon's. In his own country, the Muslim creed proscribed the consumption of alcohol so whenever he was permitted to travel abroad, which was all too infrequently, he indulged freely in the forbidden fruits that were temporarily available to him. Alcohol was one of the distinct pleasures he derived from being allowed time in Europe. As he gazed across the room at his newly arrived guest, and stared covetously at the top of her exposed thigh, the hardness that was growing in his crotch anticipated that she was soon to provide another delight that was officially prohibited in his own land.

"Happy birthday" she wished him softly as he handed her a large gin and tonic and she raised her glass to him in a toast.

"Thank you" he told her and seated himself in the easy chair opposite the sofa, clutching a large, neat vodka and ice. "What is your name?"

She gave a shrug. "Whatever you'd like it to be. But most people call me Willow."

"Then I shall do so too."

He stared at her with eager eyes. She was Chinese in appearance and she was young; in her late twenties he estimated. Her thick black hair was cut short to just above her shoulders and framed a delicately featured face where her dark brown eyes glinted above high, almost aristocratic cheek bones. Like many oriental women, her body was slim and petite but she was no skinny gamine. Her breasts were full and her perfectly balanced frame curved in all the right places.

He took a deep draught of his vodka. "And when my friends arranged this little 'birthday gift', did they say how long you were to entertain me?" he asked.

She shook her head slowly and smiled. "No. And as they are paying for my time, I am happy to be here for as long as you wish."

Nazari felt his stomach tighten with the excitement of expectation. "And what exactly did you have in mind for this little party of ours?" he enquired.

She put down her glass, uncrossed her legs and stood. Reaching to her left shoulder, she undid the clasp of her dress and it fell away, dropping smoothly to the floor. Her black lace bra and panties matched the pattern at the top of her hold-up stockings but the design of the diaphanous material rendered it almost sheer, so he could clearly glimpse the flesh beneath. She slid the straps from each shoulder and then reached around behind her back to unclip her bra. It likewise fell away to the floor, landing on top of her discarded dress, and he was provided with a clear view of her firm, exposed breasts.

"Well, as it's your birthday, I thought we'd make it a special treat" she said softly. She stepped towards him and clambered up on to his lap, resting one knee on either arm of the easy chair so she was seated above him. Taking the vodka from his hand, she leaned forward and lowered her left breast into the tilted glass until the vodka swirled around the nipple. "It tastes nicer like this" she whispered softly and leant down towards his face. He clamped his mouth over her breast, sucking and licking, as his hand reached down to her panties and his fingers began stroking and exploring her crotch. "Good boy" she told him gently. "Good boy." Placing the vodka glass on the table beside the chair, she then held his head and lifted it to face her. "I think there's more room in the bedroom, don't you?"

He nodded eagerly.

She manoeuvred herself from his lap and grabbed him by the hand, raising him to his feet. "Where is it?" she asked.

He began to lead her away towards the bedroom and she obediently followed, stopping only to scoop up her handbag as they passed the easy chair where it was lying.

A few minutes later, they were both fully naked and she was sitting astride him on the bed. "I like you" she said breathily. "So I'm going to give you something special."

His eyes burned excitedly. "And what is that?"

She held a finger to her lips. "Shh. Chinese girls know many secrets. Especially how to make a man feel the most pleasure." She sidled from the bed and picked up her handbag from the adjacent table where she had left it. Opening the small leather bag, she withdrew a pair of handcuffs. "This will be the most memorable night of your life" she promised as she crept back onto the bed and slid, almost snake like, along the length of his body to once more straddle him. She kissed him hard upon the lips and he immediately began to reach out and grope at her body. "No, no" she murmured. "Not yet. First we give you more pleasure than you have ever known."

He said nothing, but his hands relaxed and his eyes acquiesced as he rested his head back upon the pillow, content to cede control to her expert professional knowledge, delighting in the anticipation of the sensations he was about to enjoy.

Chapter Eleven

Tuesday, June 25th.

Josh awoke to the unrelenting sound of his telephone's alarm at 8.30 am on Tuesday morning. He had stayed in bed with Shelley at her apartment until well after 2 am but then, explaining that he needed to be fresh and alert for an important meeting, and that lying next to her was too much of a sexual distraction to achieve meaningful sleep, he made his way back to the Hotel Post through the quiet of the deserted, early hours streets.

Reaching out drowsily, he shut off the alarm and then rested his head back on the pillow, staring thoughtfully at the ceiling. Like most investigative journalists, logic always took second place to his instincts. It was those very instincts that had kept him alive and out of harm's way during his time in the world's trouble spots and he would always follow his gut reaction whenever the possibility of danger loomed. He had meant every word he had told Shelley at dinner the previous evening. He was *not* a hero and had no intention of being one.

Meeting the strange, shaven headed man with the laconic, terse manner who had approached him at the book signing was an ominous prospect. Logic said that accepting his invitation was unwise, to say the least. But Josh's instincts told him it was necessary. He would certainly proceed with caution, and be constantly alert for trouble, but his gut feeling was that the coming encounter would provide some of the answers he was seeking and it was not an opportunity to be missed. He had mentioned nothing of the appointment to Shelley because he knew it would only worry her. He simply told her he had to attend a morning meeting and that he would then see her at the British Council, as planned. His talk was scheduled for 2 pm so he'd promised to arrive early and be at Siebensterngasse no later than 1.30 pm. Dragging himself out of the bed, Josh went straight to the room's beverage tray and made himself a cup of coffee. He hated instant coffee, and grimaced as he took the first few sips of the hot liquid, but it would suffice until he had completed his preparations and could escape the confines of his hotel to find a decent breakfast.

Seating himself in front of the dressing table, he opened his laptop and set to work. It was only a précis, a brief summary of what he had established to date, but it was sufficient to make the broad basis of his discoveries clear to anyone reading it. He then made mention of that morning's coming meeting and added the location and time. Saving and closing the document, he opened the room safe and withdrew the USB memory stick, which he slotted into the side of his computer. Having copied the file to the USB drive, he then deleted it from his laptop. Should his laptop be stolen, the information could not fall into other hands. Returning the USB stick to the safe, and locking the door, he had but one final task. Using his local mobile, he sent a text message to Alan Denton. It read:

Will be at Tiefer Graben 8, apartment 3, at 11am. If have not checked in with you by 1 pm, take all possible action to find me. Josh.

With appropriate back-up measures complete, Josh showered and shaved and left his hotel in pursuit of a suitable café for a hasty breakfast.

The taxi cab drew into the kerb at a little after 10.30 am. Josh had told the driver to drop him at the corner of Tiefer Graben. He then walked down the street in the direction of number 8. Keeping to the opposite sidewalk, he passed by the building and made his way to a small Tabac store where, from the confines of the doorway, he could gaze back across the road to the apartment block and see who came and went.

It was an impressive building that had clearly only recently been constructed. Vienna suffered major bomb damage during the second world war and so its architecture evolved into an intriguing mix of original historical edifices that had survived the devastation, refurbishments and rebuilds that recreated the lost and damaged buildings, and brand new, diverse modern structures that sat, often incongruously, amid the older style of the rest. Much of the hurried post war construction within the city centre was now being replaced and, as with this new apartment block, it was being built with imposing and grandiose style.

He watched for more than twenty minutes but there was no sign of the shaven headed man entering the tall glass front doors. Josh crossed the street and spent a moment scrutinising the name plates on the entry panel. Some bore names, indicating they were the permanent residence of the occupants, but most, including apartment 3, merely displayed numbers, showing they were short lets. The decor of the entrance lobby, with its marble floors and gleaming brass work, announced that this was clearly a place for the rich and wealthy and did not cater for tourists on a limited budget like Josh Brody. Taking a deep breath, and acutely conscious of a clenching of his insides, Josh pressed the call button at the side of the nameplate reading 'Appartement 3'.

"Jah?" came through the small speaker.

"My name is Josh Brody" he said clearly and with as much firmness of tone as he could summon.

There was no reply, just a buzzing noise and a loud clunk as the centre lock of the two front doors clicked open. Brody pushed back the brass handle on the large glass door and stepped into the lobby. Checking the floor plan diagram at the side of the lifts, it confirmed that apartment 3, as expected, was on the first floor. Brody took the stairs that curved up from the foyer area to disappear onto the first floor landing, where he found a long corridor stretching out on either side of him. The second pinewood door to his left bore the numeral 3 and Josh braced himself and knocked resolutely on the central panel.

The door was opened by a thick-set man, with blank expressionless eyes, who was dressed in a dark, navy-blue blazer buttoned across his ample middle above a white shirt and neatly knotted tie. He said nothing and merely looked Josh up and down disapprovingly before stepping to one side to allow him to enter. There was no hallway as such, just a small vestibule area and two glass doors that gave immediately onto a large and spacious lounge. Seated on a sofa was the man with the shaven head, who looked up and stared impassively at Brody as he walked in. Shaven head said nothing but merely nodded at the thick-set guy in the blazer, who stepped to a side table and picked up a small, hand-held scanner. It looked like an oversized magnifying glass and the man held it out as he approached Josh and waved it in an upward direction, indicating that Brody should raise his arms. Josh did as he was bidden and the guy ran the scanner all around his body, under his arm pits and between the length of his legs.

"I'm not wired" said Josh.

The scanner let out a loud beep and the guy felt inside Brody's jacket, withdrawing the first of his mobile phones. It then beeped again as it was run over his buttocks and the man pulled the second phone from Brody's hip pocket. He pointedly switched each of them off and then placed both handsets onto the table before returning to complete his sonic frisking.

When he was satisfied Brody carried no recording devices or electronic equipment, he nodded to his boss and stepped to one side.

"Please take a seat" said shaven head and indicated that Josh should sit himself in one of the arm chairs opposite. Brody did as he was bidden.

For a few seconds the two men stared at each other in silence. Then shaven head spoke. "Why are you in Vienna?" he asked evenly.

"That's my business. And, if you wish to enquire into it, you'd better start by telling me just exactly who you are and why you've asked to see me."

The stranger nodded and gave an condescending smile. "I am Mr. Smith. And I have asked to see you in order to help you."

Brody grinned. "Yeah. You're Mr. Smith. And, don't tell me..." he nodded, without shifting his gaze from the man opposite, in the direction of the thick set man standing to one side... "this is Mr. Brown, right?"

Mr. Smith gave a slight shrug. "In the words of the bard, Mr. Brody, what's in a name?"

"Not much" replied Josh. "Not if you're intent on playing out this poor imitation of a Graham Green novel. So why don't we skip the pleasantries of introduction and get down to brass tacks. I am in Vienna to do a book signing, which you know perfectly well because you attended it yesterday. So why the cryptic note and why do you want to see me here instead of speaking to me at the University when you had the chance?"

"Because it is in your own best interests for this conversation to remain private and off the record. Out of sight of prying eyes and ears."

"All right" said Josh with a deliberate sigh. "We'll play the game and see what happens. But first, tell Mr. Brown over there to shift his arse in your direction and stand where I can see you both clearly."

The man said nothing but nodded a silent order to his subordinate. The minder went to the drinks cabinet in the corner of the room, picked up a bottle of mineral water and a glass and placed them on the small table at the side of Brody's chair. Then he dutifully did as he was bidden and went to stand behind the sofa.

"Good" said Josh calmly. He picked up the mineral water and poured himself half a glass. "Ok. So let's hear it. Make your pitch."

"You went to the Kriminalpolizei and made enquiries concerning the recent suicide of Fabrice Lukeba."

'Bull's eye' thought Josh. If he ever needed third-party confirmation that Fabrice's death was being covered up and masked in the claims of suicide, he had just received it. But he was well practised in the art of dissembling in an interview and his face registered not one iota of a change of expression as he simply replied: "So?"

"It is important that you understand that the circumstances of Mr. Lukeba's unfortunate suicide concern matters of which you are unaware. Matters of great importance."

"I'd say that the circumstances were more unfortunate for Lukeba than anybody else, wouldn't you? He ended up with a Sig Sauer automatic in his mouth and his brains scattered all over his hotel room. So, I'd say *that* was the matter of greatest importance as far as he was concerned, don't you think?"

The man opposite's voice suddenly took on a markedly sinister tone. "Please don't try to be clever, Mr. Brody. It doesn't become you. Whether you realise it or not, I'm trying to help you."

Brody leant forward in his chair and his face hardened. "Then stop dickering around!" he said aggressively. "We both know Lukeba was murdered. If he wasn't then we wouldn't be having this bizarre conversation. Personally, I think the Lukeba twins were a pair of conniving, evil bastards and the world's a much better place without them. But that doesn't entitle you, or anyone else, to cover up a murder. So cut the crap and tell me what it is you've got to say, or I'm walking out that door right now."

Mr. Smith gave a disdainful sniff and sat back against the plush velvet of the sofa. He gave a slight, exasperated shake of his head, almost as if he were about to address a disobedient child. "Your arrogance is astonishing. But have it your own way. I'll say this as plainly as I can. You are meddling in matters far more important than you can possibly imagine. You are correct in your assessment of the Lukeba brothers. The world is indeed better off with them gone. So allow sleeping dogs to lie and do not proceed with your inappropriate enquiries. Enquiries that could reveal nothing of value to the world but could cause untold harm."

Josh looked across at the man's staring eyes, so full of restrained anger. He wasn't sure there was too much more he could prise out of Mr. Smith but, so far at least, he was making progress and now was not the time to retreat.

"Ok" Brody replied. "You've said your piece. Now let me translate. Two unsavoury characters are dead. You're saying 'well and good'. I'm saying murder shouldn't be covered up, no matter who the victim might be. So I'm asking questions. You're telling me to back off." It was Josh's turn to sit back in his chair and stare contemptuously at his opponent. "So just who the fuck are you? And what gives you the right to tell me to back away from anything?"

Mr. Brown, standing silently behind the sofa, visibly bristled at this last tirade and Josh knew he was hitting sensitive spots within the two men. Clearly they were subordinate and superior. Was the relationship just employer and minder? Or was it one of rank? Were they military? Secret service? Police? Or possibly mercenaries? He'd come across mercenary soldiers in Libya and, despite their freelance status, they adhered passionately to the notion of rank and order of command. His thoughts ran immediately to the D.R.C., where bands of mercenaries could be found in abundance. These two would fit the pattern and the profile. But the scenario was wrong. Mercenaries might plot and carry out a murder, but it was extremely unlikely they could exercise influence over authorities in London and Vienna to cover their tracks.

All these thoughts cascaded swiftly through Josh's mind as he watched both the men he was confronting, earnestly searching their faces for some sign or indication of the true nature of their identity.

Several moments passed in silence before Mr. Smith spoke again. "How is little Saffy?" he said calmly. "Is she enjoying her new rabbit?"

Brody went icy cold from head to foot and he felt the back of his throat go instantly dry. He looked aghast at the man opposite. For a moment, every fear a father harbours as to the safety of his child came rushing in on him and his chest tightened. His head filled with devastating images of Saffy being followed and the Westcliff house being watched. Pictures of kidnapping and abduction flitted terrifyingly across his mental screen. Then, suddenly, he realised how they knew about the rabbit. 'They *are* tapping my phone' he told himself silently, confirming his original suspicions.

Mentally, he turned somersaults, desperately trying to remember when he'd last spoken to Saffy and when they discussed the rabbit. It was definitely back at home. So they'd been monitoring his English mobile since before he left London. That meant that Mr. Smith and Mr. Brown, or whomever they represented, were not just operating in Vienna. That also implied that they had followed him from England to Austria. This whole affair was instantly taking on proportions Brody had not imagined; frightening proportions that had crossed the line and made reference to his family. His piercing eyes were focussed directly upon Mr. Smith.

"You go anywhere near my daughter" he said coldly, "and, believe me, I'll bring down the wrath of Hell on your head."

Mr. Smith gave an exaggerated sigh. "Your paternal instincts are understandable, Mr. Brody, but wildly overdramatic. No one wishes any harm to your daughter. But your unwillingness to listen to reason forces me to refer to her in order to make a point. The forces with which you are meddling are far greater than you understand. Their reach is endless. So please accept that you are in no position to confront them."

He's right about their reach, thought Brody. Phone taps; influence over the police in London and Vienna; the ability to cover up murder. This is far more than a mere mercenary organisation.

Brody took a deep draught of water and then put down his glass. "What are you?" he asked evenly. "M.I.6? Interpol?"

The shaven headed man was not to be drawn. "As I said at the beginning of our conversation, names are not important. But, if it will satisfy your journalistic ego, I will simply tell you that the forces you are challenging do not fit into any of your neat little boxes and will never be known to you. So it is fruitless for you to speculate. It is now simply time for you to withdraw quietly and go home; home to your daughter and your family. I suggest you check out of your hotel and make straight for Schwechat. There are several London flights remaining before the end of the day. You are bound to find a seat on a plane back to Heathrow."

Up until a few minutes ago, Josh had felt he was gaining ground and holding his own in this extraordinary, combative conversation. But the mention of his daughter had taken every ounce of strength from him. That was a vulnerability he could not defend. He was also now certain he was dealing with some species of secret service personnel. That meant that discretion was definitely the better part of valour and, for the time being at least, he would need to retreat.

"I have to give a talk at the British Council at two o'clock" Brody explained. "It will look very odd if I don't turn up."

Mr. Smith nodded. "I agree. So fulfil your obligations and then take an evening flight."

Josh stood. "And if I don't?" he said steadily, regaining something of his previous composure.

Mr. Smith rose from the sofa to stand resolutely opposite him. "I wouldn't advise that, Mr. Brody."

There was a cold finality to this statement and Josh knew when he had run into a brick wall. Saying nothing more, he reluctantly turned, quietly gathered his two telephones from the side table, and left.

Once outside, he checked his watch. He'd been in the apartment less than twenty minutes. Using his local mobile he sent a text message to Alan Denton at The Independent:

Am safe and have left rendezvous but temperature here is rising rapidly. Need to take precautions to avoid getting burned. Will be in touch soonest. J.B.

When the handset display marked the text as 'delivered', Brody pocketed the phone and, in deeply pensive mood, went in pursuit of a cab.

The taxi ride back to the Hotel Post was a maelstrom of conflicting emotions. Whoever the so-called Mr. Smith might be, he clearly represented some form of official organisation. The influence that had been exerted on the police in London and Vienna, and the speed with which the bodies of the Lukeba twins had been repatriated, could not have been undertaken without the sanction of formal channels. Mr. Smith was clearly English but that, in itself, meant little. All covert organisations employed people of different nationalities and he could be working for any one of them. The options tumbled through Brody's thoughts: C.I.A.?, M.I.6?, S.D.E.C.E?, Interpol? Whichever group might ultimately prove to be behind the cover-up of the Lukeba murders, it had the power to tap his phone and, as Mr. Smith had so coldly demonstrated, its reach could extend to his family.

It was not in Brody's nature to allow himself to be bullied or railroaded out of a story. Had he still been a single man, he would have gone to ground, hunkered down, and risked whatever they might throw at him in order to get to the truth and print it. But Brody had an ex-wife and a daughter. Threats to his own survival were a matter for him alone; but intimidation that endangered Kass and Saffy was not to be risked. Until he could be certain his family was safe and beyond harm, he would grudgingly kowtow to the wishes of the objectionable Mr. Smith and do as he was told. It gnawed at his gut to think he was running from the fight but there was a clear difference between cowardice and rank stupidity. For the time being at least, Brody had only one option.

Back at the Hotel Post, he asked the girl at reception to make up his bill and went straight to his room. Before he packed his case, he withdrew the USB drive from the safe and plugged it into his laptop. He updated his summary document with a synopsis of the morning's strange events but left the file on the external USB drive, ensuring there was nothing on the laptop itself relating to the case in any way. He then shut down the computer, secreted the USB stick in the inside pocket of his jacket, and checked that he had his notebook and his passport and that nothing was left in the room. Then, deliberately using his English mobile, which he assumed was still being monitored, he rang Austrian Airlines and booked a flight to Heathrow for 7.45 pm. Anyone eavesdropping on the conversation would know he was leaving the country and heading home.

His last act before quitting his room was to call his ex-wife. This time he used the local phone with the pay-as-you-go SIM.

"Hello?" said Kass as the call connected. There was both curiosity and surprise in her voice as she had obviously not recognised the foreign incoming number.

"It's me" said Josh. "I just wanted to call and check that everything is ok."

"But this isn't your number. What happened to your phone?"

"It's just a local number I'm using while I'm in Vienna. It's cheaper that way."

There was a pointed pause before she spoke again. "Josh..." she began censoriously. "Have they cut off your mobile? Don't tell me you've not paid the bill. I can't believe you'd..."

He was in no mood for her customary criticisms and cut across her at once. "No Kass, they've not cut off my phone. Now please just listen because I don't have long. Is everything ok with you and Saffy? Are you both all right?"

"Yes" she replied, the obvious suspicion still evident in her voice. "We're fine."

"Good." He was trying to conceal his enormous and genuine relief but not certain he was succeeding. "And Saffy's well and happy?"

"Yes. I've told you. We both are." She was clearly puzzled. "Is something wrong Josh? You sound a little uptight."

"No. Everything's ok. I wanted to let you know I'll be catching a flight back to London tonight. But I'll be arriving too late to call you. So I'll ring tomorrow and catch Saffy when she's home from school. Ok?"

"Yes. I'll tell her. She'll be pleased to know you're coming home."

"And I'll get down to Westcliff as soon as I can. I'll bring her that chocolate I promised."

"Yes. Ok. That would be good."

"Right. Well, take care. I'll see you both in a few days."

"Ok, Josh. Have a safe flight. Thanks for calling."

He clicked off the handset, his fears allayed by the news his daughter was fine. He felt his shoulders drop a little as the tension he'd been unconsciously holding in them eased. He'd known that Mr. Smith's reference to Saffy was a scare tactic; a threat to warn him off; but there was no rationality to a father's fears and he had needed to hear Kass reassure him personally that his daughter was safe and sound.

He took his case down to reception, paid his bill and checked out.

The Hotel Post was so called because it was situated directly opposite one of Vienna's main post offices. The building was busy and full of customers as Josh crossed the street and entered through one of the tall main doors under the famous post-horn logo. He purchased a large padded envelope and carefully secreted his notebook and the USB drive inside, along with a brief note of explanation and instruction. Then, in clear, printed capitals, he wrote out a name and address on the front label and took it to the counter to be mailed, first class, to the U.K. He was fairly sure he was being over-cautious; but the echo of the so-called Mr. Smith's warning was still reverberating ominously in his head. Whatever sinister organisation he was facing, these people were powerful, and the only weapon in his armoury was the knowledge he had acquired of what they had done. That knowledge needed to be put out of harm's way and beyond the reach of his adversaries. Then, if his worst fears were realised, he would at least have a bargaining chip to use against them.

At the end of the Fleischmarkt, on the corner of Rotenturmstraße, he went into a small Tabac store and bought a large box of Mozart Kugeln for Saffy. Then he hailed a cab and twenty minutes later was walking in through the front doors of The British Council.

"You're nice and early" Shelley greeted him as she walked into reception to find him seated and patiently waiting for her. "I almost didn't believe them when they rang upstairs and said you'd arrived." Suddenly she stopped in her tracks. Despite his best efforts to appear calm and relaxed, Brody's face bore clear testimony to the way he was feeling. "What's wrong, Josh?" she asked in concern. "You look as if you've had bad news."

Brody rose from his seat and attempted a smile. "No. Nothing's wrong" he lied. "I'm fine. I just..." He stopped. He was unsure if it was simply pointless to keep hiding the truth from her, or merely that he felt he needed an ally, but, either way, all at once he knew he didn't want to continue with the pretence. "Is there somewhere private we can talk?" he asked.

She led him up the staircase to the first floor landing and along the corridor to an open plan general office that was buzzing with activity. Half a dozen people were seated at various desks, all staring at computer monitors, and a couple of secretaries were flitting in and out carrying various papers and documents. There were three large T.V. screens affixed to the back wall, one tuned to the local Ö.R.F. culture and information channel, one tuned to C.N.N., and the other tuned to B.B.C. World News. The sound was muted on each of them. Shelley led Brody to the far side of the floor where a glass panelled door gave onto a small room.

"We won't be disturbed in here."

As she opened the door and stood back to let him enter, he reached out and held her by the arm. "First I need a favour. My German's ok but it's not good enough to carry out enquiries with officialdom. Do you have someone here who can call the Vienna City Council and find out who owns or rents this apartment?" He handed her the slip of paper on which he had written the address in the Tiefer Graben.

Shelley glanced down at the note. "Yes. Freya can do that for you." She stepped across the general office to a dark-haired Viennese girl seated at a corner desk and handed her the slip of paper, instructing her to check out all details of ownership and tenancy of the property. Then she returned to Josh and ushered him into the small room, closing the door behind them.

"This is a long story" Josh began as they seated themselves on either side of the desk that took up a good proportion of the small office. "And it has to remain confidential." He reached onto the desk and, picking up a sheet of blank paper, scribbled Alan Denton's name and contact details on it. He passed the paper to her. "Keep this safe. If anything happens to me, you're to call this friend at The Independent in London. He's the editor of the World News team. He'll know what to do."

She blanched as she took the note and then reached out to grasp his hand. "Josh, you're scaring me. What do you mean 'if anything happens to you'? What on earth is going on? What are you mixed up in?"

It took him only fifteen minutes or so to give her a summary of all that had occurred. He told her everything, from his initial meeting with the pathologist, Luke Harvey, right up to that morning's meeting with the pseudonymous Mr. Smith, who had so pointedly warned him to drop his enquiries and return home. She listened attentively but deep concern was written all over her face by the time Josh brought his story to a close.

"So, for the time being at least, I have to return to the U.K. and give them the impression I have done as they requested and abandoned the whole enquiry. I hate being bullied like this but, once they mentioned Saffy, I had no choice."

"No, of course you didn't" she commiserated. "That must have been terrible to hear. And you're doing exactly the right thing. But I don't understand what's happening here. Who *are* these people?"

Before Josh could answer, they were interrupted by a knock on the door. Shelley called 'come in' and Freya, the secretary, stepped into the room.

Like all secretaries working at The British Council, Freya was bilingual. "No problem with the address" she told them cheerfully. "I thought it looked familiar when I first read it. It's one of ours."

Josh sat bolt upright. "What do you mean it's one of yours?"

"The building's owned by a development company and they hire out some of the apartments for short term lets. We use it for people on the watch list."

Josh darted a quizzical glance across the desk to Shelley. "The watch list?"

"We run a list of people who are in town that we need to know about" she explained. "You're on it yourself. That's how I first came to call you. We get a weekly update of any V.I.P.s or people relevant to our operation who are in Vienna; so we can monitor them and keep in touch; help them out and that sort of thing. It's called the watch list."

"What's that got to do with the apartment?" asked Josh, confused.

"We're sometimes asked to find accommodation for them. This apartment is evidently one of those we use."

Brody looked up at Freya. "But did you find out who is currently renting it?"

She smiled. "I didn't have to. *We* set it up."

Brody felt his stomach roll over. He had a distinct premonition that something was wrong. "Set it up for whom?" he asked.

Freya glanced down at her notes. "It was for..." she turned the page and read out the name... "a Doctor Nazari."

"Not a man calling himself Smith?"

"No."

"How long was the let you arranged? From when to when?"

"Er..." she checked her notes again... "for one week. From last Saturday to next Saturday."

Brody frowned. "Then this doctor's supposed to be there now. He's the current tenant."

Freya nodded. "Yes. He should be. It's all written down here." She placed the two sheets of paper she was holding onto the desk.

Brody exchanged a worried look with Shelley, who looked up at the secretary. "Thanks for your help, Freya. Much appreciated."

The young girl smiled broadly. "No problem." Closing the door quietly behind her, Freya left.

"Who is this Doctor Nazari?" asked Josh as soon as they were alone again.

Shelley looked down at the notes. "It says here he's an Iranian. A scientist. He's in Vienna for a week. He's attending a symposium at the U.N. centre. Apparently the Brits are chairing it."

"What's that got to do with the British Council?"

"Probably nothing. We do sometimes liaise with scientists and technical people but it's more likely we were just asked to recommend an address for accommodation."

"By whom?"

She shrugged. "By London I presume. The watch list is emailed through to us from head office, so the request was probably made at that end."

Brody stood and went pensively to the window, gazing out at Siebensterngaßse below. It was a warm, bright day with pedestrians bustling to and fro. All was perfectly normal and calm; unlike Josh's brain, that was desperately sifting through this latest revelation to try and make sense of it. He addressed his thoughts quietly and slowly to the unhearing outside world.

"How can an unknown Englishman, calling himself Mr. Smith and protected by a minder, be sitting quite comfortably in a Vienna apartment that we now know was rented, via the recommendation of The British Council, to an Iranian scientist. How can that be? How does it all connect?"

"Well, the obvious answer would be that they know each other" offered Shelley.

Josh turned to face her. "Agreed. So, *if* that's the case, then whoever is at the back of Mr. Smith is, presumably, in close contact with, or working with, this Dr. Nazari... Right?"

She nodded. "That's a reasonable assumption."

"So... is there some connection between this Iranian scientist and the Lukeba twins? That would at least give us the link we need."

Shelley glanced anxiously at her watch. "Well, in the first place, for reasons we've already agreed, you need to let this go and stop thinking like a journalist still working on a story. And in the second place, we've got a group of people gathering in the downstairs hall who are expecting you to give them a lecture in approximately half an hour."

"Oh, God. Yes, of course. I'd almost forgotten."

She took him by the hand. "Josh, you've had a rough morning. And one that's hardly conducive to giving a talk about authorship. Nobody will blame you if you don't feel up to doing this. I can just tell them you've been taken ill."

He lifted her hand to his lips and kissed it gently. "Thanks for the thought. I really appreciate it. But I'll be fine. Besides, it might help me relax and calm down a little."

"Ok. If you're sure" she said gratefully. "You wait here and get yourself together. I'll send Freya in with some coffee while I go downstairs and check everything is ready."

Shelley left the room and Josh was alone, attempting to marshal his thoughts as to what he would say in the imminent lecture and to push the concerns and worries that were nagging at him to the back of his mind.

The large downstairs room was used for lectures, slide-shows and small-scale music recitals given by visiting musicians. There was a raised platform at one end, where a small Bechstein rested under a large canvas cover and a central lectern stood facing the rows of seats that had been set out in the body of the hall. To Brody's surprise, he entered to discover around seventy-five or more of the seats were taken and the expectant faces of their occupants watched him optimistically as he made his way towards the stage.

Shelley gave a brief introduction, citing all the usual clichés about how lucky they were to have such a notable author visiting and how kind he was to donate his precious time to talk to them, et al, and then she handed over to Brody to a ripple of polite applause from the audience as she made her way to the rear of the room and took a seat in the back row.

Many of those present were students, most of whom were probably studying English Brody guessed, but the remainder appeared to be a complete cross-section of the good burgers of Wien. They varied in type and age-range from the smart suits, to the jeans and T-shirts brigade, to the just plain curious who looked as if they had mistakenly wandered in from the street during afternoon grocery shopping. Despite their diversity, they were all attentive and seemed keen to hear what Josh had to say.

He began with a brief history of his background and work as a journalist and then steered towards the actual processes of writing, focussing particularly on his Soho book, half a dozen copies of which were on display on the platform. Without revealing that he also wrote novels under a pseudonym, he explained the different disciplines required between fiction and factual history and his audience listened attentively and appeared genuinely fascinated.

When he opened matters out to a Q. & A. there was no shortage of eager hands raised. Most of the queries were expected and predictable: Where do you get your ideas and your inspiration? How do you organise your writing day? What are the difficulties in finding a publisher? Etc. etc. But several members of the audience asked intelligent questions regarding research, the mental approach to a project and his methods of application to develop form and structure. The more it continued, the more Brody found the session involving and rewarding.

Upstairs in the general office, while Josh was answering questions from his audience in the room below, the young secretary Freya was busy preparing the text for a press release advertising a forthcoming visit to Vienna by the English National Ballet company. As always with promotional material, it was necessary to find the shortest yet most effective way to describe the theatrical delights on offer and encourage people to attend the performances.

Freya sat back, racking her brains to find the most appropriate single adjective to describe the new production of Swan Lake. As her head rested on the back of her chair and she lifted her gaze, seeking inspiration from the air about her, one of the T.V. screens on the wall opposite caught her eye. It was a news flash showing on the Ö.R.F. channel. A reporter, clutching a microphone, was delivering a piece to camera in front of a set of large, glass front doors that had been fenced-off with chequered black and yellow tape. The doors struck Freya as familiar. There was something about them that she recognised.

"Who has the remote control?" she called out urgently to the office.

"It's on Gernot's desk" came a reply from across the room.

Freya hurried from her seat to the desk two stations away and, grabbing the control, un-muted the T.V. screen showing the German language Ö.R.F. channel. The Austrian reporter was coming to the end of his piece but she was able to catch the final few sentences:

The police are not yet releasing the name of the deceased but we have established that he was a prominent Iranian national on a short visit to the city to attend a U.N. conference. We know nothing of the circumstances surrounding the death but police have confirmed that they are currently treating it as suspicious. This is Kurt Lang, for Ö.R.F., reporting from the Tiefer Graben in Vienna.

The report closed and the images reverted to the studio announcer. Freya pressed the mute button and thoughtfully replaced the remote control on the desk in front of her. She was right. The large glass doors she had recognised belonged to the apartment in the Tiefer Graben that she had been discussing with Shelley Anderson less than an hour earlier. The co-incidence was odd to say the least. Freya abandoned her press release for the ballet company and made her way swiftly out of the office to hurry down the stairs to the lecture hall.

As she entered the room, Josh Brody was bringing his talk to a close. Freya spied Shelley in the back row and quietly took the vacant seat next to her. "There's something I think you should know" she whispered as Shelley looked up. "I've just heard a T.V. report."

On the platform, Josh thanked the British Council for their hospitality and the audience for their kind attention and ended his short lecture. The applause was genuine and appreciative and he felt the whole session had gone particularly well. He left the stage and, as the audience rose and began making their way out of the hall, walked back to the last row to where Shelley and Freya were in conversation. He immediately caught sight of Shelley's troubled expression and frowned.

"Was it that bad?" he asked as he took a seat in front of them. "I thought it went rather well."

"It was fine" said Shelley. "Excellent, in fact. One of the best we've had."

Brody was relieved to hear her verdict. "Then why so glum?"

She reached out and gripped his arm tightly. "Josh. Something's wrong. There's been a news report. Freya heard it on the T.V."

The look of deep concern written large upon her face jerked him unceremoniously from his post lecture satisfaction and made him instantly uneasy. "What's happened?"

Before Shelly could begin to explain, a familiar tall figure walked into the lecture hall and cast his eyes around the room. Oberkommisar Dieter Kleist was flanked by two uniformed officers of the Wiener Kriminalpolizei. When the police inspector's gaze finally settled on Josh, he walked immediately towards him, holding out his warrant card.

Josh knew instantly that the newcomer was not the harbinger of good news. "Inspector Kleist" he said as he apprehensively stood. "What are you doing here?"

"Herr Brody. You are under arrest."

Freya gave out a short cry of shock and Shelley immediately got to her feet, her face pale with disbelief.

Josh knew he had not misheard the detective, but could not quite get his head around what the man had just said. "I'm sorry?" he queried in disbelief.

"I am arresting you" Kleist told him coldly.

"What for?" interjected a stunned and angry Shelley. "On what charge?"

The reply was instant and unemotional. "Suspicion of murder."

Chapter Twelve

Forty minutes later, Brody found himself in an austere and dismal holding cell in the basement of the Wasagaße headquarters of the Kriminalpolizei.

He had suffered the ignominy of having his finger prints taken when they booked him in at the front desk. Then they had emptied his pockets. Taking his telephones, his watch and his wallet, they sealed them in a brown paper envelope; then they relieved him of his belt and shoe laces before escorting him down to the lower floor where they locked him in the cell. It was a cold and clinical, narrow room containing just a single bench bed, a small wash basin and the stainless steel bowl of a chemical toilet. The bare, ceramic-tiled walls added to the bland, impersonal and indifferent atmosphere, and the single neon strip-light, faintly humming from the centre of the ceiling, illuminated the windowless room in a stark, unsympathetic shade of lemon-yellow.

Despite the barrage of questions Brody fired at Kleist during the brief ride in the rear of the police car, the detective had remained silent throughout the journey, telling him only that he would be interviewed later and the full charges would be explained according to official procedure.

Departing the offices of The British Council in handcuffs, escorted by the Vienna police, was a strangely incongruous way to leave a building where he had only just been feted by an appreciative audience of the capital's citizens, but Brody had not made a scene or protested his ignominious exit. He knew there was little to be gained from resisting arrest and had accepted that he had no option but to allow himself to be taken until he could get some kind of handle on whatever the hell was happening.

Shelley Anderson was far less acquiescent and had remonstrated loud and long with Kleist, complaining bitterly about the preposterous charge. The taciturn detective had, predictably, paid little attention to her objections and ignored her vociferous threats to call the British Embassy. As Josh was bundled into the back of the patrol car, she called to him, encouraging him not to worry. She told him she would get everything sorted and visit him later, once she had cleared up what was obviously a ridiculous misunderstanding.

While Brody was being driven in uncomfortable silence to Wasagaße, Shelley did indeed telephone the embassy and irately reported the arrest. A polite official patiently assured her he would 'look into the incident' and requested she please leave matters to him but, dissatisfied and undaunted, Shelley ordered a taxi and told the driver to take her directly to the embassy, where she re-registered her protest in person and demanded instant action.

As Shelley was bombarding the ears of British officialdom with her heartfelt complaints, Brody was lying silently on the bench bed in his cell, trying to piece together some plausible scenario that might have caused what had so unexpectedly befallen him. He could find no possible answers.

It was close to 5 pm before he heard the metallic clicking of a key in the lock of his cell door and it opened to reveal the duty constable.

"Wir gehen oben" the guard told him, gesturing towards the ceiling with an extended forefinger, and Brody realised he was at last being taken upstairs to be questioned by Kleist.

The unfortunate prisoner was led past the office where, just a few days previously, he had spoken with the detective and taken further along the corridor to an interview room. He entered to find Kleist seated on one side of a desk with two vacant chairs opposite. The rest of the dimly-lit room was bare. In front of Kleist was a manila folder, lying next to a hard disc recorder and a microphone that was centrally positioned to cover both sides of the desk. Mercifully, Brody was no longer handcuffed but he was still very much the prisoner under arrest and the constable who had brought him from the cells remained close by, standing ominously just a few feet from the chair on which Josh sat.

Kleist switched on the recorder and spoke briefly in German into the microphone to state the date and time and the personnel present. He then looked across at his prisoner. "You are Joshua Brody?" he asked in English.

Josh let out an exasperated sigh. "For fuck's sake, Kleist. I understand you have to follow the rules but let's not play silly bloody games. I know you and you know me! And we both know this is ridiculous. So let's just behave like sensible people and get this mess sorted out. How can you possibly be holding me on a charge of suspected murder? It's crazy! What is all this about?"

The detective reached across to the recorder and depressed a finger onto the pause button. "It will be quicker, and better for you, if you cooperate with official procedure" he said coldly. "The choice is yours." He held his finger on the control, waiting for a response.

Brody realised there would be no shortcuts to obtaining the answers he wanted. He threw up his hands in exasperation but nodded reluctantly at the detective. Kleist released the pause button.

"You are Joshua Brody?" he repeated.

"Yes" Josh snapped in a clipped and curt tone.

"Why are you in Vienna?"

"To attend a book fair at the University."

"Are you not also here to report on the suicide of the diplomat Fabrice Lukeba?"

Josh raised his eyebrows in frustration. "That was not the main purpose of my visit. But, yes. I was looking into the story while I am here."

"So you have been making enquiries into the diplomat's death?"

"Yes."

"You were resident at the Hotel Post in Fleischmarkt?"

"Yes."

"But you checked out this morning?"

Josh sighed again. "Yes" he repeated dutifully.

"Where were you last night?"

Brody suddenly felt a slight shaft of optimism break into his darkness. If this arrest depended upon his whereabouts of the previous evening then he had a cast iron alibi. "I was at the Kammeroper" he said urgently. "And I can prove it."

"And afterwards?"

"At a friend's apartment."

"Who was this friend?"

Brody hesitated momentarily. He had no wish to drag Shelley into any aspect of his arrest but if it was the only way to establish the truth of his whereabouts then he had no choice. "Shelley Anderson" he admitted quietly.

"And you were with her all night?"

"No. I was there until around 2.30 am. Then I walked back to my hotel. It's only a short walk, so I must have returned at about 2.40 or 2.45."

"And what were your movements today?"

Brody obediently recited his itinerary. "I had breakfast in a café in Stephansplatz and then caught a cab to an 11 am meeting. From the meeting I went by taxi back to my hotel where I packed my bags and checked out. Then I took another cab to The British Council offices. I gave a short lecture there at 2 pm. Then you turned up and, for some reason I still don't understand, arrested me." He looked disdainfully at his interrogator. "Now we're here having this decidedly unpleasant conversation. And that was my day."

"Where was your eleven o'clock meeting?" asked Kleist, pointedly ignoring Brody's attitude.

"At an apartment in the Tiefer Graben."

Kleist nodded slowly as he reached forward and opened the manila folder that was lying on the desk in front of him. Withdrawing a couple of large glossy, black and white photographs, he placed them both carefully in front of Brody. "Is this the apartment building where you claim your meeting took place?"

Brody stared down in surprise at the images. One was a shot of him entering the premises in the Tiefer Graben that morning. The other photograph was of him leaving the building around a half-hour later. In each picture he was clearly visible and recognisable and there was a time-code printed in white lettering at the foot of each photograph that showed both time and date. The two shots had been captured from an overhead angle and appeared to have been taken from close range.

"These stills are from the building's security C.C.T.V. video footage" Kleist told him. "From the camera that covers the front door."

"Josh looked up at the policeman. "Then you have proof that I was exactly where I said I was."

"Indeed" Kleist said evenly. "And we have a little extra proof." He reached into the top drawer of the desk and withdrew a copy of Brody's book 'Soho – The Dark Side'. "This was found in the apartment. In the bedroom" he added tersely. He opened the front cover to reveal the title page and turned the book around to face Josh. It was inscribed with Brody's signature and the dedication: *To Jalil – with all good wishes.* "Is this your writing?"

Josh began to feel increasingly wary of the way the detective was assembling his facts. He had the distinct impression this was all leading somewhere specific and that the approaching destination did not bode well. "Yes" he acknowledged uneasily. "I wrote it at the book fair at the University. It was for the man I then met at the Tiefer Graben apartment this morning. That's obviously why it was there."

"And this man was called Jalil?"

"Well... I doubt that was *his* name. He was clearly English. I presumed, when he asked me to sign it, that he wanted it for someone else. People often request that."

"I see" said Kleist with an undisguised note of mockery in his tone. "Then what was the name of this Englishman?"

Brody was suddenly seized by the uncomfortable realisation that the simple truth was about to sound extremely contrived and phoney. His eyes looked downward as he reluctantly uttered: "I don't know."

Kleist sat back in his chair and took a moment to stare at his prisoner. "Let me understand you" he said at length. "You went to an appointment in this apartment but you do not know the name of the man you went to meet. Is that what you are telling me?"

"Yes!" Brody retorted animatedly. "The guy turns up at the book fair. While I'm signing his copy, he suddenly gives me the address of the apartment and tells me to be there the following morning if I want information about my enquiries. Then he walks off and disappears."

"He gave you the address?"

"Yes."

"Written down?"

"No. Verbally. He handed me a blank note and told *me* to write it down."

"So the address is in your handwriting, not his?"

Josh realised that yet again the truth was sounding implausible. He nodded reluctantly. "Yes."

"And you kept this appointment, not knowing who he was?"

Josh banged the desk in protest. "Of course I did! I'm a reporter. I was following a lead. I was less concerned with who he was than with what he might be able to tell me."

Kleist shrugged. "So what happened at this meeting with the unknown stranger?"

"He told me to refer to him as Mr. Smith. Then he got heavy."

Kleist raised a contemptuous eyebrow. "Mr. Smith?"

"All right" said Josh, becoming increasingly angry. "Let's cut the crap, shall we?! He was of medium height. He wore a black suit with a black T-shirt. His head was shaved. He didn't want to give me his name and told me to refer to him as Mr. Smith; so I did. He threatened me and told me to drop my story. That's all I can tell you about him. Now you tell me: Is he what this is all about? Is this the guy who's dead? Am I being charged with murdering this man or what?"

Kleist made no reply but leaned forward to the manila folder and withdrew another photograph. He placed it alongside the others on the desk. This picture was in colour. It showed the head and bare shoulders of an Arabic looking man of middle-eastern appearance. The mouth was open and the eyes were staring blankly from a face that seemed stretched in horror. The natural olive skin looked drained and showed an unexpected pallor. It was a face of death.

"This is a photograph of Doctor Jalil Nazari" said Kleist evenly. "He was discovered at around twelve noon today in the bedroom of the apartment you visited. Both his wrists had been slashed with a knife. On the coffee table in the lounge was a notepad. On the top sheet was written *'Joshua Brody. 11am'*. In the bedroom, on the dressing table, was a copy of your book, signed with a dedication to the doctor. Here I have photographs of you both entering and leaving the building. In the apartment itself we have found your finger prints on a bottle and a glass."

Josh was in a daze of confusion. "Wait a minute... wait a minute" he said, vainly trying to get his head around this barrage of facts. "You said his wrists were slashed. Are you telling me he committed suicide?"

"No" replied Kleist curtly. "I'm telling you I have another dead body on my hands and I have a journalist who seems to specialise in getting involved with foreigners who turn up as corpses in my city. And I'm beginning to wonder if Nazari's death was made to *look* like a suicide. *That's* what I'm telling you!"

Brody winced, as if in pain, and shook his head. "This is unreal" he said abjectly. He took a deep breath and looked pleadingly at Kleist. "Look. Think about it for a moment. You were one of the first people I called when I got here. You can't seriously believe I'd come to Vienna to murder someone and then turn up on your doorstep and announce my arrival before I commit the crime. That's insane!"

Kleist leaned forward, leaning his elbows on the desk, and fixed Brody squarely in the eye. "I have all the evidence I need for the charge of suspected murder" he whispered menacingly. "And I am getting very tired of your attitude. So *you* cut the crap and start explaining!"

Brody slumped in his chair in defeat. It dawned on him with icy cold clarity that he had not been summoned to the apartment that morning to be threatened by the pseudonymous Mr. Smith. That whole conversation had been a sham; a simple ruse to put him in the frame for a murder. His arrest was a far more effective method of preventing his continued investigations than any verbal warning to desist, and they had played him perfectly. They had offered the bait and he'd walked right into the trap. 'I've been stitched up like a kipper!' he told himself despairingly. It was time to seek an ally.

Josh fixed Kleist with a stare and nodded at the recorder. "I will say nothing more until I have a lawyer here" he announced pointedly, making it clear that he was speaking for the benefit of the recording. Then he held up a hand and mimed switching off the machine.

Kleist understood his cue and, checking his watch, declared that the interview was terminated, quoted the time, and hit the stop button. He then looked across the desk at Brody. "You wish to say something to me off the record?"

Josh nodded his head in the direction of the constable standing close by.

"Warten Sie draußen" commanded the detective and the officer quietly left the room, leaving the two men alone. The inspector looked back at Brody. "So?"

"You may be an arrogant son of a bitch, Kleist, but I think you're probably a good copper. So I'm going to gamble that the truth is more important to you than scoring points."

The detective sniffed. "Go on" he said calmly.

"If you go to your computer right now and Google an image search, you'll find several photographs of the Lukeba twins signing official documents. You'll see, in every picture, that they were both left handed. The gun that was put in Fabrice's mouth was fired from the right hand side. No left handed person could commit suicide that way. He was murdered. And so was his brother. Both killings are being covered up and I've been asking awkward questions. So I had to be removed. The meeting at the apartment this morning was a set-up to get me arrested and out of the picture. I don't know any Doctor Nazari. I've never met him. And I certainly didn't kill him. But I suspect I'm going to need your help to prove it and, unless I'm mistaken, you are going to have to help me 'off the record'."

Kleist's expression didn't change. "Why 'off the record'? he asked.

"Because before long there's going to be pressure on you from above to get this case closed quickly. And that means pinning it on me."

It was several seconds before the detective spoke. When he did, he sat back in his chair and linked the fingers of both hands, laying them in his lap like a disgruntled judge about to pronounce sentence. Suddenly, the unmistakeable trace of a grin creased his lips.

"You know something, Brody. Even an 'arrogant son of a bitch' like me knows how to use the internet. So I checked you out. You are a respected journalist. You even won a couple of awards. And you are a published author who writes factual books and gives lectures. So I ask myself a simple question: Why does a man who creates reports and books for a living invent such a poor lie to defend himself from a murder charge? Surely, a professional writer could think of something better? Wouldn't you think?"

"Yes!" said Brody emphatically. "And the reason it sounds so lame is because it's the truth!"

Kleist shrugged. "Maybe. Maybe not. But I still don't think you are telling me everything you know. So let me tell *you* something 'off the record' mister journalist. Until *I* decide where the truth lies, you are in deep trouble. Think about that while you are lying in your cell."

* * * * *

Wednesday, June 26th.

Brody awoke with an aching neck and a stiff shoulder from lying awkwardly on the hard bed. An uncomfortable night of only fitful sleep left him still tired and weary, and opening his eyes to the stark and bleak surroundings of his windowless cell did nothing to relieve his depressed state of mind or alleviate the tension that continued to engulf him. He rinsed his face with cold water at the basin and then cleaned his teeth using the toothbrush and paste that had been provided for his use.

Deprived of his wristwatch he was unsure of the time but within what appeared to be a quarter of an hour or so, the cell door was unlocked and the duty constable brought him a tray containing a cup of coffee, two bread rolls and a large slice of Almkönig cheese.

"Danke" said Brody as the officer placed the tray on the bed. "Wie spät ist?"

The constable made no reply but pulled back his shirt sleeve to show Brody his watch. It was ten minutes to eight.

In the timeless environment of his cell Brody estimated it was around an hour after he had eaten the frugal breakfast that the cell door opened once again and the same taciturn constable ushered him silently upstairs.

He was led back to the same interview room but this time, to his great delight, instead of finding the doughty Inspector Kleist at the desk he discovered Shelley Anderson anxiously awaiting him. As soon as he entered the room, she jumped up from her seat and embraced him. It felt good to feel her in his arms but the moment was short lived as the constable immediately commanded: "Nein. Nein. Verboten" and prised the pair apart.

Taking their respective seats on either side of the desk, Josh reached out to take her proffered hand but the constable again remonstrated with them and ordered there be no touching.

Shelley reluctantly withdrew her arms and retreated them to her own side of the desk. "I've been worried sick about you" she told Josh earnestly. "Are you ok?"

"Well it's not exactly the Hotel Sacher, and the bed is a major punishment in itself, but I guess it could be worse." He managed a grin. "I'm trying to use the experience as the basis of my next detective story. But I don't exactly feel inspired!"

"Very noble, I'm sure. But this is not a fiction and it's not Ian Magen sitting here, it's you! I tried to see you yesterday but they wouldn't allow it. When I turned up again this morning and started badgering, Kleist eventually gave in. But I've only been granted a few minutes and there's a lot to tell you. So please listen carefully." She looked anxiously across the room at the constable, who was now standing by the door and trying to give the impression he was not eavesdropping. "Does he speak English?"

"Not that I know of. But no sense in taking chances. So keep your voice low anyway."

"I've been to the embassy and they are trying to get this whole thing sorted out. But they can't just up and interfere with a police matter so it's going to take some time."

Brody nodded his understanding. "Yes. But it would help if they could get me an English speaking lawyer. I'd rather have my own representation than anyone the court appoints."

"It's being taken care of. But Josh, there's something else I think you should know. I couldn't just sit and wait around. I needed to feel I was at least doing something constructive. So I did some background checking on this Doctor Nazari. I thought it might help us understand what the hell is happening here."

"Yes. Good thinking. What turned up?"

"He's an Iranian physicist." She grimaced and corrected herself. "Or, rather, he *was* an Iranian physicist. He was one of the key figures in their nuclear programme, which he always publically insisted is to create domestic electricity. But the Israelis claim the Iranians are building the bomb. And guess who they name as the leading architect of Teheran's nuclear weapons programme?"

"Nazari" said Brody icily.

"Yes. And there's something else."

Brody was developing a distinct feeling of helplessness, of being caught up in something way beyond his control like a man overwhelmed by a tidal wave and knowing he was destined to drown. "Go on" he told Shelley quietly.

"Last year I was in Paris, organising an exhibition for British artists. There was a Russian dealer called Yurov who was going to make purchases on behalf of several Moscow buyers. Four days after his arrival he was knocked down and killed by a car outside his apartment block. It was a hit and run and they never found the driver. The autopsy report said Yurov's blood alcohol was so high he must have been blind drunk, so it was assumed he'd wandered into the road in some kind of stupor and fallen in front of the car." She lowered her voice further to a quiet whisper. "But it can't have been true. I'd been hosting him at several receptions and the guy didn't drink. He *couldn't*. He had a severe liver problem. He never touched alcohol and only ever drank mineral water."

"So either the autopsy report was fabricated or, more likely, someone had filled him full of alcohol and staged a road accident, is that what you're saying?"

"That's exactly what I'm saying."

Josh was unsure why she was spending precious moments of their limited time together relating this tale. "And this is relevant...how?" he asked.

Because Yurov was on the watch list! We not only wined and dined him, we were also instructed to find his apartment for him. And he ended up dead. Just like Nazari."

The parallel was all too uncomfortably clear. "And did you report the fact he was teetotal at the time?" Brody asked.

"Not to the police, no. But I had a friend in security at the British Embassy. I told him what I knew and he promised to check it out."

"And?"

"It turns out Yurov wasn't just buying and selling art. It was a cover for illicit arms dealing. He was operating on the black market, off-loading heavy duty stuff that went missing when the Soviet Union collapsed."

"So nobody was too upset to see him leave this world for the great art gallery in the sky?"

"That's pretty much what my friend said. He told me it was only a matter of time before he'd be arrested anyway. So he advised me to drop it."

"Seems sensible."

"But this Nazari business has put it all in a new light." She leaned in a little towards him, her face full of anxiety. "Josh, I think your enquiries have scratched the surface of something very serious. We could make random guesses as to who might be behind it all but, if it's leading where I think it's leading, then you really don't want to be involved. We need to get you out of here and completely disassociated with this whole affair."

"Well, right this minute, you'll get no argument from me. But I have a feeling that's not going to be easy. I've been stitched up good and proper; a really professional job. Hell, if I were Kleist, *I'd* think I'm guilty."

They were interrupted by a grunt from the constable standing by the door. They looked up to see him tapping his wristwatch to indicate their time was at an end.

"Eine Minute" said Josh, holding up one finger. He turned back anxiously to Shelley. "You're flying back to London on Sunday morning, right?"

Her eyes widened in wounded surprise. "You must be kidding? You think I'd fly home and leave you here in this shit?"

Brody was touched. Her deep concern was tangible and very real and it gave him great comfort to see how much she cared. "No. I didn't think you would. And I'm grateful. But I need to keep you out of harm's way. If they've been watching me then it's possible they're also now watching you. They may even be tapping your phone. I want to get you home and away from all this."

She managed a slight smile. "I wasn't born yesterday, Josh. I'm one step ahead of you. And SIM cards are cheap. So I'm not going anywhere until we've got you out of this. And that's non-negotiable."

"Thank you" he said softly, reluctantly accepting defeat.

"Now, I know it must be hell, cooped up in here, but you stay positive. You hear me?"

He nodded, suddenly feeling quite emotional and wishing she could stay. "I'll try."

"Zeit!" called the constable from across the room and tapped his wristwatch again."

"Ok, ok, I'm going" Shelley told him and stood. "By the way" she added carelessly. "I used my new SIM card to call your uncle Alan. I told him everything that's happened. He was very concerned and said I was to let him know at once if there is anything he can do."

"Thanks" said Brody. "I appreciate that." He was pleased to know that Alan Denton, with the power of The Independent behind him, was aware of his current predicament and available to help if needed.

The constable was impatiently holding open the door for Shelley and she stepped towards him. Turning in the doorway, she blew Brody a kiss. "Stay strong, Josh... I'll be back." She left and the officer motioned to Brody to stand.

As he was led back to his cell he felt a strange mix of emotions. The news she had brought him about Nazari, and the story of the murder in Paris, compounded his fear that the forces ranged against him were considerable and spread very wide. His chances of achieving simple justice and escaping the net in which they had so deftly trapped him seemed to recede ever further with each new revelation. Yet the brief interlude with Shelley had also lifted his spirits. It wasn't so much that he had an ally, though it filled him with relief to know he was not alone, it was more the bond that he now felt with her. The trauma of his arrest had acted like a pressure-cooker on their fledgling relationship, escalating what would normally have been a slow, gentle, emotional journey into a heightened reality and, despite the force of circumstance, he valued the way it made him feel. He'd never before experienced the kind of innate rapport he sensed between them, the unspoken understanding that was so obvious to each of them. He felt a natural affinity with Shelley that was beyond anything he had previously known; and it felt good. It made him happy. It made him all the more determined to get out of his present predicament and get back to her.

The possibility of release from the depressing confines of his cell became apparent far sooner than Brody could possibly have imagined. In the middle of that afternoon, as he was lying lightly dozing on his bed, he was jerked back into consciousness by the familiar clunk of the key turning in the lock. Josh raised himself to see the door opening and the duty officer lead two men into his cell. They were both dressed in expensive suits and exhibited an instant air of authority, as if they were accustomed to deferential treatment.

"Mr. Brody" said the first man in a clear and sympathetic voice, as he held out his hand in greeting. "My name is Miller. Stephen Miller. I'm from the British Embassy. And this is Rechtsanwalt Hans Steiner. He's a criminal barrister."

The dark-haired Miller was an imposing figure with assertive eyes and a strong, commanding countenance. Fairly tall and slim, there was a precision about him in both appearance and manner. His confident demeanour and well-modulated speech were as well-defined as the careful knot in his tie and the shine on his Jermyn Street black brogues.

As Brody shook Miller's hand and nodded at his Austrian companion, he gave silent thanks for Shelley and her redoubtable persistence. Here, at last, the cavalry had apparently arrived.

"We've just come from a long interview with Inspector Kleist" Stephen Miller continued in business-like fashion. "I don't want to raise your hopes prematurely but, according to Herr Steiner, we should have you out of here in less than twenty-four hours."

"Really?" asked Josh in delighted surprise.

"Yes. Herr Steiner has spent the last hour upstairs reading through the transcript of your interview with Kleist. Perhaps I'd better allow him to explain."

The Austrian nodded politely and addressed Josh in perfect, and beautifully spoken, English. "Technically, the evidence against you is entirely circumstantial and very weak. Firstly, the manner of death was slashed wrists. It takes some considerable minutes to die that way and is therefore an extremely inefficient and unlikely method of murder. So it clearly indicates suicide. Secondly, you yourself admitted you were in the apartment and the police have video footage of you entering and leaving the building that confirms you were there in the time frame you stated. So the critical factor becomes the *time* of death. If the autopsy report places it substantially before your arrival then the police have to explain why you would return to the scene of your crime. If it places it close to the time you spent in the apartment, then they still have to disprove your version of events."

"But isn't that just my word against theirs?" asked Josh.

The Rechtsanwalt allowed himself a slightly satisfied smile. "Not really. In court, I could tear their case to shreds in minutes. There was no trace of a struggle, and no blood anywhere except in the bedroom. More importantly, the blood flow was only around the corpse. So, unless Nazari calmly lay down on his bed, allowed you to murder him by slashing his wrists, and then lay still waiting to die, they have to explain why blood is not all over the place. Not to mention the fact that there are only Nazari's finger prints on the knife."

"But they have mine in the apartment" said Josh. "On a bottle and a glass."

"Precisely" said Steiner. So if you were careful enough not to leave prints on the knife, why would you leave them elsewhere? It makes no logical sense."

All at once Brody felt several pounds lighter. In the barrister's calm and quietly meticulous analysis, it suddenly seemed impossible that anyone could ever have doubted his innocence. His nightmare had been dispelled almost as quickly as it had so unexpectedly overtaken him. "I can't tell you how grateful I am, gentlemen. Truly."

"I'd have liked to walk you out of here straight away" Stephen Miller told him. "But Kleist is insisting on legal clarification. You know the Viennese and their love of rules and regulations. It seemed politic to allow him to save a little face, so we agreed. My best estimate is that you'll be freed no later than tomorrow morning."

Josh sat back heavily on the bed and exhaled with relief. "That's *very* good to know. Thank you!"

The urbane and ever courteous Mr. Miller turned to the Austrian beside him. "Herr Steiner. Perhaps you would be so kind as to give Mr. Brody your card?" The barrister did as he was bidden and reached into the pocket of his waistcoat to produce his business card. "You are to answer no further questions to anyone unless Herr Steiner is present" ordered Miller. "You refuse all interviews and statements and, if pressed, you refer everyone to your lawyer and the contact details on that card."

"I understand" said Josh.

"Stay positive, Mr. Brody. We'll be back as soon as we finalise your release."

The three men shook hands and Josh watched his guests depart. As the constable turned the key in the door to once again lock his cell, the familiar sound was suddenly not quite so daunting. It was strange that his physical surroundings had not altered one iota, but his perception of them had changed radically. They were still an irritation and an inconvenience, but they were no longer the precursor of doom. Brody had no reason to doubt the forthright Mr. Miller or Herr Steiner's skillful analysis of his situation. In less than twenty-four hours he would be walking out of his cell.

That night, despite the discomforts of his Spartan accommodation, Brody managed to sleep reasonably well.

Chapter Thirteen

Thursday, June 27th.

Inspector Dieter Kleist was not a happy man. The autopsy report on Doctor Jalil Nazari had landed on his desk first thing that morning and it provided more problems than answers. The pathologist's tests concluded that death had occurred somewhere between 11 pm on the night of Monday the 24th of June and 2 am in the early hours of Tuesday the 25th. Kleist knew that Brody could prove he was at a performance at the Kammeroper on the Monday evening and that he had a witness to provide him with an alibi until 2.30 on the Tuesday morning. The night porter at the Hotel Post had also confirmed that Brody arrived back at reception well before 3 am as he claimed. Unless Brody's alibi was false, which seemed highly implausible, he couldn't have been in the Tiefer Graben between 11 pm and 2 am. Not only that, but if he *were* responsible for Nazari's death, why would he not have immediately left the city instead of openly returning to the scene of the crime some nine or ten hours later. It made no sense.

Kleist's major difficulty was not so much that Brody was off the hook; he found the English reporter annoying and interfering but had never really pegged him as a murderer; Kleist's big problem was that the pieces didn't fit. Every instinct he possessed told him that Brody held the key to the puzzle and was withholding information. He'd hoped that sweating him in gaol for a few days might coax some answers from the irritating journalist but now, with the British Embassy bringing out the big legal guns like Steiner, he knew it was a lost cause. The Viennese barrister would take one look at the autopsy report and demand Brody's immediate release. Kleist would be back to square one. Worse than that, he now had an additional headache.

The detective had followed Brody's off-the-record advice and conducted a Google image search for photographs of the Lukeba twins. The damned Englishman was right. Fabrice Lukeba was left handed. That opened up a whole new can of worms. The case was officially closed and registered as suicide, and Kleist was sorely tempted to leave it that way, but something in his innate instincts as a policeman told him he couldn't simply sweep it under the carpet. Remounting an investigation into

Lukeba meant dealing with a body that had already been shipped back to Africa and buried, and asking awkward and embarrassing questions that the Austrian government would not wish to be raised.

No. Dieter Kleist was not happy. He was having a very bad day. As his internal telephone rang to tell him that Mr. Miller from the British Embassy was waiting for him in reception, he had the distinct feeling it was about to get worse.

It took under half an hour for the paperwork to be organised and Brody was then brought up from the cells to have his passport, wallet, phones and personal effects restored to him. Unsuccessfully attempting to conceal his intense chagrin, Kleist informed his erstwhile prisoner that he was officially free to go but pointedly added that he was still considered a material witness to the crime scene and that he was not to leave Vienna without prior consent and approval. With the formalities completed, Stephen Miller accompanied Brody out of the building and he stepped onto Wasagaße and into the first natural daylight he'd experienced in almost forty-eight hours.

Despite the pervasive scent of traffic fumes, the city had never smelt quite so good as Brody took a deep breath of the late morning air. "I can't tell you how grateful I am for your help, Mr. Miller" he said thankfully. "I must have put you to a great deal of trouble and I'm sorry."

"It goes with the territory" Miller told him, casually dismissing the apology." He gestured towards a large black Mercedes saloon that was parked a few metres away. "The car is waiting for us."

They crossed the street to the vehicle and Brody eased himself gratefully into the soft leather upholstery of the rear seat, settling back as the driver put the car into gear and the Mercedes smoothly pulled away into the heavy traffic. Miller remained unexpectedly silent and made no conversation.

It wasn't until a few minutes into the drive that Brody realised they had turned onto the Ring and were heading along the banks of the Donaukanal and out of the city centre. He had expected to be driven to the British Embassy but that was in Jauresgaße in the third district and the car was moving in the opposite direction.

"Aren't we going to the embassy?" he asked.

"No" replied Miller quietly, without removing his gaze from the window and the passing streets. "We're heading for Schwechat."

Josh was momentarily thrown. "I'm sorry... I don't understand. I can't go to the airport."

"You needn't worry. All your bags are in the boot. We picked them up yesterday from the British Council offices."

"That's not the point!" snapped Josh. He stopped, a little contrite, and hurriedly corrected himself. "I mean... thank you. You're very kind to take care of my luggage. But what I'm trying to say is that I *can't* leave. Firstly, I have to see Shelley Anderson and let her know I've been released. And secondly, you heard what Kleist said. I'm not allowed to leave Vienna without permission."

Miller slowly turned to him and the trace of a slightly condescending smile creased his narrow lips. "You need not worry about the officious Inspector Kleist and his diktat. Steiner will handle any problems if they arise. As regards informing people of your release, I'm afraid that, for the time being, all contact is out of the question."

Concerned, Brody sat sharply upright. "I don't understand."

A paternalistic look overtook the other man's features that silently, but clearly, declared Josh to be naive. "I am about to take you out of the country *under* the official radar, Mr. Brody. My diplomatic status allows me to manipulate the system sufficiently for us to be long gone before anybody realises you have fled this fair land. But we certainly don't threaten our departure by advertising it. There will be no contact of any description with outsiders until this operation is over and we know you are safe."

Josh felt a cold twinge of anxiety suddenly run through him at the obvious implication. "Safe?" he queried.

"All will become clear, Mr. Brody, once we've had a chance to talk through the whole business of Fabrice Lukeba and Doctor Nazari." Miller tilted his head slightly and cast his eyes warningly in the direction of the back of the chauffeur's head. "In private" he added quietly.

The airport was bustling with activity as the driver eased the large saloon into a temporary parking bay in the drop-off area of the arrivals forecourt. Brody got out of the car and went to the rear, intending to retrieve his luggage from the boot, but Miller forestalled him.

"The chauffeur will take care of the bags" he said as he stepped smartly out of the Mercedes and closed the door behind him.   With a parting nod to the driver, Miller turned on his heel and Brody dutifully followed him through the automatic glass doors marked 'Departures'. The tall diplomat led him through the crowded concourse, passing the long queues at the endless rows of check-in desks, to a discreet door on the far side of the hall where an unobtrusive sign read simply 'Privat'. There was a small electronic keypad on the adjacent wall and Miller typed in a five digit code, whereupon the locking mechanism immediately clicked and released. Brody followed Miller through the door, which quietly swung closed behind them, and was led along a short passageway

"Do you have your passport?" requested Miller as they walked. Brody reached into the inside pocket of his jacket and withdrew his passport. Unsure why it was being requested, he none the less obediently passed it to Miller who added it to his own as they reached the end of the corridor and turned into a small reception area, where a uniformed stewardess sat behind a broad, curved, mahogany desk. The girl looked up with an obligatory welcoming smile as the two men approached and she politely wished them both "Grüß Gott."

Miller handed her their passports and flashed his I.D. He then took a sheet of paper from his suit jacket and placed it on the counter. Brody couldn't see it clearly but it had an official embassy logo at the top and appeared to be some form of travel permit. The stewardess nodded a polite 'thank you'. With Josh in tow, Miller stepped past her desk and through two large glass doors that were ornately patterned in order to render them opaque and prevent prying eyes seeing through them.

As they entered, the thick-pile turquoise carpet instantly deadened their footsteps and gave a hushed ambience to the room. Brody realised he was in an executive lounge but it was unlike any other he had experienced. The plush furniture, ornate glass, gold-trimmed fittings and highly polished mahogany woodwork all silently proclaimed 'luxury'. There were only three other passengers in the room, a man and woman seated together chatting over coffee and a man on a sofa behind an open copy of the Vienna newspaper Wiener Zeitung.

This sumptuous lounge was clearly the province of the seriously wealthy, V.I.P.s, heads of state and visiting royalty. The elegant Miller seemed totally at ease within the opulent surroundings and led Brody to the far corner of the room where, almost as soon as they had lowered themselves into the wide, velvet armchairs, a waitress in a neatly-pressed black dress appeared as if from nowhere. She smiled warmly and waited in servile silence to accept their order.

"Whiskey and soda for me, please" said Miller and then looked across with a raised eyebrow at Josh.

"Actually, after the frugal catering I've suffered in the last two days, I could murder an ice-cold lager beer" Brody told him honestly. With a brief nod and a repeat flashing of her broad smile, the girl left to organise their order.

As the waitress walked back across the room, another passenger entered the lounge. He was a thick-set, black man in his mid-thirties in a dark suit that strained a little against the broad expanse of his shoulders. The girl nodded at him politely and he seated himself on a stool at the bar.

"This is not quite what I was expecting" said Josh, quietly surveying the luxurious environment. "Is this your customary level of travel?"

"Sadly, no. This lounge is reserved for those travelling by private jet" Miller explained. "I normally use a conventional, scheduled flight but, in view of the present circumstances, I felt it prudent to avoid your name appearing on any airline passenger manifest."

Brody felt another ripple of concern flow uncomfortably through him. "Is it as bad as all that?" he asked.

"Let's just say we prefer to err on the side of caution."

"So we are returning to London by private jet?"

"Yes. But we'll be flying to Manston in Kent. It's far less conspicuous. A car will take us to London from there."

"Well I appreciate the prudent approach, not to mention the expense, but either this is all getting seriously out of proportion or there's something you're not telling me. So, as it appears to be *my* neck that's in the noose, I'd like to establish a few cold, hard facts."

"That's only fair" agreed Miller. "But perhaps it would serve you best if you first allow me to give you some background? I think all will become much clearer."

"Please."

The waitress re-appeared with their drinks and placed them onto the small table in front of their chairs. Miller took a short sip of his whiskey and soda, waiting until she had retreated out of earshot and they were both alone, before he spoke.

"I was at the embassy in Vienna, engaged on another matter, when we received word of your predicament. So I was able to deal with it immediately. But I am normally based in London."

"And exactly what is it that you do?" asked Josh.

"Security."

Brody had been through a fairly traumatic couple of days but the stress of his ordeal hadn't deadened his journalist's instincts. He lifted his eyebrows and looked quizzically at his companion. "Intelligence?" he enquired.

"Security" repeated Miller pointedly, evading both confirmation and denial.

"Domestic or foreign?"

"A little of both."

Brody nodded, knowingly. He was fully aware that nobody working within a clandestine organisation would admit to it and that no amount of probing would elicit an answer. He decided that Stephen Miller was almost certainly secret service. "Ok. Then what is someone working for the British Government in 'security' doing springing me from my cell? I mean, don't get me wrong. I'm *very* happy you were there. But why didn't they send some consular official? Surely this is way outside your brief?"

"Normally, yes. But that's why I need to enlighten you. I have been concerned for some little time with certain, shall we say, unusual events. I suspect the people who organised your recent difficulties may well be the same people who have crossed my radar in relation to these matters. If so, then our need for caution is well founded."

"Ok. Now you're *really* beginning to worry me" said Brody and took a deep swig of his cold lager. "Do I take it you know who is behind all this?"

"Let's just say I have some suspicions." Miller paused, carefully observing Brody's troubled countenance. Eventually he asked: "Who do *you* think is behind it?"

Josh shrugged. "I can only make a guess. But, from what I have been able to establish, the guys who framed me must be well financed, have a wide-ranging operation, and can exert influence in high places. So, I'm thinking... C.I.A.?... Mossad?... Or maybe it's just some Mafia-like organisation? I really don't know. But the closer I get, the less I like what I'm discovering. And it's scary stuff. I mean, how do we know they're not watching us right now? Maybe they tailed us here from Wasagaße?" He cast a quick glance around the lounge and then turned back to his companion. "How do we know the big black guy seated at the bar, the one who came in after us, isn't one of them?"

Miller gave a slight smile. "Because he works for me. He covered our arrival. Now he's keeping tabs on us here and he'll be with us on the plane. If anyone had been following us, he would know."

Brody sat back with a heavy sigh. "I'm not sure whether that's a comfort or if the fact that you think he's necessary scares me all the more."

"I understand. But don't let it worry you. It's merely a precaution."

"Against whom?... Or what?" asked Josh despondently.

Miller didn't answer. He gazed at Brody for a few seconds and his expression hardened, as though he were making a decision as to whether or not to speak. "Do you know what's meant by the 'need to know' principle?" he finally asked.

"Yes, I think so" replied Josh quietly.

"It's an essential element of defence. No democracy can run an efficient intelligence service without it. Openness is completely contrary to security. The public and, dare I say it, your brethren in the press, jump up and down in vociferous protest whenever they discover we've broken the rules but, if we didn't occasionally transgress, there'd be chaos. We'd be over-run by Al Quaeda tomorrow if we *actually* ran our defences according to some ethical agenda of transparency. So, quite often, we need to undertake actions that are better left undisclosed. That means adopting the 'need to know' principle." He took a short sip of his whiskey and soda. "It's all about links in the chain. Provided each link carries out its own task efficiently, then it's not necessary to know what any other link in the chain is doing; but the overall job gets done. That's how intelligence and security functions. And it couldn't work any other way."

Brody put down his lager and looked questioningly at Miller. "I'm not sure there isn't a whole other debate about ethics and morality in there but, for the moment, let's set that to one side. Are you telling me that the people who framed me are working in some form of clandestine intelligence operation? That I'm right? That this is probably C.I.A. or something?"

Miller shook his head. "No. But, if my suspicions are correct, I think it might be part of the answer."

Brody the guy who'd just been framed for a murder he didn't commit, was feeling increasingly nervous. Brody the journalist, was uncontrollably intrigued. "I think it's cards on the table time, Mr. Miller, don't you?" he said flatly. "I have a feeling you're as keen to know why I was in Vienna, and what I've found out, as I am to know about these suspicions of yours."

"Not here" said Miller abruptly. "You're right... But we'll talk on the plane."

The twin Honeywell TFE731 engines roared as the pilot throttled the controls and the Lear 45 lifted effortlessly off the runway, its nose tilted sharply towards the open sky.

Only three of the eight, plush, beige leather seats were occupied. Miller and Brody sat alongside one another at the front of the aircraft. The anonymous black stranger who had covered their arrival and entry into the executive lounge was with them but had not yet been introduced. With a silent nod of acknowledgement to Brody, he had taken his place at the rear of the plane, where he now sat contentedly reading a magazine.

Once airborne, the solitary stewardess took their order for drinks. Josh noticed that her dark blue uniform bore a small company emblem of a feathered wing above a roundel with the name *Global-Jet* emblazoned beneath it, so he presumed the aircraft had been chartered for the trip. But he asked no questions. This time, instead of a beer, he joined Miller in ordering a whiskey and soda. The girl brought their drinks and told them food would be served shortly.

"Something you said earlier, interested me" Miller said.

"Oh?"

"About a moral and ethical debate as to the secret world."

"Well, with all due respect to present company, some of us feel that anything undertaken by the government, the armed forces or the security services, is actually being done in *our* name, not to mention at *our* expense. So there is a very valid argument that says the people who 'need to know' what's going on is actually the public."

Miller nodded. "Mmmm" he murmured slowly. "Very noble... and also very naive."

Brody was about to come back at him with a rejoinder but Miller cut him short. "I'm sure there's little I could say to influence a committed libertarian such as yourself so, before we enter into fruitless discussion, allow me to relate a little story. It might at least illustrate how I was converted from once thinking just as you do, to my present acceptance of hard realities. May I do that?"

"Please" said Josh invitingly.

Miller took a sip of his whiskey and soda and then held the glass between the fingers of both hands, rotating it thoughtfully. "Many years ago I was a student in London, entering my first year at University. One evening I went with a group of friends to the Almeida to see a play called *All For Love*. Do you know it?"

Brody nodded. "I know *of* it. It's John Dryden isn't it?"

"Yes. It's a seventeenth century play, written in blank verse. It's a long piece; in five acts. But the time flew by. Dianna Rigg was the star, and she and the entire cast were excellent. It was a fine production and, as you might expect, was hugely successful; great reviews and full houses. Yet at the time, the Almeida, like all theatre companies, was completely strapped for cash. It never knew from one week to the next how long it might be able to survive and was entirely dependent upon subsidy and support."

"I dare say it still is" commented Josh.

"Exactly. A theatre that continually produces work of that quality, and yet it is permanently holding out a begging bowl. And that's what made such an impact on me. You see, that same Saturday night, the London Palladium was housing a sell-out production of *Joseph and The Amazing Technicolour Dreamcoat* and the show that was topping the T.V. ratings was a quiz programme called *Blind Date*. Now I have nothing against popular T.V. shows and nothing against commercial musicals. In fact I took my own nephew and niece to see *Joseph* and found it very entertaining. But it made me realise how important it is that popular taste doesn't eclipse and extinguish great art like Dryden's play."

"Well that's why we have subsidies" interjected Brody. "To ensure that art survives."

The trace of a smile formed on Miller's lips. "Indeed. And that's why, on that distant Saturday night, my fervent democratic and social values began to unravel. You see, many millions of tax-payers regularly watched that T.V. programme and other shows like it. By comparison, the numbers who go to the opera, to art galleries or the ballet, are a mere handful. And those like me, who went to see that Dryden play, are even fewer; a drop in the ocean. So what is so democratic about spending the majority of the arts budget on works that only the minority of the population wants to see and experience? At that time, I was a student; I contributed nothing to the tax coffers. But I'd have been the first one to the barricades to protest if the government had removed the subsidy that made that play possible."

"But that's how we structure society" argued Josh. "Everybody contributes to the common pot and then all needs are catered for. That's what makes us civilised, isn't it?"

"Yes. And that's precisely my point. Somebody somewhere makes a decision about what those needs are and what priority they are given. It's anything *but* democratic. Some small committee of a few individuals is holding the purse strings and deciding what is good for us and what is not. That is elitism. And, as unpalatable as it might be, I realised that night that it was essential. Without it, there'd be no performances of Dryden and we'd all be watching a diet of crass T.V. programmes and commercial theatre."

Brody was beginning to get an uncomfortable sense of where this particular philosophical ideology might be leading. "So, you're basically telling me that democracy occasionally needs to be side-stepped. Is that what you're saying?"

"I'm saying that it *is* side-stepped. Constantly. Because the vast majority of the populace constitutes the lowest common denominator. And the future of culture, art and science rests with a *very* small percentage. So, ultimately, the people in power have to make decisions about what is good and what is bad for the public at large."

"Isn't that one step away from Fascism and dictatorship" asked Brody?"

"Yes. It is. Abhorrent, isn't it? And that's why that Saturday night had such a profound effect on me. I realised that if we were not to drift towards that kind of extremism, then my egalitarian beliefs were going to have to accommodate practical compromises."

Brody was far from convinced. "Is that a convoluted way of saying you sold out?"

Miller allowed himself a slight laugh. "No. It's a way of saying that I grew up." He looked Brody squarely in the eye. "And that's why I told you that openness is completely contrary to security. There are sometimes things that have to be done for the greater good that do not stand up to public scrutiny." He leaned forward a little in his seat and his tone suddenly became sombre and serious. "And I think you've run into a group of people who have extended that argument and are acting upon it."

Brody took a fortifying swig of his whiskey as the truth finally began to settle on him. "Wait a minute" he said with a heavy sigh. "Let me get this straight. Your little arts and philosophy lecture was your way of gearing up to tell me that we're not necessarily dealing with the bad guys here? We might be dealing with the good guys who may have just been 'over-stepping the mark'? Is that it?"

"I'm telling you that, if my suspicions are correct, then we may not simply be dealing with a few villains that we can arrest and bring to trial. I think you may have unfortunately stumbled into a legitimate group, but one that is operating of its own volition and being concealed by the 'need to know' principle."

Brody considered this revelation carefully. "That makes them a pretty scary bunch, doesn't it?"

"It means we have to tread very cautiously, yes."

"But I'm stuck in the middle of this thing. And once they know the police have let me go, they're going to be hot on my tail. So where does that leave *me*?

"As soon as we get you back to London, we give you a full debriefing. I need to know everything you can tell me about your visit to Nazari's apartment and everything you've got on the Lukeba suicide. If we put it all together with what I've already established, then we might get a conclusive picture of just what, or whom, we're facing."

Brody put his hands to his head and rubbed his temples in exasperation. The more he learned, the more he wished he'd never started down this particular road.

The stewardess reappeared carrying two meal trays and served them food, so the discussion was abandoned and it seemed to be tacitly agreed that nothing further would be said until they were safely back in London.

Half an hour later, the captain of the plane spoke over the address system to tell them the aircraft was benefiting from a strong tail wind and he expected to make better time than expected. True to his word, the plane eventually touched down at Manston Airport fifteen minutes ahead of schedule.

Brody was surprised at how quickly and smoothly the departure procedure was completed. He was well accustomed to long waits at baggage carousels and queues at immigration and passport checks, so it was a novel experience to find that travellers by private jet suffered no such irritations. As they descended from the aircraft, a uniformed airport hostess met them at the foot of the stairway while a porter was already offloading their bags from the hold before they stepped onto the tarmac.

Escorted by the hostess, Miller, Brody and the minder from the rear of the plane, whose name Josh had now learned was Carter, were whisked through immigration without a question being asked and the porter pushing their luggage trolley followed close on their heels. Two minutes later they were in the concourse car park to be met by a waiting Jaguar XF saloon, with gleaming black paintwork and darkened window glass. A navy-blue Ford Focus was parked with its engine idling a few metres away and the minder, Carter, climbed into its front passenger seat as Miller and Brody seated themselves in the Jag. With the bags loaded, the two vehicles set off in convoy into the green of the Kent countryside, making their way along the A299, heading for the M2 motorway.

Brody was in a deeply reflective mood and, for most of the journey, said very little. He'd endured the dangers of Egypt and Libya, and knew what it was like to be under fire, but in conflict zones it was usually fairly clear as to who was who and what their objectives were. In his present predicament, he had only a vague notion as to who the enemy might be and even less of an idea as to how they might strike. There were no green zones or red zones, no safe areas, no clear lines of demarcation as to what was home ground and where bandit territory began. If Miller's assumptions were right, and Brody had stumbled into some rogue, clandestine operation by members of a legitimate security service, then, in theory, their reach might be limitless. That meant there was nowhere to hide. It was a frightening prospect.

"Do you know what puzzles me most?" he suddenly said to Miller beside him. "The whole Nazari business. It makes very little sense. The message to go to the apartment was delivered to me the previous day, when we know Nazari was still alive. So his death was planned and scheduled. But if they wanted to put me in the frame and get me arrested, why make it look like suicide? Why not make it look like what it was? A murder."

"Yes, it's puzzling" agreed Miller. "My only guess is that they were building your credibility as a killer. Implying that *you* had made it look like suicide to try and cover your own tracks."

It was a sobering thought and Brody suddenly experienced a threatening sense of isolation, as if he were an animal caught in a trap, helplessly awaiting the arrival of the hunter. It made him immediately think of his family and he felt the need to speak to Saffy and hear her voice. He reached into his inside pocket for his wallet. Opening it, he withdrew the SIM card he had bought in London. He took his mobile from his jacket and unclipped the back cover in order to remove the Austrian SIM and replace it.

"What are you doing?" enquired Miller.

"I need to call my ex-wife and daughter. They were expecting me to be home on Tuesday evening. They'll be wondering why I haven't called. I need to let them know I'm ok."

Miller gave a slight shake of his head. "As I told you before. I'm afraid outside contact is out of the question" he said gently.

"Yes, I understand. But this is a pay-as-you-go SIM. I bought it over the counter; so nobody has this number. It can't be monitored."

"No" agreed Miller. "But your ex-wife's phone might be."

Brody was crestfallen. He hadn't considered that possibility and his concern showed clearly in the look of deep disappointment that instantly covered his face. He knew Miller was right and, as badly as he needed to hear Saffy's voice, the last thing he wanted was to bring Kass and his daughter onto the radar of his adversaries. "I hadn't thought of that" he said sombrely. "I knew they were listening in to *my* phone, but it didn't occur to me that they might be covering the line at home."

"They're probably not" said Miller encouragingly. "But it's a risk we don't need to take."

Brody silently nodded his understanding.

The normally undemonstrative Miller suddenly appeared touched by Brody's evident sadness. He checked his watch and then leaned forward in his seat and addressed the driver. "Where exactly are we?"

"A few miles this side of Dartford, sir" replied the chauffeur.

"Take the M25 and head for the tunnel, will you?"

"As you wish, sir."

Miller turned to his disconsolate companion. "Westcliff is a detour of only a few miles. I'll call our watchers in the car behind and we'll set up something."

"Thank you" said Josh sincerely as Miller took out his phone and began to call Carter in the trailing car. "I appreciate it."

Chapter Fourteen

The procedure was simple but effective. The Jaguar dropped Miller and Brody outside the group of seafront cafés known as The Arches and they entered The Mermaid, Saffy's favourite. By prior agreement, Stephen Miller took a place at a pavement table and Brody made his way inside to the seating at the rear. While the two men were separately ordering coffee, the minder Carter was half a mile away, ringing the doorbell of the Brody family apartment.

Kassia at first assumed the sound of the bell heralded yet another door-to-door salesman, probably offering grants to remove the flat's beautiful Victorian wooden window frames and replace them with characterless double-glazing; but the build and general demeanour of the man she found standing in her doorway instantly disabused her of the notion.

"Mrs. Brody?" he asked unemotionally.

"Yes."

"I have a message for you. Mr. Brody will be in The Mermaid café for the next half an hour. He would like you and your daughter to meet him there."

Kassia was confused. She had long ago learned to expect the unexpected in anything involving her ex-husband but this was particularly puzzling. "I don't understand. Why hasn't he called me? And who are you? Why isn't he here himself?"

Carter's impassive expression didn't alter and his dark brown eyes looked piercingly at his inquisitor. "I am a friend of his. He will explain everything to you. But please be quick. He doesn't have much time." Carter turned and began to walk back down the front path towards his waiting car.

Alarm bells were starting to ring and Kassia called after the retreating messenger. "Wait a minute! You can't just leave. What's all this about?"

Carter turned and pointed to his wristwatch. "Half an hour" he said slowly and then departed.

Less than five minutes later, Kassia herself was walking down the front path with an inquisitive Saffy at her side, holding her hand.

"Where are we going?" the child asked, a little nonplussed by her mother's obvious haste.

"To see Daddy."

The little girl was delighted. "Where is he?"

"The Mermaid." Kassia was trying hard to sound nonchalant and hide the concern she was feeling.

"Oooh. Can I have a milkshake?"

"Yes. Whatever you want."

Content that their hurried pace was merely bringing her closer to her promised treat, Saffy obediently accelerated her stride to keep up with her anguished mother. It was only a short walk along the promenade to The Arches and they covered the distance in under ten minutes. As they entered the café and Saffy caught sight of her father, she ran to greet him with open arms and a cry of "Daddy!"

Scooping her up into his embrace, Josh squeezed her tightly, never more grateful for the feel of her little body close to him. She fired off a dozen excited questions, wanting to know about his trip and what he had done, but her chief concern appeared to be whether or not he had remembered to buy the promised chocolates for her and her friend Chloe. Josh assured her they were in his suitcase and that he would nip back to the car and fetch them for her before they parted.

"Saffy. Why don't you go to the cabinet and pick out a nice cake?" said Kassia. "One for you and one for me."

"And one for Daddy?"

"Yes. Of course."

Kassia waited until the little girl was out of earshot and fully occupied with the delights of the patisserie display.

"What the hell is all this about?" she whispered vehemently, her voice ringing with genuine anxiety rather than anger.

Josh reached across the marble table-top and gently held her arm. "I'm sorry about this, Kass. But I have to explain before Saffy gets back so please listen carefully. It's all going to be fine. It's just that the story I'm working on has thrown up some trouble and I need to keep a low profile until it's sorted out. The authorities are helping me and this will all be over soon. But, just to be ultra-cautious, I don't want to be seen coming to your flat. I don't want to draw attention to you and Saffy."

This was hardly a comfort. "What do you mean you 'don't want to be seen'?" Her face creased in further incredulity as the logical conclusion slotted uncomfortably into place. "Are you being followed?"

"No... I'm just being careful." He was vainly trying to sound convincing but the slight hesitation before he answered told her all she needed to know.

Kassia slowly shook her head, and real fear was evident in her eyes. "Oh my God, Josh. What have you done? Why did you come here?"

"I needed to see you and Saffy" he protested. "And there's nothing to worry about. It's all fine. I would never put you or her at risk, you know that."

"If there was no risk, you could have knocked on the front door like any normal parent" she hissed at him. "How dare you drag us into harm's way?!"

"Please Kass. Try to understand..."

He broke off, unable to continue as Saffy returned excitedly to the table. "I chose strawberry for me and Dad and cheesecake for you Mum" she declared enthusiastically. "Can I have a milkshake now?"

"No" snapped Kassia. "We'll take the cakes with us in a box. We have to leave now."

"But you promised!" complained the little girl bitterly. "And we only just got here. Why do we have to go?"

Brody reached out and lifted her onto his lap. "Well, Mum has lots to do, darling. But I'm sure there's enough time for a milkshake." He lifted his eyes accusingly to his ex-wife. "Isn't there?"

Kassia reluctantly nodded. "All right. Just one" she said unwillingly, deciding to avoid unconvincing explanations to her daughter. The child was young but nobody's fool, and she had long since learned to detect the tension that could arise between her parents and mastered the art of manipulating it. As uncomfortable as Kassia felt, she knew it was the easier option to allow the child to stay a little longer.

The next twenty minutes passed in overtly polite conversation as both adults sought to minimise the stress of the meeting and concentrate on Saffy. The little girl told her father about school, her friend Chloe, the newly acquired rabbit, which for some unaccountable reason she had christened Marmaduke, and anything and everything to do with the full and ever eventful life of a seven year old. Brody was greatly comforted simply to sit and listen to her talk. Amongst all the violence and detritus of life that was all too often the focus of his reporting, her innocence was the one thing that gave him a sense of optimism and allowed him to believe in hope for humanity.

As soon as she felt a suitable interval had elapsed and the moment was apposite, Kassia told her protesting daughter it was time to leave.

Brody stood and gave Saffy a final hug. "Be a good girl for mummy." He looked up at his ex-wife. "I'll be in touch" he said as reassuringly as he could. "And if you need to reach me, use this." He handed her a slip of paper on which he had written the number of his untraceable pay-as-you-go phone. "But please only call me from a call box. Don't use your mobile or the home phone."

With a look of disbelief, Kassia reluctantly accepted the note and nodded her head despondently. To hide her words from Saffy, she reached in as though kissing Josh on the cheek. "You will not contact us again until this is over" she whispered harshly in his ear. "Or I'll take her away and you won't know where we are."

Before Brody could respond, she pulled back and took her daughter by the hand. "Say goodbye, darling."

To the little girl's chagrin, she took her leave of her father and was swiftly led by the hand out of the café and onto the promenade. Brody sank back disappointedly into his seat. It had not been the reunion he had wanted or anticipated but, the more he thought about it, the more he could see his ex-wife's point of view and understood her fear. She was right. His desire to see Saffy should not have outweighed his natural caution or the need to keep her completely removed from the circumstances that had overtaken him. He was sure the meeting had been harmless. Stephen Miller would never have allowed it if there was any risk involved. Yet, only vaguely appraised of the facts, Kassia could not be expected to understand. He should not have come. He should have stayed away. And that cold reality only served to make him even more aware of the gulf between himself and the daughter he loved so much. It depressed him mightily.

"It didn't go well?" enquired Miller as he took the seat opposite Josh and saw his sad expression.

Brody shrugged. "It was good to see my daughter. Thanks for that. But I think it's best if I have no further contact until all this is over."

Miller nodded. "Very wise."

"Oh, damn!" exclaimed Josh. "I forgot to give her the chocolates."

Miller raised an eyebrow.

"Mozart Kugeln. Little chocolate balls. I promised I'd bring them back for her. There still in my bloody suitcase."

"I shouldn't worry" said Miller reassuringly. In a few days you'll be back. You can give them to her then."

The journey into London along the A13 was contrary to the flow of evening traffic, which was mostly heading out of the capital and into the commuter towns of Essex, so the Jaguar made good time. Brody passed almost the entire drive in silence and Miller was content to leave him alone with his thoughts. When the car left the Highway and looped through Minories to turn in front of The Tower of London, Brody checked his watch. It was approaching 7 pm. It had been a long and eventful day and he was looking forward to the end of his journey, not to mention an evening meal that the pangs in his stomach were informing him was long overdue.

"I could do with something to eat" he announced to Miller.

"Yes. Me too. But we're almost there. We'll organise dinner as soon as we arrive."

Unsure exactly where 'there' might be, and choosing not to enquire, Brody settled back in his seat to wait out the last stage of his mystery tour. The Jaguar travelled the length of the Embankment and rounded Parliament Square to head into Victoria Street. As the well-known landmarks flashed by Brody's window, the customary sights and sounds of the capital's ever crowded streets brought undeniable relief. It felt good to be back on his home territory. Although his situation was still one of great uncertainty, there was at least some sense of security about being on familiar ground.

Just before the road reached the main junction in front of Victoria Station, the driver turned off into Carlisle Place and steered the Jaguar through the back turnings, around the side of Westminster Cathedral, and into Morpeth Terrace. He brought the saloon to a gentle halt in a resident's parking bay at the far end of the narrow road.

Brody looked out to find himself in a street of elegant, six-story, Victorian redbrick apartment blocks. The main entrances to each identical terrace were ornate plaster-work porch-ways, where half a dozen polished marble steps led to sturdy, oak-framed front doors. At pavement level each building was fronted with wrought iron railings, all decorated with well-tended flower boxes that bloomed above the well of the basement flats below. It was a far cry from Brody's tiny Soho eyrie above a pole-dancing club.

Constructed in an age when the street would have echoed to the regular clip-clop of horses pulling Hansom cabs, the apartments had originally housed the newly emerging Victorian middle class, where top-hatted men in frock coats and their long-skirted wives in broad bonnets propelled the surge in commerce and business that fuelled the Empire. The appalling price of property in modern day London meant that such dwellings were now far from the reach of mere middle class entrepreneurs. This had become the land of the rich and seriously wealthy.

Entering the last block on the right, Miller led Brody through the vestibule. Producing a set of keys from his pocket, he opened the door to flat three on the ground floor. The inside of the apartment was impressive. Whoever had been responsible for the decor and furnishings had tastefully installed modern fixtures and fittings without detracting from the natural elegance of the Victorian high ceilings and tall windows. A large green Chesterfield leather suite took up the centre of the lounge and the casements were hung with matching green velvet drapes. The plain walls were painted in a quiet cream colour and hung with prints depicting London scenes. There was a large television set in one corner, facing a pair of double-doors that opened into an adjacent dining room, where a table was laid in readiness for a meal.

"Make yourself at home" Miller invited. "Carter will bring in the bags and show you to your room."

"When you said we were going to a 'safe house', I envisaged a small semi in Hounslow, somewhere out near Heathrow airport" Brody told him as he gazed in surprise at his well-appointed surroundings. "This is not exactly what I expected."

Miller allowed himself a contented grin. "Well, there are many drawbacks to working for Her Majesty's government, but at least it's been around long enough to acquire some decent accommodation for its humble servants."

"And how does one of its humble servants get to commandeer such an elegant safe house?" asked Brody pointedly. He still had no notion as to who Miller really was, and even less of an idea of his official status or rank, but the private jet, the minder Carter, and now the expensive apartment in S.W.1 left little room for speculation or doubt. Miller had to be a senior officer in S.I.S., or M.I.6 as it was more commonly known. "Care to account for your undeniable influence?"

As they ate, Brody revealed most of what he knew about Dikembe and Fabrice Lukeba and Miller listened attentively, only occasionally interrupting to check on minor details. The main course was followed by baked cheesecake and coffee and by the end of the meal, when they retired to the lounge with a glass of Armagnac brandy, Miller knew almost as much about Brody's investigation as Josh did himself.

What the inquisitive Miller did *not* know, were the names of Brody's contacts. Like any good journalist, Josh protected the identity of his sources. Luke Harvey, Daniel Fowler and his escort Sophie, Sean Finnegan and Gerhard Weber were all referred to in the third person or simply as 'my connection'. The one person Brody could not exclude from his report was Shelley Anderson, who had first rung alarm bells at the embassy in Vienna and was obviously already known to Miller, but he avoided all mention of her in connection with Yurov and Paris, leaving Miller to infer that Brody's own research had turned up the goods on the Russian's murder.

"This was quite a formidable undertaking" said Miller thoughtfully. "Doesn't a freelance like you normally acquire backing for something this big? Surely you must have approached a T.V. station or a national newspaper?"

Brody nodded. "Yes. I took it to The Independent" he confided. "Unofficially, though. I called in a few favours so I had help in reserve if I needed it."

"Very sensible. I'd have done the same."

"The great irony of course is that I was *that* close to walking away from the whole affair" said Brody, holding up his hand to Miller and forming a slight gap between his thumb and forefinger. "But once I knew I was being followed and that someone was very concerned about the questions I was asking, there had to be substance to my suspicions. So I went digging."

"But do you have *proof?*" asked Miller emphatically. "The circumstantial evidence may be strong but to give me the leverage I need to get these monkeys off your back, I need proof. Nothing less will frighten them away."

It was time for Brody to reveal his trump card. "I have video footage, stills photographs and a time sheet that prove Fabrice Lukeba was shot in his hotel room by a female assassin."

Miller sat bolt upright. Brody couldn't tell if the man's concentrated expression signified relief or concern but the tangible tension in the ensuing silence, as Miller pensively set down his brandy glass and then slowly stood, demonstrated the full import of this new information. Preoccupied, Miller turned and stepped towards the large window frame, gazing through the fine net curtain into the late evening shadows that were enveloping the street outside. It was several seconds before he spoke.

"Do you have this proof with you?" he asked Brody unemotionally over his shoulder.

"No. But it's safe."

Miller turned to face him. "If I'm to get you out of harm's way, then I need this evidence as a matter of urgency."

Josh nodded. "I can get it within twenty-four hours. Two days at the most. But first I'd like to know just who are these 'monkeys' on my back, as you put it? And how can you remove them? What is it you haven't told me?"

Stephen Miller thought for a moment and walked across the room, as though carefully weighing his words before declaring his hand. He stopped in front of the empty fireplace and stood with his back to the mantelshelf.

"What do you know about Yurov?"

"He was an arms dealer masquerading as a buyer of art."

"Correct. And Dr. Nazari?"

"A scientist, whom the Israelis cite as developing a nuclear bomb for Iran."

"Again, correct. And you are obviously well acquainted with the crimes of the Lukeba brothers. So what does that tell us?"

Brody shrugged. "They were all..." he broke off his sentence as the true significance of the obvious connection suddenly struck him. He looked up at Miller. "They were all *bad* guys."

"Exactly."

"And not many people would be mourning their departure from this world."

Miller nodded. "On the contrary. A great many would be celebrating."

Brody eased himself back into his chair and took a swig of Armagnac. "Are you telling me...?"

Miller interrupted. "I'm not in a position to tell you anything. But I will remind you of our previous conversation. The 'need to know' principle means that orders are usually legitimately carried out by operatives who know only what they have been told to do; not 'why' they are doing it."

"I'm not sure I like where this is heading" said Brody. "But carry on."

"Certain services, like the C.I.A. and Mossad, are able to publically declare their defence of their nation states. After the hostage killings at the Munich Olympics in '72, the Israelis made no secret that they would pursue and assassinate every single identified kidnapper. And they did. After 9/11, the C.I.A. announced they would hunt down and kill Bin Laden. It took them ten years, but they did it. But in many countries, including the United Kingdom, such actions would not have been possible."

Brody raised his eyebrows. "Why not?"

"Because no one in any of our security services can authorise a state assassination. Only an elected member of government, which means a cabinet minister, can take the responsibility for deciding when a killing is necessary in the interest of national safety. And nobody ever does because it would have to stand up to later public scrutiny."

Brody was not sure he fully understood. "You mean, if 9/11 had happened in London instead of New York, we wouldn't have mounted the operation against Bin Laden?"

"Oh, I'm sure we would have mounted the operation, but it would have been to arrest him and put him on trial. It would *not* have been sanctioned to kill him. It couldn't be. Unlike the U.S. or Israel, it's against the law of the land. Even a self-confessed mass murderer like Bin Laden is assumed innocent under law until proven guilty and must be offered a fair trial."

"But that would mean havoc!" protested Josh. "If the Yanks had put Bin laden in gaol, and gone through the motions of a trial, there would have been Christ knows how many bombings and atrocities all around the globe to try and force his release! His followers would have caused hundreds or maybe thousands of more deaths."

Miller nodded. "Precisely. There was no way he could have been brought back alive. So, to answer your question, had it been a British operation, we'd have organised a cover story. An S.A.S. bullet would have dispatched him on the ground at first sight, but there would have been an official explanation of 'shot while trying to resist arrest'." He fixed Brody squarely in the eye. "It's what I was trying to explain to you earlier. Sometimes, for the benefit of the greater good, the expediency of the moment has to take precedence over the rules."

Despite the warmth of the summer evening, Brody felt a distinct chill coursing through his body. "So Yurov, Nazari and the Lukebas were all a matter of 'expediency'. And I got in the way. Is that where we're at?"

"I don't have an official response" Miller told him coldly. "But, in your position, my assumptions would not be dissimilar to your own."

"But who's watching the watchers?" protested Josh. "This is unchecked vigilantism. It's a one way ticket to chaos!"

"Agreed" snapped Miller. "That's why I need to put a stop to it."

"How?" Brody demanded. "If this is all cover-up upon cover-up, how do you propose to reach whomever is responsible? How can you get to them to expose what they've been doing?"

"Up until now, I couldn't. I had a series of unlikely co-incidences and some well-founded suspicions but I lacked the proof. Now, thanks to your intervention, I can lay the evidence in front of the right people."

"And they can get the dogs of war off my tail?"

"The people pursuing you are merely foot soldiers. They do as they're told without knowing why. So we have to tackle this from the top down. Once we remove the head of the beast, the rest of it dissolves. And you can resume your former life."

"It sounds deceptively simple" said Brody, the doubt very evident in his voice. "And I'd like to believe it. But there must be some pretty big guns behind what's been going on. I'm not sure they'll roll over so easily, are you?"

"That's *my* responsibility" Miller told him confidently. "Yours is to provide the proof." There was a slight pause before he spoke again. "Where is it?"

"I posted it. To a London address. If went first class so it ought to have arrived by now. I can pick it up tomorrow."

"You need to stay under wraps. We'll give the address to Carter and he'll collect it for you."

Josh gave a wry smile. "He can't. I sent strict instructions that it was only to be released to me."

Miller shrugged. "Ok. That was sensible, I suppose. But Carter and an extra man will go with you. No point in running unnecessary risks now that we're in the home straight."

"That's fine by me" Josh told him, welcoming the protection. He raised his brandy glass. "To the home straight."

Stephen Miller bent and picked up his own drink and joined the toast.

Brody looked up across the top of his glass. "Can we get a message to Shelley Anderson at The British Council in Vienna? She must be wondering what the hell has happened to me by now. I'd just like her to know I'm ok. Or is that out of bounds?"

"It wouldn't be wise" Miller told him regretfully. "The only safe option is total operational silence until this is all over. I'm sure she'll understand once you are able to explain. And, all being well, you'll be free to get in touch in a few days and thank her yourself. You just need to be a little patient."

Josh reluctantly agreed. "Ok. I understand. In that case, if it's all right with you, I think I'll turn in. It's been a tiring day."

"Of course. We'll speak again in the morning. Mrs. Rawlings usually serves breakfast at around 8.30."

"Thank you." Brody stood. "Then I'll say 'good night'." He drained the last of his brandy and set down his glass. With a final, silent nod to Miller, he turned and made his way to his bedroom.

The warmth and softness of the bed was a welcome haven of relief after the stark discomforts of the Vienna prison cell and, for the first time in more than three days, Josh felt he would be able to achieve restful sleep. With his head on the pillow, he gazed up at the shadows of the high Victorian ceiling. Hopefully, Miller was right. In a little while his ordeal would be over and he would be free to contact Shelley and pick-up the threads of their fledgling relationship. Miller was clearly a capable man and obviously held significant rank in the echelons of the security services. If the Lukebas and Nazari were assassinated by some rogue element within the covert word, there was good reason to believe that Miller could reach the appropriate hierarchy and put a stop to its vigilante operations.

Brody should have been greatly relieved and feeling optimistic. But his journalist's instincts were nagging at him. He was certain Miller was carefully rationing what he would and would not reveal and, as a reporter, it bothered him that he still didn't have all the facts. As he wrestled with his concerns, his eyelids became heavy and he finally slipped into much needed sleep.

Chapter Fifteen

Friday, June 28th.

Brody awoke before the alarm went off. Hauling himself out from under the duvet, he crossed the room and pulled back the drapes on the tall French windows to discover the outside garden bathed in clear, bright sunlight. It was going to be a beautiful summer's day and, after a full night's rest, Brody was in a determined frame of mind and keen to face it. He tried the handle, intending to open the door and let a flood of fresh morning air into the room, but it was locked.

He quickly showered and dressed and made his way to the kitchen where he found a place set for him at the broad oak table that sat in the centre of the room. Mrs. Rawlings was standing at the large stove, adding a light trickle of olive oil to an iron frying pan.

"Good morning, sir" she wished him as he entered. "There's porridge in the saucepan and fresh coffee in the pot. How do you like your eggs and bacon?"

"Any way it comes" replied Josh as he took his seat and helped himself to a mug of black coffee. "Is Mr. Miller not joining us?"

"The gentleman breakfasted early and went out, sir. He said he'll be back in an hour or two. The other gentleman also ate early but he is in the lounge if you need him."

The breakfast was good and Josh ate his fill. Carter appeared briefly to help himself to coffee but was as uncommunicative as ever and offered only a curt 'morning' before retreating to the lounge with his replenished cup.

Brody thanked Mrs. Rawlings for the meal and then went back to his room. His chin sported several days' growth of stubble and he wanted to shave. In the bathroom he filled the sink with hot water, soaped his face, and pulled a new Bic plastic razor from his toilet bag to deal with his emerging beard. He always wet shaved and disdained the use of electric razors, which irritated his skin and were never as efficient as a blade. As he watched his reflection in the mirror above the basin, he was thinking about Shelley and wondering how long it would be before he could see her again when he momentarily lost concentration and the sharp, new razor nicked his cheek.

"Damn!" he cursed as he hurriedly rinsed away the lather to inspect the damage. The cut was only small in length but was quite deep and running freely with blood. It would need to be covered. He grabbed a sheet of toilet paper from the holder affixed to the wall and tore off a segment, laying it against his skin, but it was ineffective and did nothing to stem the flow so, holding the rest of the sheet against his cheek, he walked back to the kitchen to ask Mrs. Rawlings if she could provide a sticking plaster or small dressing.

Brody found her with both flour-covered arms immersed in a large bowl, mixing pastry. When he explained what he needed she started to abandon her task, intent on helping him, but Brody insisted she continue.

"Please!" he said firmly. "Don't let me disturb you. Just tell me where to look and I'll find them myself."

"There are plasters in the medicine cabinet, sir" she explained, grateful not to have to extricate herself from the dough. "It's in the en-suite, in the main bedroom at the end of the hall."

Brody thanked her and left the kitchen. Back in the hallway he opened the door to Miller's room and stepped inside. It was a little bigger than his own, containing a double rather than a single bed, but was otherwise similarly decorated. Opening the door on the inside wall, Brody entered a compact en-suite bathroom. There was a small cabinet on the wall to the left of the washbasin, just as Mrs. Rawlings had described. Josh opened it to find two shelves lined with the usual array of bandages, dressings, aspirins, and half a dozen small bottles of various medicines and potions. But he could see no sticking plasters. Reaching inside, Josh moved some of the bottles and discovered a small box marked Bandaid in the rear corner. He was about to withdraw the box when his eye was taken by one of the glass bottles he had moved. In pulling it forward he had rotated it and the label on the front was now visible. It had the words *St. Bartholomew's Hospital Pharmacy* printed in green letters across the top, but it wasn't the label title that caused him to double-take and stare in shock at the glass phial. Written across the centre, in the clear typeface of the pharmacist's printer, was: *Suxamethonium Chloride.*

For a moment Brody froze, almost transfixed by the sudden evidence of his own eyes. His mind raced back to his conversations with Luke Harvey. There was no mistake. The pathologist had referred to it colloquially as 'Sux', but, ever keen on accurate detail, Brody had asked him to spell out the name and clearly remembered writing it out in full in his notebook. He also remembered Harvey telling him that it was a highly dangerous drug and available only for hospital anaesthesia. So there was no possible domestic scenario to account for the presence of Suxamethonium Chloride, the drug that had killed Dikembe Lukeba, being in a bathroom medicine cabinet.

As the full import of the tiny bottle standing on the shelf in front of him became chillingly obvious, the status of Miller moved instantly and alarmingly from friend to foe. It seemed impossible and Brody experienced a flash of disbelief. Somehow there had to be a perfectly reasonable explanation for what was confronting him. Yesterday the man had been a compassionate ally. He'd extricated Brody from his frame-up in Vienna and flown him home. He'd even authorised an unscheduled stop to allow Brody to visit his wife and child. Then, all at once, Josh realised with icy clarity that he'd never disclosed Kassia's address in any conversation; yet the Jaguar had taken them straight to the Westcliff seafront on Miller's personal instruction. He already knew where Brody's family lived.

Josh's stomach convulsed in a tight knot and he felt a surge of panic rising in his chest. Miller wasn't *pursuing* the clandestine organisation he'd been describing; he was *running* it.

Brody's natural first instinct was to run. But he forced himself to stop and think. Why hadn't he already been dispatched with a bullet in the head or an injection of the Sux? There had been plenty of opportunity. Clearly, Miller needed him alive. Why? It had to be due to the evidence Josh had assembled. Miller's careful questioning of the previous night had been to establish exactly what Brody knew.

Suddenly, all Josh's unresolved questions seemed to have answers and the vague, nebulous doubts that had relentlessly nagged at him crystallised and made all too uncomfortable sense. Miller would continue to play out this charade until all the proof Josh had collected was safely in his hands; then, and only then, would Brody be removed from the equation. Josh now realised he was under a death sentence. Secreted in Miller's elegant Victorian cage, he was simply awaiting execution; he had to act, and act swiftly.

Withdrawing a plaster from the box of Bandaid and peeling it open, he sealed it across his still bleeding cheek. Then he carefully replaced everything in the cabinet, leaving it exactly as he had found it.

He moved back through the bedroom and out into the hallway, silently closing the door behind him so as not to alert Carter, who was still reading in the lounge, as to his whereabouts. A few further steps took him into the sanctuary of his own room and he quietly shut and locked the door. Taking his wallet and passport from his jacket, Josh put them deep into the pockets of his jeans. Removing his shoes, he withdrew his trainers from his suitcase and changed into them, tying the laces tightly. Finally, grabbing both his phones, he shoved one handset in each hip pocket.

Guessing that the front door to the apartment was bound to be locked, he walked back into the kitchen, with as relaxed an expression as he could manage. He found Mrs. Rawlings now rolling out her prepared pastry.

"Did you find the plasters, sir?" enquired the housekeeper.

"Yes. Thank you" said Josh casually, pointing to the Bandaid that now adorned his cheek. "Wondered if there was any coffee left in that pot?"

"Oh, it'll be no good now, sir. I'll make you some fresh."

"No, no. This will be fine. I only need a mouthful." He poured himself a cup of the now lukewarm liquid. "Looks like you're making something nice."

"It's a pie."

"I never know how to get the pastry right" Josh told her with an idle smile. "You don't want it crispy like a biscuit but you don't want it too soft or floppy either. How do you manage it?"

"Ah, it's all in the mixing" she said with pride.

As Mrs. Rawlings began to wax lyrical about her pastry technique, Josh moved gradually towards the back door and casually leant against the frame. Sipping from his coffee cup as he feigned listening to her, he surreptitiously lowered his other hand and tried the door handle. It was locked and held firm.

He remained where he was, allowing the housekeeper to finish her brief instruction on the finer points of baking, before he thanked her for the coffee and, placing his cup in the sink, made an excuse and left the kitchen.

There was only one possible route to escape remaining; but first he needed to check on his minder, who, he now realised, was actually a gaoler. He walked into the lounge, where Carter immediately looked up from his newspaper. "I'm going to make some fresh coffee" said Josh nonchalantly. "Want one?"

Carter gave a gentle shake of his head. "I'm fine." He returned to reading.

"Ok." Brody turned and left. With Carter engrossed in The Daily Mail, Josh went straight to Miller's room, quietly opened the door and then closed it behind him.

In the en-suite bathroom, the window on the side wall gave onto the rear garden. The casement was small but big enough to allow egress. The Victorian window was divided into two and still bore the original, ornate metal handle on the left-hand half that clipped into a receiving plate on the other. It was locked, and looked as if it hadn't been opened since the last time it was painted, but the screws fastening the handle to the frame were tiny and the woodwork was old. Brody wrapped a towel around the handle and levered it upwards with all the strength he could muster. It took three attempts before there was a resounding thwack and the handle snapped away from the frame, leaving it suspended with the top end still locked into the receiving plate. Brody climbed up onto the toilet seat and threw the full force of his weight against the left half of the frame with his shoulder. It gave at the second thrust and, with a complaining crack as the paintwork finally split and parted, the window swung open.

Brody cambered up onto the washbasin and, with his right foot in the sink, manoeuvred his left leg and then his head and upper body through the opening. He was almost out and free when his trailing foot caught a glass on the small shelf above the basin and sent it tumbling into the sink, where it broke with a loud crash against the hard ceramic surface and shattered.

Hurriedly lowering himself, Josh half climbed and half fell onto the grass below the window. His ankle twisted slightly as he landed and sent a sharp pain shooting into his lower leg but it was nothing serious and he quickly picked himself up. The wooden fence at the rear of the garden was around two metres high but he reckoned that with a run and a leap he could grab the top and gain enough purchase to haul himself up and over.

Inside the apartment, the noise of breaking glass brought Carter swiftly from the lounge to investigate. It took only seconds to discover that Brody's room was empty and to move into Miller's bedroom and find the open en-suite window.

Josh ran full pelt at the fence and, despite the throbbing pain in his ankle, launched himself at it with the desperate power of a man in genuine fear for his life. He clutched the top of the fence and was dragging his legs up behind him when he heard Carter's voice behind him shouting "Hold it!"

Scrabbling up the wooden panel, Josh was half over the top when he heard the shot. Instantly there was a loud cracking noise of splintering wood as a bullet ripped through the denim of his jeans, painfully grazing the surface of his calf, and exploded into the fence. As he dropped to the earth on the other side, he heard a distant shout of "Fuck!". He knew he had only seconds in which to make good his escape, while Carter negotiated his bulkier frame through the small window.

Josh found himself in the rear garden of an apartment block in Carlisle Place, which backed onto Morpeth Terrace. The gardens of all the houses in both streets were entirely enclosed, with no possible exit to the roadway. Running to the back door of the house, he frantically pulled at the handle. It was locked.

Near the door, there was a small coal bunker against the garden fence. Brody jumped up onto it and launched himself over the fence and into the adjacent garden. This time the back door of the neighbouring house opened as he tried it. He burst into the kitchen where he was met with a cry of surprise by an elderly woman in a dressing gown who was seated at her table sipping tea. Ignoring her bewildered protestations and demands to know what was happening, he tore out of the kitchen and into the hallway, making for the front door. There was a bunch of keys hanging from the lock, where the front door key itself was still inserted in the brass Chubb handle. Paying no attention to the shouts of the elderly woman, who had irately pursued him into her hallway, Brody yanked the key around and opened the door. It was a matter of only a few strides to cross the building's vestibule and in seconds he was through the main door of the block, down the front steps and onto the street.

Turning immediately right, with his heart beating furiously in his chest, he ran up Carlisle Place, making for the junction with Victoria Street at the top. His ankle was still throbbing, and the graze of the bullet was bleeding through the side of his jeans, but he barely noticed either as he desperately pounded the pavement. The road was several hundred metres long but he knew that the northern end would be crowded with people and, if he could reach the intersection, he could lose himself in the throng.

He had travelled around twenty frantic paces when he heard the deafening clang of bursting metal and the whine of a ricochet down low to his left. A bullet had hit the rear wing of a Volkswagen Golf parked in the kerb beside him and bounced off the wheel arch. Brody turned to see Carter at the very bottom of the street. Standing with his feet squarely apart in a firing pose, he was brandishing an automatic that had a silencer fitted to the barrel. Even at such a distance, Brody could see the fury in his taut, black features. Darting between the Volkswagen and the vehicle parked in front of it, Josh ran a few further paces, keeping to the centre of the road. A quick glance over his shoulder told him that Carter had also run into the middle of the road and was again levelling his gun. Brody immediately dashed to his left and heard a second bullet ricochet off the tarmac near his feet as he disappeared between two more parked vehicles. He leapt onto the opposite pavement and managed a few more energetic strides northwards.

Every step he took brought him nearer to the safety of a crowd, and every second Carter wasted in trying to fix a bead on him, increased the distance between them.

After another half dozen frenetic strides, Josh darted back into the road. Six paces later he moved back onto the pavement. His zigzagging was preventing Carter taking accurate aim, and Brody was now only seconds away from the top of the street. Risking one final look over his shoulder he saw Carter running towards him. He had obviously given up on trying to make a shot and was now holding his left wrist to his mouth, shouting instructions as he ran. He was clearly fitted with a wire and was calling for back-up.

Josh made the end of the street and scurried left into Victoria Place. Weaving desperately in and out of the crowd, he threaded his way around the corner to the top of Vauxhall Bridge Road. The traffic was against him but he leapt onto the crossing, narrowly avoiding collision with a van and eliciting loud blasts of the horn from several motorists as he reached the opposite pavement and then sprinted over Wilton Road onto the concourse outside Victoria Station.

There was a piercing screech of brakes some way off to his left and he looked up to see Carter's blue Ford Focus of the previous day pulling up sharply into the kerb on the other side of Wilton Road. But it wasn't the thick set black man who hurriedly exited the vehicle. To Brody's amazement, he saw the shaven headed 'Mr. Smith' he had encountered in the apartment in the Tiefer Graben in Vienna. And he was accompanied by the same minder who had been sarcastically referred to as 'Mr. Brown'. The two men began frantically checking the street in all directions and clearly had not yet spotted Brody. Using the large concourse news-stand for cover, Josh edged around the front of it and dived into the crowd heading down the subway steps to the Underground.

As he feverishly worked his way through the swarm of people, bumping shoulders with annoyed passengers, he was desperately trying to second guess what his pursuers would be doing. As he reached the station hallway and saw the ticket barriers in front of him, leading to the train platforms, he realised with a chilly foreboding that he was doing the all too obvious. The Underground system was both out of sight and the fastest method of evacuation from the area. It was the first place a fugitive would choose. Undoubtedly the men chasing him would think the same. Turning to his right, he hastened through the tunnel and rushed up the far stairs, heading back above ground and ascending into the inside of the mainline station. Hurrying to the far end of the concourse, he came out of the station and quickly crossed the road to the bus terminus, where there were half a dozen buses parked.

A few metres in front of him stood an inspector with a clipboard, deep in conversation with a colleague. Brody positioned himself behind them, so he was hidden from view from across the street. "Which is the next bus out?" he demanded frantically.

Clearly annoyed at the brusque interruption, the inspector gave him a disdainful look but none the less glanced down at his clipboard. "The 38 to Clapton Pond leaves in six minutes" he said a little acidly. "The 507 to Waterloo is leaving now."

Without another word, Josh dashed to the 507 bus. He leapt onto the platform as the doors emitted a loud swishing sound and swung closed behind him. Moving swiftly down the aisle to the rear, he hurriedly settled himself into a seat by the window. Keeping his head back in the shadows, he risked a final glance at the station concourse as the bus pulled gently away and turned into the junction. Mr. Brown was running towards the subway stairs to the underground. The shaven headed Mr. Smith was in animated conversation with a distraught Carter, who was gesticulating at him wildly. Clearly, they hadn't seen him board the bus. Josh sank back into the hard upholstery of his seat and exhaled a deep breath of relief. He had managed to elude his pursuers and, for the time being at least, was free.

The temporary safety of the 507 bus furnished Brody with valuable respite and time to think. He reached down and lifted the leg of his blood-stained jeans. Carter's bullet had left a neat hole on both sides of the denim where it had torn through from the back and immediately exited.

Fortunately, the graze on Brody's calf was only slight and the trickle of blood had already subsided and begun to congeal. A wash with a little water and the application of a plaster would be all the attention it required. A centimetre closer and the bullet would have embedded itself in the muscle and prevented him from running. He realised he had been *very* lucky.

Then it suddenly struck him that both the shots in Carlisle Place had been at low level, one striking the wheel arch of the adjacent Volkswagen and the other hitting the tarmac near Brody's feet. Neither had struck at torso height and Carter couldn't have been so far off target twice. He was a professional and had fired the first shot when Josh was in full view, straddling the garden fence less than twenty-five metres away. On each occasion, he must have been aiming for Josh's legs, intending to disable him rather than kill him. It was of only slight comfort; but it was highly significant. They definitely still needed him alive.

The 507 made its way sedately across Lambeth Bridge and curved around the small central roundabout to turn left and pass by the walled gardens of the Archbishop's London palace. Once it was south of Westminster Bridge, it turned into York Road and Brody disembarked. Walking down Belvedere Road, he turned onto The Embankment. At one of the numerous street stalls, selling souvenir trinkets of London and general tourist junk, he bought a pair of large, dark sunglasses and a baseball cap with a deep brim. With the cap planted firmly on his head and the peak pulled low, and with the glasses covering his eyes, he kept to the riverside, hidden within the summer crowds flocking to the arts centres on the south bank, and headed towards the National Theatre. He was thinking clearly. Miller and his cohorts would expect him to run, to put as much distance as he could between himself and London. So he would do the opposite. He would stay in the capital that he knew so well.

In the foyer of the theatre, he went to the washroom and tended to his leg wound, tying his handkerchief around it until he could later find a plaster. Then he purchased a large cup of black coffee and, ensconced in a shadowy corner of the wide and extensive foyer, settled into a chair to assess his situation and plan his next move.

* * * * *

Miller was incandescent with rage. Returning to Morpeth Terrace, he had been nervously informed by his team that his house guest had flown the coop.

Like miscreant children reporting to the headmaster's study, Carter was standing in line next to his two cohorts, Lucas, the shaven headed man Brody knew as 'Mr. Smith', and Podolski, the silent minder who had been referred to as 'Mr. Brown'.

The contrite Carter was sheepishly attempting to relate the events of Brody's disappearance. None of them could explain what had prompted the journalist suddenly to make a break and escape but, whatever had triggered Brody's flight, he had clearly become aware of the reality of his situation and Miller's carefully planned operation, that was so close to fruition, had been blown.

"I gave chase and called for back-up, but we lost him in the crowd" said Carter defensively. "I could have taken him out ...but I didn't think you'd want it."

"No" snapped Miller, relieved that his operative had at least shown some initiative and forethought. "No, under the circumstances, you did the right thing."

"The boys spent an hour out in the car, scouring the area" Carter explained. "But there was no sign of him. And he'll be long gone now. Do you want me to alert the police and put out an A.P.B. on him?"

Miler stepped towards the fireplace and stood drumming his fingers agitatedly on the mantle shelf, considering his options and their possible consequences. "Yes" he said eventually, turning back to face Carter. "But make it a Code 'D'. Total press and media blackout. We have to avoid this going public if at all possible. Get a description and a photograph to all police forces, ports, airports and exit points, and start with the Met. Make sure every London beat bobby has his description. But stipulate that he's *our* pigeon and if there are any sightings they're to stay on his tail and wait. Nobody picks him up except us. Got it?"

Carter nodded. "Got it. But he knows now that we're after him. So what if he goes to ground and just hunkers down? It could take a very long time to flush him out."

"Yes. And time is something we don't have" said Miller bluntly, addressing all three men in front of him. "It's still essential to try and take him alive if at all possible. But the longer he's at large, the greater the risk he becomes. So, if we can't locate him within the next twenty-four hours, then we have to look at damage limitation. From now on, if it becomes a choice of losing him or killing him, then you take him out. Is that understood?"

There were nods of cold agreement and unemotional understanding.

"And I want full surveillance of all his known friends and contacts" added Miller. "Especially that girl in Vienna. He's mentioned her several times."

"Anderson, sir" said Lucas helpfully. "Shelley Anderson."

"Yes. What's the latest on her?"

Lucas flipped through some sheets he was holding until he came to the appropriate page. "Since we started monitoring on Wednesday evening, she's had nine phone calls, three text messages and fourteen emails. All of it either family or British Council business. Nothing significant or worthy of note and nothing referring to Brody apart from the calls between her and the embassy in Vienna, which we already know about."

"Do we know when she's due back in the U.K.?"

"The airline ticket register shows she's booked to fly on Sunday morning, sir."

"Send someone to Heathrow and put a tail on her when she lands. I've a hunch Brody will want to contact her."

Lucas's eyes widened. "Would he really be that stupid?"

"Probably not" said Miller dismissively. "But we'll watch her anyway."

Josh spent most of the day hidden away in the foyer of the National Theatre. Like a typical journalist, he mentally assembled a list of his priorities, working through what was possible and what would be too risky.

In severe need of an ally, at 2 pm he put in a call to The Independent using his pay-as-you-go mobile which he knew could not be traced. He asked the girl on the switchboard for the World Affairs Desk but, when he was put through, the call was answered by a female voice that he didn't recognise.

"World desk. Can I help you?"

"I'd like to speak to Alan Denton please."

"I'm afraid Mr. Denton isn't here."

"Do you know when he'll be back in the office?"

"I'm afraid he won't be here for some considerable time. He's on extended leave."

Josh felt his neck involuntarily go tense and his grip tighten on the handset. "I don't understand" he said hurriedly. "What do you mean by extended leave? Is he sick?"

"No, no" said the operator reassuringly. "He's perfectly well. But he's been granted special leave of absence."

'Christ!' thought Josh. 'They've got to him already' and he winced to think he had brought down such trouble on the head of his friend.

"Is there someone else who can help you?" asked the girl politely.

Josh didn't reply and merely clicked off the handset to end the call. It was less than twenty-four hours since he had revealed to Miller that he was backed by The Independent and, quite deliberately, he had not revealed Alan Denton by name. Yet the editor had already been removed. Brody didn't know if Miller himself was pulling the strings or if he was simply reporting to someone higher up within the echelons of power but, whoever was wielding control, the tentacles of their reach were demonstrably long and formidable.

His immediate thought was that if they had already removed Denton from the picture then Shelley Anderson might well be next in the line of fire. Miller had no reason to suppose she was aware of Brody's Lukeba investigations; but she was the one person, other than Denton, who was connected to Josh's time in Vienna, and she had made a considerable fuss over his arrest. It made her a possible risk to Miller's need for secrecy.

Josh felt sick to his stomach to think that Shelley's association with him might have placed her in danger. It was now vital to reach her and warn her of all that had happened; to get her out of harm's way. Slowly, as he considered his limited options, the kernel of an idea began to develop. It would certainly mean a risk; if Shelley was being watched and monitored then any form of contact would be hazardous; but there was a strong chance it might work.

By 6.30 pm, when the early evening patrons were beginning to gather in all the venues along the south bank, he felt the outside crowds were sufficient to provide necessary cover. Wearing his dark glasses, and with the brim of the baseball cap low across his forehead, he left the National Theatre.

His first port of call was an ATM machine on the riverfront near the Festival Hall. He inserted his cash card, tapped in his number and waited for the banknotes to be dispensed. There was an unaccountable pause and then, to his surprise, a message flashed onto the screen declaring that there was an error and 'for the security of this account' the card would not be returned. He suffered an immediate foreboding but took out his credit card and nervously tried a similar withdrawal. It produced exactly the same result. He knew at once that his cards had been cancelled. By depriving him of cash, he was being forced further into a corner and movement was being rendered ever more difficult.

Brody thought for a moment. Alan Denton had been removed from the equation but that didn't necessarily mean Miller had discovered the project account the editor set up to finance Josh's investigation. Mentally crossing his fingers, Brody took the appropriate cash card from his wallet and inserted it into the slot at the top of the machine. This time there was no problem. He ran a balance check and there was still just under four thousand pounds in the account. Withdrawing the daily maximum of £1,000, Josh placed the notes carefully in his wallet and said a silent prayer for the faith and trust of his friend, Alan Denton. He would remove the entire balance over the next three days before the account was discovered and blocked.

Leaving the south bank, Brody walked up the stone stairs at the southern end of Waterloo bridge and crossed the road. A wait of only a minute or so ended when a black cab, its yellow 'for hire' light shining brightly in the early evening dusk, turned onto the bridge and headed in his direction. Brody waved down the taxi and clambered into the rear, telling the driver to head north for Tottenham Court Road. Fifteen minutes later the cab dropped him outside the Dominion Theatre.

Once full of well-known stores selling furnishings and household goods, now only the solitary Heal's remained to reflect the street's former glory days of domestic retail. The long road now consisted almost exclusively of electronics shops selling every possible modern device from hi-fi and television to computers and telephones and all the conceivable peripherals that accompanied them. It was a techie's paradise and Brody knew he would find what he needed.

In a little shop run by two young, smiling and keen-to-please Pakistani guys, he bought a new smart phone, capable of running the internet and email, and a new pay-as-you-go SIM card to give him a new untraceable number. He then paid a £5 fee to have them transfer all his contacts files from his original mobile to the new phone. That meant he had all his address book numbers and details on the new handset.

Coming out of the shop, he walked a little further along the road and then turned left into Googe Street, where he found a small internet café. There were several people seated among the three rows of monitor screens, most of them with the youth and appearance of students, and nobody looked up or paid any attention as Brody entered through the front door. At the counter, he purchased an hour of computer time, a coffee and a muffin, and made his way to a corner terminal at the rear of the premises.

Once in his seat, he navigated the internet to the site for Hotmail, only to discover it had been replaced by something called Outlook. It still provided the same web mail service and he opened a new email account. Then, checking her address from the contacts file on his phone, he headed up an email to Shelley Anderson. Sitting back in his small wooden chair, he stared at the screen. It was a 'now or never' moment. Once sent, an email could not be retracted; and once released into cyberspace, it was vulnerable to interception and monitoring. He already knew how he would disguise his true identity and hide it from prying eyes but the content of his message also needed to be camouflaged to deflect scrutiny. Brody hesitated; but then his gut instinct took over. As an author, he was well practised in creating a character and adopting a fictitious persona. Carefully and deliberately, he began to type onto the keyboard.

Hi Babe,
Are you back from your trip? How was Vienna? All Strauss and Strudel I bet! I've really missed you! Loads to tell you – you won't believe what's happened while you've been away. I'm desperate to see you and share the gossip! Let's catch up soon.
Love, Ian x

His finger momentarily hovered over the mouse. Then, with a surge of resolution, he clicked the SEND button and the email was gone.

Anyone monitoring the email would find it an innocuous enough message and he had deliberately composed the flamboyant text to ring with faintly 'gay' overtones. Shelley worked in the arts and it would be natural for her to have gay friends who might write in such a chatty, over familiar style. It only added validity to the message *not* being from Josh. But the key was in the name. He signed it 'Ian' and the address from which he sent it was Ian.M@outlook.com.

Only his agent, his publisher, and a few close friends knew he wrote under the nom de plume of Ian Magen. But Shelley knew it and she would instantly register the curtailed reference in the address. Now all he had to do was wait for a reply.

Leaving the small café, he turned off into Charlotte Street and made his way through Rathbone Place to Oxford Street, where he crossed the main thoroughfare and entered Soho.

It was dangerous to be on his own stomping ground and he skirted widely, taking an elongated route so as to avoid Old Compton Street, where he was certain his flat would be under close surveillance. He walked east and then down towards Leicester Square in order to approach Wardour Street from the south side. He kept a wary eye open for any sign of the law. If he saw a police car approaching he made for the nearest shop doorway, turning his back and pretending to examine the contents of the window. When pairs of officers patrolling on foot came into view, he crossed the street and gave them a wide birth, keeping his head down and his face hidden. It was a nerve racking journey but one he had to make. He knew exactly where he was heading and, with a little luck, would soon find an ally that not even the extended arms of Miller could reach.

Chapter Sixteen

For once, Brody was pleased to find himself in a crowded bar. O'Neill's Irish pub was, as usual, packed to the gunnels and the atmosphere was boisterous and lively. When he eventually elbowed his way through the throng and reached the small stage area, the band was setting up, getting ready for the first set of the night's performance.

"Can I buy you guys a drink?" Brody enquired amiably.

"That's uncommonly decent of you, friend" said the Bodhran player in the melodious accent of Southern Ireland and with a broad smile on his chubby face. "A Guinness all round would certainly be welcome."

It took almost fifteen minutes for Brody to reach the bar, be served the drinks and then skilfully manoeuvre his way back through the crush to the musicians with five pints delicately balanced on a tray, but he managed it without spilling a drop.

A little idle conversation ensued but it was not long before Brody casually asked if Sean Finnegan might be joining them.

"Well, with Sean, you never really know" said Owen, the fiddle player, philosophically. "But he wasn't here yesterday and he's never been known to miss two nights in a row when he's in town. So, if I were a betting man, I'd say it's worth a wager that we'll see him tonight."

Ensconced in a dark corner at the rear of the pub, where he checked his new phone every ten minutes to see if Shelley had replied to his email, Brody settled himself apprehensively to wait. He had carefully chosen a position next to a fire exit door so that, should sudden departure prove necessary, he had a ready means of escape.

The violinist's prediction eventually proved correct when, an hour and a half later, Sean Finnegan's tousled auburn head could be seen edging its way through the crowd in the direction of the bar. Brody watched and waited patiently as Sean exchanged pleasantries with several of the regulars before collecting his pint of Guinness and weaving his way to the bandstand. Josh couldn't hear the conversation but the fiddler Owen nodded in his direction and Finnegan turned to gaze at the stranger in the baseball cap who had been enquiring after him. Brody gently raised his glass in greeting as Sean made his way towards him but it took the puzzled Irishman several paces before he eventually recognised who it was that was waiting for him. His face lit up and he beamed with a guileless smile that stretched from ear to ear.

"Brody, me darlin', how the fuck are you?" he asked as, one arm resolutely clutching his pint glass, he threw the other around Josh's shoulder and hugged him. "I thought you'd buggered off to Vienna in search of Tweedledee?"

"I did" said Josh, extricating himself from Finnegan's bear-like embrace.

"And how was it? Did you solve the mystery of the bastard's checking out?"

"Yes. And that's why I'm here. I need your help."

There was an unfamiliar urgency to Brody's manner and a look of real tension in his eyes that instantly disarmed Finnegan's natural bonhomie. "What's up, Josh?" Sean asked, suddenly concerned. "You look troubled."

Brody lowered his voice. "I'm in deep shit, Sean. I've ruffled the feathers of some very heavy people. And they're keen to see me disappear."

The Irishman looked at him in silence for a moment as he digested this unexpected news, sensing the genuine fear underlying his friend's words. "You're serious, aren't you?"

"Yes. And I've no right to involve you and put you at risk. But I'm fast running out of options and I couldn't think of anyone else who might help me."

Finnegan's stubble-covered face creased into a grin. "Now, who else would you turn to when it's time for a scrap? Whaddya need?"

Brody reached out and squeezed Finnegan's hand in gratitude. "Well, first I urgently need to get off the streets and find a place to crash. Then I need you to look at a few naked women."

Sean laughed aloud. "Sounds like my kind of assignment!"

Forty minutes later the two men were in Finnegan's small flat in Covent Garden, sharing a bottle of Jameson's. Like the Irishman himself, the apartment was untidy and dishevelled but Brody had never been more grateful for the security of its unkempt surroundings.

He spent an hour bringing Sean up to date on everything that had happened in Vienna and on the bizarre nature of his escape from the 'safe' house in Morpeth Terrace. Finnegan listened attentively and said very little until Josh reached the end of his sorry tale.

The Irishman shook his head gravely. "The big problem is that the bad guys are technically also the good guys" he told Brody solemnly. "They're sitting inside officialdom. Christ, they *are* officialdom!"

"Yes. And they're clever. It always bothered me that when I was stitched up for the Nazari killing it was faked as a suicide, and not a straight murder. It was all too improbable. But the case against me was *meant* to collapse. It gave them the chance to get me off the hook and released from gaol. They came charging in like the cavalry and I swallowed it hook, line and sinker. They were my rescuers. So naturally I was going to trust them."

"And hand over the evidence you'd put together on the Lukebas."

"Exactly."

"And once they'd got it..."

The sentence didn't need completion.

"I'd say you're well and truly buggered" summarised Sean and took a large swig of whiskey. "What's your next move?"

"Well I'm not going to spend the rest of my life in hiding. And I've only got one card left to play."

"The Vienna evidence."

"Yes."

"So where is it?"

Brody managed a smile. "That's where the naked women come in."

The bouncers, Eric and Ernie, were standing like sentinels at the front doors of La Gattina as the taxi dropped Sean in Old Compton Street at just before midnight. The Irishman cast a wary eye around but there was no sign of anyone obviously watching the door to Brody's flat. Not that he had expected to see anything. If Josh's pursuers were as powerful as he claimed then their surveillance would be covert and well hidden.

Sean paid his entrance fee and entered the club, which was as packed as ever with a typical, raucous Friday night crowd. The majority of the punters were jammed into the area in front of the stage, encouraging each other with alcohol-fuelled gibes of phoney machismo to stuff money into the thongs of the dancers who teased them with their naked contortions, so Sean was able to secure a vacant stool at the bar. Beckoning to the nearest of the two barmen, Finnegan ordered a whiskey. Just about managing to conceal his shock at the highly inflated price, he settled himself to wait for an appropriate moment.

The on-stage act came to a close and there was an instant rush to the bar to replenish drinks before the next performer made her appearance. Sean was impressed with the way the two barmen dealt swiftly with the sudden demand and managed to serve every order without error. A loud blast of rock music announced the imminent arrival of the next pole dancer and the group assaulting the bar dissolved as quickly as it had formed, returning boisterously to the bear pit of the stage apron. Sean undertook a swift mental calculation as to how much cash had flooded into the till during those frantic few minutes and decided he should probably give up photo-journalism and open a strip club.

Taking advantage of the temporary lull, he leaned forward and spoke to one of the barman, "I have a message for one of the girls" he told him.

The barman, whose nametag pinned to his shirt pocket identified him as Tim, threw him a slightly patronising look. "You and every other guy in the room."

Sean nodded. "Yeah, I know. But this is personal. And she'll want to receive it." Before Tim could offer further protest, Sean cut him short. "Just tell her, Josh says how's your little boy?"

The message certainly pulled the rug from under the barman. In his years at the club he'd witnessed all variations of crude and lewd in punters trying to get notes passed to the girls, but he'd never heard anything remotely like this missive. Deciding something so odd was probably genuine, he reluctantly nodded. "Which girl?"

"Carla" said Sean quietly. "The one they call 'Angel'."

Fifteen minutes later, Carla appeared and took a seat next to him. She was wearing a long dress of deep crimson with a low, provocative neck line and side splits that exposed most of her shapely legs as she settled herself on the adjacent stool.

"May I buy you a drink?" Finnegan asked politely, furtively admiring the view of her exposed thigh and hoping she hadn't noticed.

"Depends who's asking" she replied, the suspicion very evident in her eyes.

"I'm a friend of Josh Brody."

"And I'm close pals with William and Kate."

Sean laughed aloud. "I can see why he likes you so much. And he said you'd be a tough nut to crack. So he told me to ask you a specific question."

"Which is?"

"Did your son get the football boots he was asking you for?"

Carla thought for a moment and then smiled. "I'll have a gin and tonic" she said calmly. Sean nodded to the hovering Tim and he left to carry out the order. "How is he?" asked Carla.

Finnegan lowered his voice. "Not good. Between ourselves, he's in a heap of trouble. But he'd like to see you."

"When?"

"Tonight. It doesn't matter how late you finish. He'll be waiting for you." Sean reached into his pocket and pulled out a folded slip of paper. "He asked me to show you this."

She opened the message. It read:

Carla.
This is Sean Finnegan. You can trust him. My last note asked you to keep something for me until you could hand it to me in person. Sean will tell you where. I'll be waiting for you. Heartfelt thanks. Love Josh B.

She folded over the paper and handed it back to him. "It could be three or four before I finish."

"No problem." He passed her a twenty pound note. "Josh says this is for the mini cab."

Carla smiled. "Typical. Now I *know* you're from him. But tell him this one's on me." She smiled warmly as she handed back the money. "Where am I going?"

Sean gave her the address in Covent Garden and she repeated it back to him to ensure she had memorised it correctly. "What's your telephone number?" she asked.

Sean borrowed a biro and an order slip from the barman and scribbled down the number of his mobile. "You can call at any time" he assured her as he handed her the note.

Carla nodded and slipped the paper into the inside of her bra. "Tell Josh I'll see him later." Swiftly downing the remains of her gin and tonic, she eased herself up from the stool. "Thanks for the drink" she said politely and, with no further word, made her way back to the dressing rooms to prepare for her next set.

It was twenty minutes to four in the morning when Sean Finnegan's cell phone rang. Brody was awake, lying on the sofa and staring at the ceiling, deep in thought, but the Irishman was dozing in an easy chair. The insistent ringing roused him quickly from sleep and he reached into his pocket and withdrew the handset. Brody sat upright and looked expectantly at his friend.

"Hello?" said Sean, blinking and shaking his head back into consciousness.

"It's Carla. I'm outside, across the street in a mini cab. Tell Josh to show himself at the front door so I can be sure it's him. If he's not there in five minutes I'm telling the cabbie to drive on, and I'm taking the parcel with me."

"You've got it" replied Sean and snapped shut his handset. "Downstairs. In the front doorway. Now!" he commanded. As Brody raised himself up from the sofa and made for the hallway door, Sean let out a laugh. "That's one hell of a girl, Brody me boy. I *like* her! I'd lay you odds there's some Irish blood in those sultry veins of hers!"

It took Josh less than a minute to descend the hallway stairs to the front doors of the building. As he stood in the porch, he saw a Mondeo parked in the shadows on the far side of the road and watched as Carla opened the rear door and clambered out. The cab drove away and she hurried across to the building. "Just wanted to be one hundred per cent sure it was you" she told Josh as he ushered her inside.

Once within the safety of the apartment block and hidden from view, Brody embraced her and hugged her tightly. "I'm sorry for all this" he whispered. "I would never have sent you the package if I'd known it was going to get this crazy. But I can't tell you how grateful I am."

She managed a knowing smile and shrugged. "Like I told you before, Josh. This isn't Never Never land. It's life. And we all have to shovel our share of shit."

Brody took her by the hand and led her back up the stairs to Finnegan's second floor flat.

"Whiskey?" offered Sean as the pair entered the tiny lounge. Carla shook her head. "No thanks. But I could murder a cup of tea."

Sean was more than a little startled to see the change in appearance of the woman seating herself next to Brody on the sofa. Like most girls who earn their living being professionally attractive, Carla preferred to be unremarkable and anonymous when she wasn't working. The paint and mascara was gone and her face showed not a trace of make-up. The glamorous, revealing dress had been replaced by a worn pair of denim jeans and a plain woollen jumper under a shapeless anorak. But the strength of the woman beneath was as evident as ever and Sean was smiling admiringly as he stepped into the kitchen to make his newly arrived guest a cup of tea.

Brody began the conversation with a brief attempt at explaining his predicament and his reasons for mailing her the package from Vienna, but she held up a hand and stopped him in mid-sentence. "I don't want to know, Josh" she said calmly as she handed over the padded envelope. "What I don't know can't hurt me. And I have a son to consider. So it's better for all of us if I'm out of the loop."

Brody nodded contritely. "You're right." He lifted the flap of the unsealed envelope. Inside, wrapped around with the brief letter he had written to Carla, instructing her that under no circumstances was she to hand the package over to anyone other than Josh in person, were his notebook and the USB drive. They were the only weapons in his arsenal and it felt good to have them back in his possession. "And thanks again" he said softly.

The three chatted for a brief while as Carla drank her tea and then she told them she was tired and wanted to get home. Sean rang for a taxi and it was outside the building five minutes later. Repeating his gratitude for both her help and her friendship, Josh escorted Carla downstairs and watched her drive away. By the time he was back in the apartment, Finnegan already had the USB drive in his laptop and was looking at the photo files with the expert scrutiny of his professional photographer's eye.

"I can sharpen these up for you" he told Brody as he looked at the oriental features of the Chinese girl. "And I can bring up the clarity of her face."

"Enough for us to get a good make?"

"Sure. But that's not the problem, is it?" said Sean as he turned to his friend. "You can have the most accurate portrait in the world but it doesn't mean you'll match it to anyone. Girls in her profession are not exactly listed in the Yellow Pages under 'Assassin'. She lives in the shadow lands; off record."

"Probably" agreed Brody. "But at least we have somewhere to start." He checked his watch. It was almost 4.30 am. "Now I think we both need some sleep. Tomorrow's going to be a long day."

* * * * *

Saturday, June 29th.

"Clever" said Shelley Anderson quietly to herself. "Very clever."

When the email first arrived, her immediate thought was that it had been sent in error and was meant for someone else but, as she scanned the text for the second time, she recognised the name 'Ian M' and realised it could only mean Josh. Puzzled, she read the text over again, trying to fathom the need for his pseudonym and a cryptic message.

She had first learned of Josh's abrupt Thursday morning release from police custody when she tried to visit him later that evening. The desk sergeant at the Wasagaße station of the Kriminalpolizei was unable to provide any detailed information. Reading from the daily log, he merely told an anxious Shelley that Herr Brody's lawyer had secured his release and he had left the premises. When pressed, the uncooperative sergeant regretted he could offer the Fräulein no details as to where Herr Brody might be and, no, Herr Oberkommisar Kleist was not available for comment.

Surprised to have heard nothing from Josh himself, and more than a little concerned that he was not answering his mobile, Shelley called the British Embassy but, as it was after 6 pm, it was closed for business and it was not until Friday morning that she was able to speak to someone. Her disquiet only increased when she was informed that nobody within the embassy knew where she might find Mr Brody.

"But I raised this matter with you myself" protested Shelly. "I came to see you and reported the arrest and you sent somebody to see him."

"Yes, Madame, we have a note of the case. And, according to our information, Mr. Brody has now been successfully released from custody. However, he has not informed us of his present whereabouts. I'm afraid there's nothing more we can do to help you unless he makes contact with us."

Shelley had worked within official ranks long enough to recognise a standard 'brush-off' when it was presented and, just as with the Vienna police, she knew she would make no further progress along this particular avenue of enquiry. She was pleased to know Josh was no longer in gaol, but completely mystified as to why he had not telephoned. It was the final day of the book fare and she had a full work schedule. There was no option but to get on with her day and wait until Josh finally called.

By Saturday morning, still without contact, her genuine concern was becoming tinged with anger. Wherever he might be, and no matter how pressured his situation, there had to be a few minutes available in which to call her. But it was over forty-eight hours since his release and there was still no word. She was beginning to think that perhaps the elusive Mr. Brody was not all she had believed him to be when she opened her laptop to check her emails and discovered the bizarre message.

She read it through several times. By using his 'Ian M' alias, Josh was telling her he felt unable to write as himself. That could only mean trouble. She stared long and hard at the text in the small window of her smartphone.

Hi Babe,
Are you back from your trip? How was Vienna? All Strauss and Strudel I bet! I've really missed you! Loads to tell you – you won't believe what's happened while you've been away. I'm desperate to see you and share the gossip! Let's catch up soon.
Love, Ian x

The email was written in a style about as 'un-Josh-like' as it were possible to be. He would never call her 'Babe' and he was more likely to tell her he was flying to the moon than to suggest they 'share the gossip'. So he was further disguising himself. She had assumed that his release from custody meant his ordeal was over but this cryptic message was telling a different story.

She re-examined the text, discarding the manner of expression and sifting the facts. A great deal had happened; it was hard to believe; he was desperate to explain and wanted to meet her as soon as possible. But it all sounded like some chatty friend just wanting to blather and share apparent trivia.

"Clever" she repeated to herself. Anyone monitoring the message would never equate Josh with the sender of the email. Her reply had to be equally innocuous and carefully constructed and continue the deception.

Several cups of hot coffee later, surrounded by numerous scribbled attempts on paper, Shelley felt she had the necessary answer and began to type apprehensively on the keyboard of her laptop as she addressed an email to Ian.M@outlook.com.

Hi Sweetie!
Book fare was great – big success – but personally Vienna has been a drag! Got involved with a guy (yes I know – typical me!). Anyway – he turned out to be a whole heap of trouble and after I'd run around after him helping to extricate him from the shit, the bastard has dumped me. Can you believe it? Just up and left without a word!
Ok, ok - I can hear you saying 'silly bitch, she's done it again'! – and yes, you're right! So I need a shoulder to cry on and a large bottle of wine! I'll be back Sunday morning – tell me when and where and we'll get drunk and swap sob stories!
Lots of love, Shelley x x

Hoping she had matched Brody's skillful artifice, she clicked the SEND button and the email instantly disappeared from her screen.

Saturday morning for Brody and Sean Finnegan began with an early alarm call. Brody had spent the night wrapped in a duvet on Sean's sofa and he struggled wearily to his feet, stumbling bleary-eyed across the lounge to knock on the bedroom door and rouse Finnegan. They had agreed that they would endeavour to manage on just four hours' sleep and would rise at 8.30 am.

Finnegan went out to Covent Garden market to purchase fresh bread rolls while Brody showered and shaved and then made a pot of strong, reviving coffee. After their breakfast, it was Sean's turn to shower and, remarkably for a man who'd had so little sleep, by 9.45 am he stood before Brody looking smart and alert and ready for the day.

Josh handed him the cash card for Alan Denton's project account and told him the PIN. "The daily maximum is a grand. Withdraw the whole thousand. You'll have more than enough to cover whatever bribes you need to make and still leave plenty in reserve but, whatever it costs, pay up. Take a cab there and back and be as discreet as you can."

"Got it" said Sean in business-like fashion as he pocketed the cash card. With a promise to be back as soon as he could, and a reminder to Brody to stay hidden in the apartment and not venture out, Finnegan left on his mission.

Brody refilled his coffee mug and settled himself in front of Sean's laptop. He wanted to spend the morning running extensive and detailed searches on Dr. Jalil Nazari and the Russian so-called 'art dealer' Yurov. If he could build a profile of each of them and track as much information on them as the internet held, then he could add it all to his existing file on the Lukeba twins. With everything collated, he might be able to unearth common denominators that would support his claims to their murder.

It was a little after 10.15 am that he logged onto his Outlook account to once again check his inbox. Shelley's reply was waiting for him. Brody punched the air in delight, loudly yelling "Yes!" to the empty room, as he read the opening line of her response. He realised at once that his ploy had worked and she had picked up on his ruse and followed the thread. "Smart girl!" he declared as he read through the email and recognised that her reply was even better disguised than his original. She referred to him as 'a bastard' and as having 'dumped her without a word'. It was perfect.

Brody's overriding concern was that Shelley's obvious connection to him might put her under threat from Miller and he wanted somehow to get her to safety. But the text of her email had cleverly broken that connection at a stroke. Hell hath no fury like a woman scorned, and if Miller was reading her emails then he'd be certain she felt both scorned and furious and had washed her hands of the whole affair. It had totally changed the emphasis. She might well still be under surveillance, but Miller would no longer believe she was directly involved or had knowledge of Josh's whereabouts.

Now Brody had to think carefully and compose the details of how and when they would meet. Even under the guise of his alter ego, he didn't want to state a time and place in plain text. If she were being tailed, as was still possible, then openly announcing a rendezvous venue in advance would be an un-necessary risk. Better to leave the location hidden from prying eyes and remain cryptic.

He sketched a few ideas, searching for something she would recognise and clearly understand, but his options were few. They had known each other for such a relatively short period that they had yet to establish the little details of a relationship that would be known only to a couple themselves and would pass un-noticed by outsiders.

Suddenly, he was struck by inspiration. His mind was tracing the all too brief time they shared in Vienna when he remembered the sunny day they spent walking the streets of the capital, ending up at the Prater park. Instantly he knew where they would meet in London. A few rough drafts on a sheet of paper produced the text he needed and he set about copying out the email.

You poor Baby!
How could you end up with another loser like that?! What a shit! Good riddance is all I can say. Let's meet Monday for wine and tears and dishing the dirt - I want to share all the juicy details!!!! There's more to this than meets the eye! What about 11 am where you had your first lime kiss??
Love Ian x

In her Bäckerstraße apartment, Shelley was sitting at her computer, anxiously waiting for Josh's reply. When it dropped into her inbox, she nervously opened it to see what he had written. It was a few seconds before she understood the hidden reference. Then she smiled and hit the reply button. She typed:

I'll be there! S x x

She sent the email and firmly closed the lid of her laptop. It was time to clear her apartment and pack her bags, ready for the following morning's flight home.

The black taxi dropped Sean Finnegan right outside the imposing Georgian facade of the Radisson Vanderbilt Hotel in the Cromwell Road. As he walked up the few marble steps of its columned portico, Sean could easily imagine the grandeur of its days as a privately owned house, with an army of servants living in in its basement rooms and running at the beck and call of the wealthy family occupying its five stories. The interior was beautifully appointed, carefully preserving the style and furnishings of the original period, with highly polished woodwork, large oil paintings in ornate golden frames and spotlessly clean marble flooring.

Exuding every ounce of Celtic charm that he could muster, Finnegan beamed his widest smile at the girl behind the reception desk as he produced his N.U.J. card and held it open for her to see. "Good morning" he wished her ebulliently. "I wonder if you can help me?"

In his lilting Irish brogue, he spun a yarn about writing a piece on hotel security and claimed he'd heard the Radisson group had some of the best systems in place in London. He wondered if he might have a word with whomever ran the Vanderbilt's security to find out what made their operation so efficient and effective. The girl obligingly summoned the duty manager and Sean repeated his story, stressing that it would mean great free publicity for the hotel chain when the article went to print because, so far, it seemed to be far ahead of all its rivals. Sensing he might gain valuable brownie points with his employers, the manager was only too happy to give him a guided tour.

After half an hour of copious nodding of approval, and scribbling endless futile observations in his notebook, the tour of the hotel finally brought Sean to his target destination, the C.C.T.V. control room, where he was introduced to Wayne, the young technician on duty.

"It's all *very* impressive" he told the manager's eager ears. Do you think I might be allowed to sit here and watch for a little while to see how this all functions?"

With a promise to meet him later in the reception area, the manager was only too pleased to leave Sean in situ to admire the hotel's video monitoring system and abandoned him to the company of the young operator.

"So is all this recorded to a hard drive?" Finnegan asked casually.

"Yup. We've got ten terabytes down there" said Wayne, exhibiting the pride that all techies seem to take in the details of their equipment. "It'd take you a year to fill that lot."

"Sure, but presumably you don't keep it all forever?"

"Nah. We run an edit at the end of every month. We keep anything important and bin the rest" He grinned widely. "And you'd be amazed at some of the stuff we pick up. People seem to forget they're on candid camera and get up to all sorts. Especially in the lifts!"

Sean laughed. "I bet." He pulled a wad of notes from his inside pocket. "So, if I wanted to see the footage for a particular night, you could show it to me. Right?"

The young man instantly lost his erstwhile grin, wary of the sudden new direction the conversation had taken, but his eyes widened visibly at the sight of the money and Sean was fairly sure he had him hooked. "What's all this about?" Wayne asked quietly.

"Simple really" said Sean, counting out five, crisp twenty-pound notes. "I'm interested in one room only. The night of Friday the 7th of

June. I'd like to see everything you've got between 6 pm and midnight. And there's a hundred quid in your pocket."

Wayne sat back in his chair and pulled a disdainful face. "Yeah. You and everybody else."

"What do you mean?" asked Finnegan.

"This is about the black guy, right? The one who had the heart attack. The police were in here earlier this week asking about the same night."

This was not good news. "What happened?" asked a worried Sean.

"Just like you, they wanted to know if we'd got footage. I showed them the files but they never even asked to run them. They just insisted it was all wiped. That night, the day before and the day after; all deleted. They said it was a security issue. Top priority. The manager signed off on it, so I did as I was told."

"Bugger!" said Sean bitterly. "So you didn't get a look at it? You don't know what was on the recording?"

Wayne leaned in towards the journalist and lowered his voice. "What's it worth?"

"I'll tell you when I know what you can remember."

"I can do better than that" said Wayne softly with a confident grin. "Our system runs auto-copy. They told me to clear the files, so I did. The original's wiped. But they never asked about the back-up drive."

Finnegan's eyes lit up. "So you've still got the recording?"

"Two hundred quid and it's yours."

Sean pulled a USB drive from his jacket pocket and handed it to the smiling technician. "Everything you've got on this. And mum's the word, right?"

"You're on!"

Taking the proffered memory stick, Wayne swivelled around eagerly in his chair to begin the copying process. Finnegan counted out another five, twenty-pound notes.

Chapter Seventeen

It was just after 2.30 pm when Sean Finnegan returned to the Covent Garden flat. He discovered Josh bent studiously over the laptop. The morning's diligent Google search had returned numerous further articles on the Lukeba twins, several news reports on the Iranian scientist Nazari and a few paragraphs on the Russian Yurov but, to Josh's intense frustration, nothing appeared to serve as a link between any of them. Despite Brody's best efforts to discover otherwise, the Congolese brothers appeared to have no connection with the other two victims.

"I hope you've had better luck than I have" said Josh despondently as Finnegan walked into the lounge. "So far, I've come up with zilch."

"Well, I'm afraid Miller beat us to it" Sean told him as he flopped onto the sofa with a sigh. "He sent the boys in blue around earlier this week to wipe the hotel's recordings."

"Shit!" said Josh vehemently. "He's ahead of us at every frigging turn."

Finnegan's face creased into a satisfied smile. "Not quite, me bucko!" He pulled the USB drive from his pocket and held it up in triumph. "It cost you two hundred smackers, but I think you'll be pleased with what you bought."

With a celebratory glass of Jameson's each, Sean related the full story and they plugged the USB drive into the laptop to study the fruits of the trip to the Vanderbilt. There was nothing in the foyer or lift shots but the footage of the corridor leading to Dikembe Lukeba's room eventually yielded the images they were hoping to see. With her head bowed and her face hidden from view, it was impossible to identify the features of the woman who walked along the hallway, keeping close to one wall, and then knocked on the door of Lukeba's room. But the frame and the stature were unmistakeable.

"It's her!" declared Josh with delight. "It's the same woman."

They watched as the door was opened from within and the Chinese girl stood talking to the unseen occupant of the room. A few moments of conversation passed and then she stepped across the threshold and the door was closed.

"But the girl from Elite Escorts told you Lukeba called off the gig, didn't she?" asked Sean.

"Yes. He'd booked Sophie. But he called in sick and cancelled her."

"Then I don't get it! What was Lukeba thinking when little Miss Asia turns up on his doorstep unannounced? Why does he calmly let her in?"

"Because *he* didn't make the call" said Josh, looking up at his friend. "Don't you see? Miller, or more probably one of his cronies, calls the agency pretending to be Lukeba and cancels out Sophie. Then Dragon Lady here arrives at the appointed time. She says Sophie is unwell and she has been sent in her place. Lukeba is expecting a hooker and here is a beautiful Chinese girl. Ok, it's not the woman he booked but is he going to turn her down? Not very likely. So the assassin walks right in."

"Christ, it was that simple?"

"The most effective plans usually are."

"Let's run both recordings side by side" said Sean. "Just to be doubly sure." They copied the file to the hard drive and then ran both recordings side by side, playing the original footage from the Vienna hotel alongside the Vanderbilt recording. As they looked from window to window, comparing the shadowy figure moving furtively in each corridor, the similarities were obvious and undeniable. There was no mistake. It was the same girl.

"We know she was in London on the night of Friday the 7th and in Vienna on Wednesday the 12th" said Josh. "That gives us a relatively small time window in which she left one capital and entered the other."

"Agreed. And the odds are that she flew, right?"

"Right."

"So, even if she took a roundabout route to cover her tracks, there should be a photo record of her passing through airport departures here and entering arrivals in Vienna."

"Yes."

"Well, Vienna's a long shot but do you have any contacts who could get access to the security camera footage at Heathrow and Gatwick?" asked Sean hopefully.

Brody smiled. "No. But I know a man who does!"

While Josh made a call to a journalist friend called Ethan Taylor, Sean set to work at his laptop with his photo editing software. His years of experience enabled him to work swiftly and accurately and, within less than ten minutes, he had completed his task of cleaning the print. The still shot of the Chinese girl, captured from the foyer video footage of the

Intercontinental in Vienna, was now a clear, and almost pin-sharp, full face image. It gave Finnegan a strange feeling to be looking at the eyes of a woman who had calmly murdered both the Lukeba twins. There was nothing in the face staring back at him from his computer screen to suggest she was a killer. On the contrary, the features were attractive and impassive; but Finnegan's years in Africa had long ago taught him that appearance meant very little. Anonymous looking men, women, and even children with startlingly innocent faces, were capable of pointing a gun and pulling a trigger. The look of the Chinese girl in front of him meant nothing. Her deeds were what defined her character.

Ethan Taylor answered Josh's call in welcome surprise, delighted to hear unexpectedly from him after such a long time. Taylor was an experienced B.B.C. reporter who worked as a security correspondent for T.V. and radio news. Josh had known him for more than ten years, since the days when their contracted periods at The Independent overlapped. Whilst Brody would not have described Ethan as a 'close' friend, their relationship was firm and trusted. It was the sort of friendship where they might not see each other for a year or more but were then able calmly to pick-up where they left off, as if they had parted company only the previous day. They exchanged the usual pleasantries and then Josh got down to the purpose of his call.

"I won't beat around the bush or feed you a line, Ethan. I'm in trouble and I need your help. It's in your own interest to remain in the dark and not get dragged into this. So I'm going to ask you a big favour without telling you why. If you say 'no', I'll understand and there are no hard feelings. But you're the only guy I know who can help me. So please give it some thought."

Whether he was moved by the genuine anxiety in Josh's voice, or simply the trust of one journalist for a fellow professional, Ethan Taylor didn't hesitate. He simply said: "What do you need, Josh?"

A few minutes later, Sean emailed the newly cleaned photograph to Taylor. An hour after he received it, having made a couple of strategic phone calls and left messages for his contacts, the B.B.C. correspondent obtained the go-ahead he requested and forwarded the image to the security teams at both Heathrow and Gatwick.

* * * * *

Sunday, June 30th.

The age of international terrorism brought many horrors to the world but it also delivered swift and far-reaching improvements in security procedures, especially at airports where passengers and planes are particularly vulnerable to attack. In the U.K., photo recognition programmes were among the top priorities of software developers so that the anti-terrorist squad could conduct wide ranging identity searches. With millions of passengers passing through Britain's airports every year, and every single one of them photographed as they entered or exited passport control, the computer programmes checking names and faces had to operate across a breath-taking range of data and do so at lightning speed. With a specific and narrow date span to check, it was not long before the team at Heathrow produced a match for the photograph Ethan Taylor had sent. The head of security mailed the details back to the journalist and he forwarded the email to Josh Brody. The entire process, from initial phone call, to the return of results, took less than twenty-four hours. Such was modern technology.

At 11 am, when the email arrived, Brody and Sean Finnegan were sitting drinking coffee. They both peered nervously at the screen as Josh clicked on the email and opened the attachments. Neither man could believe their luck. On Saturday the 8th of June, at 11.15 in the morning, the day after Dikembe Lukeba's murder, a young Chinese woman passed through passport control at Heathrow airport. Unlike the Vienna photograph at the Intercontinental Hotel, where her face bore bright red lipstick, heavy eye-shadow and mascara, this face was bland, pale and showed not a trace of make-up. The hair was mostly concealed under a head scarf and her expression was neutral and impassive; but there was no mistake. The computer facial recognition software was not deflected by the change in her outward appearance. It was the same girl. She was travelling on a British passport, issued in London, and the accompanying data sheet stated that she was booked on an Austrian Airlines flight to Vienna. Her name was stated as Tsu Li.

"It's probably an alias" said Josh philosophically. "But if Miller is behind her then you can bet the passport is genuine. And, alias or not, now we've got an identity!"

Apart from Sean's brief visit to a local ATM machine to withdraw the remaining balance of Alan Denton's project account, the two men spent the rest of Sunday safely ensconced in the Covent Garden flat. By mid-afternoon they had assembled all their evidence, cross-referencing dates, photographs and video footage, and typed a detailed report. It made a clear and incontestable case that the Lukeba twins had been murdered by a slim, petite Chinese girl named Tsu Li.

The indictment against Miller and his team was more tenuous. Josh's personal account of his time at the safe house in Morpeth Terrace was the only accusatory testimony. It was one man's word; but, allied to the provable facts that Miller had employed the lawyer Steiner, secured Brody's release from custody in Vienna and then flown him out of the country, there was no way to deny his involvement. Both men felt that, even circumstantially, they could mount a convincing case.

The next issue was how to proceed and utilise the information they held. Before they could address that all important question, there was the urgent matter of Shelley Anderson to consider.

Miller had no reason to consider her as anything more than a bystander; but reality was different. Josh had shared the details of the Lukeba case with her and she herself had suggested the possible connection between the Nazari murder and the death of Yurov in Paris. Once the 'shit hit the fan', as Sean eloquently put it, her knowledge would make her a prime target for 'silencing'. So the immediate issue was to warn her of the true nature of Miller's activities and to remove her from harm's way. That would require judicious and meticulous planning.

Finnegan telephoned the nearest Pizza Express and ordered a delivery and, with endless cans of Guinness stored in the larder and a still half-full bottle of Jameson's on the table, the two men spent several hours carefully devising a strategy to get Shelley to safety when she appeared at the following day's rendezvous.

"We need a car" declared Josh soberly. "But hiring one is out of the question. You have to provide too much documentation and proof of I.D. We can't afford for either of us to be traceable."

"I'll call Declan" said Sean thoughtfully.

"Declan?"

"Declan Lynch. He's got a couple of lock-ups in Southwark. He runs a business re-conditioning gear boxes but he's always got a couple vehicles for sale. He does up old bangers that local dealers take in part-ex and don't want on their forecourts, so don't expect anything posh, but it'll run ok."

"Will he hire us one 'off the book'?"

Sean laughed. "He'd hire you his own mother if the price was right. How much cash do we have now that we've emptied uncle Alan's project account?"

"Much more than we need. Just over three grand."

"Right. I'll set it up"

A phone call to the acquisitive car mechanic produced a promise to have an Audi saloon waiting for Sean Finnegan at nine o'clock the following morning. Fifty pounds, cash in hand, would cover a single day's rental and a further hundred would ensure there would be no questions asked, no hire agreement and no need for insurance. The deal was sealed.

Josh and Sean ran through the details of their plan many times, taking it in turns to play Devil's advocate and suggest possible problems. When they were convinced their preparations were sound, they finally relaxed.

Sean raised his glass and offered a toast. "To tomorrow. And beating the bastards at their own game!"

Brody lifted his whiskey in salute, silently praying that their optimism was well founded.

* * * * *

Monday, July 1st.

The modern office building imposingly dominating the south bank of the Thames beside Vauxhall Bridge, on the site of the famous nineteenth century Pleasure Gardens, is known within the intelligence community as 'Legoland'. The regular, angular sections of its construction bear a striking resemblance to the famous children's toy and quickly gave rise to the affectionate nickname when it opened in 1994 as the newly built home of the Special Intelligence Service, known as M.I.6.

In marked contrast to previous, long-standing government policy, when the very existence of the service was never officially acknowledged, the striking new edifice beside the river was publicly declared to be its headquarters. The new, self-imposed doctrine of 'openness' within the corridors of power dictated that even the location of the nation's security services should be admitted. In reality, little changed. The clandestine keepers of the country's intelligence flame merely continued as they had always done, working to a secret agenda, while an adept and able P.R. department produced anodyne, pacifying statements for public consumption.

Stephen Miller and his team were so deeply concealed within the layers of deniability that, officially, they did not exist. Their H.Q. was located in a nondescript office block in Millbank, on the north side of the river, looking enviously across the water at the modern command centre of their glamorous cousins. Like the bastard offspring of olden day royalty, they had been conceived and born on the wrong side of the official blanket and, while supported financially by substantial off-the-book funds, would remain forever unrecognised and denied by their progenitors.

The state-of-the-art, specialised facilities within M.I.6 were all available to Miller but, just as with any operational requirement, the technicians who ran and managed the banks of data, computers, satellites and audio-visual monitoring were only aware of the information they were processing and had no knowledge of its purpose or utilisation. Indeed, the stringent exigencies of the 'need-to-know principle' meant that only three of the most senior occupants of 'Legoland' knew of Miller and the existence of his small, carefully chosen group.

The unit's regular Monday morning briefing began promptly at 9 am. Carter, Lucas and Podolski were all seated at the conference table, not looking forward to the arrival of their boss.

"What have we got?" demanded Miller as he strode into the meeting room and took his seat.

"Nothing" said Carter, despondently. "It's almost seventy-two hours since our bird took flight but there's been no trace of him. The entire greater London police has his description and a photo but it's produced no sightings as yet. Ports, airports, stations and all exit points have been circularised as you requested but have also drawn a blank. We are therefore presuming Brody has gone to ground and is staying hidden."

"Known contacts and associates?" asked Miller.

Lucas shook his head. "No contact so far. We've drawn up a list of likely friends and colleagues he might turn to but he hasn't reached any of them yet. We can't know *all* his connections of course but his personal circle actually seems quite small so we think we've covered most of the possibilities. We're tapping his agent's office and naturally we're watching his Westcliff home, listening-in to his ex-wife's calls and reading her emails; but there's been no contact of any kind."

"What about the girl, Anderson? Wasn't she due back from Vienna?"

"Arrived yesterday" replied Lucas, checking the notes in front of him. "We've got a team of three watchers on her, working eight-hour shifts, but she went straight home from the airport and hasn't surfaced again yet."

"And do we have full monitoring on Denton, the newspaper editor? He's the most likely to receive whatever evidence Brody has assembled."

Lucas checked his notes again. "His mobile, home phone line and broadband were co-opted yesterday just after mid-day. No traffic of any significance and no calls or emails from Brody. But we have a man watching the house."

"I think he's hunkered down, sir" offered Carter with a pessimistic shake of his head. "And it's going to take huge resources to flush him out."

Miller sat back in his chair with his linked hands resting in his lap and his two thumbs slowly tapping together. "Maybe" he said thoughtfully. "Maybe not. Any fish can be caught eventually. Netting it just depends on how well you bait your hook." He checked his watch and looked across the table at Carter. "Order up the car. You're coming with me."

Shelley Anderson left her Putney apartment at just after 10 am. She had plenty of time in which to make her short journey but, above all else, she did not wish to be late. She was concerned to look as inconspicuous as possible but, at the same time, wanted to be sure Josh would easily recognise her among what she knew would be a large crowd. Her compromise was to wear the same powder blue cotton jacket and denim jeans she had worn on the first day they met. She had rejected heels and chosen to wear trainers, just in case whatever was in store involved the need for extended walking. It took only a few minutes to reach the Underground station and the service was running on time and to schedule. Boarding a District Line train, she headed east and alighted at Westminster, where she left the subterranean station concourse and emerged to enter the bright morning sunshine outside the Houses Of Parliament.

Like most of the world's major capitals, London is a prime, year-round tourist hub but the four summer months between June and September, known to native Londoners as 'the silly season', is when the majority of overseas visitors flock to the city's landmarks. The area around Westminster Bridge, where tourists can stand with the tower of Big Ben rising majestically behind them, is the number one spot in which to be photographed and Shelley found herself surrounded by eager groups of holiday-makers from a bewildering range of nationalities. She had to elbow her way through the throng in order to cross the street and walk across the bridge to the south bank.

Her stomach was tight with nerves as she continued through the crowds and every step took her nearer to her long awaited rendezvous with Josh. She had no idea what might lie ahead of her and no option but to trust in Brody's judgement. All she knew for certain was where Josh wanted her to be at 11 am.

The text of the email from Ian Magen was clever and adroit. Her first *'lime kiss'* had taken place at the very top of the Riesenrad, Vienna's famous Ferris wheel, when she and Josh were joking about the film 'The Third Man'. Josh was standing by the door of the gondola, in just the position where Orson Welles, playing Harry Lime, had stood. Then he kissed her for the first time. There was only one equivalent venue in London, and the preceding sentence of the email had confirmed it perfectly. *'There's more to this than meets the eye!'* could only mean meeting him at The London Eye, the giant Ferris Wheel on the south bank.

From Westminster bridge, Shelley gazed across at the enormous circular frame of gondolas, suspended, as if by magic, around the edge of what looked like the spokes of a colossal bicycle wheel. It was an imposing, impressive structure and the sun glinted from the glass of the highest of the thirty-two gondolas as it rose to crest the top of the circuit, giving its occupants wide-ranging views of the capital that stretched for miles in every direction.

As usual, The Embankment beneath The Eye looked choked with tourists and sightseers, with long queues of people snaking across the walkway and stretching back into Jubilee Gardens as they waited patiently to board for their half-hour ride. If Josh was seeking crowds to conceal their meeting then he had chosen wisely.

Shelley crossed the bridge and continued on past the old County Hall building, turning left into Belvedere Road where she found a small Italian café. Ordering an espresso, she checked her watch and settled down to wait, determined to time her arrival at the foot of The Eye for exactly 11 am.

Unknown to Shelley, as she stepped through the front door of the café her arrival was immediately reported back to Stephen Miller's headquarters. A copper-haired man in a grey, check jacket had tailed her all the way from Putney and was now stationed across the street. His closed circuit radio was linked directly to the Millbank office and he lifted his wrist and spoke into the small microphone that was attached to it.

"This is Fisher. Subject has just entered a café in Belvedere Road. Do you want me to go in or remain outside?"

The voice of Lucas played into his earpiece. "We were expecting this. She's waiting for somebody. She had an email from some faggot friend arranging to meet, so she could be there a while. Go in and have yourself a coffee, see who turns up and then report back."

"Got it." Fisher obediently crossed the street and casually entered through the café's front door. Taking a seat at a table in the far corner, where he could keep Shelley within his peripheral vision, he ordered a coffee from the smiling waitress and took out a small paperback from his jacket pocket. Opening the book on the table in front of him, he pretended to read.

Josh Brody made his way steadily through the crowd of tourists. The section of The Embankment between Waterloo and Westminster Bridges, on the south side of the Thames, was full of street entertainers and vendors, all competing for the attention, and cash, of the thousands of pedestrians walking along the river frontage. The constant hubbub and ever changing action provided Josh with more than adequate cover as he walked slowly towards his rendezvous, dark glasses covering his eyes and his baseball cap pulled low across his brow. Like Shelley Anderson, he too was timing his arrival as precisely as he could. Waiting around in a public place was not a good idea for a man on the run and he needed to complete his planned operation as quickly and efficiently as possible. He nervously checked his watch for the tenth time in as many minutes. He was on schedule.

In the Italian café, Shelly Anderson was also keeping a careful eye on the time. As the hands of her watch clicked onto five minutes to eleven, she rose from her seat and left.

Her watcher, seated in the far corner, was taken by surprise. He had been expecting someone to arrive to meet his target and anticipated a long and boring wait while they talked and probably ate an early lunch. Her unexpected departure caught him off-guard. Throwing a couple of pound coins onto the table to cover the cost of his coffee, he hurriedly got to his feet and followed his quarry out of the café. As he entered the street, he spoke again into his sleeve microphone.

"This is Fisher. Subject has left café. Heading east."

"Stay with her" said the unemotional voice in his ear, and Fisher set off in pursuit.

Brody positioned himself alongside a souvenir stall, where a tourist family of two parents and three children were chatting noisily over the goods on offer. Close enough to be taken for one of the group, he continued to hover, occasionally picking up and examining some of the souvenirs as if considering buying them. He was constantly monitoring the entrance to the London Eye, just some fifty metres or so ahead of him, and continually looking down at his watch. As 11 am arrived he could feel his shoulders tightening and a knot forming in his gut. For an unsettling minute, he thought he had perhaps made a misjudgement. Maybe she had not correctly understood the coded message. His fears proved unfounded as, a few moments later, he spotted her blue cotton jacket and at last caught sight of her moving among the crowd. She walked calmly up to the entrance gate where she stopped, apparently reading the information board.

It was time for Brody to act. Pulling a five pound note from his pocket, he stepped away from the souvenir stall and stopped a teenage boy who was ambling past carrying a skateboard. "Like to earn an easy fiver?" he asked the youth, flashing him a broad smile.

The teenager appeared to be around fourteen or fifteen years of age and was wearing a T-shirt with the message 'Fuck Art – Let's Dance!' emblazoned in large letters across his chest. He looked warily at Josh. "Maybe" he said suspiciously. "What I gotta do?"

Shelley felt nervous and on edge. She didn't want to look about her, drawing attention to the fact she was expecting someone, so she cast her eyes back to the top of the information board and began reading it for the second time. She was just beginning to doubt she was in the right location when her shoulder was abruptly jolted and a teenage boy bumped into her.

"Sorry" he apologised immediately and turned away but, as he left, he furtively took her wrist, keeping it at hip level, and deftly placed something in her palm, firmly closing her fingers around it. By the time Shelley glanced down to see the mobile phone in her hand, the youngster was gone.

For a few seconds she was confused but the disorientation of the moment was quickly broken as the handset rang and vibrated within her grasp. She hesitated momentarily but then clicked on the receive button and apprehensively lifted the phone to her ear.

"Hello?"

"Don't look 'round" commanded Josh. "Just smile and act normal; as if you were idly chatting with someone."

"Josh" she blurted out with immense relief. "Where are you? And what's happening? Are you in trouble?"

"No questions" he told her swiftly. "I'll explain everything in a few minutes. Right now I just need you to listen and do as I ask. Ok?"

"Ok" she agreed anxiously.

"Now smile and give a little laugh; as though you're joking with a friend."

She did as she was bidden, nodding and laughing out loud.

"That's good" he encouraged.

"Wait a minute. Are you watching me? Where are you?"

"I'm really close. But don't look for me. Give all your attention to the call."

"Ok. I don't understand any of this but we'll play it your way. What next?"

" I want you to start walking along the river front in the direction of Waterloo Bridge. I'm going to be a little way behind you but don't turn around. Just keep talking to me and move casually."

Shelley nodded again and set off as directed.

Josh followed at a safe distance, watching her carefully. "You look good" he said softly into the phone. "I've missed you."

"I've missed you too" she confessed emotionally. "I was furious with you for a while when I thought you'd just run off without a word; but then I got your email and realised something was wrong."

"Are you still furious?" he asked with the trace of a smile in his tone.

"No. Now I'm just a little frightened. Why are we behaving like we're in some espionage B movie? What's going on?"

"Trust me" he encouraged. "We're just being ultra-cautious. It'll be all over in a couple of minutes and I'll explain everything."

Fisher was a little confused. He'd seen his quarry waiting by the entrance to The Eye and assumed she was waiting for her expected meeting but suddenly she was talking on the phone and moving away. He guessed that whoever was supposed to meet her had called to cry off but, ever the efficient watcher, he decided to report back.

"This is Fisher" he said into his microphone. "Target was waiting on The Embankment but is talking on the phone and now walking away, heading east."

"Follow" instructed Lucas, seated in the control room of the Millbank office. He looked across the room at one of the three computer operators, whose terminals were all logged into the main operations centre across the river. "We're still monitoring Shelley Anderson's mobile, aren't we?"

"Yes, sir" came the immediate reply.

"Tap into it and tell me who she's talking to and what they're saying, will you?"

"Sir."

Lucas waited patiently for his technician's computer to check into the main frame where the monitoring software was reading all chatter and traffic on designated lines. The operator peered at his screen with a puzzled expression and then re-typed instructions onto his keyboard, but the data in front of him didn't change.

"Negative, sir" he called back across the room. "The line is not operating."

"But she's on her phone now. The watcher's looking at her."

"No, sir. Not on the quoted line. That number is quiet."

Lucas suddenly realised something was very wrong. "Stay with her!" he barked to Fisher. "Whatever you do, don't lose her. We're on our way." He called across the room to Podolski, who was seated and idly reading a newspaper. "Get the car!"

Under the sprawling span of Waterloo Bridge, outside the riverfront entrance to the National Film Theatre that nestles within the bridge's arches, the pedestrian walkway was spread with numerous trestle tables, all filled with a seemingly endless display of second-hand books. Taking advantage of the shelter of the bridge above, street traders had turned the area into a regular book market, drawing large crowds on most days of the week. Shelley found herself surrounded.

"I'm under the bridge" she said into the handset. "What now?"

"Almost there. As you come out from the bridge, turn right in front of The National Theatre and head away from the river along the side of the building."

"Ok. Are you still with me?"

"Yes, I'm close by. On the left hand side you'll see the National's little café."

It soon came into view. "Yes. I've got it."

"Just a few steps further on there are some metal stairs leading down to the underground car park. Can you see them?"

"Wait a minute... Oh. Yes. I see them."

"At the bottom of those stairs is a maroon coloured Audi. The driver is a friend called Sean. Get into the rear of the car and keep your head down. Sean will drive you out of the car park. I'll be with you in a couple of minutes. Got it?"

"Yes" she said nervously, clearly unconfident. "But I don't like this Josh. Please be quick."

"I will" he promised and clicked off the handset.

Brody watched her turn into the stairwell and descend to the car park below. Then he quickened his pace, moving along the walkway at the side of the theatre towards the road at the far end where he would meet the Audi.

Fisher rounded the corner just in time to catch a glimpse of Shelley's blue cotton jacket as it descended the steps and disappeared below street level. Another two seconds and Brody's carefully executed plan would have succeeded; she would have been home and safe, as if she had simply evaporated into thin air; but Fisher had been just close enough to see where she had gone. Realising she was heading for a car, and guessing that Brody might well be driving it, the watcher ran immediately to the metal stairs and they clattered loudly under his frantic feet as he rushed downwards, pulling his automatic from the holster under his left arm. He heard the sound of the engine before he reached the bottom and arrived just in time to see the brake lights of the Audi as it rounded the turn at the end of the aisle, heading for the exit.

Fisher had two options. He could run in pursuit of the car, knowing it would probably be through the barrier and out of the car park before he could catch it, or he could dash back up the stairs and head for the road. If the Audi turned left when it exited the car park, it would be gone; but if it turned right, and headed towards him, he might be able to shoot out the tyres. Fisher chose to turn around and, panting hard to fill his lungs, tore back up the stairs.

By the time he reached ground level, Brody was well ahead of him and waiting at the far end of the street. Fisher had no notion as to the identity of the man in the baseball cap whose back was towards him but, as the maroon Audi pulled sharply into the kerbside and the rear door opened to allow the man in, the stranger turned to the side and the watcher saw his profile. He recognised it at once.

Fisher was still at least fifty metres from the end of the street. It was too far to issue a command to 'freeze' and the clinical words of his instructions flashed into his head: *'If it's a choice between losing him or killing him, then take him out.'* The obedient watcher took a stance, steadied his aim by gripping his right wrist with his left hand, and fired. The shot struck the door frame of the Audi, no more than two centimetres from Brody's left shoulder, only missing his head because he had lowered his upper body to clamber into the rear of the vehicle.

The next few seconds were a maelstrom of chaotic noise and movement.

The report from the gunshot bounced loudly off the long, flat concrete walls of the National and the Film Theatre, rebounding back and forth between the two buildings like a sonic ping pong ball. The crowds at The Embankment end of the street were instantly startled and there were several screams as people realised a gun had been fired and, not knowing from where, started running frenziedly for cover in all directions.

In the Audi, as the bullet smashed deafeningly into the steel bodywork, Shelley also let out a loud scream. After a dumbfounded second, Sean realised they were under fire and yelled "Get in the fucking car!" Brody needed no further prompting and dived onto the back seat as Sean revved the engine and threw the Audi into gear. With the wheels spinning violently, frantically seeking traction on the tarmac, the tyres screeched and the car pulled away, the back door still open and flapping behind Josh.

Fisher let loose a second shot. The bullet smashed through the window glass of the Audi's rear door, as it swung back on its hinges, and ricocheted off the steel of the bodywork. Fisher was running full pelt towards the vehicle as it sped away, desperately trying to read the number plate. He reached the end of the street in time to catch sight of the last three letters as Sean threw the car to the left and hurtled up the slip road towards the roundabout at the southern end of Waterloo Bridge.

"It's Brody" Fisher yelled loudly into his wrist microphone. "He's with the girl; in a maroon coloured Audi. Registration ends in Charlie, Delta, Uniform. I may have winged him."

The anxious voice of Lucas broke into his ear. "We're your side of the river. We're in York Road. Make yourself scarce and get out of there." He reached to the seat behind him, seized a battery-operated blue warning light and quickly switched it on. Opening the side window, he thrust it out onto the roof of the Ford where the magnetic surface of its base adhered to the metal with a loud clunk. Podolski threw a switch on the dash board and the vehicle's siren began to wail as he gunned the Ford Focus and pulled across the central white line, speeding along the wrong side of the road and weaving swiftly between the traffic as it ceded passage and moved aside.

As the Audi sped around the Imax cinema, that took up the whole of the centre of the large roundabout, the three worried occupants could hear the wail of the approaching siren. Brody was frantically thinking. "Jump the lights!" he commanded and Sean pulled the car sharply to one side, cutting up a van and a motorcycle and ignoring the protesting horns that were furiously sounded as he ran the red light. He skidded across two lanes and then, darting in front of a double-decker bus, threw a left to head north across Waterloo Bridge.

Podolski was a trained pursuit driver and expertly steered the Focus through the traffic. The Ford reached the large roundabout in time to see the rear end of the Audi disappearing onto the bridge. "There!" yelled Lucas and the Focus set off.

The shocked driver of the bus had been forced to slam on his brakes and swerve when Sean sped in front of him and the irate man, cursing loudly, was fully occupied with pulling his vehicle back into its correct lane. Podolski was about to manoeuvre in front of the bus when he realised the driver hadn't seen him and wasn't going to stop. He had only a split second in which to avoid a crash. Braking hard, he swerved to his right. The front wing of the Focus glanced against the rear end of a truck, throwing Lucas and Podolski violently forward against the restraint of their seat belts and stalling the engine. The small collision bought precious extra seconds for the fleeing Audi.

"Where do you want me to head?" demanded Sean as the car sped towards the north end of Waterloo Bridge. The three options were left into The Strand, right into the Aldwych, both of which meant jumping the traffic lights, or down into the underpass to rise up in Kingsway.

"Take the tunnel!" Josh told him. He reached out and grabbed Shelley's hand. She was speechless with fear. "Hang on!" he told her urgently.

Brody needed to make a decision and to make it fast. "They mustn't catch *you*" he yelled at Sean. "If they do they'll find the flat and everything we've got. Then we'll *all* be dead."

"I'm not arguing" called Sean over his shoulder, as he steered the Audi towards the underpass entrance. "But how the fuck do we get out of this? There'll be police cars all around us in no time!"

Even as Sean was prophesying an onslaught of police, Lucas was on the radio in the Focus calling for back-up while Podolski re-started the car, reversed back from the truck and accelerated hard towards the bridge.

"I need Met. cars *now"* ordered Lucas into the microphone. "A maroon Audi saloon, number ending Charlie, Delta, Uniform, heading north across Waterloo Bridge. All units in pursuit!"

The Audi tore into the tunnel, careering around the narrow curve to the right and speeding past the tile covered walls that echoed to its engine's roar as it headed for Kingsway.

"As soon as we hit the road, pull over" instructed Josh. "You take Shelley and make a run for it. Wait for me at the flat."

"No!" cried Shelley. "For Christ's sake, Josh. They'll kill you."

"There's no time to argue!" he told her. "It's the only chance we've got."

Sean didn't like leaving his friend any more than Shelley did but, right or wrong, discussion was not an option. Their pursuers had guns and were only seconds behind. As the Audi broke daylight and emerged from the northern end of the underpass into Kingsway, Sean veered to the left and pulled the car to a screeching halt at the side of the road.

"Go!" yelled Josh to Shelley as Sean leapt from the front of the vehicle and Brody scrambled forward, clambering into the driver's seat.

Shelley, in a flood of tears, was scarcely out of the rear door as Brody floored the pedal and drove off.

Finnegan ran to Shelley and grabbed her arm. "Quickly!" he told her urgently, hauling her away from the roadside and across the pavement towards the porch-way of the nearest office building. Pushing her ahead of him, he forced her through the revolving doors and into the foyer, where he turned her face away from the street and stood with his considerable bulk in front of her so she was hidden from view. Within the shadows of the vestibule, Sean dared to lift his head and look out. As he did so, the Ford Focus, its siren wailing and a flashing blue light flickering from its roof, tore out of the underpass and flashed by.

Now only a couple of hundred metres ahead of the tailing car, Brody desperately scanned the road ahead of him. If he continued to the very end of Kingsway he'd land at the major junction with Holborn where traffic lights regulated the flow from three different directions. His flight would grind to a halt. He had to turn off the road. Hitting the horn furiously to warn pedestrians, he tore over the crossing at Great Queen Street before throwing an immediate left into Parker Street. The Focus was close enough behind to see the tail lights of the Audi as it braked hard and then disappeared.

"In close pursuit" Lucas said into his microphone. "Heading into Parker Street."

As Josh completed the turn and straightened his vehicle he gasped in horror. It was a narrow one way street and there was a junction just seconds ahead where a large refuse truck was slowly entering from the left to pull in front of him. Brody punched the bottom of his clenched fist down onto the horn in the centre of the steering wheel and held it there. The loud blast alerted the driver of the truck who, horror-struck to see the Audi speeding towards him, jammed on his brakes. Josh pulled his car to the right, mounted the kerb, and sped through the gap between the front of the truck and the wall of the corner building. The truck driver and three of the refuse men, who were collecting rubbish bags from the street, all yelled and swore as Brody's car squeezed by them. Shocked and dumbfounded by the reckless driving, they had just about recovered when they heard a screech of brakes and turned to see a dark blue Ford Focus, a police light flashing on its roof, turn violently around the corner and start heading towards them. The truck driver braced himself and the men on the street dropped their bags and ran as Podolski accelerated towards them and took the same route as the Audi, tearing into the narrow gap between the truck and the wall.

Parker Street widened into two way traffic and Josh kept the car in a straight line, speeding towards the end T-junction with Drury Lane. He was frantically trying to decide whether he should make a right or a left, attempting to picture what lay ahead in either direction, when the road sign at the corner made the decision for him. The fast-approaching section of Drury Lane was one-way only and he dare not turn into oncoming traffic and risk a head–on collision. His only option was to turn right. A lightning glance in the mirror told Josh that the Focus was gaining ground as he braked hard, veered right and, hitting the horn to announce his arrival to possible pedestrians and advancing cars, jerked the steering wheel clockwise and skidded around the corner. Vehicles were parked on both sides of the one-way street and the rear of the Audi banged into the nearest car as Brody fought to straighten its nose.

As he drove like a maniac towards the end of Drury Lane, Josh could hear another siren. It had a different pitch from the Ford that was chasing him and sounded as if it might be approaching from the north; but there was no way of pinpointing it or knowing whether he was avoiding this new threat or heading straight for it.

Suddenly he heard a metallic clang and realised that a bullet had hit the rear of his car. He darted another look at the mirror and caught a glimpse of a shaved head hanging out of the passenger window of the Focus and aiming a gun. He was unsure whether his pursuer was trying to shoot out his tyres or attempting to put a bullet into him through the rear window and only the violence of the chase was rendering aim inaccurate. It made little difference either way.

He saw there was a turning to his left and swung the Audi viciously towards it, mounting the pavement outside the Travelodge and narrowly missing an elderly couple who had just crossed the road. He found himself in Shorts Gardens, another one-way street. Speeding past a block of flats to his right, he pressed the palm of his left hand hard against the horn, holding it down to sound an alarm and broadcast his imminent approach. People stared and heads turned as he flew down the street towards the next junction.

Podolski threw the Focus left and followed the Audi's path. "We're in Shorts Gardens heading west" Lucas spat into the microphone. "Where's the fucking back-up?"

Praying there were no vehicles or pedestrians about to cross the junction with Endell Street, and that all and sundry had heard his loud, incessant blaring of the horn, Brody accelerated and drove clean across the junction without stopping. He was vaguely aware of a large shape looming to his left and heard the piercing squeal of panicked braking, followed by the furious blast of a horn, but his attention was fully concentrated on the street in front of him. Alarmingly, it was narrowing. The pavement on either side was suddenly bordered by thick, intermittent wooden posts that were meant to warn approaching traffic as the road tapered to what Brody suddenly realised, to his horror, was a pedestrianised area.

The tailing Focus was not so lucky as it entered the junction with Endell Street. The large shape Brody had missed by a whisker turned out to be a Transit van. Stamping on the brakes to avoid colliding with the Audi that was screaming across the junction in front of him, the Transit driver had wrenched his vehicle to the left, causing it to turn broadside as it skidded to a halt, ending up at ninety degrees to its original direction. Podolski frantically slammed down both feet but the Focus was travelling too fast to stop and careered violently into the rear of the van. The air bags exploded into inflation as Podolski was jerked brutally forward, only saved by the seat belt that locked viciously against his right shoulder, and the cushioning air bag that enveloped his head.

Lucas was less fortunate. He had released his seat belt in order to be able to lean out of the side window and fire at Brody. With nothing to restrain him, he was catapulted forward. Despite the efforts of the air bag to halt his progress, he was hurled through the windscreen and out onto the bonnet of the Focus as it crumpled into the rear of the Transit van.

Brody heard the din of the crash behind him as he concentrated on keeping his car in a straight line between the posts on either side of the narrowing road but he had no conception of the serious accident that had occurred. A momentary glance in the rear view mirror told him nothing more than that the Focus was no longer immediately on his tail. Whatever had transpired behind him, he had a brief moment's respite. The street surface itself was now cobbled and had become a pedestrian precinct where passage for vehicles was possible but restricted and intended only for deliveries. It was the end of the line. Brody could still hear the approaching sound of the second siren and knew his options were limited.

With another swift look in the mirror to check there was no immediately chasing vehicle, he suddenly braked and halted, leaving the car at a slight angle so that it filled the narrow space and blocked passage. He switched off the engine and grabbed the key from the ignition as, to the amazement of passers-by, he dashed out of the Audi, leaving the driver's door swinging open behind him. He ran hell for leather towards the end of the road, heading for Seven Dials. It was a fortuitous location. If he could make its circular junction, anyone later questioned by police and reporting his flight from the Audi would have no idea as to which of the seven possible exits he had taken.

Panting and gasping for breath, Brody reached the end of Shorts Gardens where the famous obelisk stood in the centre of the converging roads. He heard a siren close by and looked up to see a white B.M.W. with the livery of the Met. police emerging from Monmouth Street to his right. It tore around the junction and swerved left by the Cambridge Theatre into the southern half of Earlham Street. As it swept by him, Brody turned his back and hid himself within the doorway to The Crown pub. The car passed and its occupants appeared not to have noticed him. Maybe his luck was holding.

Not wishing to be too conspicuous by running, Brody forced himself to travel at only a walking pace as he crossed the central island with its sun-dial adorned pillar and headed in the opposite direction to the police car. Aiming for the market stalls in the northern end of Earlham Street, he slipped into the crowd of shoppers and slowly, as the panic in him started for the first time marginally

to subside, he felt his tension ease a little. He began to believe he had perhaps, once again, escaped Miller's forces. In an urgent effort to control and regulate his breathing, he began to inhale slowly and deeply, willing his shoulders to drop and relax and attempting to compose himself as he stepped warily through the throng and finally walked out into a busy Shaftesbury Avenue.

Irrationally, he immediately felt exposed, as though all eyes were staring at him, but he fought the illogical fear and, keeping close to the walls of adjacent buildings, turned right. Holding to the shadows, he made his way along the pavement, keeping a constant eye on the road. Shaftesbury Avenue was one of the West End's major thoroughfares and he knew there had to be numerous cabs among the approaching traffic. The first three he saw were all occupied but, within a few minutes of anxious waiting, he found what he was seeking. The yellow 'For Hire' light had never been more welcoming as Josh stepped away from the comfort of the nearby wall and walked to the kerb with a raised arm. To his immense relief, he saw the taxi indicator flashing and the driver pulled over and stopped.

Brody quickly clambered into the rear of the cab, slumping onto the vinyl seat as he gratefully pulled the door closed behind him. For the time being at least, he was out of sight. For the time being, he was safe.

Chapter Eighteen

Badly shaken and traumatised by their ordeal, and both desperately worried about Brody, the immediate priority for Sean and Shelley was to remove themselves from the streets and return to the safety of Finnegan's flat where, hopefully, they could wait for word from Josh. Keeping to the back streets, away from the scrutiny of passing police patrol cars, they left Kingsway and in less than twenty minutes were stepping through the door of the Covent Garden apartment.

Their first act was to switch on the T.V. and select the BBC News channel to see if the morning's events were being reported. For almost an hour there was nothing. Then, a little after 1 pm, as Sean handed Shelley yet another cup of strong black coffee and they sat anxiously together on the sofa in front of the television set, they saw the first newsflash.

The rolling marquee at the bottom of the picture started showing *'Breaking News – a shooting incident on London street'*. They sat glued to the screen but it was a further couple of minutes before the female anchor referred to the item.

"We're getting reports coming in of a shooting incident in London's West End earlier today. We have few facts as yet but sources are saying that a police car was involved in a pursuit and shots were fired. The chase ended in a car crash. We have no confirmation of details but eye witnesses are reported as saying at least two people were injured with one possible fatality. We'll of course bring you updates as soon as they come in."

The colour instantly drained from Shelley's face and she slowly turned to her equally worried companion. For a moment neither spoke, but each knew what the other was thinking.

"Don't let's presume anything" Sean offered tentatively. "Nothing's confirmed yet and, even if someone was hurt, we don't know it was Josh." His effort to comfort her was appreciated but the lack of conviction in his voice told her he was just as fearful as she was.

"Why haven't we heard from him?" she asked meekly. "If he's ok, he would have called us wouldn't he?"

"Not necessarily" said Sean, struggling valiantly to maintain some sort of optimism. "Calls are traceable."

Shelley held up the mobile handset she had been given that morning on The Embankment. "This isn't traceable. That's why he got it to me this morning. "Why hasn't he rung this number?"

Sean shrugged. "He's probably lying low. We mustn't jump to conclusions."

She was unconvinced. "I'm frightened, Sean. The news said there was a crash. I have a terrible feeling..."

Before she could finish her sentence the apartment's land line rang. The two of them exchanged an apprehensive look as Sean quickly got up from the sofa and hurried across the room to the telephone.

"Hello?" he said cautiously into the receiver.

"I'm in a call box across the street" Brody told him. "Is it safe to come in?"

Sean's eyes closed and his head fell back as he exhaled loudly with relief. "Thank Christ!" he said to the unhearing ceiling. "I'll come down and let you in."

Before he had hung up the phone, Shelley was off the sofa and dashing across the room. "Is it him?!" she demanded. "Is he ok?" More overcome by emotion than he realised, Sean could only nod. Shelley burst into tears. A tidal wave of relief swept over her and she threw her arms around the Irishman and began to sob on his shoulder. "Thank God" she blurted out. "Oh, thank God."

Five minutes later she was hugging Brody himself as he stood in the flat's small lounge holding her tightly. He was exhausted and badly shaken but, in answer to Shelley's silent prayers, he was alive and unharmed. When the emotional reunion was over, Finnegan poured them all a large whiskey each and he and Shelley settled themselves to listen as Brody recounted the horrifying events of the car chase once he had left them at the kerbside in Kingsway.

"I can only presume they were in a pile-up somewhere behind me" he said in conclusion. "All I knew was that, for the moment, they were off my tail. So I abandoned the car and legged it." He looked regretfully across at Sean. "I'm afraid Declan Lynch is not going to be too happy with us for what we've done to his Audi."

Sean grinned. "It's ok. I rang him as soon as we got back. He's reported the car stolen. He told the local police he arrived at work this morning to find it nicked. I promised we'd cover his loss of course but the car was only worth a few hundred so it won't be too painful."

"That's good of him" said Josh. "We owe him one."

"Declan is the least of our worries" Sean told him. "Right now, we're sitting here hiding in a small flat while Miller and his cronies have half the police in London looking for the two of you. Now, don't get me wrong. I enjoy your company and you're both welcome to stay as long as you like. But we are in the proverbial shit and we can't just sit here like Mr. Micawber, waiting for something to turn up."

"Agreed" said Josh. He held out his empty whiskey glass. "So let's top-up our courage and decide exactly what we're going to do."

Sean obligingly refilled their glasses and Brody began by giving Shelley a complete update of all that had happened since he'd last seen her in Vienna. He held back nothing, giving her every last detail of the complex plot in which she was now inextricably entangled.

"My intention this morning was just to explain everything to you and then get you out of harm's way." He reached out and held her hand tightly. "But all I've done is to drag you further into this whole bloody mess and put you at risk. I can't tell you how sorry I am."

She lifted his hand and gently kissed the back of it. "I'm not sorry. I would have hated knowing you were in such trouble and that I was out of the loop and unable to help. At least, this way, we get to share the problem and solve it together."

"You're a darlin' girl" Sean told her affectionately, "and far too good for the boyo here" he added with a wink at Josh, "but solving the problem is not going to be easy. We need to understand the limited cards we're holding and, frankly, this is not much of a hand!"

"You're right" agreed Josh. "But we have evidence. And Miller must fear that evidence or he wouldn't be prepared to take such risks to eliminate us. It's the one weapon we have that we can use against him."

"But where do we go with it?" asked Shelley. "We don't know the extent of the hierarchy involved in this. If we make contact with the wrong people we could be playing right into Miller's hands."

"So we need to pool our connections and draw up a list of contacts and associates we can trust; people we can use clandestinely and be sure they won't leak. Agreed?"

Sean and Shelley nodded.

The next couple of hours or so was spent in forensic analysis of their situation and gradually a possible scenario came together whereby, with careful tactics and cautious approaches, they might plan a route to securing help. The mood lifted and they were each feeling a little more positive when, at just after 4 pm, Brody's pay-as-you-go mobile rang. Any phone call was ominous until they were sure who was calling and why and, initially, the three of them exchanged apprehensive glances. Then Brody looked down at the handset's display. He recognised the area code for the number. It was Southend. "It's ok" he told his companions. "I think it's Kass."

His assumption was correct but he was not prepared for the onslaught that immediately assailed his ears as he answered the call.

"Where is she?!" Kassia's voice screamed from the handset. "Why have you done this without telling me? How dare you interfere like this without my permission?! I told you to stay away from us, didn't I?!"

It took Brody several seconds to calm his ex-wife and persuade her to stop ranting long enough to explain. As she finally relented and curbed her anger sufficiently to clarify her accusations, Brody went icy cold from head to foot. His stomach convulsed and he felt close to throwing up.

When Kassia had turned up to collect her daughter at the end of the school day, a surprised staff told her that Saffy had already left with her father. Kassia was calling from the school secretary's office to vent her anger and insist on an immediate explanation.

"This is totally out of order, Josh!" she complained bitterly. "You can't just take it into your head to pick her up without telling me! If you wanted to give her the bloody chocolates that badly then you could at least have told me."

"Chocolates?" said Brody vaguely, not really listening, and frantically trying to come to terms with what he now knew had occurred.

"The bloody Mozart chocolates. The secretary said she was handing them around to everyone, telling them her wonderful Dad brought them back from Austria. It's just not on, Josh. You can't buy your way into her life with presents and you can't just waltz in and out without telling me!"

His head was spinning. If he told his ex-wife the awful truth, she would firstly be hysterical and then she would immediately call the police, who would eventually join up the dots and make the connection between the man on their wanted lists and the disappearance of his daughter. The hunt would immediately go public and nationwide. The entire country would be on alert, looking for the missing girl and her father. But Brody knew exactly who had collected Saffy from school and handed her chocolates apparently sent from her Dad. He also knew how simple it was going to be to secure her release.

"Listen to me please, Kass" he said as evenly as his churning emotions would permit. "I'll have her back with you very soon, I promise."

"That's not the point!" she protested acidly. "You have no right..."

He cut her short. "No. I know. And I'm sorry. It was meant to be a surprise" he lied with seeming conviction. "You were supposed to be told but there have been some crossed wires and the message obviously didn't get through. I can only apologise. But I promise you she's fine and I'll get her back in no time. Got to go now. Speak to you later."

He clicked off the handset and slumped back into the sofa, ashen faced.

"Miller's got Saffy" he said quietly.

Shelley gasped in shock and clutched a hand to her mouth. Sean was struck dumb. For several moments nobody spoke. Their previous tentative optimism was shattered at a stroke. The unthinkable had happened.

"What can we do?" asked Shelly plaintively. "There must be someone we can go to. Someone who can help." She looked imploringly from Brody to Sean and back again but their stony expressions offered her no shred of hope.

"It's over" said Josh coldly. "He's won."

Sean slowly stood and looked sympathetically at his friend. "What do you need us to do?"

Before Brody could answer, three short tones beeped from his pocket. He withdrew his original mobile phone and stared down at the text message in the display window. It simply said:

Please call Saffy on this number.

Josh lifted the handset and showed it to his two companions. "And so it begins" he told them grimly as he hit the appropriate buttons to call the sender.

"Daddy?" said the voice in Josh's ear as the call connected.

Brody was in unbearable turmoil but, for the sake of his daughter, battled to defeat his surging anxiety and keep his emotions under control. "Yes, darling. It's me" he managed to reply. "Where are you?"

"I'm in a car."

Brody could hear the natural apprehension in her voice but, to his immense relief, she didn't seem particularly frightened. He wanted to say nothing that might cause her to worry or become alarmed. "And who is with you?" he enquired as casually as he could.

"Your two friends. They're bringing me to see you. But it's taking ages."

Brody's face screwed up in anguish. The tension of knowing she was beyond his reach and in the clutches of Stephen Miller was almost unbearable and he winced in pain as he strove to prevent fear entering his voice. "Are they looking after you?"

"Yes" she said softly. "But I want to see you."

"I know, darling. And you're going to see me very soon, I promise. So just be a good girl and be a little patient. I'm on my way to pick you up. All right?"

"Ok."

"Now let me have a word with the man."

"Ok, Dad. Bye!"

There was a brief hiatus while Saffy was clearly handing over the phone, then Brody heard the heavier breathing of an adult as the receiver was taken. "She's very well and happy and looking forward to seeing you" said Miller's voice in his ear.

"Listen to me very carefully" Brody told him icily. "You harm one hair on her head... and I'll kill you."

Miller chose to ignore the threat and, for the benefit of the little girl beside him, continued in casual tone. "She'll be waiting for you. Mrs. Rawlings will look after her until you arrive. You need to bring everything with you. And I mean *everything*. Is that understood?"

"Yes."

"Good. Then we'll expect you at 6.30 pm. And I'd advise you not to be late."

The line went dead and the disconnected tone purred ominously in Brody's ear. He lowered the phone, his face a picture of helplessness and misery.

"He wants to trade?" asked Sean.

Brody nodded silently.

"We have to *do* something" protested Shelley, frantically clutching his arm. "You can't go to him just like that; alone."

"I can. And I must" Brody said calmly. "He has my daughter. So we play this his way. There's no other choice." He looked up at his two sorrowful companions. "But I'm going to need your help."

As Brody stepped out of the taxi cab, he saw the familiar Jaguar saloon parked in the resident's bay at the end of Morpeth Terrace. It gave him an uneasy, sickening feeling to think of Saffy naively riding in the back of it, all the way from her school in Southend. One minute she was spending a perfectly normal day then, with the trusting innocence of a child, she was whisked away and driven here where sinister men play out their deadly games under the legitimate cover of officialdom. Swallowing hard, Josh crossed the street and made his way to the entrance doors of the Victorian apartment block.

Despite his all-consuming concern for the safety of his daughter, he felt strangely calm as he pressed the button on the panel that was inscribed *Flat 3*. He presumed it was the natural reaction to knowing that, no matter what the consequences, he had no other choice but to do what he was doing. Fatalistic acceptance of the inevitable had removed almost all his fear and he was thinking clearly as he heard a buzzing sound and the lock mechanism released the front door to the building. He walked through the vestibule to the flat and knocked on the heavy door.

It opened and he found himself looking at the dark, expressionless features of Carter. Brody stared coldly at the man who three days previously had taken shots at him as he made his escape from this very apartment. Carter said nothing and merely stood back to allow Brody inside.

Passing through the hallway, Josh entered the lounge to find Miller standing by the fireplace, awaiting his arrival. In an easy chair, close to his boss, sat the stocky minder Podolski, whom Brody knew only as Mr. Brown. One hand was covered in little scratches and cuts and his right arm was supported in a sling. He frowned angrily as Brody entered but said nothing. He merely continued to stare at the newcomer as he idly fingered the automatic that was lying in his lap with a silencer affixed to the barrel.

Carter followed Josh into the room and closed the door behind them.

"Where is my daughter?" asked Brody evenly, looking directly at Stephen Miller's somewhat smug face.

"In the bedroom with Mrs. Rawlings."

"I want to see her."

"And you will."

"Now!" commanded Josh emphatically.

Miller acquiesced and gave a nod to Carter, who disappeared from the room. "She's a charming little girl" said Miller casually. "You must be very proud of her."

Brody had a strong impulse to rush across and punch Miller hard in his patronising mouth, but he remained still and silent. A moment later the door opened again and Saffy was led in, holding the hand of Mrs. Rawlings.

"Daddy!" she cried and ran to Josh. He scooped her up in his arms and hugged her tightly, kissing the top of her head. "Why have you been so long?" she demanded.

"Sorry, poppet" he said, still squeezing her close. "I was held up. But I'm here now."

"Are we going home?" she asked innocently.

"That depends on what your Daddy brought with him" said Miller in an overtly avuncular tone that Brody found almost obscene. Miller fixed him in the eye. "Doesn't it?"

Josh eased Saffy down beside him and held her hand. "There's a taxi outside across the street" he told Miller bluntly. "When she's safely inside it and underway I'll receive a telephone call. When the call comes in, and *only* when I know she's safe and away from here, you'll have what you want."

Carter stepped towards Brody and spoke for the first time. "And what if we simply take it now?" he whispered acidly.

Miller gave a slight sniff of disapproval at his operative's naive assumption. "Oh, Mr. Brody is far too canny to carry anything on his person" he told his subordinate. "And, after all, we have him here now; and fair exchange is no robbery. So we'll allow him his little victory." He turned to Mrs. Rawlings. "Please escort little Saffy outside to the cab."

The housekeeper nodded and extended her hand. Josh bent low and smiled warmly at his daughter. "I want you to go with Mrs. Rawlings and she'll take you to a taxi. It will take you all the way home to Mum. Ok?"

"But aren't you coming too?" asked Saffy, puzzled.

"Not just yet. I have some business to do here. But I'll see you later, all right?"
The child nodded reluctantly. "Ok. But don't forget."
"I won't" he promised. Suddenly, as he watched her walking away with the housekeeper, he was seized by an overwhelming fear that he might never see her again. "Saffy!" he called, and his daughter turned abruptly around to face him. "I love you lots."
"Me too, Dad" she said, disarmingly unconcerned, and left the room.

Outside, in the taxi cab, Shelley Anderson was anxiously watching the apartment block with her eyes fixed permanently on the large oak-framed front doors. When she saw them open and a woman appear leading a little girl by the hand, she was seized by conflicting emotions. Relieved that Josh had secured the release of his daughter, she was also terrified that Brody himself was still inside.
Mrs. Rawlings brought the child to the taxi cab and Shelley helped Saffy climb into the rear.
"Hello. My name is Shelley" she said as comfortingly as she could. "We're going to take you home to your Mum."
Josh had given her a large wad of cash and promised the cabbie they'd cover his entire night's takings to persuade him to drive the pair all the way to Southend. With the little girl strapped securely into a seat belt, Shelley told the driver to get going and the taxi pulled away.
Sean Finnegan was standing a little distance along the street, watching the cab's departure. He watched Mrs. Rawlings return to the apartment block and disappear inside. Then he waited patiently, ensuring nobody else came out of the building and no tailing car was leaving in pursuit of the taxi. After five minutes, he took out his mobile phone and rang Josh's number.
"Taxi left safely. Nobody on its tail" he said clearly.

Inside the apartment, Josh clicked off his handset. "Ok" he said tersely and reached into his pocket. He withdrew a small key on a large, green-coloured fob and tossed it onto the coffee table in the centre of the room. "The left luggage store in Victoria Station. Platform Eight. There's a briefcase. Everything you want is inside."

Miller looked across at Carter and nodded. His operative bent and gathered the key fob and immediately left the room.

"Well" said Miller with a sigh. "It will take him a good twenty minutes before he's back. We may as well settle ourselves and wait." He gestured to the chair in the corner of the room. "Please take a seat."

Josh did as he was bidden.

"Mrs. Rawlings!" Miller called out. She appeared at the door in a matter of moments. "I think a pot of coffee is in order, if you wouldn't mind." The housekeeper obediently left to carry out her task.

"I confess, you've been a considerable thorn in my side, Mr. Brody" said Miller unemotionally as he leant an elbow against the mantle shelf, his body half turned away. "I will be glad to be finally rid of you. As, indeed, will Mr. Podolski here." He nodded in the direction of his minder, who continued to stare mutely at Josh with anger burning fiercely in his eyes. "He suffered a nasty accident this morning, thanks to you. And his partner is now in hospital in a coma, having been thrown through the windscreen of their car."

"That would be the man who was trying to shoot me in the back of the head" said Josh calmly. "So, you'll pardon me if I don't shed a tear."

Podolski visibly bristled, but stayed silent. Miller merely smirked. "Brave words, Mr. Brody. Well said. But, sadly, bravado will not assist you now. I'm afraid your meddling has led you out of your depth. *Way* out of your depth."

"That appears to be true" said Josh resignedly. "But do you really think this will end with me? You can't keep this sort of monstrous operation secret for ever. Someone else will stumble onto your antics and expose you. It may take a few months, or maybe a year or so, but it *will* happen. I may be deprived of the pleasure of bringing you down personally, Miller, but you'll end up nailed just the same."

Miller gazed at him contemptuously. "You know, for an intelligent man, your naivety is staggering." He turned fully around to face Josh head on. "Do you *really* think I'm running some rogue, wildcat operation that is somehow moving around the world with impunity? Just *what* do you think you've stumbled into here?"

"Megalomania" said Josh caustically.

"You fool" Miller told him, his voice full of derision. He pointed to the telephone resting on the coffee table. "I could pick up that phone right now and ring a dozen different governments. And they would *all* take my call."

Josh felt the hairs on the back of his neck rising as, for the first time, he glimpsed the true magnitude of what he was up against. It was as if he had suddenly rounded the final bend in a long, arduous road to find himself facing a granite mountain. He frowned at Miller. "Just what are you trying to tell me?"

"The simple facts of life. It's not such a wonderful world out there, my self-righteous friend. There are men who murder and maim; who rob and rape entire countries; who wage war and kill thousands; yet they can't be touched. They're protected by the trappings of government and the weight of authority. So, sometimes, to protect the innocent, we have to bend the rules. It's the only way; because these 'untouchable' men have to be stopped."

"That's why we have international law" Josh protested. "The U.N. and the courts in the Hague."

"Tell that to the villagers around the Sankuru river where Thorium was discovered. Oh, wait a minute. You can't. Because the Lukeba brothers annihilated them. Wiped them off the face of the map. Men, women and children. Gone, as if they never existed."

He stepped across the room and stood by Brody's chair. His voice lowered but it was full of menace, every word burning with barely suppressed anger. "And two weeks after they'd done it, the Lukeba twins were sipping champagne at a cocktail party hosted by the United Nations." He leaned down and brought his face close to Josh's own. "So sometimes, while the lumbering, ineffectual, hopelessly inadequate processes of international law look on like impotent eunuchs, other action becomes necessary." He looked accusingly into Brody's eyes. "And the last thing we need is some meddling bloody journalist making the task even more difficult than it already is. Are you getting this?"

Brody felt his fists clench. He loathed this man who was berating him. Not only had he endangered Brody's own life, he had kidnapped Saffy and taken her hostage. That was unforgiveable. Brody's instinct was to reach out and strangle him for the threat he had made to his daughter. But he kept his anger in check. He was beginning to understand that Miller was the front man for something much bigger than he had ever thought possible and his own fragile position would not be helped by any angry outburst.

"So, basically, you're running an international vigilante group. Is that it?"

Miller shook his head with a scornful sneer and raised himself up. "If only I were. That would be much easier to manage" he said with a sigh. "No, Mr. Brody. Despite what you may think of me, I report to a dozen different nation states and nothing... I repeat *nothing*... can be done without their express prior approval."

There was a knock at the door. "Come" called Miller, and Mrs. Rawlings entered the room with a laden tray. She placed cups and saucers and a large pot of coffee on the small table and then quietly began to pour, passing each of them a cup.

The brief hiatus gave Josh precious moments in which to think. Why had Miller spoken so candidly and revealed so much? It could only mean that he had no intention of allowing Brody to live to repeat any of it. Josh's mind was working frantically. He knew Sean Finnegan was still outside but there was nothing Sean could do to extricate Brody from his situation. If Josh tried to run then the man Podolski, who was still pointedly fingering the loaded automatic that rested in his lap, would drop him in a second and before he'd even made the door. His only recourse was to steel his nerves and wait out the return of Carter. Then, he would play the one remaining card he had left in his hand.

Mrs. Rawlings completed her task and quietly left the room.

Miller and Podolski drank their coffee in silence. Despite the fact that his throat was dry, Josh couldn't drink. He was seated opposite a man with a gun who might well be instructed to shoot him within a very short time. It was not conducive to calmly swallowing coffee.

Another agonising, mute ten minutes passed before they heard the sound of the front door of the apartment slamming closed to announce the return of Carter. He walked into the lounge with the briefcase under his arm. Miller reached down and removed the tray, allowing Carter to place the case on the coffee table.

"Combination?" asked Miller evenly.

"Nine-three-four, Nine-three-five" Josh told him.

Miller rotated the wheels to the appropriate numbers and flicked open the locks. He then lifted the lid. "Well, well" he muttered gently. "Aladdin's cave."

Reaching in, he withdrew the contents and set down everything on the table beside the open case. There was the full report that Brody and Sean had compiled, all the photographs they had printed and the two USB drives containing the video recordings from both The Intercontinental in Vienna and The Vanderbilt in the Cromwell Road. Miller seemed particularly preoccupied with the stills photos of Tsu Li. He picked up the picture of her in the Intercontinental's foyer, holding it alongside the Heathrow departure gate shot and comparing the images.

"Taken from the hotel's internal video footage, I take it?" he enquired. Brody nodded.

Miller stared at the full-face shot and tutted. "Very unfortunate" he said calmly. "And very careless of her." He turned back to Brody. "And this is everything?"

"Yes" said Josh quietly. It was time to play his only card. "But there is one other copy."

Miller's expression didn't alter. "And?"

"It's my insurance policy" Josh told him. "You've already clearly demonstrated that you can reach me or my family at any time. And everything I've heard here this evening only reinforces that threat. So you can be sure that, for the sake of my daughter and her mother, this information will all stay buried."

"So?"

"So if anything ever happens to them; or if I don't walk out of here tonight in one piece, then the lawyer holding the copy of this information will go public."

"Ah" said Miller with a smile. "You're attempting to blackmail me."

"I'm telling you that if I end up in a hit and run like Yurov in Paris, or with a dose of Sux in my toe, or if anything out of the ordinary sees me unexpectedly cashing my chips, then all this is released. You can carry on with your private war. I don't care. I don't want to know. But you leave me and mine alone. Understood?"

Carter and Podolski looked at their boss, wondering how he would react to this undisguised threat, but Miller remained impassive, showing no response. "You over estimate the power of what you hold. Mr. Brody" he said calmly. "I look forward to reading your report, of course" he added with sardonic bite, "but, however detailed it might be, your evidence against me is entirely circumstantial. In the final analysis, in a court of law, it will simply come down to your word against mine."

Brody pointed to the contents of the case, laid out across the table. "Those photographs are not circumstantial. And they're time-coded and dated."

Miller nodded. "Yes. Unfortunately they are. But, once again, you're viewing this from entirely the wrong angle." He nodded his head at Carter who turned and left the room. "You see, Mr. Brody, if only you had co-operated with me from the outset, we might have avoided this unpleasantness. But your obstinacy has left me with no alternative."

The door opened and Carter returned. Josh's jaw dropped in surprise as he then saw who followed him into the lounge.

"Allow me to present Miss Tsu Li" said Miller. "She is one of my most successful and efficient operatives."

Brody gazed in shock at the diminutive Chinese girl. She was dressed in a plain blouse and jeans and her face bore very little make-up. If he had not known who and what she was, Josh would never have believed the slim, quiet woman standing so near, and seeming so feminine and gentle, was actually an assassin.

"Sadly" said Miller, "as the contents of this briefcase proves, you do indeed hold irrefutable evidence against Miss Li. It unfortunately forces my hand." He nodded at Podolski.

Podolski stood, removed his right arm from its sling, and calmly lifted the automatic with the silencer affixed to the barrel. Josh's whole body tightened in terror as the minder raised his weapon and, with a contemptuous sneer, pointed the gun directly at him. Brody's face screwed up and he caught his breath in awful anticipation of the bullet he was about to receive. But Podolski suddenly turned to his right and fired. The dull thwack of the silencer was the only sound as the bullet left the gun, hitting the unsuspecting Chinese girl directly between the eyes, and she dropped to the floor like a stone.

Josh gasped and collapsed backwards, crumpling onto the chair as if he'd been punched hard in the gut. He felt as if he was about to throw up. He was shaking, simultaneously convulsed by acute shock at what had occurred and intense relief that he himself had not been shot. Never, in all his time in Egypt and Libya, had he witnessed such a cold, callous and instant despatching of life.

Podolski simply sat down again as Carter gathered the girl's corpse from the floor, lifting her under the arms, and manoeuvred her out of the doorway. Suddenly she was gone and it was as if the whole thing had never happened. It was bizarre. Less than a minute had passed between the woman entering the room and her dead body being dragged out of it. Brody was stunned and unable to speak. Stephen Miller reached for the coffee pot and filled a cup with the strong, black liquid, passing it to Josh.

"Drink this" he commanded.

Still in something of a daze, Brody accepted the cup and forced some of the coffee between his lips. "I can't believe what I've just seen with my own eyes" he said eventually. "How could you do that? It was murder."

"If you had refrained from meddling in matters, it would not have been necessary" Miller told him coldly. "But your investigation produced proof. She was exposed. And an exposed assassin, even one as efficient as the beautiful Miss Li, is a fatal liability."

Brody looked at him, seething with contempt. "And now, of course, she can't be traced to you. Right?"

"More to the point" rejoined Miller acerbically, "your photographs are now somewhat redundant. The woman no longer exists. And you will discover she never did. Tsu Li was of course not her real name. And there will be no record or photograph of her on any official files, anywhere. I can assure you of that."

"How very convenient for you."

Miller gave a disdainful sniff. "It's actually more convenient for *you*, Mr. Brody. Your evidence is no longer a threat to me. Therefore I need detain you no longer. You are free to leave."

Josh could not believe his ears. "Just like that?" he asked incredulously.

"I would advise you to erase the last month from your mind. Whilst your circumstantial evidence is of little worth, the people for whom I work would not take kindly to the irritation of you creating a fuss."

"And what I have just witnessed was a demonstration of how 'irritations' are dealt with?"

Miller fixed him squarely in the eye. "What you have just witnessed should serve as a reminder to stay away from matters that don't concern you. You have a sweet little girl, Mr. Brody. She's growing up in a dangerous world and she needs a father. Don't let your bourgeois, misguided sense of morality deprive her of that right."

Josh was speechless. He was standing in the shadow of something cruel and deadly that he was powerless to control and from which it was futile to try and flee. Yet, unbelievably, he was being offered an avenue of escape. No matter what his logical mind might tell him was right or wrong, his one imperative was to grab the chance he was being given and put as much distance as he could between himself and the horror that surrounded him.

Without another word to Miller, Brody turned on his heel and walked swiftly from the room and into the hallway. With his heart still pounding, he let himself out of the apartment and hurried across the vestibule and out through the main front door. The cool evening air felt good and reviving and he inhaled deeply. The familiar sounds of distant traffic in Victoria were comforting and, all at once, he began to feel he was emerging from a condemned cell and back into a world of reality.

Sean Finnegan, holding his small Nikon, was still standing across the street, patiently waiting and observing the apartment block. He could scarcely believe his eyes when Josh Brody emerged from the shadows of the building alone and unaccompanied, and apparently free. Ever cautious, and sticking rigidly to the pre-agreed plan, Sean made no movement. His instructions had been to wait at a distance from the apartment and to photograph all coming and going so that, if needed, there was some evidential basis to prove Brody had entered the building and, if he ever emerged again, a record of who was with him. But Brody was alone and nobody was on his tail.

Sean watched in semi-disbelief as Brody crossed the road and walked slowly towards him. He looked badly shaken, and his face was drawn and pale, but to Finnegan's immense relief, he was in one piece and, apparently, unharmed.

"Christ, bucko, you're a sight for sore eyes!" he said quietly as Josh arrived next to him. "Did it work? Are we home and dry?"

Josh gave a slight nod of the head. "In a manner of speaking. It was not quite what we expected but... yes. It would seem we're off the hook."

Sean reached out and enthusiastically embraced his friend. "That's great news!" he told him as he patted his back hard. "For God's sake, call Shelly and tell her. She's been on the phone to me every five minutes asking for updates. The poor woman is worried sick about you."

Brody obediently reached into his pocket and took out his mobile, but he was acting as if on auto-pilot, pre-occupied and moving almost without thinking. "Yes" he murmured. "She needs to know. We'll call her now." His face was still set firm in deep consternation. It was not the look of a man who had just been freed from a possible death sentence.

"What is it, Josh? What happened in there?" asked Sean.

Brody looked his friend in the eye. "For your own sake, I think it's better you don't know" he said softly. "I think it's better for all of us that *nobody* knows."

"That bad, huh?" asked Finnegan sombrely.

Josh nodded. "I need a drink, Sean. A large, stiff whiskey.

"You've got it!" said Finnegan. He put a comforting arm around Brody's shoulder and led him away towards Victoria to find the nearest pub.

Chapter Nineteen

Monday, July 29th. Bern, Switzerland.

The view from the fourth floor of the elegant, nineteenth-century building was breath-taking. The picturesque city of Bern lay spread out around the horse-shoe bend of the river Aare, with its green, tree lined banks and the Nydeggasse Bridge rising high above the russet tiled roofs and cream-coloured stone work of the old town district.

The meeting was to be held in the 'long room', originally a banqueting hall used by the city's main Masonic lodge, and now owned by a Swiss Asset Management Company and used for special occasions and entertaining important high-net-worth individuals and corporate clients. A waiter in a crisp, white linen jacket and matching gloves completed his task of laying out the refreshments and beverages on the dresser that was positioned against the side wall. He turned and contentedly surveyed the centre of the room. The large, circular table was in place and the twelve comfortable, leather-faced swivel chairs were carefully arranged around it, each equidistant from its neighbour. Satisfied that all was in order and his work was done, the waiter left the room. He had been instructed to absent himself before the first guests arrived.

Within the next fifteen minutes, a regular flow of taxis and saloons began punctually to arrive in the street outside to drop off their occupants, who each discreetly and unobtrusively entered the building and made their way to the fourth floor. The range of accents heard as the visitors bade a polite 'Guten Morgen' to the reception staff in the vestibule, was an indication that the various delegates had arrived from several different countries. To the casual observer, it appeared that yet another of the company's senior management committees was in plenary session to discuss world markets and international finance.

The atmosphere within the long room, as each of the representatives entered and exchanged greetings with their counterparts, was convivial and far from sombre, despite the gravity of the morning's agenda. The members had long since learned to disassociate themselves from the sinister purpose of the business in hand. Indeed, they had each been appointed to this committee precisely because they were able to apply themselves dispassionately and objectively to the cases under consideration and remove all personal emotion from the decision making process. They viewed the task before them as no more than a job to be done.

Whilst, for obvious reasons, there was no documentation stating the articles of association of the group, and no written definition of its purpose, the central tenet of its ideology was to serve the greater good; where the rights of society at large were weighed in the balance against the unscrupulous acts of certain individuals. Each person seated at the round table supported that conviction. To them it was a matter of simple justice. Justice *without* a blindfold, but justice none the less.

In civilised, ordered societies around the globe, the judicial system was founded upon the time honoured notion of: 'let right be done'. In practice, right was all too seldom done. There was a wide gulf between what was legal, and fulfilled the requirements of statutes, and what constituted actual justice. Manipulation of the system, clever interpretation of the code, and expert presentation and argument were too powerful, and too lucrative. They frequently over-rode and denied the application of simple justice. So the twelve participants gathered in Bern on this July morning had no qualms or doubts as to the validity of their work or the need for the contribution it made in order to 'let right be done'.

When they were all settled and seated around the table, the door opened and the familiar figure of The Convenor entered. He wished them all a polite 'good morning'. None of them knew Stephen Miller by name. None of them required or expected his identity to be revealed.

He passed copies of an agenda sheet to each member of the group and placed a large document folder in the centre of the table. In accordance with the usual custom he then withdrew two dice from his pocket and rolled them gently alongside the bulky file. They ended up displaying a two and a four.

"Seat six will be today's reader" declared The Convenor, and the occupant of the designated chair pulled the document file towards him and opened it.

"At the top of your agenda sheets, you will notice a brief report on the actioning of the last decision reached by this committee" announced Miller. "The matter was dealt with successfully."

"Excuse me" came a voice to his right, and he turned to see one of the women representatives with her hand half-raised just above the level of the table top.

"Yes, Madame?"

"Following our last meeting, I was part of a diplomatic mission visiting Vienna. I was naturally aware of the subject of our previous discussions and so I wasn't surprised when the matter was referred to during a reception at the British Embassy. However, I *was* a little concerned when I heard there was a complication and the embassy had become involved. Are you able to elaborate?"

"Yes, Madame. It was nothing major or important. There was a brief period when the press became a little too inquisitive but it was immediately dealt with."

"The press?" said one of the men sitting opposite, clearly uneasy. "There's nothing about it here in the report."

"No, sir" replied Miller calmly. "Because, as I said, it was immediately dealt with. There were no repercussions and the integrity of our operation was, as always, preserved. Security was impenetrable and never under threat. There was nothing whatsoever to concern this committee."

The Convenor's confident assurance was all the delegates needed to hear. He was his customary highly efficient self and they had every faith in his competence and the precision and professionalism of his work.

"Are there any further questions?" enquired Miller politely. Nobody spoke. "Then I will leave you to your deliberations. May I please remind you to leave all papers within the room and to take nothing with you. All documentation will of course be placed in the burn bag once the meeting is over." There was a general murmur of consensus and understanding around the table. "I will be outside the room if you need me."

With a slight inclination of the head, Miller turned and walked smartly from the room, firmly closing the door behind him.

Once outside, he seated himself near the doorway. Lifting his left wrist, he spoke quietly into the microphone of his closed circuit radio link. "This is station one" he said firmly. "Call it in please."

One by one, the operatives on duty called in to confirm their positions and status. Miller had one man on the floor below, two in the vestibule and three in cars in the street outside. Every station reported. The 'all clear here' was given by every operative.

Miller sat back in his chair with an air of quiet satisfaction. The committee was once again in session.

Epilogue

It took Josh Brody several weeks to readjust and pick up the threads of his life. The events of that fateful summer left permanent scars on his psyche. As a reporter, he had covered many war zones and conflicts but the shock and horror of those terrible hours when he feared for the very life of his daughter and then witnessed at close quarters the callous and cold blooded murder of Tsu Li, affected him like no previous experience. His nights were subject to recurring, frightening dreams and, all too often, his waking hours brought periods of sad reflection when his mind suddenly and involuntarily replayed the scene in the Morpeth Terrace apartment.

On the fateful night itself, once Sean had led Brody to the nearest bar and poured a large glass of whiskey into him, events had moved swiftly. Josh's first task was to call an immensely relieved and highly emotional Shelley Anderson and assure her he was safe and well.

Shelley delivered little Saffy to her mother's flat where Kassia, still furious with her husband, was somewhat pacified by the return of her daughter, apparently unscathed and untroubled by her unscheduled trip. As instructed, Shelley said nothing of the true events surrounding the girl's disappearance from school and, having conveyed Brody's repeated apologies, returned in the cab to London to be reunited with Josh and Sean.

Although their ordeal was over, none of them felt like celebrating. The three of them spent a quiet, sombre evening in Finnegan's Covent Garden apartment, glad of each other's company and grateful to be secure. Brody told them only the basics of what had transpired at Morpeth Terrace and, for their own protection, withheld all details of the killing of Tsu Li. During the ensuing weeks, however, she inhabited his thoughts a good deal.

The Chinese girl should have held little claim to his emotions. She was, after all, a professional and apparently highly effective assassin who had despatched her victims as dispassionately and pitilessly as she herself had then been killed. In the moral balance, there was a distinct evening out of the scales. 'Those who live by the sword, die by the sword' Josh reminded himself. The death of a trained killer was hardly deserving of his sympathy. Yet, illogical or not, Brody was intensely saddened by her demise. He was unsure why. He thought perhaps it was not just her brutal slaying with a bullet between the eyes that stirred his feelings, but rather the waste of her entire life. Why had a young, attractive woman, who was clearly intelligent and daring, embarked upon a murderous career? What might she have achieved if her life had taken a conventional course? No one would ever know.

More than anything else, Brody was haunted by his failure to produce the story he had set out to find. His investigation into the apparent suicides of the Lukeba twins had unearthed an international conspiracy and a clandestine operation that would have made banner headlines around the world. It was the scoop of the decade. Yet, to protect himself and his family, he was forced to bury it. It went against every journalistic instinct he possessed; but silence was his only option.

Once the dust had settled, he reported, apologetically, to Alan Denton. With as much mystery as his initial removal, Denton was suddenly recalled from gardening leave by his superiors and reinstated to his position. The editor was a wise enough hand to know that no explanation would be forthcoming. Brody's remorseful and severely edited account of events, together with what little he already knew, was sufficient to tell the newspaper man that the hand of officialdom had been wielded from on high.

"All I can tell you is that I am unable to write the story" Brody told him with regret. "And even if I were foolish enough to do so, you would never be allowed to print it. So I'm afraid it's a dead end." He reached into his pocket and produced a bundle of cash. "This is all that remains of the project fund" he said, placing the wad of notes on the desk. "There's about fifteen hundred quid left. But you might like to know that, although the money you provided hasn't produced a story, it quite literally saved my life."

"I'm glad" Denton told him with a grin. Then he passed the cash back to Brody. "But keep it. Buy something nice for little Saffy. After what you've been through, it's the least the paper can do."

With grateful thanks, and a promise to provide him with another story as soon as he could, Brody took his leave of Alan Denton.

Sean Finnegan, with typical insouciance, treated his role in the strange and terrifying events of Brody's plight as no more than part of the job of investigative journalism and merely chalked up the entire episode to experience. The resilient Irishman resumed his day to day life as if little had changed. Within a couple weeks he undertook an assignment to cover the latest conflict in Mali, where French forces were assisting the nation's army to repel the advance of Islamist rebels and push them north. Finnegan was keen to return to his beloved Africa and, to celebrate his new mission, took Josh and Shelley to several nights of farewell revels at O'Neill's, where he joined the band and regaled the crowd with the full extent of his vocal repertoire.

Freed from the turmoil of their initial time together, Josh and Shelley were able to make a fresh start on their burgeoning relationship and it blossomed and grew faster than either of them anticipated. Brody spent so much time at Shelley's Putney apartment that, after only a few weeks, he vacated his tiny Soho flat and moved in with her. Contrary to his expectations, his new relationship and domestic arrangements met with the approval of Kassia and Saffy. His ex-wife managed to set aside her territorial jealousies and genuinely seemed to like Josh's new partner. Kassia appeared to be glad that her daughter's father had at last acquired what she saw as a stabilising influence in his life. Saffy warmed to Shelley immediately and, like most modern children, appeared to have no difficulty in sharing her affections between three adults and enjoying the added benefits of two separate family units.

Josh Brody's world had become settled and steady and, for the first time in his life, he felt the road ahead of him was well defined, ordered and optimistic. He should have been a happy man. Yet, the untold events of his investigation were still a raw nerve. His journalistic instincts continued to rankle and nag at him. It was a sense of imbalance that was his problem. He knew that some might view Miller's activities as a necessary evil in the modern world; as no different from a war-time agency undertaking secret strikes against the enemy; and there was a valid argument that villains like the Lukeba twins and the arms dealer Yurov were indeed an enemy to civilised peoples. But there was no debate. No discussion. No consensus. It was the secret autonomy of Miller, or at least the nation states he claimed were behind him, that disturbed Brody's sense of moral equilibrium. Perhaps Miller had a point;

perhaps the expediency of the moment was sometimes a greater protector of the public than the obfuscating processes and grinding pace of so-called justice. But Josh couldn't reconcile himself to that argument.

He found himself listening to broadcasts and scouring newspapers for articles on apparent suicides or the unexpected deaths of dubious individuals, wondering if each such reported demise was actually as stated or whether Miller and his clandestine forces might be behind the surprise passing. It was a constant thorn in his side but a problem he was reluctantly struggling to accept when, one afternoon in late September, sitting in his agent's office, he underwent a sudden epiphany and realised he had a route to resolution.

Adele Sanders was her usual effusive self as Josh seated himself opposite her desk in her Poland Street office. He had fobbed her off with a carefully prepared excuse as to why his Vienna trip had not resulted in the promised book and, though very disappointed that her wayward client had again not delivered a manuscript, she was philosophical.

"Darling, Orion was delighted with the book-signing you did and really chuffed to hear you had followed it up with the British Council thing. Apparently, the University has put the Soho book on its reading list for their English course. So, all in all, we've clocked up a serious amount of brownie points and the trip was very worthwhile."

"I'm glad" Josh told her, genuinely pleased that she had something positive to tell him and he was not merely to be berated for the non-appearance of a manuscript.

"So!" said Adele, meaningfully. "They're asking me what's on the agenda. I was a little economical with the truth and implied you were working on a new novel. If we play our cards right, I think we could obtain a small advance. So what about another crime thriller?" She leaned forward onto her desk, intent on focussing the mind of her recalcitrant author. "Why not utilise your Soho knowledge to create a plot woven into the bad old days? Protection, gambling, vice; it's all there. And you've already done the research! If you set it in the fifties it will be too distant to rattle anybody's cage. So you could really go to town on the police corruption behind it all and base it on some of the guys who were actually active at the time. Change the names of course. But use the academic work you've already put in to feed a new fiction." She sat back, evidently pleased with her motivational idea. "What do you think?"

Suddenly Brody couldn't understand why it hadn't occurred to him before. It was so obvious. His factual case could no longer be proven and the power of Miller, and those who inhabited the shadows behind him, was too strong and could reach too far to risk arousing their wrath. But no one can control fiction. It would mean changing locations and names, and removing direct links, but the essence of the story could remain. The very power of fiction was in its ability to cause the reader to think; to imagine the unlikely and the seemingly impossible; to deliver an association of ideas that would resonate with everyday life. Josh Brody could not risk publishing a factual exposé; but Ian Magen could write a new novel.

"No" said Brody decisively. He leaned forward in his chair, his face full of eager optimism and his eyes brimming with promise "We can keep that idea up our sleeves. But I already have the plot, the characters, and the setting for a new novel set in the present day. If I work around the clock, I think I can get the first draft to you in around three months; maybe four. And I promise you this will outsell everything else I've ever written."

Adele was surprised but delighted. The words 'new novel' were the most favourable any client could utter, and her agent's ears rejoiced whenever she heard them. "I'll let Orion know at once" she told him gleefully. "Too late for the Christmas market of course, but we'll plan a Spring campaign for the release. Can you give me any idea as to what it's about? I can prepare a teaser."

"No" instructed Josh. "No teasers. This is too important. It's better that we arrive with an unexpected bang and raise eyebrows." He stood. "I'll keep in touch when necessary but, basically, I'm about to hibernate. So don't panic if you don't hear from me. Just trust me."

Adele had no idea as to the subject matter of his proposed book, but she could sense Brody's enthusiasm and it was infectious. "Don't worry, darling. Leave everything to me. You just sit and write!"

Brody began working on the new book that very evening. The first blank page of the first draft of any novel is an awesome and frightening prospect for every writer. The knowledge that a couple of hundred sides of A4 need to be filled with original, engaging and affecting narrative makes the task ahead seem a long and arduous road but for Brody, unlike any other starting point he had encountered, this daunting embarkation was not a journey into the unknown. The whole novel was already written in his head and he knew he could set it down with devastating and accurate authority and convey the true emotions of the principal characters.

He typed his chosen title across the header of the first page. *The Presidium*. It defined the senior, ruling council in a dictatorial state where decisions were made by the chosen few, affecting the lives of the many, whilst avoiding the need for the democratic process and where no redress was possible. It seemed the perfect description.

True to his word, Josh completed the first draft of the manuscript in just over twelve weeks of constant writing. His editors were full of praise for the work and, after only minimal revisions and alterations, the final draft was signed-off and sent to the presses. Orion was delighted with the book and, at Adele's prompting, allocated a significant budget to the marketing campaign.

The Presidium, by Ian Magen, was launched in April 2014. It received rave reviews and within three weeks of release had entered the best seller lists. Many critics praised the audacity and ingenuity of the plot; one or two even suggested that fiction is sometimes a signpost to fact and pondered the feasibility of such a clandestine organisation actually existing.

Brody often wondered if Miller and the people behind him ever read the novel. He hoped they did. When Adele later received an offer for the screenplay rights and a film company announced they were turning the book into a movie, Josh was certain that Miller, and those behind the *actual* Presidium, would become only too uncomfortably aware that the modus operandi of their clandestine group was, in theory if not in practice, at last within the public domain.

Ian Magen's third novel remained in the best seller lists on both sides of the Atlantic for ten months. It's financial returns gave Josh Brody the security he had always sought and made him an established author, albeit under a pseudonym which, for obvious reasons, he preferred to keep in place. Even more valuable than the success it brought him as an author, the book provided Brody with a release; a catharsis; a way to purge his soul of the events of the dangerous summer of 2013. Events that had been dictated by the unfettered power of *The Presidium*.

The End   © All Rights Reserved

FIVE OTHER NOVELS
by
MICHAEL HEATH

Available in paperback and e-book
from

CABERNET BOOKS

DEVEREUX ...and a question of class Powerfully evoking the atmosphere and mood of 1930s London, DEVEREUX ...and a question of class is an engaging crime novel that introduces a brand new private detective - Clayton Devereux.

Former military intelligence officer, Clayton Devereux, resigned his commission in 1930 and set-up his own detective agency, which he runs with his secretary Rose and the occasional hiring of his street-wise cohort Ollie Jones. Their routine work of divorce and petty crime usually bores the urbane Devereux so he is intrigued and keen to help when a former colleague asks him to assist unofficially in the search for an M.I.5 operative who has gone missing. In a plot that is woven against the actual political and social tensions of the period, the story twists and turns as Devereux's clandestine investigation gradually uncovers a dangerous and sinister threat to national security and the stability of the country. Solving the case and finally defeating the forces set against him costs Devereux far more than he was prepared to lose.

CONQUERED HEARTS In a carefully researched and detailed narrative, CONQUERED HEARTS tells a moving and engaging love story set in Jersey during the German occupation of the Channel Islands during World War Two.

The discovery of a skeleton on a Jersey farm in the summer of 2010 leads a local reporter to elderly Belle Legallienne, whose amazing personal story takes the journalist back seventy years to the German occupation of 1940. Her poignant and touching tale relates the strength of spirit and humour with which the Legallienne family and the entire island population endured five long years of hardship and oppression under the heel of Nazi rule. The eighteen year old Belle grows to womanhood in a gripping account of courage and daring that shows the best and worst elements of human nature and salutes those who stood against injustice and the loss of liberty. As her story finally reaches the liberation and the island is free, the reporter brings the interview to what he thinks is a close; but Belle has one more secret to reveal. She takes the reporter back again to 1945, to a surprise twist in the tale that finally provides the answer to a decades long murder mystery.

LEGACY is a crime thriller with a plot that continually twists and turns and wrong-foots the reader right up to the final shocking denouement.

James Mackintosh, a high profile journalist, receives a bizarre telephone call announcing a series of three murders. The first of the caller's predictions comes true and the police are called to the macabre crime scene where an ex-army officer lies crucified to the floor. As Detective Chief Inspector Paul Chard leads his team to find the killer before the second murder takes place he runs headlong into Major Pennington of military intelligence who is trying to restrict and undermine the investigation. Chard's only ally in his struggle to catch the killer is his new psychological profiler Dr. Sadie Haslett but, as the two draw ever closer in both their professional and personal relationships, even she is not all she at first seemed. When the murder hunt reaches its extraordinary conclusion, the killer's last act causes shock waves that reverberate around the world.

WILLOW MOON is a historical adventure story set in China in 1872 that tells the moving story of British trader, Richard Covington, and Lihua, the Chinese girl he loved.

In Christie's London auction rooms in 2012, a painting by Chinese Master Bingwen, called The Willow Moon, sells for a record price. As the delighted buyer, James Covington, leaves the auction he is confronted by a young Chinese woman. She produces an old sepia photograph showing The Willow Moon in the possession of a beautiful Chinese girl named Lihua and standing beside her in the photograph is an Englishman whom James instantly recognises as his ancestor Richard Covington. The exciting and deeply moving tale the girl then relates, handed down by each generation of her family, is the story of Tián Shuǐ, a small village in China. James learns that Richard Covington was a hero who saved the rural community from the terrorising bandit leader Meng and married Lihua, the daughter of the head man. Their wedding gift was the painting by Bingwen of the rare lunar eclipse called The Willow Moon. But the extraordinary story of the painting and its strange and wonderful journey to Christie's one hundred and forty years later, brings James Covington more than the true history of a work of art.

THE ALBION CONSPIRACY* is an exciting and intriguing espionage novel that tells the story of a man alone against the all-powerful state and his fight to survive.

In Switzerland, a British tourist dies suspiciously on the ski slopes. In Russia, a top scientist conducts cutting-edge research under the scrutiny of the state secret police. In France, a world-weary detective hunts Islamist terrorists bombing the streets of Paris. In England, the Special Intelligence Service secretly monitors an international conference of The World Health Organisation. As these apparently unrelated threads gradually converge, the fly caught in the spider's web is Alan Russell, a British Government interpreter. On a quiet road his vehicle collides with a car driven by Nina Petrova, an attractive Russian journalist. The consequences of that seemingly innocent collision reach to the very top of British Intelligence and change Russell's life for ever. He is overtaken by events beyond his control and plunged into the callous and violent reality that is the world of espionage, leaving him no choice but to participate in *The Albion Conspiracy*.

* **Cabernet Books has a limited number of new, original edition, hardback copies of this novel, signed by the author, available for purchase.**

For full details of the Cabernet Books catalogue - for both printed and e-books – visit our web site:

www.cabernetbooks.com